SPEAK WITH THE DEAD

E. C. TAYLOR

Hardcover ISBN: 979-8-9991076-0-2
Paperback ISBN: 979-8-9991076-1-9

Cover and Interior Design by Ashton M. Smith Designs
Art by Marta Riva (Marta Into The Forest) and Anna Jones (wolfmumma)

For anyone who has lost someone.

And for those that would like to escape.

Telluth
ALTUMBURG
EYSA
LUMINPORT
Casus Ocean
KASTARUS
LAKOONA
Solanis Ocean
AMGEN
VELLES
OSBOROUGH
HILLCREST
DORE
WALLSET

1

THE DAY AFTER ANNALYNN HALE'S DAD DIED, SHE RAN AWAY.

Anna felt smothered, strangled for months in a way she couldn't even begin to describe. Not that there was anyone she could talk to if she could find the words. But the woods listened. They heard her shouts and sobs, cushioned her running feet, and enveloped her in a calm that was impossible to find at home. Not anymore. But here—away, outside, alone except for the flora and fauna and wind—here she could *breathe* again.

She had spent six long—but too short—months tending to her dad with her mother as he became too sick to care for himself. The disease had worn down her father like the carts and hooves and feet wore down the dirt road around the edge of town. At first, he'd had occasional nausea and stomach pain. Then it had become constant. He lost his appetite, and then lost too much weight. He grew so tired that he had a difficult time getting out of bed. His skin and eyes yellowed—a visible sign the disease had taken over. His body wasn't his anymore.

Early on, the other people in their life were helpful. They would bring over meals, fetch what her mother needed from the shops, visit to chat, but as the weeks wore into months and he only grew worse, they stopped helping and stopped coming over. It was clear her father was dying. Nobody wanted to talk about death. Nobody wanted to be around death. It was bad luck, and it was tempting the gods. No one wanted to invite Morterra in.

The only person who stayed was the village healer. Mister Saul Farney wasn't Blessed—no one from Wallset had been Blessed since before Anna had been born, and it had always been rare—but he was a genius with natural medicines. Echinacea for colds, willow bark for pain, peppermint and ginger for nausea, and chamomile for so many things. He visited every day to administer medicine and teach Anna and her mother what he was doing. Some nights, he'd spend so much time showing Anna how he made his tinctures and salves that he'd stay well through dinner.

When Anna asked him why he kept coming back, even after he knew her father was dying, he told her, "Your father's still very much alive. Until that changes, I'll do what I can to give him the best days possible, under the circumstances. Everyone deserves that dignity."

And then her mother started crying.

The months were a blur of gathering plants for Mister Farney, reading her mother's cheesy romances to her father while he pretended to find them silly, and helping her mother in the bakery whenever she needed. And then, suddenly, it was mid-morning. She'd just given him the tea Mister Farney prescribed, and then gone out front to help her mom with the morning rush. When she came back to check on him, he was gone.

She'd spent the day getting their affairs in order as her mom broke down. And now that the wake was set, his burial ordered, and the news spread, Anna ran into the embrace of the trees.

In her tear-stained haste, she didn't see the rock until her ankle rolled. She missed the crumbling stone staircase that disappeared into the ground until she was falling down it. At the bottom, stunned by pain, she gathered the wits she'd left in town.

How long was I running? Where am I?

As her wet eyes searched around her, she found the familiar structure of an old stone basement. Many homes in Wallset had them. This one was far from town and missing a house.

Carefully, Anna stood up. Pain shot through her ankle when she tried to put weight on it, so she limped over to the dirty wall and leaned against it. Her hands gathered the hem of her tunic and lifted it to wipe at the tears and snot on her face. Eyes clearer, she looked around the room. Sunlight streamed through the opening at the stairs, fading to darkness at the corners of the room. A table sat in the center of the room, covered in decades—maybe centuries— of dust. There were tracks where birds and rodents had crossed the tabletop.

Anna took an unsteady breath in. She was not supposed to be here. The ruins in the woods were expressly forbidden. Everyone in Wallset knew it. Parents and teachers warned children with stories of strange, old magic that would turn them into a wolf, turn their flesh to stone, or simply kill them in any number of excruciating ways.

As Anna looked around, however, the basement didn't feel strange. Damp and musty, sure, but she felt no sensation of change.

I could be a wolf. Forever in the woods. No more awkward conversations or taxes.

There was a bookshelf in the corner. She limped over, holding herself against the wall as she went. The shelves were bare, so she opened the cabinet doors at the bottom. A metal lockbox was inside, its door slightly ajar. She lifted a hand to open it, paused to reconsider the whole wolf thing, and then grabbed the door and pulled. The metal creaked, but her hand remained unchanged.

There was a small glass bottle. It was similar to the containers Mister Farney used to store his tinctures, but the glass was decorated with an intricate floral pattern. She reached in and picked it up. The liquid had a pink hue in the dim light. She unstoppered the cork with a *pop* and lifted it to her nose. It smelled like wildflowers and hot afternoon sunshine.

Perfume.

She resealed the container and put the bottle back, then leaned against the wall next to her.

So... I'm not a wolf. And I'm still alive. There's no more magic in this room than in my bedroom.

Anna contemplated living the rest of her days in the ruins. Her father had taught her how to hunt and gather. They'd spent countless days out in the woods together. Maybe she could dedicate her life to her father's memory, the way the monks in Lakoona were said to dedicate their lives to patience or knowledge or whatever.

I'd never have my mom's brioche or croissants again.

More tears pricked her eyes at the thought of her mother. If she were to leave, her mother would be alone. She'd lose her whole family.

"It's not fair," she said to the darkness as she slid down the wall to sit in the dirt. "It's not fair. Why him? Why now? *Why*—" Her sob interrupted her. Her shoulders shook and fat tears rolled down her cheeks. She held the backs of her hands to her eyelids, not wanting to get dirt in her eyes. Slowly, she choked back the sobs.

She was talking to the god of death. As expected, there was no answer.

Too busy stealing people's dads.

It was at this moment that Anna decided there were no gods, because, if they were real and they let such awful things happen—*did* such awful things—they were truly terrible.

No. She wiped at her eyes. *They're nothing but stories made up to explain things that aren't understood. As real as the warnings about the ruins or the fairy that brought a gift and hid it in the house the night before your birthday. Lies fabricated to please the listener.*

Anna sniffled and stood. She hissed when her throbbing ankle hit the ground, but pushed through. Tears still falling, she started the long, painful walk home. After hours of limping through the trees and into town, her mother greeted her with a tight hug and they held each other as they cried.

2

Years had passed since the day she had fallen into that basement. As she hunted for meat and furs, she kept her eyes open for ruins. She loved the thrill of uncovering these old, unfamiliar spaces and the strange objects they held within. She always found a way inside, despite the ancient locks and traps in her way.

The first trap she'd encountered had almost cut all of her exploring short. In an old hallway buried in the dirt, she stepped onto a tile and heard an ominous *click* as it depressed with the force of her foot. Before she could stop her momentum, the floor in front of her fell away to reveal a pit full of rusted spears, and she was plunging toward them.

She twisted her body, released the burning torch in her hand, and flung her arms back at the floor now rising up behind her. Her fingers scraped against stone until they caught the lip of the depressed tile. Her knees slammed into the wall framing the pit as her torch clattered to the ground at the base of the spears. Then she began the arduous process of pulling herself back up. As she lay on the dirty stone floor, her chest heaving as she caught her breath, she vowed to return the next day. As she felt her way back through the dark hallway, she formulated a plan to create a makeshift bridge from thick branches and small tree trunks.

After she had built her bridge and made her way to the far end of the buried hallway, she uncovered a small cabinet filled with a handful of crystal goblets.

Some ruins were like the basement she had claimed, crumbling and barren, forgotten and with little of interest inside. Others held secret doors that she spent all afternoon getting open, or more mechanized traps she learned to take apart or find a way around. She learned what to look for—clean-cut stones and boards in the floor, barely too smooth to match the rest of the ground, a thick compartment around the lock on a rotting door, or the shine of taut wire as it connected an object to the ceiling or wall.

These traps often led to her favorite finds. A handful of random cutlery from the dust-covered kitchen of one earthen structure. A small library in a half-standing stone tower full of the most interesting books in an unrecognizable language, one of them gilt in gold. A small house with a hidden nook containing old perfume bottles. A chest built into the floor of a cabin, hiding a small locked box with jewelry inside.

Anna had created a haven for herself in that long-forgotten basement. To make it easier to gather fruits and vegetables for her mother, she planted the most common around the stairs to her hideaway. This left her with more time to explore. She'd claimed the space as her personal museum, and the items she retrieved greeted her as she jumped down into it now. They sat next to each other on the long wood table that she kept clean. She ran her fingers over the silver cutlery as she walked by, forks with too many tongs and the spoons with scoops that were turned at a slight angle. Her finger tapped one of the glass goblets, upended so that it didn't fill with dust, and she smiled at the resounding *ping*. At the end of the table was her favorite piece—pieces, really. It was a small wooden box with a metal lock built into the top. The wood had rotted enough for her to dig her hunting knife into the joint and pry it apart. It had bent her hunting knife, and her mother had scolded her when she'd found out, but it was worth it for what was inside.

The treasure chest held a necklace, a small, teardrop-shaped blue gem dangling from a delicate silver chain. The clasp was not made in a way she had ever seen, but she hadn't seen much jewelry. The gem was about the size of the fingernail on her pinky. The stone glittered in the low light as she lifted it out of the box. As the light hit it, it glowed softly, slightly, just enough that you would notice if you were paying attention. Anna let the silver chain of the necklace gather in her hand, tickling her palm with its cool touch. The blue gem glowed against her skin, tiny lines spreading outward at its facets.

Satisfied, she lowered it back into the box. It cast a subtle blue glow over the wood inside. She shut the lid, not because it would deter any actual theft, but because it made her feel better to keep it hidden.

She knew her finds were most likely worth something substantial to the right buyer, but she would have to travel out of her small town to sell them. Her neighbors would suspect thievery, and if they found out it was from the ruins, they'd curse her for even bringing it near them. Besides, she and her mother made do. There was no reason to stir up their little life by bringing in cursed treasures. She was content hunting and gathering, then coming home to keep the books for the bakery, just like her dad used to—just like her dad had taught her to.

So she kept her treasures here, far from anyone else, for herself to enjoy.

After checking on her collection, Anna found two rabbits in her snares, and the rhubarb plant nearby was ready to harvest. Before she headed home, she stopped at the little graveyard at the edge of the woods. Her father was buried near the tree line—Anna had insisted on it. Paxmortium flowers vined across the grass and up onto the headstones. The little, white flowers looked like circular stars against a green sky. She sat in the shade of the trees next to the large, round river stone they had placed as his headstone, and she traced her fingers over the letters of his name carved there, clearing them of debris.

"That rain the other day almost washed out the Jeffersons' herd," she said with a little laugh. "The dip in the woods where they live is great for keeping in the sheep, but it always floods when we get a late spring storm. Mom's told them to trench it, but they always say they'll get to it later. So now the sheep are scared of the rain." She laughed again. "I counted three cardinals today. Two of them were a pair."

She looked down at the vines creeping up the stone, and she plucked one. She laced it around her fingers, and the white flowers stood out from her hand like bright gems. "Mom's on a rhubarb kick again, but you know that's fine with me. There's never too much rhubarb pie. The town must agree, because they bought us out of them last week."

She sighed, and her hands fell into her lap. "That's all I've got today. Maybe someone will get engaged, and I can tell you about the cake Mom will make. That always seems to happen in spring." She stood, dusting off her pants. "Bye, Dad."

When she came home, she showed off the day's spoils to her mother with a smile.

"That's good, Lynnie," her mother nodded distractedly. "Thank you."

Anna's mother, Bren Hale, was a hand shorter than her daughter, with the same auburn hair that shone bright red in the summer sun. Flour covered her simple blue dress and white apron, and there were streaks of it on her face and hair. Her deep brown eyes were locked onto the oven across the room. A small fire was lit underneath it, and there was something cooking inside—meat pies, from the smell of it.

Anna had gotten her green eyes and love of nature from her dad.

"Something wrong with the oven?" Anna asked.

Her mother shook her head and looked over at Anna with a smile. Her eyes crinkled up with her grin as she said, "I was just thinking how nice it will be to have another."

"Mm." Anna shrugged nonchalantly and picked the rabbits up again so she could move them outside to clean them. "That would be something!"

"I've put in for another," her mother said carefully. "They said they'd have it built in a week."

Anna spun toward her mother, her shoulders tight. "We can't afford a second oven. I know, I keep the books!"

"Your father left a small amount when he passed. It turned out to be just enough for an oven!" Her mother smiled excitedly, but her brown eyes didn't match that joy. They watched Anna's face intently.

Anna's brow furrowed, and she frowned. She pulled open a drawer in the counter and took out a leather-covered journal. "Dad never said anything about leaving us money. None of the notes he left in the book mention—"

Her mother put a hand on the book before Anna could open it. "He wouldn't have."

Anna stared at her mother skeptically.

"It was a safety net."

Anna sighed. That sounded like him. Her father had started teaching her how to do the accounting shortly after she learned her numbers and letters. He was always squirreling some away for a new bow or new clothes for them. Even after death, he was looking out for them.

"He would be so proud of you," her mother said, eyes shining with tears.

Anna softened at her mother's expression and put the book away. "He'd be proud of *us*," she corrected.

Her mother nodded, blinking away the water in her eyes. "Anyway, I'll be able to bake twice as fast. It'll earn back the money I've spent on it in no time."

Anna nodded, chewing on the inside of her cheek. *She can certainly bake more with another oven, but there are a limited number of people in town, with limited coin purses.*

"You'll see," Anna's mother held both of her daughter's arms and rubbed them soothingly. "We'll be able to afford a third!"

Anna laughed at that. *Maybe this could work. Maybe we could sell bread to the tavern. Jo always complains about baking. How much would it be worth to him to not have to?* She teased, "Three ovens? Who are we, the governor's bakers?"

"Mm," her mother hummed and nodded, an easy grin on her face. "We'll be living like it!"

Anna laughed again, then picked the rabbits up and went to clean them in the backyard.

Soon, the local construction crew came around to build the oven, and a handful of days later it was ready to use. Bren beamed as she put the first rolls inside. Anna celebrated the moment with her, each of them having a slice of rhubarb pie with extra sugar sprinkled on top.

As Anna sat with the accounting book late one night, she stared at the numbers from recent days. There was a small increase in profit from more sales, but they had given more away, too. While she appreciated feeding those less fortunate, their upcoming taxes still made her nervous. The line between her little family and those they donated to was growing thinner.

The oven won't pay for itself anytime soon.

3

ANNA'S BASKET WAS HEAVY WITH BAKED GOODS AS SHE FOLLOWED HER mother through town. She tucked the fabric covering the food in tighter against the light rain. The square was quiet. The tall chapel at the end loomed over the open space, as if staring down the Registrar's office on the other side. Its stained glass windows flickered with ever-burning candle light as its stone face darkened from the falling rain.

The Hales were not religious. Anna had never attended a service at this chapel or prayed the Following before bedtime. Occasionally, her mother would pray—during especially harsh winters, when the neighbor had a fire, or when her father was sick. Those prayers were scattered trains of thought, a last effort to fix things when she thought others wouldn't notice. Anna wondered if her grandparents had been part of the Creed, if they'd raised her mother in it. When she asked, her mother would only say that she'd attended services a long time ago.

She hadn't heard her mother pray since her father died.

Anna followed her mother around the side of the chapel to the structure behind it. A woman in a simple, light green cotton dress and a matching veil embroidered with white flowers greeted them at the doors and ushered them inside. She thanked them for the donation as she took their baskets and asked them to stay where they were. She would be back.

The room they stood in was a tall, open space. There was a large fireplace, and cots lined each side of the room—some occupied, others empty, but all made neatly with linens. The smell made Anna's nose wrinkle—dirt and sweat and human waste—and someone was moaning in pain at the back of the room.

Most of the people here were homeless, and most of those were sunburnt—addicted to a drug called solim, so named because it was said to make you feel the euphoria of sitting in warm sunshine all through your body. Addiction to solim was steadily rising, and the affliction hadn't missed the little town of Wallset.

Anna looked for the source of the moans, and her eye landed on an old man, writhing slowly on a cot as another woman in green attended to him. He was slick with sweat and covered in dark splotches of dirt from the streets. His clothes hung off his frail frame and his crazed eyes stared through the roof. The woman wiped his brow with one hand and held him down on the cot with the other. The same dark stained the front of her dress.

"Don't stare," Anna's mother chastised in a whisper.

Anna's eyes snapped forward to the woman returning with their empty baskets. *But not really empty.* They always returned the baskets with a small gift of gratitude. It was springtime, so sitting gently atop the fabric they'd used to pack their baked goods was a single white calla lily.

"Thank you," Anna's mother smiled. "It's beautiful." It was customary to thank them for the gift, but Anna knew her mother would have done it regardless. She used to wonder if the process ever devolved into an endless cycle of thanks with the people that were the most pious.

The Creed servicewoman bowed her head and led them out.

As they rounded the corner to walk down the side of the chapel, three men stepped out, blocking the path forward.

Anna's brow furrowed as she slowed, stepping slightly in front of her mother. "Excuse us. We need to pass." Not recognizing any of them was enough to raise her hackles.

The man in the middle stepped forward with a cold grin on his face. He was tall and thin, with a wisp of blonde hair on his head. His wool pants and vest told Anna that he was of some status, but he seemed dirty. There was no *visible* dirt on him—he was actually incredibly clean—but Anna could feel it around him, like an aura. "'Fraid we have business with your mother."

The two men behind him nodded. The one to his left was just as tall, but about three times as thick. He wore a gray button-down shirt and black pants with shined black boots, and the shirt clung to the muscles of his arms as he crossed them. The man to his right was shorter and stout. Red hair fell from his head and then braided into his long beard. Bright rings danced on his fingers as he flexed his fists at his side.

"You must have us confused with someone else." Anna didn't move.

"Bren Hale," the tall, thin man smiled, revealing a golden cap amidst yellowing teeth, "and her daughter, Annalyn Hale." He put a hand in his pocket, playing with something on the end of the gold chain that looped down from his vest.

Anna's breath caught at the sound of her mother's name from his mouth. She felt a hand on her arm, and her mother stepped around her to stand in front.

"Mom, what are you doing?"

Her mother's eyes caught Anna's, trying to communicate too much at once. All she could read was an apology. *But for what?*

Then her mother turned to the men. "I'm Bren Hale."

The man's gold tooth flashed as he tilted his head slightly to the side. "Good. You know why we're here."

Anna's mother nodded, but her shoulders shook and her knuckles were white around the handle of the basket they held.

"Good, good," the man sighed. "It's been a month and a half, awfully generous of him. If he doesn't receive the agreed payment in seven days, he'll send us back to collect."

"What? Who are you?" Anna stepped up next to her mother, even as her mother held an arm out to keep her back. "What payment?"

"Hush, Lynnie," Anna's mother scolded her in a whisper.

"Ah." The man grabbed the lapels of his vest and rolled back on his heels, then forward again. "Name's Crocker. Leonard Crocker. Pleased to make your acquaintance. This here is Cricket and Luke." He thumbed behind him to the redheaded dwarf and then the muscle man. "I'd say see you again soon, but," he shrugged and the cool grin returned, "you don't want to be seeing us again."

Bren's jaw was tight as she said, "He'll have his payment."

"I hope so." Crocker nodded, and his right hand moved back into his pocket. His eyes narrowed at Bren, and then at Anna. "Or the next chat we have will be less…friendly."

Luke cracked his massive knuckles and Cricket rubbed his hands together. Sparks flew from the movement, scaring the women.

"Come on, boys." Crocker turned to walk back toward the square, and the other men followed.

Bren let out her breath only after they disappeared around the chapel.

Anna stepped forward to look her in the eye. "What's going on?"

"If Jo wasn't so stubborn, they'd already be paid," she mumbled, looking down at the hem of her sleeve as she played with a loose thread.

"Mom," Anna said sternly, grabbing her arm.

Her mother sighed and looked up at her, and the eyes that met hers were sad and tired. "I'll explain when we get home."

The walk home was painfully long. Her mother seemed unable to hide the pain in her back, or the strain in her knuckles as she held the large basket in front of her. It took all of Anna's patience not to steal the basket away and rush her along. The rain pattered softly on her head and shoulders as they walked.

Even when they got home, her mother wouldn't talk until she put the flower in a vase. She set it in the middle of the table before sitting.

Anna sat quietly across from her, knowing that if she pushed, it would only take longer.

Her mother smoothed her skirt, then said quietly, "I took out a loan to cover the cost of the oven."

Anna sucked in a breath. The only loans available to people like them would be predatory, with high interest that they'd struggle to pay back. They'd never recover. "How could you? Dad would be ashamed."

Bren looked like Anna had slapped her.

Anna stiffened.

Frowning, her mother looked down at the corner of the table. "With Governor Woufle raising taxes the way he is, we need to make more money. In order to sell more, I need to bake more."

"The taxes won't last forever." Anna shook her head. "You said they might last a couple of seasons, maybe three, before everything calms down again."

Her mother's brown eyes found hers, the same message in them as she had seen there in front of those men. "I was trying to be optimistic, Lynnie, but there are rumors all over town now of a war coming. The governors need coin to pay their armies. This looks like it's just the beginning."

Anna's face heated. *Rumors all over town.* She might have heard them, if she wasn't constantly in the woods. She might have seen hints at home, if she were there helping her mother. Maybe then, she could have pieced together what her mother was doing, and she could have stopped her. Guilt tasted like burnt molasses in her mouth, heavy, dark, and bitter. "How much is the loan for? What were the terms?"

"Just enough to cover the oven. 3,000 gold, paid back over two years."

Annalyn's head reeled back, and the heat drained from her face. *That's more money than we make in a year. Monthly payments without interest had to be...*

She did the math in her head and came out with around 125 gold, not including interest. Their little bake shop made around 120 gold a month, most of which went back into the shop to pay for ingredients and living expenses for the two of them. After a moment, she recovered enough to ask her second question again. "And the terms? What's the interest?"

"Fifteen percent."

Anna almost choked. " How could we ever afford to pay that?"

"With the second oven, we should bring in twice the profit. Word hasn't spread yet, but once it does—"

Anna shook her head, holding it in her hands. Tears stung her eyes. "We'd never be able to double our profit. There isn't enough demand. We can't sell more than what people will buy."

"But if we can convince Jo to let us bake for the inn—"

"I've talked with Jo and his son. They won't do it. They'll stick to their dry, cheap bread until Jo dies."

"If— If..." Bren tried to come up with another idea, but trailed off as she fell short.

"We have to end this loan. Can we sell back the oven?"

Her mother shook her head. "Even if we could, we wouldn't get the money back that we paid for it. We'd be responsible for the labor of dismantling it, and..."

Anna put her head in her hands again and shut her eyes. *Think, think, think. What would Dad do? He would've stopped her.* That train of thought would get her nowhere. Her mind jumped to her collection of valuables buried deep in the woods. *No, where would I sell them? Who would buy them? Maybe the Creed needs something for their services. It would be small coin, but it would be something.*

She looked up across the table at her mother. Bren looked ashamed and guilty and small. Anna felt betrayed—lied to—but seeing her mother like this, all she could think about was how to fix it. They'd have to figure it out. There was no other way.

"We'll get the money," Anna said more confidently than she felt. "I don't know how yet, but we'll get it, pay the damned thing off early, and avoid as much interest as possible."

Her mother's eyes brightened a little, and she nodded.

Anna's mind raced. There were only so many options in this little town to explore, and almost none that they hadn't investigated before. *Mother's Children. I should've paid more attention. How could I let this happen?*

4

ANNA STUCK CLOSE TO HOME THE NEXT DAY, SCAVENGING WHATEVER food she could from the forest. She didn't want to leave to hunt again until she found a solution to their problem. It felt wrong to turn around and head back into town without wandering, though. She came back with four bundles of asparagus, three rabbits, and a small adult deer slung over her shoulders. She was carrying too much to stop at the graveyard, so she went straight home.

She cleaned the animals and sold the furs the following day, holding tightly onto the few coins she got in return. The day after, she made her way to Jo Wilcott's, hoping that one last try would convince him to change his mind about offering their baked goods at his inn. He was as resistant as he had ever been, though, and told her harshly that she shouldn't ask again.

She held the strap of her bag where it slung across her chest, trudging back into town. Her boots clunked against the pavers, the treads worn and leather scratched. She would need new ones next year, if not by winter. Her dark green pants were tucked into them, and the thick material was soft against her legs.

Her blue shirt hung down to her thighs, the sleeves billowy until they gathered at the ends. It was one of her dad's old shirts, fitted to her smaller frame with her own mediocre sewing skills. Sometimes, she imagined it still smelled like him, like cut wood and leaves. Or maybe that was what *she* smelled like now.

The noise of the square broke through her thoughts, and she looked up at the spire of the chapel.

Anna drew in a deep breath and made her way toward it. She didn't mind the people of the Creed, but she was wary of some of their overly devout members, the kind that took everything literally or to the extreme. When she'd been little, she had seen a preacher on the street, standing on crates, shouting to the crowds. Their intensity had scared her, as she now understood it was meant to, but she had held onto that fear when it came to the church, and stayed cautious when discussing religion.

She appreciated the charity the followers did, though. They fed and clothed the less fortunate, helped orphans find homes, even taught basic courses for those who hadn't been schooled when they were young.

Anna touched the bread at the bottom of her bag, reassuring herself it was still there, and then she stepped inside the chapel. Rows of benches lined the floor, facing toward the front of the building, which held three altars covered in burning candles. An old woman with a black veil sat at the far end of a bench in the middle of the room, hands held together in front of her while she whispered quietly, rocking back and forth. The windows on the sides of the room were etched to keep attention inside the building. Little scenes played out in stained glass at the tops of the windows.

In the first, white, shining stars spread across dark glass. Connected, they created an open hand, a constellation Anna recognized as Mother's Hand. Her father had taught her how to navigate with it at night. In the second, water poured from two cupped hands, the wave in the glass making it look like the water was moving, ever-flowing. The third showed a rudimentary map. To the west was the Casus Ocean, one green blob at the bottom showing the Western Isles. In the center was a large green land mass—Telluth, outlined on the vast, main continent.

To the east was the Solanis Ocean, with the Eastgreen Peninsula reaching down into its gulf. The fourth and last panel on the left side of the room was a group of people, all genderless, humanoid shapes. The first was human, a familiar silhouette. The next was a dwarf, shorter and stout, with long hair and a pronounced beard. The next was an elf, a tall body with pointed ears and long limbs. The fourth was the biggest, the silhouette of a Vasbrute, taller and thicker than the rest, with large hands ending in claws and sharp teeth. Even represented in the creation story, they looked vicious.

On the right side, the four panels depicted each of the Well-Mother's Children. The first was Sollis, god of the day. Their sunshine-golden cloak shifted to a rainbow at the bottom as they smiled down into the room. Next was Noctis, god of the night. An androgynous figure with dark skin stood in a cloak of starlight with a bright white mask covering their face. Their deep navy and violet accented with white mirrored the constellation across the room. To their side was Viterra, goddess of life. A pale woman with red hair stood wearing a green gown covered in flowers, with clean white sheep resting at her feet. Lastly came Morterra, god of death. A man with dark hair and tan skin stood wearing a robe striped gray and black, with a scepter in one hand and a sword in the other.

Footsteps echoed across the room, and a man in the same green as the other Creed members walked down the center aisle toward her. White flowers edged the hems of his shirt, and a simple matching cap sat atop his head.

"Mother's blessings," he greeted. "What are you in need of today? You've come at a good time for reflection." He gestured around him at the quiet room.

"Actually," Anna began, "I was hoping I could help you with something."

His eyebrows rose and he waited for her to continue.

Anna pulled the buttery rolls out of her bag. "We own a bakery. I was wondering if you needed help for any of your functions." She presented the rolls to him.

"Oh, those are lovely," he said, "but we bake our own rolls for our services."

Anna was familiar with the rolls they served. They were twisted to form circles, supposedly meant to represent the eternity of the Well-Mother. They were given out during holidays, too, so she knew they were usually overcooked and under-seasoned. "Right, I thought we could offer to take that work off your hands. We wouldn't ask for much."

The man's eyes saddened, and Anna felt as if he saw right through her. She realized suddenly what she was doing—begging the church for work. Shame scraped inside her chest, but she pushed it down with a hard swallow.

"Unfortunately, that's not something we can accommodate at this time," he said. The words behind those also came through. *I'd like to help. Maybe if this were a larger parish, there would be something I could do.*

Then he seemed to have a thought, the sadness in his eyes leaving. He glanced up at the panel for Viterra, then back at Anna. "The summer solstice is approaching. We usually spend weeks preparing the food, but we could contract you for what we need."

Anna fought a frown. The summer solstice was months away, but it could be a useful venture in the future. "Yes, we'd be happy to help."

"We can't pay you as much as–"

"I understand," Anna interrupted him. "We'd still be happy to accept the work. I'm Anna Hale and my mother is Bren Hale. Our bakery is down on Birch Street."

The man nodded and smiled. "We'll keep you in mind."

"Here." Anna held the buns out to him. "A gift."

"Thank you." The man took the buns and bowed slightly. "Wait here a moment."

Anna nodded, waiting for him to return with another flower. She was right. He held a white daisy in his hand, but there was a wide, white ribbon wrapped around its stem. Anna took it from him, said her thanks, and then left.

Her eyes burned as she left the square, her hand tight on the stem of the flower, crushing it. She felt the edges of something hard in the ribbon. She lifted the flower and undid the bow. A roll of paper and one gold coin fell out. Anna's jaw clenched as she clutched the coin in her palm and unrolled the paper. Neat, looping handwriting filled the small slip.

May the Mother guide you during this difficult time, and may this coin bring you closer to what you need.

Her ears heated. She felt like a beggar. And even the church had mostly refused her. She felt a hot tear roll down her cheek. Quickly, she wiped it away with her sleeve and took a deep breath. She stuck the coin at the bottom of her bag and tossed the paper and flower onto the cobblestones.

5

ANNA HAD TO WAIT UNTIL THE END OF THE WEEK TO GO BACK INTO THE forest. She needed the excuse of hunting as a cover. She'd tell her mom that she had found everything in a bag at the side of the road, and then she would go to Hillcrest to sell them. Her precious finds would fetch at least enough for a single payment, potentially more. She had two days left.

She jumped down into her museum and paused there, wanting to take it in just the way it was before she disrupted it. After a deep breath, she walked over to the bookshelf. All four books went into her bag, the gilded one on top. The weight of them on her shoulder was substantial. She hoped their worth in coin would be the same.

Then, she turned to the table. She made sure the perfume was stoppered tight before wrapping the little cerulean glass in fabric and putting it in her bag. Next, she rolled the assortment of silverware into one long cloth and placed it next to the perfume. She hesitated at the goblets, then wrapped them in the remaining fabric and placed them carefully at the top of her bag.

Last was the necklace. She opened the box and lifted it out. The silver chain glittered and the gem shone like the water in the stained-glass panel flowing from the Well-Mother's hands. She didn't want the delicate chain to tangle, so she undid the clasp and pulled it around her neck. She tucked it under her shirt. The gem hung just below her collarbone, chain hidden by the collar of her worn cream tunic. It stayed cool to the touch, giving her goose bumps.

On the way back into town, Anna collected a small bag of cherries and two more rabbits. She tied the rabbits together and slung them over her shoulder.

She hadn't been to this side of town since their run-in with the debt collectors. That was one reason she hadn't been back to her father's grave, but the other was that she was avoiding it. Now, as she stepped around the paxmortium vines to the headstone, her face set into a tight frown. She stood there for a moment, staring down at his name and the flowers.

Finally, she said, "I'm sorry. I should've been there more. I…I didn't want to—"

A frustrated sigh left her. "She always talks about you. What you used to do, why you'd be proud of me, how you're *gone*. But I should've been around to know what was going on. I should have talked her out of the second oven. I'll fix it," she said. "We can fix it. I'll be there now, and we'll figure it out. I won't let you down."

Her heavy bag bounced against her hip, making the trek home longer. When she reached the cobblestones, her boots clunked gently against them until she paused.

The street was quiet. Usually, there were children running around or people working outside. The only sound she heard was a distant rolling cart.

And then a scream.

She broke into a sprint, holding her heavy bag steady as her feet clattered against the ground. The door to their home was cracked open. She threw it open and stepped inside, panting.

The front curtains had been closed, and the room was dark. A large, muscular man—Luke—stood to the side of the door. Cricket stood by their small table, a half-eaten sweet roll in his hand. Crocker, the tall, thin man stood over her mother, teeth bared at her and fist raised.

Bren Hale cowered in the corner, still standing, but barely. She raised her arms as she leaned into the wall to get as far away as she could, brown eyes wide in fear. Her hair was a mess and her cheeks were red.

No. Is that a bruise?

Anna's nostrils flared as she sucked in a breath. "Get away from my mom."

Crocker's head turned lazily, and then he looked at Luke and gestured with his chin toward her. The hulking man turned, reaching for Anna's shoulder. She ducked and spun out of his grasp to the side of the room. The heavy bag at her side slowed her down, but Luke hadn't been expecting the move.

"Hey!" Luke protested. "None of that!"

"Wait!" Anna threw one hand up at Luke and the other at Crocker. Cricket seemed to enjoy the entertainment, taking another bite of the roll in his hand. "We have two more days!"

Luke stepped forward to grab Anna again, but a dismissive wave from Crocker stopped him. The gold tooth glinted in the low light as Crocker chuckled, a rumbling that Anna thought should rattle his whole frame. "We grew impatient. 'Sides, if you don't have the money by now, you won't have it in two days."

Anna tossed her rabbits and cherries onto the counter. "But I *do* have it!"

A handful of cherries rolled across the counter, bouncing off the floor as she swung her large satchel in front of her. She pulled out the goblets and the silverware, still wrapped in cloth, and set it on the counter close to Crocker so that he could see. Luke made a move to grab it from her, but Crocker put a hand up and shook his head. Anna unrolled the cloth and revealed them. All their scratches and bends suddenly jumped out to her eyes.

Crocker eyed them curiously, his mouth a thin line. "I don't know what we could do with old dinnerware."

"They're silver and crystal," Anna said, glancing between Crocker and the counter.

He remained unimpressed.

Anna's hand shook as it dove back into her bag. "I have more! I was going to sell them. We would've had your payment." She pulled out the perfume and set it next to the silverware, and then the books.

Crocker frowned as he picked up the bottle, unstoppered it, and held it to his nose. His nostrils flared as he turned back to Anna. "Perfume? What would we do with perfume!?"

He lifted the hand with the bottle and swung. Anna flinched back as the glass shattered at her feet. The blue in the glass seemed to leach out and disappear. Terrified, she looked back up at Crocker. He swung his arm across the counter with an angry grunt, knocking the goblets to the ground, where they shattered, too.

"And books? What would they do for us?" Crocker picked up a book as if to throw it, noticed the script on its spine, and then tossed it back into the pile. "And books we can't even read!"

"I-I was going to sell them." Anna's voice shook as she repeated herself. "We would've had your gold."

Crocker snickered, looking down his nose at her. Her breathing shuddered as she realized they were never meant to pay.

"No, no." Crocker stepped back from Anna slowly, shaking his head. "This won't do. There's a lesson to be learned here." He cracked his knuckles and then reached into his pocket. He pulled out the object attached to the chain on his vest, hidden in his palm until he put his fingers through it. Gold-plated brass knuckles, the face of them blunt but polished to a shine.

Anna's breath caught. Crocker turned to her mother with a wicked smile.

"Oh, Lynnie," her mother breathed. "Run!"

But she couldn't, even if she had wanted to. Luke stepped up behind her and took hold of her arms. His large fingers dug into her biceps painfully, and when she kicked, he simply picked her up off the ground.

"No!" Anna shouted. "No! Stop! Please!"

Crocker lifted his fist and swung down hard. A crack sounded as her mother's cheekbone shattered. He lifted his fist again.

Anna kicked and pushed against Luke's hands, but his hold was like stone. She swung her head forward, trying to bring it back in a headbutt even though she'd most likely contact his chest. She felt a spark of heat on her chest, and one of her feet made hard contact with his knee.

Luke cried out, and his hands fell away.

Anna scrambled to her feet as Luke fell to his knees in her peripheral vision. She jumped over the counter and pulled out her hunting knife, pointing it at Crocker. "Get away from her!"

Crocker frowned. "Cricket!"

Cricket had finished his roll and was staring at Luke in amusement. At the sound of his name, he locked eyes with Anna, then stared at her little knife. His hand spun in the air. She cried out as the blade heated red-hot, and she released it. It clattered to the floor, hissing against the dirt. She clutched her burnt hand to her chest.

Luke, now recovered, strode around the counter in two big steps. He grabbed Anna's shoulder and slammed her into the wall behind her. She felt her back splinter the wood, and her head cracked against the boards. She shouted in pain.

Luke held her against the wall as she watched Crocker adjust the weapon in his hand and then raise his fist again. Dazed, she called out, "No! Please!

Anything! I'll do anything!"

Crocker paused, hand still in the air, and looked at Anna. "Anything?" His eyes flashed and the wicked grin returned.

"Yes," Anna begged. There was too much pain in her head, her back, for her to shiver in fear at that look directed at her. "*Please.*"

Crocker's smile turned into an amused grin as he glanced at Luke. Some kind of inside joke. He looked back at Anna. "I'm sure you've heard the governor's building his armies. If you joined his forces, any money you earn would go toward the debt your mother owes. It would take the full two years, but your mother would be free to run her little shop, rather than sit in a dirty cell because her debt is past due."

Mother would be free. Anna didn't have to think about it. "Yes! Yes, I'll do it!"

"Looks like we've got a fighter on our hands, boys," Crocker called to the other men. He pulled a white handkerchief out of his pocket and cleaned off his brass knuckles. Without looking up from the task, he said, "We'll be out front. You have ten minutes."

The three walked through the door, Luke standing in front of the open doorway and blocking the light.

Anna helped her mother stand upright, taking in the bruise around a long cut on her mother's swollen cheek.

"You have to run," her mother told her quietly, watching Luke's back. "Get out of here."

Anna shook her head. "No, they'll take it out on you. I'm not letting that happen."

Her mother cried, "I won't let you go. I can't let my baby fight a war." She wrapped Anna in a hug, as if to keep her there.

Anna hugged her back tightly and said into her hair, "It'll be all right. It'll all be over in two years. Maybe sooner, if you save what you can and put it toward the loan." She felt her mother crying, her body heaving with each breath. "They might grant me leave. I could visit before then."

"I'm so sorry," her mother said. "I'm so sorry. I'll never forgive myself."

"They trapped you," Anna told her mother sternly.

Her mother was still muttering, "I'm sorry, I'm sorry. I can't lose you, too."

Anna stiffened, then pulled away from her mother so she could look her in the eyes. "I swear it on the Well—no, I swear it on Dad's grave, I *will* come back. And I'll write, if they'll let me. When this is all over, it will be like it never happened."

Her mother wiped at her tears, nodding.

"We don't have much time. Would you help me pack?"

The two went into the little back bedroom. Anna rolled her clothes and put them in the empty bag that still hung at her side. Three pairs of pants and three shirts, socks and undergarments, one thick wool jacket. That was all she had. Her bow and quiver, she strapped to her back. Her mother gathered some food and swaddled it in cloth before giving it to Anna, who tucked it in on top of her clothes. She looked up to see her mother pulling the strings tight on a small leather coin purse, which she then handed to Anna.

"Here. I don't know what you may need, but this will help."

Anna opened the bag and looked inside. There had to be a hundred gold in it. "No, this is too much!"

"You have no armor, no weapons. You'll need it," her mother insisted.

"Fine," she conceded.

She walked behind the counter and bent toward her knife. It looked normal, no longer red hot. She reached down, hesitated, then grasped it. It was warm. She stuck it in her belt.

"You haven't changed your mind, have you?" Crocker's voice called from outside.

Anna hated the idea of the neighbors seeing strongmen stationed outside their home. The thought distracted her enough to get on with it. She turned to her mother. "Call for Mr. Farney. You know old Jim down the road? His son hunts every day. I'm sure for a small price, he could get you what you need to eat and to bake."

Her mother started crying again.

Anna willed herself to keep going, even as her eyes brimmed with water and her ears heated. "A-and I'm sure Jo would be happy to cook for you now and then if you get lonely. You'll just have to ignore his bread. Tell everyone it's my fault. Tell them I got bored and ran off to join the army."

Luke ducked back inside, and Anna took a shuddering breath. She squeezed her mother into another hug.

"I love you, Mom."

"I love you, Lynnie," her mother cried.

Luke tugged at Anna's arm, firm, but gentler than Anna had expected.

"No!" her mother cried, reaching for her.

"I'll be back!" Anna called to her as she stumbled outside.

She heard her mother praying before the door slammed shut.

6

ANNA HELD HER BAG TIGHTLY AS SHE MET THE MEN ON THE STREET.

"What's wrong?" Crocker teased. "You've just saved your mother's life." Quieter, less cheerily, he added, "Few people survive Woulfe's prison."

Anna's jaw tightened and she mumbled, "She should've never been allowed to take a loan."

Crocker's brows lifted. "You'll have to take that up with Ivan. I don't have anything to do with the dealmaking, I just make sure what's due gets paid."

Anna shook her head.

They led her north on the road out of Wallset. She stared at her feet for a while, then picked her head up to look ahead. The gate out of town was wide open, as it usually was, revealing trees and grass and birds beyond.

She felt eyes on her. Turning slightly, she found the dwarf staring at her, his eyes such a vibrant brown that they shone red in the sunlight like his hair. She remembered her knife burning red hot in her hand and quickly looked away.

"It's late," Luke's deep voice rumbled behind her. "We won't make it to Hillcrest 'til tomorrow, even if we walk through the night."

"This is our last chance for a bed before Hillcrest. We'll get a room," Crocker told him, gesturing vaguely at the Wallset Inn. It was barely an inn, with only three rooms to rent. The chimney lazily released smoke from the top of the large wood-beam framed building, and like most places in town, anything that happened there was common knowledge within twelve hours. Alvin, the innkeeper's son, was out front sweeping the steps. She gave him a stiff nod and a stiffer smile. He nodded back, and then kept staring. Anna sighed.

Her lips tightened into a line. "I don't mind walking through the night."

"You will," Crocker said, "when you get to Hillcrest and the commander makes you prove you can fight."

Anna's brows furrowed. "What do you mean?"

"All new recruits go through a trial," Luke explained as he adjusted the pack strapped to his back. Crocker eyed him curiously, a thin frown on his thin lips, as Luke went on. "They won't take in people with no skill."

Anna shook her head, confused. "They don't train people?"

Crocker scoffed. "Of course they do, but if there's nothing there to begin with, it's not worth their time. Let's hope you're good with that bow and knife." He eyed each weapon dubiously.

Anna's jaw set. *I'll have to prove myself, then.* She wanted to tell Crocker that she could show him firsthand, but didn't want to jeopardize her precarious position. After she imagined sticking her knife into Crocker's shoulder so that he'd never be able to swing his fist again, the anger passed and doubt crept in. She cringed at the waver in her voice as she asked, "And if I fail? If they don't let me in?"

Crocker returned his gaze forward. "You'll come back home with us, and we'll be taking your mother."

"That won't happen," she said. *I'll make sure of it.*

"We'll see." Crocker interlaced his fingers and pulled them against the back of his neck leisurely, letting the hold carry his arms. "All right," he sighed. "Let's pay for a room and get some food."

Cricket led the group into the inn. Alvin ran around the back as they approached. Once inside, Cricket crossed to the large fireplace, grabbed a short stool from nearby, and sat in front of it. There weren't any flames, but Anna was sure Jo would start it as soon as the sun set and the air chilled.

Crocker nodded at Luke, who nodded back before taking a step closer to Anna. Crocker walked up to the bar to get a room.

Jo stood there, pretending to clean the bar top, but shooting nervous glances at the men that had walked in with Anna. He stiffened as he talked with Crocker.

Anna found a little comfort knowing that her mother would be hiding at home for the time being. She wouldn't come running to talk to Jo and find them here.

Luke looked Anna over briefly, eyes searching for something specific. "You can use that bow, that knife?"

Anna's eyes narrowed. She nodded.

"Good," he nodded, seeming a little relieved. "It's different, using them against people," he told her, "but if you know how to use them, you'll learn. You'll make it."

"What…?" Anna's question trailed off as she realized she didn't know what to ask. *What are you doing? Why are you acting… concerned?*

"I have a mother, too," he said in answer, his dark eyes softening. Then he nodded and turned back toward Crocker.

The thin man was making his way back over. "Grab a seat. They'll bring out food."

Luke led Anna around a table and toward Cricket. He gestured for her to sit at the end and took the seat next to her, putting her in between the two men. Crocker sat across from her.

"Cricket," Crocker said.

The dwarf snapped his fingers, his rings shining faintly in the candlelight. A small spark jumped from his hand, faded and disappeared, and then the fire roared to life.

Anna gasped.

Cricket turned to smile at her.

"How-how did you do that?" she asked.

"Magic," Cricket said, his voice like small stones turning in a rolling bucket. It was higher than she expected.

"My friend here is *blessed* by the Well-Mother," Crocker mocked with a teasing grin. "One of many reasons we keep him around."

The dwarf grinned coolly at Crocker, his eyes narrowed and hard. "You'd be lucky for the Mother to step on you. Be glad she's kind even to those who don't believe."

Crocker rolled his eyes and then turned them to Anna, firelight flickering across them. "Are you part of the Creed?"

Anna shook her head slightly. "No."

"The Creed." The dwarf said it like he was discussing the rear end of a sick horse. He shook his head, a frown on his face.

Crocker sighed at his friend, apparently familiar with his feelings on the subject.

Jo brought out four bowls. Chicken, peas, and potatoes filled each of them, with a little gravy spread over top and a dry piece of bread. He set them down and hovered for a moment, looking at Anna with worry in his eyes.

"The ale, too," Crocker waved at him.

"Uh, yes, sir." Jo nodded and rushed back behind the bar.

After his first bite, Crocker announced, "It's no Hillcrest tavern, but it'll do."

Jo returned with four mugs of ale. As he set them down, he tried, "Might

I ask what brings you gentlemen into town?" He raised his eyebrows at Anna and deepened the creases across his forehead.

Anna discretely shook her head. *Now is not the time to get involved.*

Crocker took a drink and then grinned at him. "This young woman has volunteered to join Lord Woulfe's armed forces." He gestured at Anna with his mug. "She wants to fight some Vasbrute vermin! We're going to deliver her to camp."

Jo's eyes grew big. "A-ah," he laughed nervously. "What a...brave thing to do."

"Indeed." Crocker turned his smile to Anna, then said to Jo, "That'll be all, thank you."

Jo sighed, gave Anna another pitying look, and then turned to walk back to the bar. Alvin was peeking from the kitchen, until his father pushed him back inside and shut the door.

It was quiet as they ate, until the question bothering Anna came out between bites. "Have you always had your..." Anna searched for the right word, "abilities?"

"No," the dwarf said, stroking his beard with his free hand. He had finished most of his food. "And that's not a story for this fire."

"So dramatic." Crocker rolled his eyes. "You ever consider the theater?"

Cricket glared at Crocker and sent him a crude gesture.

Crocker sneered at the dwarf, who turned back to the fire. The thin man lifted a curious brow at Anna. "How old are you?"

Anna saw Luke bristle slightly, but decided there was no harm in answering. "Twenty-four."

Crocker hummed thoughtfully, and it reminded Anna of that feeling she'd had when she first saw him. The vibrations from his throat felt off—not out of tune, but like they didn't belong. He looked her over again, slowly, blatantly.

"Is anyone in town going to miss you? Besides your mother."

She swallowed the lump that formed in her throat. She had friends, but they were distant friends she only talked with during town festivals or around birthdays. They probably wouldn't even notice she was missing until Jo and Alvin spread the news through town. "Yes." She tried to sound convincing.

"Well," Crocker didn't recognize the lie or didn't care, "if you *do* return in two years, they'll surely have moved on. But that's probably for the best." He picked at something under his nails. "They'll have been getting *married* and having *babies*. You'll be getting carved up by Vasbrute."

Luke seemed to settle at this response. Anna fidgeted, wondering how what Crocker had said was better than what Luke had been imagining.

"Then we *are* going to war?" she asked.

Crocker sighed sadly. "We've caught scouts on this side of the wall. That's more than enough to break the Treaties."

Anna reminded herself to breathe. *I'm joining up at the worst possible time.*

"You just have to make it two years," Crocker reminded. "If you don't, your mother will still be expected to finish paying her debt."

Anna's head shook slightly and her sharp eyes shot daggers at him. "What?"

"You're not earning anything if you're dead." He smiled coolly, and she shivered. "The debt will still be here, even if you aren't."

Cricket mumbled something that Anna couldn't discern. A frown spread over his features. Luke looked down at his food with a scowl on his face.

They slept in one room with two single beds. Anna slept on the floor with Luke, who laid in front of the door. The bruises forming on her back made it impossible to get comfortable on the hard wood boards. She held her bag to her tightly and absentmindedly played with the pendant on her necklace as she listened to the men sleeping around her. She tried her best to avoid thinking of her father, and what he would think of this. It was a long night.

7

LEONARD CROCKER HAD MEANT IT WHEN HE SAID THEY WOULD RISE before dawn. Light was just beginning to touch the sky when Anna woke to a boot kicking her ankle.

"Up and at 'em," Crocker's voice called. "We have a lot of walking to do."

Anna sat up stiffly. Her joints were aching from sleeping on the floor, and she could feel all the bruises from the day before. Her hand stung from the burn across her palm. She stretched and yawned, then rubbed her tired eyes. She ran her fingers through her hair, pulling any loose strands back toward the braid, and then stood with the men. A single mourning dove called in the distance, but the rest of the town was still asleep as they left the inn.

Anna was tall, but Crocker and Luke's long legs made longer strides. She struggled to maintain their pace. Cricket was apparently used to the speed. This close, Anna could see that the dwarf was a full head shorter than her, but at least twice as thick. Every time she fell out of pace, Crocker would tell her to hurry, but she noticed Luke would slow slightly. The strong man avoided looking at her. He spoke only in response to Crocker, who always seemed to have plenty to say. Cricket was silent as ever.

The walk was long, and Anna was quiet. Their conversation last night had left a bad taste in her mouth. It was clear Crocker only revealed useful information when it would hurt Anna, so she kept her mouth shut and kept her questions to herself.

As they passed through small villages on the road, the people turned away, went inside, found somewhere else to be. Nobody thought of debt collectors fondly, and Crocker's little band was obvious. They looked at her with pity. She stared down at her old boots.

It was evening and the sun was low in the west when Hillcrest's great walls appeared over the slope in front of them. The trees had opened up to grassland. There was still a good distance to the cobblestones, but it was encouraging to see their destination ahead. The men seemed to be relieved, but they also sped up.

White stone encircled the city, a shining beacon in the late light. The bright walls were two stories high, and the open, wooden doors centered on the path were just as tall. They were covered in iron banding that curled into two wolves. The wolves lunged at each other when the doors were closed and lunged into town when the doors were open. She knew the hard-packed dirt path changed to neat cobblestone at the threshold. Anna had seen it once when she was young, but she couldn't remember anything specific, only bustling crowds, big smells, and bright sunlight. Her town was surrounded and covered in trees. The only shade in this city came from its buildings. She saw a gathering of tents and people to the east of the city. Apparently, that was where Lord Woulfe was gathering his troops.

She risked Crocker's cruel tongue as she asked, "Are we going into the city?"

"*You* won't be," the tall man answered. "We'll drop you with the commander, make sure what you earn gets sent to us, and then leave you to it." His hand waved in the air lazily.

One of Anna's hands found her bow, the other held the handle of her small knife, grounding herself as her world shifted around her.

Massive green-and-white-striped tents were spread out near the eastern base of the wall. Banners with a snarling green wolf on them flapped in the breeze from their peaks—Governor Woulfe's crest. Smaller, simpler canvas tents spread from there, the space in between filled with people. Shouts and chatter rolled over the field to her ears.

A simple wooden desk stood at the front of the nearest tent. There was a man wearing leather armor seated at it. Crocker approached him while the rest of the group held back. As he discussed Anna with this man, she took the time to get a better look at the camp.

She could hear metal clanging in the tent next to her, and people walked out of the nearby opening holding armor and swords. Across from the tent was a small trail of smoke rising into the sky and the smell of dinner. Next to this large tent was a smaller tent that was closed up, and after that, there was a long, wooden structure built against the wall of the city. This was a stable, she recognized.

A large opening filled the space between these structures, and a hundred small tents. A million footprints had beaten the ground between. She watched the group of people on the other end of the opening. Most of them sat at long tables, eating. Some were still training, a small group moving in sync as someone shouted orders. *I hope they don't expect me to have any sword training.*

The man at the front of the group dismissed them with a call and a wave of his arm. They dispersed, and the man walked toward the desk.

He was tall, and he wore full plate armor that reflected sunlight into Anna's eyes when he turned a certain way. His light brown hair was cut traditionally close to his head, and he had a short beard. A long sword swung at his side. He leaned forward next to his seated friend, looked over whatever had been written down, and stood back up, frowning at Crocker. Crocker waited patiently—the first time Anna had seen him act with respect. After some shared words Anna couldn't hear, the armored man walked around the table and toward her. She set her shoulders back and waited for whatever was coming.

"I am Commander Lyon," he said in a deep voice. "You are Annalyn Hale."

She met his brown eyes and nodded. "Anna, sir."

He looked her over quickly, over the bow, the quiver, the knife, and then returned his gaze to hers. "What can you do, Anna?"

"I'm good with a bow. I can do a little with a knife," she answered confidently, but honestly. She could talk herself up, but she wouldn't lie. She glanced down at the blade strapped to his hip, then back to his eyes. "I've never held a sword."

He grinned in amusement. "Most people haven't." His hand settled on the hilt of his sword. "Have you ever used a longbow?"

Anna shook her head.

"Follow me." Commander Lyon turned to walk through the large opening between the tents.

Anna followed, ignoring the urge to glance behind her.

The commander led her through the tents and into the open area on the other side. Here, archers were practicing with targets set up at different distances. They stopped and waited as he approached, the closest moving out of his way. Anna guessed the furthest target was 150 yards. He stopped in front of the nearest target, which stood about fifty yards away, and then gestured with his gauntleted hand. "Show me what you can do."

She was aware of the eyes on her. *Of course it's a spectacle when someone comes to try out. How many fail?*

She pulled her bow from her back and nocked an arrow. Her hands shook slightly as she drew back the string. She felt the pain in her right palm and her bruised back as her muscles went taut. She glanced at the commander, who was taking in her form. His brows were low over his eyes, and he had crossed his arms.

There was no telling how high the bar was. If she wanted to impress him, she might have to do more than make this shot. She drew in a deep breath, trying to calm her nerves and steady her aim. At the last moment, she decided to try something she had only succeeded at once. As she exhaled, she shot her first arrow. While it flew, she nocked a second, pulled the string of her bow back a little further, and shot it.

The first arrow thumped into the center of the nearest target. Second arrow still flying, she nocked a third, pulled back as hard as she could, aimed, exhaled, and released. The second arrow hit the outside of a target seventy-five yards away, left of the center. The third wedged itself into the wooden leg of a target a hundred yards away, to the right of center and low.

If anyone nearby hadn't been paying attention, they were now. Jaw tight, she lowered her arms and turned to the commander.

The corner of his mouth was lifted in a grin as he stared across the open field at the targets. "Well done. I thought reaching a target at that distance with *that* bow," his hand lifted toward the old shortbow in her hands, "was impossible. You've proved me wrong."

She let out a relieved breath. Glancing back at the targets, she wondered if she should retrieve her arrows. Before she could ask, he said, "We'll get a read on your hand-to-hand next."

Anna's heart stuttered. "Hand-to-hand?"

"Don't worry." Commander Lyon grinned and turned to walk towards the wall. Anna followed him. "You passed the test. This is to understand what other training you need. Just don't hurt yourself so badly that you can't use a bow."

Anna sensed that was a joke, but she wouldn't underestimate whatever challenge was next. He led her to a large square of dirt that was marked in the corners with yellow flags. People gathered around, waiting to watch.

"Taggert!" The commander's shout startled Anna.

"Yes, sir." A tall, young man stepped out of the crowd wearing simple leather armor. His blonde hair shone in the sunlight and his blue eyes glanced at Anna before holding the commander's gaze.

"Show us what Hale can do," he told him.

"Yes, sir," Taggert nodded.

The commander turned to Anna. "You don't know how to use a sword, so no weapons. You can surrender at any time, but this is for us to assess your skill, so it would benefit you to show us. Keep away from the eyes, and if you break my soldier's knee, elbow, or shoulder, I'll be very upset."

Anna's eyebrows rose. *He thinks I can break that guy's knee?* She nodded and turned to Taggert.

"Same to you," the commander called more loudly to Taggert. "No eyes, and she needs her arms and legs."

"Yes, sir," Taggert said, and then took a deep breath and stepped forward. He took off the belt that held his sword and tossed it to the edge of the square. He lowered himself into a crouch, arms ready in front of him.

Anna's heart beat loudly in her ears. She set her weapons on the ground and stepped toward the center of the space, facing Taggert. She tried to mirror his stance. She knew it must be obvious she didn't know what she was doing, but Taggert confirmed it as he eyed her skeptically.

"Ready?" the commander asked her.

She nodded.

Commander Lyon held a hand in the air. It flew down as he shouted, "Fight!"

The crowd around them broke into cheers as Taggert immediately charged forward. Anna's breath caught and she thought it would be over just as it started, but her instinct kicked in at the last moment. She lowered herself and scuttled around him, coming up behind him. His arms swung into nothing. Adrenaline rushed through her, and the crowd roared.

Anna had no fighting experience. Her father had only taught her to hunt, and she never needed to punch wildlife. He'd taught her what to do in case she ran into a bear, but the bottom line of that lesson had been to get away, eyes on the bear so that it knew you weren't giving it an opening, arms out to look as big as possible.

If you can't run, she heard her father's voice in her head, *you'll have to trick it. Bears are big and fast, but they can also be dumb. Throw some food at it, distract it, and give yourself the opportunity to get away.*

As Taggert turned, Anna imagined him as a bear. But this bear didn't want food. He wanted to beat her. She'd let him think he had.

Taggert aimed a kick at her side, and she shifted her weight to her back leg. She felt a spark of heat at her collarbone. His foot came forward and she threw out her arms. The impact stung her hands, but she grabbed and pulled, dragging him off balance, and he fell forward. Anna brought up her knee, and it landed hard against his stomach. His leathers may have taken most of the blow, but he still grunted in pain.

The crowd roared with cheers and laughter. Anna's knee burst into pain. She jumped back, hobbling on her stiff knee and flexing her bruised hands. "Ow, shit," she hissed.

Taggert steadied himself and shot Anna a glare. Now he was angry. He charged her again, faster than before. She wasn't quick enough to get out of the way. His shoulder met her waist and then she was off the ground. Taggert threw her into the dirt, knocking the air out of her and hitting every bruise from the day before.

Lack of breath cut off Anna's cry, and she wheezed as she tried to draw in air. Pain sent stars soaring across her vision, and the surrounding noise sounded far off.

"That's enough!" Commander Lyon's voice broke through the crowd and everyone quieted. Taggert stopped with his knee on Anna's chest. "Ease off, Taggert, you've won."

The man kneeling over her straightened his leathers, stood, and then extended his hand. The anger in his eyes wasn't gone, but he didn't seem angry at Anna anymore. She put up her hand and he pulled her up. She shifted her weight to her uninjured left knee and rubbed the back of her head. Tears had welled in her eyes at the pain, and she quickly wiped them away while trying to catch her breath.

Commander Lyon stepped out into the open square, looking amused. "Thank you, Taggert. You're dismissed."

"Yes, sir," Taggert nodded, and he walked into the crowd. A few people caught him, giving him light shoves as they teased him.

"I doubt he'll ever leave himself so open in a kick again," Commander Lyon mumbled to Anna, quietly enough only she could hear. Then he turned to face her. "You all right?"

She nodded and stood up straight. "Previous injury."

The commander frowned slightly, glancing back to where Crocker was still waiting. Anna wondered what he was thinking. He sighed, the smile returning to his face, and turned his gaze back to her. "Well, we'll get you checked out, and then we can get you armed. I can see you have no previous combat training. You'll start tomorrow."

"Uh, yes, sir," Anna nodded, copying Taggert's responses.

"There'll be plenty of time for *yes, sir* later," the commander said with a wave of his hand. "Come on, follow me."

As the commander led her through camp, he told her she would get her own tent, bedroll, and blanket. She was expected to keep them clean and in good condition. They provided three meals a day, the first just after the morning horn, the second at midday, and the third in the late afternoon or early evening, just after training finished. She was allowed one ale at each meal, but if she wanted more, it would come out of her pay for the week. Similarly, the weapons and armor she'd be given were considered hers and would either be paid for when she received them or would come out of her pay.

The commander took her into a tent and left her with a nurse, saying he was going to settle things with *her friends.*

"Tell the man at the armory that you're a level three archer," he said before ducking out of the tent.

The nurse was an older woman in a simple, dark gray dress with a heavy apron over it. She gave Anna a physical, hummed in disappointment at her bruises, and then led her on to the armory.

Between the medical tent and the city wall was an open-air blacksmithing forge. A thick man stood outside, pounding red hot metal against an anvil. He was covered in hide to protect him from his work, and his face was dripping with sweat. She was so distracted by the noise and motion that she didn't notice the long wooden counter directly to her right, or the tent full of armor and weapons.

"Here we are." The woman lightly touched Anna's arm and then directed her attention to the counter. A man sat behind it, waiting for something to do. He perked up as Anna looked at him.

"Thank you," Anna said to the woman before she left. She turned to the counter. "I was told I'm a level three archer."

He got out of his chair, somewhat slowly, and stepped toward her. He was old, with a small hunch in his back. He had a gray mustache and thinning gray hair. "A third level archer," he mumbled to himself as he started to round the counter. "Let's get you a bow to match."

She followed him over to a rack of bows. There were three kinds. Most of them were shortbows, more elegant versions of the one she had strapped across her back. Next were the longbows, flat weapons that were dyed green. Last was a short row of longbows that were slightly bigger than the others, gilded with small wolf carvings at their grip and little golden accents at the tips of the bow.

The armorer pulled off one of the simpler longbows and handed it to her. It was as tall as she was. It also came with a belted quiver full of arrows, the tips of which were sharp, bright metal. Anna took them and followed him to an area with a variety of swords, long, short, thin, thick, curved, straight. She had no idea of their names or how to use them. When the man held out a short, thin blade in a leather scabbard, she took it.

"Now, armor," the old man said, making his way toward the leather armor hanging in the corner of the room. He eyed several sets before pulling one off the rack. "Set those down."

Anna set her weapons on a chair. She pulled off her old bow and knife and set them with the rest.

"Try this on," the man told her. "Pull it on from the side."

She took the armor from him and then attempted to slip into it. It was heavy. He had to help her figure it out. When she got the clasps at her waist and shoulder shut, he stood back and held a hand to his chin as he inspected it.

It was fitted for a man. The shoulders were loose and the hips were tight. The old man stepped forward, humming to himself in his hoarse voice as he unsnapped something at her shoulders and then something at her waist, and finally at her hips. The whole thing came loose and fell down onto the tops of her shoulders. He snapped something again at each shoulder, fitting the joints to her form. When he was done at her waist and hips, it felt like a stiff, thick second skin. The weight of it diminished as it sat correctly across her body.

"There we are," the old man sighed, pleased with himself.

He showed her how to wear her belts around it and where to attach her weapons. He had her move in the armor, pulling her bow back, putting it away, and slowly swinging the sword. He unsnapped something on her shoulders and then refitted it together. She moved her arm in a circle. Now there was full range of motion, with no pinching or tugging.

"Thank you," she told him as he rounded the counter.

"It's only my job," he told her. "Can't have our people running around fighting Vasbrute unable to lift their arms."

"Right," Anna breathed, nodding in agreement.

"That'll be 100 gold for the lot. You can pay now or have it come out of your pay in installments until it's paid off."

"How much…do I get paid?" Anna asked hesitantly, wishing she had asked the commander before he left.

"As a third seed archer," the man said, "you'll get around 130 gold each month."

"I'll pay now, if that's all right."

"'Course," the old man shrugged.

Anna took out most of the money in her coin purse and set it on the counter. He gathered it into a large bag, and then locked it away under the counter in a hidden cabinet. As she was about to ask him where she should go next, she heard someone call her name behind her. Turning, she found the young man she'd sparred with standing at the entrance.

"I'm going to help you find your tent," he told her.

She nodded to him, turned to give the armorer a wave, and then followed him outside. She looked around. Her debt collectors were nowhere to be seen.

"Here." Taggert held out a folded piece of paper. "It's a copy of your contract."

Anna took it from him. She'd look at it later. "Thanks."

"I'm Pyran, by the way. Pyran Taggert." He glanced over at her as they walked.

"Anna Hale. Nice to meet you, Pyran."

"You don't have much skill," Pyran said, as if commenting on the weather, "but what you did with my kick was quick thinking."

"Thanks," Anna said quietly, not entirely sure it was a compliment.

"The tents are gathered into a few different groups," Pyran told her as they walked towards them. "It's mostly split into regiments, because they train together in the morning—swordsmen with swordsmen, archers together, some healers, and there's a small group of mages."

"Mages?" Anna asked, unfamiliar with the term.

"Those with magical abilities." Pyran wiggled his fingers. "Blessed by the Well-Mother, or whatever. The ones who have magical skills they can use in battle are in own regiment, but we only have a handful here. They train outside of camp."

"Why?" She tried to picture Cricket in the middle of some great battle, but she couldn't.

"So they don't burn it down, or lock us into stone or something, I guess," he shrugged. "Anyway, the archers' tents are in the back to the left. This way."

She followed him between the tents. Each of the regiments had one big bonfire built at its center. The tents were numbered with white paint near their peaks. Her tent was A-14.

"You can leave anything you want in your tent. There hasn't been any trouble with stealing, Commander Lyon won't have it, but there's a lockbox in there for anything you want to keep safe."

"Okay." Anna swallowed nervously and stared at the tent's entrance.

"They'll blow the horn for supper soon. It's best to get in line quickly so you don't get the last of it. The toilets and showers are against the wall, next to the stables. Best time to use the shower is before the first horn. That way, they've just been cleaned."

"Thanks," Anna told him sincerely.

"Don't worry about it." He hesitated, then said, "I remember my first day at camp. Someone showed me around after they beat me, too. We all have something we can learn from each other."

"I appreciate it." Anna nodded to him.

"You can come find me for dinner," he said, "Lucy's a little cold at first, but she'll warm up to you."

Anna's brows rose. "I'll think about it."

"My tent is I-9," he thumbed behind him, presumably in the direction of his tent, "with the other swordsmen, if you ever need anything."

I-9? "I thought A stood for archer?" she questioned, looking at the white numbers on her tent.

"I for infantry," he explained. "A for archer. H for healers and M for mages."

"Got it," she nodded.

He waved and walked off.

Anna held her new weapons and glanced around. Small groups of people were walking between the tents, chatting and laughing. None of them took notice of her. She ducked into the tent and took a breath.

I did it. I made it. Now I just have to survive.

8

ANNA FELT DIRTY, BUT AS MUCH AS SHE WANTED TO SHOWER, SHE KNEW it would be better to wait until morning, like Pyran had told her.

She could stand up in the middle of the tent, but had to crouch if she walked to the sides. There was a small bed against the back wall, raised off the ground on a short platform. It was layered with one thick blanket over one thin blanket, and had a small pillow. To the left of the bed was the chest that Pyran had mentioned. It was wooden, with metal strapping and a large metal lock, and the key sat on top of the chest. There was a short table on the other side of the bed, holding a single white candle. A waxed canvas tarp covered the ground beneath her.

This was the first place she'd ever had wholly to herself. The thought had snuck up on her. She thought about the small room she'd shared with her mother, the sound of her mother gently snoring next to her, the smells that drifted in from the kitchen during an early morning of baking. And then she thought about her mother, baking alone, eating alone, and sleeping alone. This space she stood in now felt empty. Other people surrounded it, and yet it felt dark and cold. It was as if she could feel her mother's loneliness in it…and maybe her own.

Anna let out a rough sigh and moved to the chest, opening it. Inside were a handful of candles and a box of matches. She took out a match and lit it. She pulled herself across the bed enough that she could grab the candle and light it before replacing it again. *A little better.*

She set her bag in the chest, taking the food out. She contemplated taking her armor off and stowing it away. *Will the others eat in their armor with their weapons strapped to them? I hope not.* Even though the leathers were fitted to her, she felt uncomfortable in them.

In the end, she decided it didn't matter, and she took them off. It took her a while to remember how to undo the fastenings. She set her knife on top of her armor, resting her two bows and quivers against the chest. From her bag, she pulled a little comb. She took the braid out of her hair, brushed through the mess, and then braided it again. The braid came to nearly her elbows, ending in a knot of black ribbon.

A horn sounded three blasts. Remembering Pyran's warning about being late, she made her way out of the tent. She noted that most of the people walking towards dinner were not wearing armor.

Everyone congregated in one long line that split into two at the main tent. The line moved more quickly than she would have guessed. She was given a plate full of hot beef stew and a mug of ale. The food smelled good, if a little bland. The ale seemed average compared to the homebrew at the Wallset Inn. She wandered toward a large grouping of picnic tables on the grass by the tent, where people were gathered talking and eating. She noticed the eyes that followed her, the people who turned to say something quietly to the person next to them. While she was wondering if she should find Pyran or eat in her tent, she saw a hand raise into the air and wave once.

Pyran looked at her from under the arm, and he lowered his hand when their eyes met. He sat next to a slightly older, tan woman with brown hair and soft hazel eyes that seemed to contradict the stiff frown on her face. Her mouth shifted into a terse grin as Anna sat across from them.

"Lucy, this is Anna. Anna, this is Lucy," Pyran introduced. "Lucy's one of the infantry trainers."

"Nice to meet you," Lucy nodded. "What brings you into *Lord Woulfe's* military?" She said the governor's name in a snobby tone. "Escaping the family business like Pyran here?" The corner of her mouth lifted into a smirk as she teased him.

"Shuddup," Pyran told her between bites of food.

Lucy rolled her eyes and turned to Anna expectantly.

"Uh, something like that," she said nervously.

Pyran said, "For the record, I was supposed to take over my father's business, but I was terrible at it. Believe me, it would've been a disaster. So I left. I got out of my younger brother's way. He's much better suited for it than I am—and I get to do what I like."

"Throw a sword around?" Lucy asked jokingly.

"Train," Pyran corrected, shooting her a glare. "I want to be a commander one day." His chin lifted.

"Keep working on your sword form and you might get there someday," his mentor teased him again.

"You both fight with swords?" Anna asked.

"I prefer a sword and shield," Lucy responded.

Pyran rolled his eyes. "She thinks she's special."

"I am." Lucy grinned.

"Arrogant," Pyran mumbled into his food.

"It's not arrogance if it's true," Lucy said. She turned to Anna. "Never let anyone tell you that you're bragging when you're just stating what you can do. I hear you prefer a bow. Sounds like you're pretty good with it, too. You did quite the trick with the targets earlier."

Anna shrugged. "I tried that once on a herd of deer, but I missed them, too."

"How old are you?" Lucy asked her.

"Twenty-four."

"Another young one," Lucy sighed. "I thought Pyran was too much. Luckily, you've fallen into the right group. We'll have you fit and ready in no time."

"Did you hear?" Anna heard from the table next to her. "The Vasbrute have invaded Dore."

"No, no," another voice from the table argued. "They're *planning* to invade Dore."

Anna thought of her mother, alone and so close to the wall. "Is that true about Dore?" she asked Lucy.

"Hm?" Lucy turned to Anna with her mug at her lips. She swallowed and set it down, then glanced at the table behind her where the chatter was coming from. "Oh, I don't think so. This town is the biggest rumor mill in Telluth. Some people will say anything for attention."

Anna nodded, but kept her ears open.

"They'll be hard-pressed to get through Lady Gratadia's forces."

"Those bastards'll die at the wall before they ever set foot on our land."

"Didn't you hear? They already have."

"That's why I joined the forces. Going to take out some Vasbrute vermin."

Anna had heard that word used to describe the Vasbrute before, but she always thought it was odd. Even if the Vasbrute were cruel invaders, they were physically quite the opposite of any vermin she knew of. They were intimidating, taller and stronger than any other being. Still, most of the people gossiping puffed up their chests and talked about how many they'd kill, given the chance.

As Anna ate, she tried not to think about what would happen if she came face to face with Vasbrute. *I don't think I'd walk away from that.*

ANNA SPENT THE FOLLOWING DAYS GETTING USED TO HER LONGBOW IN THE morning and training in melee in the afternoon. Commander Lyon often walked by, checking her progress. She shared meals with Pyran and Lucy.

At the end of the first week, she was exhausted. Her arms burned from the weight of drawing the longbow, which had been adjusted by her trainer to be more difficult so that she could build muscle. Her legs were sore from training herself to maintain a combat-ready stance. Even though her previous bruises were fading and her hand had healed, new injuries popped up. Lucy liked to hit her pupils with the flat of her sword wherever they were off their form, but she cheered the loudest when someone completed a move correctly. And while the others rested on their weekend, she spent the time with Pyran, catching up on basics.

The second day of weekend training with Pyran, she broke down. She stumbled and fell as they worked through a mock-fight, a mistake that would've killed her if she was really in battle, and she burst into tears. Pyran hovered over her, looking concerned but unsure of what to do.

He raised his hands as if to do something, then paused. "Are you all right?"

"No, no." She tried to quiet her sobs. "I shouldn't be here."

"What do you mean?" Pyran sat on his haunches next to her.

She shook her head, red face growing hotter. "I'll never make it. Those Vasbrute are going to kill me."

"Hey, hey," Pyran attempted to sound comforting. "We're a long way from fighting any Vasbrute. No one is good at this at first, and you mostly started from scratch."

"Oh, Sons and Daughters," Anna put her head in her hands.

"I didn't mean—" Pyran said quickly, "I was just trying to say you have time. You'll get better!"

"What if I don't?" Anna said into her palms.

Pyran sighed. "You already have. You're just too sore to see it."

"Really?"

"Definitely."

She wiped her tears and took a deep breath. She was ashamed of herself for reacting so emotionally. "I'm sorry. I don't know what came over me."

"That's all right. You're exhausted." He moved to sit on the ground next to her. "Why don't we take the rest of the day off?"

She nodded.

"You can talk to me, you know. I won't tell Lucy."

"Thanks." She could feel the truth in his words. She wanted to trust him, but all she could do was sit quietly and avoid meeting his gaze.

"All right." He stood up and held out his hand to her. "Let's get you a snack and a nap."

A huff of a laugh escaped her, and a corner of her mouth lifted as she took his hand.

9

A MONTH OF TRAINING PASSED, THEN TWO. SHE GOT A LETTER BACK FROM her mother, telling her that the Creed had asked for help in baking sweet buns for the summer solstice. Anna responded with all the skills she'd learned. Hopefully, she'd spend two years here on the grounds, perfecting her skill with the bow and then training others.

She fell into a routine, and although she could not sneak into the woods during the day, she found a sense of contentment in it. Eventually, she could hold her own during spars, though she rarely won. She was stronger and faster than she had ever been, and she was thankful to her new friends. They continued to sit together during meals and go out on the weekend. She showed them the healing that Mister Farney had taught her and became their medic when sparring got too rough.

She was sparring with Pyran on a particularly hot day when the commander approached, trailed by three men.

Two armored men in bright breastplates with a wolf embossed across them flanked a portly man in dark green finery. His graying red hair fell in waves and his matching beard covered most of his throat. He looked out over the training grounds with his chin raised, looking down his nose at the people he passed. They paused twenty feet from the square Anna and Pyran were in.

"Come on," Lucy called to her trainees, ignoring the newcomers. "You wouldn't stop a fight just because someone interesting walked up, would you?"

Anna and Pyran turned back to each other, sharing a puzzled glance. They returned to their spar, but Anna couldn't shake her distraction. She glanced at the commander and the rich man speaking quietly to each other and looking their way. His many rings sparkled in the sunlight. Pyran took the opportunity to knock the sword out of her hands. She hissed as her hands stung.

"Pay attention!" Lucy scolded.

Anna frowned and picked up her sword. "Is that who I think it is? The governor?" she asked quietly.

"Pretty sure, yeah," Pyran answered in a hushed voice.

Anna settled into her ready stance. "What's he doing here?"

Pyran shrugged.

"Start!" Lucy commanded.

They circled the ring for a moment, until Pyran lunged. Anna blocked with her own sword, metal clanging, and then spun into a strike. Her spins and swings were still slow and clumsy, and he easily caught her sword with his and shoved her back. The clash left her arms vibrating.

"You're holding your sword too tightly again," Lucy told her. "Loosen your grip."

Anna was still trying to grasp how you could hold a sword *too tightly*. She flexed her fingers on the handle of the weapon as she and Pyran circled again, a frown on her face. Then Pyran charged. She attempted to parry, but the force of his swing shoved her sword completely out of the way and knocked her off balance. She stumbled back and fell, her butt landing outside of the confines of the ring.

She hissed in pain. "Mother's Children, do you have to swing so hard?"

Lucy sighed, and began to walk over. Anna was sure she was about to feel the flat of her sword after she helped her up.

"You hold your weapon as if you're afraid of it," Lucy said, looking down at Anna. She held out a hand, and Anna took it, rising to stand. "Let me see your grip."

Anna held her sword out in front of her, the way they had taught her to.

"Do you see these?" Lucy pointed at her white knuckles. "Your hands should be relaxed unless you're blocking or striking, and even then, most blows don't require white knuckles. Relax. Like this." She held up her own sword, showing Anna her fingers.

Anna flexed her fingers and tried to relax her grip.

"Better." Lucy didn't seem satisfied. "This is a shortsword." She swatted at Anna's left hand. "It doesn't require both hands all the time. Your other hand should be free to stab or block or choke the life from your enemies."

Pyran grunted a laugh.

Lucy raised a disapproving eyebrow at him. When she turned back to Anna, she said, "We're going back into form work."

Before she and Pyran could groan their complaints, they heard the commander speak up.

"Sir, I would recommend another—"

"No."

Anna glanced behind her to see the governor's eyes on her. He wore a chilling smirk across his lips.

"I want her," he said.

The hair at the back of her neck bristled.

"You've said yourself she's familiar with the woods. She'll be an asset to the team." The governor turned his whole body toward the commander as he looked up at him, a challenge.

Commander Lyon's face grew pink in frustration, partially hidden by his beard. It looked like he was fighting to keep his face from dropping into a scowl. "Yes, sir," he said reluctantly.

"Good," Lord Woulfe grinned and turned to scan the training camp again. "It's settled. Thank you, commander." He nodded to the armored men he'd come with and they left.

"That's enough staring," Lucy said, but her voice didn't hold the authority it usually did. "Go stand next to Pyran."

The commander wiped a hand down his face, glanced at Anna, then at Pyran. He walked over and crossed his arms, a shallow frown on his face. "Anna Hale, Pyran Taggert, follow me."

He walked away and they followed, sharing a questioning glance. Lucy's lips were pressed into a tight frown as Anna passed by, but the woman offered her a hand on the shoulder and an attempt at a reassuring smile. She only made Anna more nervous.

The commander led them to his tent. Anna had never been inside. "Come in."

A large desk sat in the center of the room, a tall high-back chair behind it, and two smaller chairs in front of it. The commander gestured to the chairs, and they sat. He took the tall chair on the other side. Anna's back was tense and straight as she fisted her hands on her knees, her short nails digging into her palms.

Commander Lyon steepled his gauntleted hands in front of him and looked thoughtfully between the two of them. "The Vasbrute have become exceedingly active at the wall. We need to understand why. The Council has decided to send a small troop to gather information and decipher their strategy."

Anna glanced at Pyran, but he remained quiet. "What does that have to do with us?" she asked.

"The Council voted to create the troop they'll send from all over Telluth to ensure each area has representation and to maintain integrity." He shifted uncomfortably in his chair. "Governor Woulfe has chosen you, Anna."

Anna slowly sucked in a breath, her back stiffening as her stomach dropped.

The commander swallowed, and then continued. "There was nothing in the directive to say we couldn't send two soldiers. I've decided Pyran will accompany you. This is only a reconnaissance mission. You may never have to use your weapons.

"Pyran," the commander turned to him, "I know you've been looking for a way to prove yourself. While I don't wish for hostilities, those are the best chances we have to progress as military personnel. This chance is yours." The corner of his mouth lifted into a small smile.

Pyran was already nodding. "Yes, sir. I won't let you down."

The commander turned to Anna, his grin dropping as he took in her shock.

"You—" Anna started, breathy, "You think I'm ready for that, sir?" Her mind flew to her sparring, and she imagined a Vasbrute in the place of her opposition. Her heart stuttered.

The commander leaned back, taking a breath. His plate armor rose and fell. He considered her thoughtfully, eyes trained on her face. "You've proven yourself to be a fast learner. You'll make a damn good scout, better than any of these city folk I've got. I'm also aware of your...situation." After a moment, he added, "You'd each receive 500 gold upon your return, and Anna, half of your debt would be paid for your service."

Anna glanced at Pyran, her ears heating at the mention of her secret. It only took a fraction of a second for that embarrassment to turn into surprised excitement.

The commander explained, "We need to send you out by the end of the week. Take a couple of days to prepare while we get your supplies ready. You're excused from training." He stared thoughtfully at them for a moment, as if he were reading them. He nodded, satisfied, and finished, "I look forward to seeing you off."

10

PYRAN HURRIED TO HIS TENT WITH EXCITEMENT. ANNA'S LIMBS MOVED like she was wading through water, slow and stiff. The usual bustle and noise of the camp faded away around her as she focused on one thing—what her letter to her mother would say.

She spent the rest of the afternoon writing, crossing out, and wasting good paper and ink. The horn sounded for dinner, and she set it aside to eat.

"Congratulations," Lucy offered. "Pyran told me about your mission."

Anna's cheeks warmed as she sat next to her trainer. She caught Pyran looking at her. "Thanks." Her tone fell flat, despite her attempt otherwise.

Lucy bumped her with her shoulder. "It's okay to be nervous."

Anna nodded, taking a deep breath. She thought aloud, "Why do you think the governor picked me?"

Lucy sighed. "Your familiarity with the woods? Your skills with a bow? That's a question we might never get an answer to, and its not worth worrying over. Trust your skills and your gut. You've both got good guts."

"Why didn't they pick you?" Anna asked her.

"If there's going to be war, the commander will need people he trusts to make sure we're ready and to keep the ranks together. We haven't seen an actual battle since *the* War. He probably needs me here."

"400 years is a long time," Pyran said.

THAT NIGHT, ANNA STAYED UP LATER THAN USUAL WRITING HER LETTER. She eventually settled on something simple.

Mom,

I've been given a chance to pay back half of what we owe. I'm being sent to the capital to prepare for a mission. It's reconnaissance. I shouldn't even have to unstrap my bow. Pyran, someone I've been training with, is being sent with me. I won't be alone. We're going to meet up with people from all over Telluth.

I don't have an address for where we're going, but I'll write to you when we get there. I love you.

Lynnie

AFTER BREAKFAST THE FOLLOWING DAY, PYRAN LED HER TO HIS TENT AND lifted the flap to let her in. She glanced at the table by the bed and noticed a small picture, recognizing a younger version of Pyran. Behind him with her hand on his shoulder stood a woman with the same blonde hair and blue eyes, her cheeks lightly freckled. Next to her was a man with brown hair and serious, dark eyes. His tan matched Pyran's. His hand rested on the shoulder of the boy next to Pyran. This boy was thinner, more of an average build. He had the man's eyes and the woman's nose.

"Your family?" she asked him, pointing at the painting.

He glanced to where she pointed before turning to the trunk. "Yeah."

She picked up the picture and put it next to the clothing he was setting onto the bed.

After several shirts and pants had been laid out, he pulled out an elegant navy jacket, trimmed with shiny gold buttons. It was a little wrinkled from sitting in the trunk, but it was obviously worth more than his other things. He caught her staring at it and said, "It was a gift from my dad. He said every young man should have a dinner coat." He tried to smooth out a wrinkle.

"It's very nice," Anna told him.

"Thanks," he said and turned back to his trunk. "I haven't gotten a chance to wear it."

From the bottom of his trunk, Pyran pulled out a simple shortsword. It was small for him, and the edges of the blade were rusting. He grabbed an older, more worn shirt and wrapped the sword in it before setting it on the bed.

"Lucy would be disappointed in the state of that sword," Anna told him.

"That sword is none of Lucy's business." Pyran rolled his eyes.

Anna huffed a laugh. "Did I hit a nerve?"

Pyran frowned tightly. "It was my first sword, okay? My…friend gave it to me."

After everything was laid out on the bed, Pyran pulled out his pack, a large leather bag that he wore on his back with straps across both shoulders. It was a much nicer bag than the small one Anna had brought from home. It looked like it was made for adventuring. Then he started packing all of his things inside. When he was done, he looked up at her. "Your turn."

"I don't have much," she said as Pyran led her out of the tent.

"Neither do I."

Less than that. Anna pursed her lips and steeled herself for their entry into her barren little tent. Before they could get there, Lucy found them.

"There you are," she said, glancing between them. She held an empty pack in her hands. "I've been looking for the two of you."

"We're packing," Pyran shrugged.

"I know." This time Lucy rolled her eyes. "Here." She held the bag out to Anna. It was like Pyran's, but worn and wrinkled. The top was faded, as if it had sat in the sun for a long time before the leather had been oiled again.

"Oh, no, I couldn't—" Anna protested.

"Don't worry about it, I've already got a new one," Lucy insisted, putting the bag into her hands and forcing her to take it. "There's no way you'd last the four days on foot to Kastarus without it."

"Thank you," Anna told her sincerely, opening the bag to look at its spacious interior. It smelled like grass.

"Where's your tent?" Lucy asked.

"You don't have to—" Anna started.

The trainer shrugged. "I get the afternoon off if I help you pack."

Anna smiled. "All right, come on."

She led them into the archers' regiment, and then to her tent. The bed was neatly made and her armor and weapons rested near the closed chest in the corner. The side table was littered with her failed attempts at letters to her mother, which she jumped toward, quickly gathering them into a messy pile before she shoved them into the small space between the bed and the table.

Lucy chuckled from behind her. "What was that? Love letters?"

"What? No!"

Lucy blinked, startled by Anna's overreaction to her joke.

Pyran sat on her bed. "They can't be love letters. We're the only people she talks to, and we know she's not in love with either of us."

Anna huffed and let her shoulders relax. "You're right on that."

She moved over to her trunk and pulled out her clothes. When all four outfits were sitting on her bed, Pyran teased, "Your dad didn't gift you a dinner jacket?"

"Nope." She stood and crossed her arms.

Moments later, Lucy and Pyran had her clothes tucked into her new bag, and Lucy was showing her how to strap on her longbow so that it didn't trip her up as she walked. She would have to remember it was attached to her back if they had to travel the woods, or she'd risk getting stuck walking between trees.

"Who will I beat up on during training now?" Lucy wondered with a sad sigh. "The commander won't let me do that to the others."

"You'll have to find replacements," Anna laughed. "Or maybe he'll make you learn how to properly train someone."

"Ha-ha," Lucy elbowed Anna. "Don't forget your stretches and training, *every* day."

"Is this the part where you get sentimental and say goodbye?" Pyran asked, joking.

"No," she scowled. "I'll see the two of you at dinner." Then she turned and walked out of the tent, leaving Anna and Pyran to laugh at her response.

11

ANNA AWOKE TO THE MORNING CALL, SHOWERED, AND MET PYRAN AT the back of the big tent where the cooks prepared the meals. A dwarven man met them there, confirmed who they were, and then disappeared. He came back with two bundles full of food. There was fresh bread, soups in stoppered bottles, dried meat, fresh vegetables, and a couple of apples.

Commander Lyon stood at the entrance of the camp waiting for them, his armor flashing in the morning light as Anna and Pyran approached.

"Good morning," the commander greeted them. "You both look prepared."

"Good morning, sir," they responded in unison.

"The cooks are sending us off with plenty of supplies," Pyran added.

The commander shot him a knowing smirk. "I told Roderick not to spare you anything. We need you both strong and healthy once you get to the capital." Anna noticed he was holding two rolls of parchment. He held them out, saying, "These are your authorizations. Put them somewhere safe. You'll need to show them to the Council guards when you arrive."

"Yes, sir."

It felt light but thick in Anna's hands. She noted the pearly Hillcrest seal on it and the wolf stamped next to it. She slid it into her pack, and then closed her bag and swung it back over her shoulders.

The commander gave them a once-over. Satisfied with what he found, he said, "They'll keep me somewhat informed after you get there—when they send you out, estimated timing, things of that nature—but I would appreciate some direct communication from the two of you. I'm sure there are certain things you won't be able to share via letter, so use your discretion." His brown eyes dug into theirs.

Anna nodded.

"Yes, sir," Pyran replied.

The commander nodded to each of them, and then turned. "One last thing." He stepped toward a table nearby and picked up another scroll, this one much larger than the first two. He handed it to Pyran, and then he stepped closer to speak more quietly. "A map. There's been talk of this mission for some time now, and I wanted to be as informed as possible, so I sent scouts. You can look at it later." He smirked. "This is, of course, separate from the Council's preparations, and it should only be shared with those you trust. Wouldn't want them to think we were working behind their backs."

Anna knew that the Council the commander referenced included their own Lord Woulfe. She thought of the commander's interaction with the governor when he'd been forced to select her, and wondered if the rest of the Council were as difficult to work with.

"Good," the commander said with his normal volume and stepped back. "That's all I have for you. May the sun shine on your journey. And remember, you represent myself and Hillcrest."

"We won't let you down, sir," Pyran said.

"Thank you, sir," Anna told him.

He nodded, and then said, half-teasing, "Now get out of here. You're losing daylight."

THEY WERE QUIET AS THEY WALKED THROUGH HILLCREST. ANNA, STILL UNused to carrying a pack this big, fiddled with the straps on her shoulders. She was used to holding onto the single strap of her bag as it crossed over her chest. Eventually, she found she could hook her thumbs under the straps of her new bag and let her elbows fall to her sides. She drummed her fingers against the straps anxiously.

Moments later, she was walking toward the northwest gate of the city, walking through it, and then beyond. She paused, blinking into the morning sun. Ahead, she could see the bridge crossing the river that slipped out of Long Lake, made from the same white stone as the city. Behind her…

Anna turned. The noise and hustle of Hillcrest continued, completely unaware of her.

"Anna," Pyran's voice called. "What is it?"

She spun forward quickly, her face flushing in embarrassment. "Sorry," she apologized, and stepped forward once…twice…and paused again. "Uh," she shook her head, flustered. "I'm sorry."

"What's wrong?" Pyran asked, confusion on his face.

"Oh, uh," Anna sucked in before deciding her best option was to be honest with him. "This is the farthest I've ever gone."

She waited for him to get annoyed, but it didn't happen. Instead, his eyebrows rose in slight surprise before his face fell into a soft, nervous grin. He walked back to her, his right hand fiddling absently with the adjuster on his strap, and said, "Me, too. I've been to Lake Town to the west, but I've never gone east."

Anna nodded. She took a deep breath, then another. Some of the heat left her face. Pyran waited patiently. "Okay," she nodded. "Let's go."

They started walking again, and the sound of the city behind them dimmed. Anna felt her heart beating hard in her chest and put a hand over her necklace through her shirt. *How stupid. I can walk into whatever ruins I want in the woods, but I struggle to leave Hillcrest?*

Pyran started to talk. He talked about how his father was an avid historian in his free time, and liked to tell the stories he researched to his kids. He talked about how the bridge they were approaching was most likely as old as the governor's home high in the city, the oldest building in town. Some sources said that they had been built long ago, before the War, before time was tracked the same way. Some well-to-do person during ancient times had wanted a house high on a hill, away from others. They had built the bridge to match. It was suggested that in these ancient times, when magic was still abundant, the bridge had been enchanted with a glamor, hiding the path from most visitors to the new castle.

"This is all historical rumor, of course," Pyran added. "But it's a fun story to tell your kids after you've been gone all week for work."

They were on the bridge now, and Anna's heartbeat had calmed. She turned, taking in the bridge and considering who might've built it. She let out a soft "oh," as she saw Hillcrest in the distance and Long Lake next to it. The city was like a beacon of light on the hill, reflecting the morning sun. The lake next to it glittered like a pool of navy gems. Sunbeams bounced off the lake and waved against the north wall.

"Huh," Pyran took it in next to her. "I've never seen it from the bridge."

Anna nodded. "It looks completely different from this side."

"Well," Pyran turned, "let's go."

ANNA AND PYRAN WALKED UNTIL LUNCH, AND THEN THEY FOUND A SHADED rock to perch on while they ate. The road here wasn't as wooded as the path from Wallset. Farm fields and homes broke up the patches of forest. It still made Anna more comfortable than she had been leaving the city. The sounds of woodland creatures filled the silence between them until Pyran spoke.

"So...you didn't leave Wallset very much?"

"No, not really." She shook her head.

"Not really?"

"I hunted around the area. I'm familiar with most of the woods around my town, but that's as far as I went."

Pyran nodded in understanding as he chewed. "I stayed in Hillcrest almost my whole life. Occasionally, my dad would take me to Lake Town when he went for work, but that stopped once it was obvious I wasn't interested."

"What does your dad do?" Anna asked.

"Accounting," Pyran grumbled.

Anna smiled to herself. "I think you made the right choice. I can't picture you lining up numbers."

"Yeah, my younger brother is going to take over the business."

"When did you know you wanted to be a soldier?"

She felt Pyran shrug next to her before saying, "I've always been good at the physical stuff, always been one of the biggest my age. My friend's dad is a blacksmith, and he taught him how to use a sword. They let me train with them after I asked my friend about it. We were eight, I think, when we started."

Anna smiled. "My dad made me this little bow when I was five and taught me how to use it. None of the little arrows he gave me had points on them, but I still drove my mom crazy."

Pyran snorted and elbowed her, and then started to tuck his food away. "Come on. If we're lucky, we'll get to the crossroads before the sun sets, and that's one less night we'd have to spend in the woods."

"All right," Anna sighed and tucked her own food away.

PYRAN KEPT THEM MOVING AT A GOOD PACE. SHE WONDERED IF HE WAS keeping track of the time and the distance they covered, because whenever they started to slow, he'd urge them on a little faster. As the sun started to hang lower, she asked him if whatever tavern they found would be worth the pace they'd set today and their sore muscles. He grunted at her and told her that she'd want a bed after all this walking, and she'd feel differently in a couple of days when it wasn't an option anymore.

She let him lead her on at his pace. They passed by clumps of woods, surrounded by farms and open fields. Ranches stood on hills in the distance. They walked by a group of cows that greeted them with low sounds. Anna laughed when Pyran gave the large animals a wide berth.

When the sun hung low in the sky, Anna wondered if even Pyran's quick pace wasn't enough to get them to the crossroads. Her calves burned and hips ached, all to end up sleeping in the trees.

Just as she was about to voice this thought, they heard noises in the distance. Far up the road, people were talking and silverware was rattling against plates. Someone was trying to play a kind of stringed instrument in the middle of it all.

Pyran must have noticed, because his pace quickened even more.

"Hey!" she called to him. "You're almost running! Slow down, Pyran!"

He didn't. She hurried after him until she found herself at the big wooden doors the noise was coming from. They were shut. In her rush to keep up, Anna only saw that the large building was made of stone and was two stories tall before Pyran pushed the doors open and stepped inside.

After walking along the quiet road all day, it was like walking into a hurricane of civilization. The room was full of tangled conversations, vigorous eating, and the crackle of a large fire in the giant hearth. The sound of an instrument was trying to cut through all of it.

The smell of a delicious, slow-cooked roast smacked her in the face, along with wine and burning wood. Fat candles hung from chandeliers over the tables, bathing everything in a warm light. Six large, rectangular tables took up most of the room, their long benches covered in people. Most chatted loudly within their group over the din, but a few leaned in close to a neighbor to speak more quietly. Anna found the stringed instrument being plucked by an old man who sat next to the fire, and she realized he was singing. His deep voice mixed with the hum of the crowd, becoming almost indistinguishable in a way that seemed to tie everything together.

As she marveled at the room, completely different from what she had ever experienced at the Wallset Inn, a woman walked up to them. "Welcome in! Would you like a meal? How about a spot to sleep?"

"Both," Pyran nodded, glanced at Anna, and then back to the woman. "Two rooms, please."

"It's a gold per room for the night, and dinner comes with it. You'll get breakfast in the mornin', too." She held out her hand.

Pyran nudged Anna, and she came out of her daze enough to swing her pack to one side and retrieve a gold coin. They each placed one in her waiting hand, and she tucked them into a pocket in her skirts.

"Thank you. Find a seat." She tossed an arm at the tables behind her. "I'll bring you dinner and your room keys. Drink's extra. The ale's all right, but we make our own wine. That's what I'd recommend."

She gave a hurried nod-curtsy before spinning away behind the bar at the back of the room. A tall man stood behind it, wiping at something with a rag.

Another man, shorter, younger, but with similar features, walked around with cups, handing them out as he wound between the tables.

"Have you never been to an inn?" Pyran was looking at her with a puzzled expression.

Anna felt heat rise in her ears, and told herself it was the warmth in the room. "The Wallset Inn is nothing like this."

Pyran let out a grunt of acceptance before finding the open end of a table to sit at. It was near the fire, which was probably why the spot was left open. The room was warm enough that the fire seemed excessive. Anna sat across from him, setting her pack next to her and then tugging the hems of her sleeves up her arms.

The musician sat kitty-corner to them, still plucking at the instrument. Anna could see it better now. It had a long neck and a small round end with a hole. A handful of strings lay over it, and she could feel them buzz as he plucked them, now that she was closer. He was playing a sad song, and she found herself trying to decipher the story as he sang in his low rumble.

The woman who'd greeted them at the door returned with two large, shallow bowls full of food. She set these down in front of them, and Anna's mouth watered. A perfectly cooked roast sat piled with potatoes and carrots and onions, all in a bath of their own stew. As steam rose from the plates, Anna could smell warm wine and herbs. The base of the stew must have been their homemade wine.

Hand now free, the woman reached into her pocket and pulled out two large brass keys, setting them between them. Lastly, she asked, "What'll it be, wine or ale?"

"Wine," Pyran answered with a shrug.

"Wine," Anna nodded, looking down at the food in front of her as if she could inhale it by sight.

"I'll start your bill at the bar. You can pay in the morning. Be right back with those cups." She hurried away again.

Pyran grabbed his fork, then asked, "Still annoyed that we hurried here?"

Anna huffed and grabbed her own fork. "Not at all. Thank you, Pyran," she said with enthusiasm, digging her fork into her meal.

Almost finished with his food, Pyran sat back with an annoyed sigh and sipped from his cup.

"What is it?" Anna asked between bites.

"All these old songs are the same," Pyran told her. "Some fair lady or young boy gets lost and either meets a tragic end or is saved…tragically."

Anna huffed a laugh and glanced at the musician. He seemed to be in his own world. His eyes were shut as he sang and moved his fingers along the instrument.

"Old men love playing the old elven stuff," Pyran said.

"It's an old elven song?" Anna asked.

Pyran huffed in exasperation. "Do they not have music in Wallset, either?"

"The Creed have their hymns, and we were taught a few songs in school," she answered.

"So you're all pretty much isolated down there, huh?"

Anna hadn't thought about it much, but she was starting to realize he was right. Rather than agreeing, she turned back to her food, and he did the same.

When she finished, she pushed the bowl forward with finality and set her fork in it. Then she let her hand rest on the cup of wine in front of her, where her fingers slowly turned the glass. Without looking up, she asked, "Are there a lot of old elven songs?"

Pyran's eyebrows were high when she glanced up at him. "Loads. They must have loved to write music, and with all the time they have, they just played and played all those songs."

"Serial musicians," Anna added with a small smile, playing along.

"Criminals are what we should call them," Pyran told her with a serious nod. "Or maybe our musicians are the criminals for being lazy and not writing their own material."

"Stop it," Anna hushed him with a small laugh, but the musician's eyes were still closed, and he had moved on to another song.

That night Anna slept on a small bed in a small room upstairs, across the hall from Pyran. The bed was soft and warm, but creaky. It reminded her of the bed she'd shared with her mom back home.

I'll have to tell her what a real, busy inn is like.

12

THE NEXT MORNING, PYRAN KNOCKED ON HER DOOR TO MAKE SURE SHE was awake as she was putting on her boots. When she met him downstairs, he already had two hot plates. She sat across from him again, and he slid the second plate in front of her, biscuits underneath hot gravy. From the smell, she assumed the cook had made it from the leftover stew. The food was just as delicious as last night. Halfway through her meal, Anna had a full enough belly to look around.

The room was quieter than it had been last night and half-empty. A few small groups sat quietly, eating breakfast. She recognized the musician from last night sitting at the bar and eating.

"We'll have to pay for our drinks last night," Anna remembered.

Pyran shook his head nonchalantly. "Don't worry about it. I already did."

"How much do I owe you?" Anna turned to dig through her bag for her money.

"I told you not to worry about it. It wasn't much."

"You didn't have to do that," Anna said with a small frown.

He shrugged. "You can get the next one."

Anna was pretty sure there weren't any more taverns between here and Kastarus. When she narrowed her eyes at him, he told her, "Hurry up. I want to cover as much ground as possible today."

She let it go. "You said that yesterday."

"Yeah, well, we'll be sleeping in the woods tonight, so I'd like to be as close to civilization as possible."

They walked for hours through flat countryside before stopping for a late lunch, and Pyran only let them rest long enough to eat before starting off again. Anna spent most of the day listening to farm animals or watching farmers in their fields with heavy equipment pulled by horses or cattle. She counted the birds again, most of them a parade of ducks that had crossed their path. A couple of carts drove by, one full of people and another full of canvas bags stacked high. Anna and Pyran waved politely at the drivers, who returned the gesture with a smile. Pyran slowed when the sun sank to the top of the approaching tree line.

"We should probably find somewhere to build a fire and sleep," he said, looking defeated.

Anna grinned at his annoyance, walking off the road and into the woods. "Come on, then," she called back to him.

He followed as she picked her way through the grass and then through the trees. In the woods, she found a small, open circle away from the road, just big enough for them to sleep and set up a fire. She set her pack down and leaned it against a tree. When she turned back to Pyran, he was frowning at the clearing.

"What?" she asked. "You don't like this spot?"

He let out a huff, slung his bag down, and then sat on it. "I don't think I'll like any spot."

"Have you never camped in the woods?" she asked, imitating his tone when he had asked her about being in an inn.

He looked up at her and crossed his arms. "No, I haven't."

"You can sit there, and I'll get us some firewood." She pulled her shortbow and a couple of arrows from her pack.

"What do you need those for?" he asked, eyeing the woods behind her.

She turned back and shrugged. "In case I see a rabbit. You'd love fresh rabbit."

Reassured, he nodded and let her go.

Anna took a deep breath as she walked further into the trees. It had been months since she had last been surrounded by trees and no one else. She threw one last thought to hoping Pyran didn't get too nervous while she was gone before she started gathering sticks and branches, monitoring the underbrush for rabbits. It didn't take long for her to fill her arms with wood and have to turn back to camp. When she got back, she found Pyran laying out her bedroll, his own already laid out across from it with a blanket over top.

"Thanks," she greeted him.

"Thanks for getting wood," he told her, and then pulled her blanket out of her pack and unrolled it over her bedroll.

"Of course." Anna set the wood down, and then began clearing a spot for a firepit. Pyran sat on his bedroll and watched as she built a little tower from half of what she'd brought and then retrieved her matches. She struck one against the back of match case and it ignited. She held it under the tower where she had placed some smaller sticks and dry leaves. She blew gently into the flames until they licked at the larger branches, and then took a seat on her bedroll.

"What did you do in your free time, if none of it involved the woods?"

He thought for a moment before responding, "Sometimes we'd fish in the lake, but mostly there was a small group of us that would run around the neighborhood playing when we were little."

Anna remembered being young and playing with other kids around town. That had slowed as she grew older, and stopped after her dad passed. "I'm not any good at fishing. I've tried twice."

"Well, it's not like a bow and arrow. You have to wait for the fish to come to you."

She nodded her head to the side. "Yeah, I was never any good at that. It's hard to see them under the water."

It was quiet for a moment, except for the crackling fire between them, until he said, "So, I've told you why I joined up. What about you?"

Her mouth pushed into a thin line, and she rose from her seat. He watched her dig out food from her pack. She glanced at him as she sat back down, pulled out a bottle of soup, unstoppered it, and set it over the fire to heat up. She rested her hands on her lap. "It's a long story."

"We're here all night." Pyran waved a hand at the surrounding trees. "Maybe a story before bed will help me sleep."

Anna sighed, unable to stop the small smile that appeared on her face. "Fine, but get your food. I don't want to keep you from eating."

"Sure." Pyran grabbed an apple along with his bread and meat, and settled in.

"My parents have always run a bakery in Wallset," she started, looking down at her food to avoid his gaze. "Growing up, my dad taught me everything he could. Even the accounting." She looked at Pyran with a small smirk.

"You're good at math?" he asked, surprised. "People who are good at math rarely join the local regiments."

"You're right." Anna frowned and returned her gaze to her food. She took a bite, chewed, and swallowed.

"My dad got sick and died when I was thirteen." She didn't dare chance a look across the fire, or she might freeze and start choking on her words. Anna felt her chest grow hollow from talking about her father. It always made her think of what could have been—of what she was missing. "I took over his part of the business. I foraged and hunted, and I checked the books when I got home. But my dad was a better hunter than me, and my mom never quite did as well as when he was around.

"Then Woulfe raised taxes and it became harder. We got by, but my mom always felt like she should do better for me. One day, I found out she had taken out a loan to pay for a second oven, and with the interest on it, it was impossible for us to pay back." She cleared her throat and found she had been driving her nails into her palms again. "Rather than have them jail her for defaulting on her payments, I agreed to join up. Almost all of my pay goes toward our debt."

"Oh," she heard Pyran say quietly across the fire. "That's what Commander Lyon meant."

She nodded.

"And that's why you were so *intense* when we sparred, the day I met you."

She looked up at him. "If the commander wouldn't take me… I needed him to take me."

He nodded.

"I'd rather you didn't say anything…to anyone," she told him.

He met her eyes. "I won't. It's not my story to tell."

She nodded. "Thank you," she said, and then carefully took the bottle of soup off the fire, using her blanket as an oven mitt.

They ate quietly for a moment. Anna frowned as she sipped the soup, and Pyran seemed to be inspecting every item before each bite. He leaned back onto one hand and sighed before saying, "You know my friend? The one that gave me that sword." He gestured toward his bag, where she knew that small, rusty sword sat wrapped within.

She nodded. "Sure."

"Yeah," he looked down at the bread in his hand. A nervous smile spread his lips, and she caught the corners of his cheeks reddening. "We're actually… We're dating."

"Really?" she asked, surprised.

He nodded. "I've never told anyone that before."

"What's his name?"

"Adrian." His smile grew. "Adrian Lockert."

She put the leftover soup back into her pack before settling in a cross-legged position, resting her elbows on her knees. Her palms held her chin up as she asked, "What's he like?"

He rolled his eyes at the question, but his smile never fell. "He's got dark hair and blue eyes. He likes to make stupid jokes and do sword tricks."

"I'm sure it's the stupid jokes that hooked you," she teased. "Is he as strong as you?"

"Yeah, about."

"Do you miss him?"

He nodded. "What about you?" His eyebrows scrunched together as he took in her oversized shirt and messy hair. "Is there someone in Wallset you miss, besides your mother?"

"No, no one like that. I don't have an Adrian."

The night was quiet again as they both got lost in their thoughts. Camping in the trees like this reminded Anna of her time with her father, and she drifted off in the memory.

THE NEXT MORNING, PYRAN ROSE WITH GROANS OF DISCOMFORT. WHEN Anna eyed him with an unamused expression, he waved a dismissive hand at her and used the other to rub his lower back. They ate quickly, and it surprised Anna how much food she had already eaten during their journey. She would still have more than enough, but walking all day certainly made her hungry. She took a moment to stretch out her limbs before donning her pack and leading Pyran out of the woods.

"How much longer do we have?" Anna wondered aloud. "One more night?"

Pyran nodded. "Yeah, one more night, and then we should reach Kastarus in the early afternoon."

Anna's feet were beginning to grow sore in her boots. They were well worn-in, which meant no blister, but it also meant there wasn't much support left under her feet. She frowned as she thought about the hours and hours left of walking.

Today's trek had fewer farms and more forest. At one point, they passed over a small bridge over a creek. It was wooden, but well-maintained. Curious, she looked over the railing and found a couple of geese underneath. A fungal frog sat in the mud at the edge of the water, waiting for its mushroom cap to attract an insect.

Two more, that makes seven birds today.

"Come on," Pyran told her. "We don't want to waste any time."

"Of course not," she pulled away from the railing to follow after him. "You wouldn't want to miss your appointment with the forest floor this evening."

"Ha-ha," he mocked.

After a third day of walking, they were both sore and tired by the time they started looking for a place to sleep in the trees. Pyran offered to help Anna gather wood for the fire, but still seemed less than enthused when she accepted his offer. They split up, and when Anna came back, she found Pyran sitting on his made bedroll with a pile of wood next to him. She started the fire and then went about laying out her own bedroll.

"You haven't been around mages much, have you?"

"No," Pyran dragged out his answer in curiosity. "Why?"

Her shoulders lifted and fell. She sat down. "I hadn't either, until recently. I met a dwarf, and he could start fires by snapping his fingers."

He hummed thoughtfully. "Sometimes I wish I had the Well-Mother's powers, but then I think about it and decide it's not worth it."

"Not worth it?"

"Some of them, their own families are scared of them. And for good reason—without proper control, you could do a lot of damage."

She nodded in understanding. There hadn't been a mage in Wallset for years, since before she was born. She remembered her mother telling her about a girl that she had grown up with who had run away and left after she was done with school. Her mother had heard nothing about her after that.

"I thought all mages had to be part of the Creed—that's how the Creed talk—but the one I met hated the church."

"Not the religious type?" he asked.

She shook her head. "He believes in the Well-Mother, but he doesn't like the church."

"I've met some Creed who think they're entitled to your entire purse only because they asked nicely. There were others that seemed genuine, though."

"The church in Wallset wasn't very big, but they always seemed to be helping people."

"It's probably easier to be genuine in Wallset. You can't get very greedy if there isn't as much to take."

Pyran wasn't wrong, but it still stung slightly to hear her hometown described that way. When Anna didn't respond, he hurried to recover. "I'm sorry, I only meant—"

Anna waved a hand across the fire at him. "It's fine. I didn't come from Hillcrest, with its big schools, busy market, and one of the oldest buildings in Telluth."

Pyran watched her for a moment, then said, "Hillcrest isn't all great."

"No?"

"No, we have a surplus of silver spoons from so many of us being born with them in our mouths."

They both laughed, and Anna threw a small stick at him, which bounced off his shoulder and made him laugh harder.

"Shut up," Anna said, smiling.

13

IT WASN'T UNTIL MIDMORNING THE NEXT DAY THAT THEY SAW KASTARUS high up on a hill, still miles away. It appeared from behind the trees as they rounded a bend in the road. From this far, it was so small that it would have fit on Anna's thumbnail. Still, she marveled at what she could make out of its high walls and wide, tall castle. She could tell the city spread massively from where the castle sat at the highest point. The stone was some kind of deep blue-gray, which made up the main structure and then surrounded it twice in two massive walls. An abundance of towers reached into the clouds, where pinprick flags waved, too small to show a specific color.

"That's really far, right?" Anna asked.

"Pretty sure," Pyran said.

"And really big?"

"Yeah."

"Damn," she swore under her breath, not a common occurrence. Her mind immediately thought of five different kinds of punishment from her mother.

"Damn," Pyran agreed.

Traffic on the road increased as they got closer to the city. Carts went by, going both directions, and occasional single horse riders or walkers passed them. They stuck to the side of the road when traffic passed, holding their packs tightly. They were too eager to stop for lunch as the city grew bigger and bigger in front of them. The forest relented again to farmland, which stretched right up to the city walls. The outer wall grew higher and higher, until the castle was only towers reaching above it, high on a hill. As Pyran and Anna approached, they arched their necks up at the parapets on either side of the gate. They must have been three or four stories up.

Anna realized her heart was starting to race as they reached the bottleneck in traffic. It had been easy to forget where she was in the monotony of walking the country roads, but now their destination loomed before them. The gates were open, but armored guards stood in the open pathway, stopping anyone going in or out. Pyran swung his pack over to one shoulder so he could reach across with his other arm and dig around in it for his papers. Anna did the same. Her hand fumbled around inside her pack as they approached the guards. They were dressed in dark gray armor that seemed to mimic the stone of the walls on either side of them. Even their boots were gray. The dirt path turned to pressed gravel under their feet.

"What's your business?"

Anna almost jumped as a guard stepped in front of them. He was maybe in his late forties with a long mustache. He hooked the thumbs of his gauntleted hands on the straps of his breastplate as he looked them up and down.

She tugged out her papers and held them in front of her.

"We were sent here from Hillcrest," Pyran said as he handed the man his authorization after her.

The man took the scroll from Pyran's hands, gently unsealing and unrolling it. His eyes scanned the page, his lips pressed into a thin line, and then he glanced at both of them again. He took Anna's papers, unrolled them, and read that as well. In one smooth motion, he rolled both up together and turned his head to the side to shout, "Jen!"

A female guard ran up from somewhere near the wall. She looked to be about the same age as the man in front of them. Her blonde hair was braided to one side. "Here, sir," she greeted.

He held the scrolls out to her, saying, "Escort these two to the Barracks. Introduce them to Captain Heiser."

She took the scrolls from him, eyed both of them curiously, then turned on her heel toward the city. "Yes, sir. Follow me!"

Anna glanced at Pyran, and their eyes met before they both took off after the woman.

"Have you ever been to Kastarus?" the woman called back to them without turning her head.

"No," Pyran shouted through the commotion at the gates.

"Stay close," she turned to meet each of their eyes. "It's a busy city."

Anna nodded and focused on tracking the woman's movements as she navigated through the streets. They wove through the crowd and then around the little carts selling their wares to people entering the city. The street led them uphill. Small houses filled the streets here, and Anna found the pointed top of a Creed cathedral a couple of blocks over. Little restaurants and shops were sprinkled in here and there in the first levels of some homes. The whole place smelled like *people,* the good and the bad.

It took them a long time to get to the inner wall, and by that time, Anna's veins were buzzing from all of the activity around her. She stuck close to Pyran, who was glancing over at her every now and then to make sure she was keeping up. This woman walked faster than Pyran racing for that inn, turning suddenly down streets, weaving ever closer to the next wall.

Their cheeks were red from the walk as they passed through, and doors shut behind them.

As soon as they did, the hustle and bustle dulled to a slow, consistent flow of walking people. The streets themselves were clear for carts to go by. Paths on either side allowed those walking to stay out of the way. The sound of wheels and footsteps pounding across the gravel and chatter from the crowds was replaced with the steady trot of occasional horses on cobblestone and the light clatter of boots and heels. The array of smells dulled.

Anna took a deep breath as the buzzing inside of her lowered to a hum.

"That's better." The woman glanced back at them with a smile. "It's always noisy in the outer districts. You can hear yourself think again, right?"

Anna nodded, a nervous smile across her face.

"I don't know how long you folks are staying in town," she went on, "but if you're looking for a good home-cooked meal, the Lavender Room has the best food." She gestured to her right side.

Anna followed her hand and found a two-story restaurant with a balcony on the second floor. Fresh lavender hung off the sign.

"Thanks for the suggestion," Pyran said.

"I'd avoid the Tipsy Tiger and Left Leg," she added. "Not crowds you want to get mixed up in."

"Duly noted," Pyran nodded. His eyebrows were high as he looked over at Anna, who sent him a shrug in response.

As they speed-walked through the city streets, Anna wondered how this woman managed in all of her armor. The dark gray metal did not appear light. By the time they approached their destination, Anna was huffing and puffing.

The Barracks turned out to be a massive two-story building made entirely of stone that flanked the castle. A third, smaller wall surrounded the castle grounds, and the Barracks was built into this wall. *It must be acres wide.* Anna looked down the length of the building and tried to catch her breath. The outside was incredibly blank except for small, square windows at consistent intervals and three large doors, one on each end and the last in the middle. They stopped at the nearest doors, and Jen turned to go inside.

Anna followed, squinting as her eyes adjusted to the dark interior. A young man sat at a desk just inside the doorway, and Jen waved to him as she passed and said, "Afternoon, Bill. Just making a delivery."

"Go on, then," he said without looking up from the paperwork in front of him.

Still trying to catch her breath, Anna hurried down a couple of long corridors, and then Jen knocked on one of the many plain wood doors. A small plaque next to it read *Cpt. Nathaniel Heiser.*

"Come in," a man's voice called from inside the room.

Jen swung open the door and stepped inside. Anna and Pyran followed.

"I've got two for you, captain," she told the man sitting behind the desk.

He was older, with salt-and-pepper hair and a matching, trimmed beard and mustache. He wore a gray military uniform, and there was some kind of fancy brooch pinned on his left breast. He reminded Anna of a military man on the cover of one of her mother's romances. He was handsome enough for an older man. He was frowning down at some papers and only managed to glance up at Jen as she entered. Without looking up again, he said, "Thank you, Parker. You may leave them with me."

"Yes, sir," Jen set the scrolls at the front of his desk, smiled at both Pyran and Anna, then turned and left.

Anna was trying to keep her breathing under control. She didn't want to look weak in front of this captain person, but the walk here had left her breathless, and she was just beginning to get it back. She glanced at Pyran, who was only slightly better off.

"I apologize." The man shuffled some papers on his desk into a pile and then straightened them into a stack. "If there were a speed-walking tournament in Kastarus, Jen Parker would win." His green eyes met Anna's and then Pyran's. "I am Captain Nathaniel Heiser." He picked up their authorizations, noting the seal on them both. To himself, he said, "Hillcrest," before unrolling them and scanning the contents.

After he was done, he let the papers roll back up and looked at Pyran and Anna again. "I like Commander Lyon. He does good work. I hope I can see the same qualities he demonstrates from the two of you."

"Yes, sir," Pyran told him.

Anna nodded, realizing she was meant to respond, and followed it with her own, "Yes, sir."

"Good." The captain gathered his hands and set them in front of him on his desk. "Tell me about yourselves. What are your skills? Why are you here, Pyran Taggert and Annalyn Hale?"

Pyran glanced at Anna, and then turned back. "I'm a swordsman, sir. Commander Lyon also believes me to be a strong strategist. I hope I can lend you my skill with a sword and learn from you, sir."

Captain Heiser nodded appreciatively. He looked Pyran over. "Very good. And you?" he turned to Anna.

She sucked in a breath and answered, "I use a bow, sir, and I'm resourceful. I've spent most of my life in the woods north of the wall, and I know how to get around."

The man behind the desk considered her for a moment. An eyebrow had quirked at the mention of the wall. He looked her over, noted her pack and her bows, along with the dagger and shortsword at her hip. Her right hand fidgeted at her side as he inspected her.

"You're not from Hillcrest?" He phrased it as a question.

"No, sir," Anna shook her head and swallowed her nervousness. "I'm from Wallset."

"Wallset." The captain leaned back into his chair, crossing his arms. "Now there's a place you hear little of," he said thoughtfully, then asked more directly, "You're a hunter, I take it?"

Anna glanced at Pyran, wondering why she was getting an interview, then turned her eyes back to the man in front of them. "I kept my family fed and our bakery stocked."

The captain nodded appreciatively. "It's amazing how much being in a city can disconnect you from the world. It'll be good to have you with us."

She nodded reluctantly, unsure what he meant.

The captain sighed and leaned forward again to pick up one of the papers on his desk. He scanned it and told them, "We're still waiting for most of the members of our team to arrive. When they do, we'll convene to discuss the mission and its goals. You'll be given rooms here at the Barracks and you'll train in the courtyard. It is of the *utmost* importance that we all work together. I want you to take this time to introduce yourselves and get to know the others."

"Yes, sir," they both responded.

The captain thought for a moment, looking through them, then rose from his chair. "Follow me."

Anna took a deep breath as he passed her, and she turned to follow. Pyran nudged her gently with his elbow as they headed out of the room, offering her a reassuring smile. She shot a nervous glance back.

As they walked down the hall, Anna noticed that the torches lighting the way were not normal torches. The light they gave off was a pale yellow, and rather than flicker, they seemed to breathe faintly in and out. There was no smoke. Curious, Anna reached a hand close to one as they passed by, and she sucked in a breath. It wasn't giving off any heat.

Captain Heiser turned his head at the small noise she made, and then his expression split into an amused smile. "Ah, the mage lights. Extremely efficient."

"I've never seen them before," Anna explained.

"I would think not," Heiser agreed. His stoicism was suddenly replaced with a bit of excitement. "These came from Luminport only a few years ago. It'll be awhile before they show up in Hillcrest...or Wallset, for that matter." With a little laugh, he continued walking. "Our mages at the academy in Luminport spent years optimizing an archaic enchantment to create these. They're a great progressive achievement."

Anna heard Pyran mutter quietly, "Progressive? But you said the spell already exists."

"It's been hundreds of years since we've been able to produce such a spell at this scale," Heiser went on. Anna wasn't sure if he heard Pyran and was responding, or if he was just continuing his speech. "It's been adjusted to use less energy and give more light."

"Are they just in the Barracks?" Anna asked. "Or are they all around the city?"

"The castle is full of them, along with this building. You may see some scattered around town, as well." He waved a hand towards the outer wall of the building.

"Do you know a lot about magic and enchantments?" Anna wondered aloud.

"Everyone in Luminport knows a little about these things," he answered. "It's the location of the biggest academy for mages in Telluth."

He walked up to someone sitting at a small desk in front of a large storage room. "Presley," he greeted the young man, "these two need rooms near the others. Could you show them the way?"

"Yes, sir." He nodded and stood, turning around to retrieve something from the neatly stacked piles behind him.

"I'll see both of you in the courtyard in the morning." Captain Heiser addressed Pyran and Anna, his face serious again. "I'll be there tomorrow for training."

"Yes, sir," they both responded.

He nodded in acknowledgment and then turned on his heel and walked back toward his office.

"Here you go." Presley returned and shoved a bundle of bedding into Anna's arms, then another into Pyran's. "Follow me, please."

He led them down another hallway, turning left at a four-way intersection. The buzzing returned as Anna wondered how she would ever find her way around…or out.

"Your rooms are on the second floor on the west side. You'll meet for training in the courtyard every morning at seven, shortly after the horn. From your rooms, it's down one floor and out the inner doors," Presley said.

Anna looked for a window to determine which way was west. She couldn't find one.

Presley led them up a staircase and then around another corner. "The building is big, but it's just a rectangle, so if you keep moving and you're on the right floor, you'll get to where you're going eventually. The cafeteria is in the northwest corner. Breakfast is at six, lunch is at noon, and dinner is at seven. The courtyard is open for training every day, and it sounds like Captain Heiser wants you out there tomorrow. You can get there from the inner doors on the west side, too."

He stuck his hand in his pocket and pulled out two keys. He opened one door on his right and another one just past it, then set each key on top of the bedding in their hands.

"My name's Tom Presley. I'm down in the storage room for now, if you're missing anything."

"Thank you," Anna said.

He gave a small wave over his shoulder as he walked back to the stairs.

Anna glanced into the first room, and then looked at Pyran. She could hear the muffled noise of other people in the building. "Which room do you want?" she asked.

Pyran glanced into one and then the other. "I'm pretty sure they're exactly the same."

"All right." Anna walked into the room that matched her key. She found a bed in the corner, a small window with a curtain at the center of the far wall, and a simple desk in the other corner, a stool tucked underneath it. The walls were bare stone. The door was thick wood. *The tent in Hillcrest was cozier.*

She set the bedding onto the bed—more of a cot, really—and then set down her pack. She stepped up to the window and looked across the street from the Barracks. There were several little shops and restaurants. She could make out a smithy. From this high on the hill in the city, she could also see over the tops of some buildings and out over the surrounding area. Even Hillcrest hadn't felt this high.

Slowly, the buzzing faded. As Anna calmed, her stomach rumbled.

She turned from the window and walked to her door, intending to grab Pyran and find food. She rounded the corner just as she heard laughter coming down the hall. Turning, she found two people coming up the stairs and walking toward her. The one who had been laughing was a tall woman in metal armor carrying a large shield. The other was a young man in black leathers with a smirk on his face. He looked away from the woman next to him and locked eyes with Anna. His golden-brown irises narrowed as he took her in, and he stopped walking.

"What?" the woman asked him, then followed his line of sight. "*Oh.*"

14

"Hello," Anna offered, after a silent moment of staring. "Captain Heiser said—"

"She's another one!" the woman announced, extending her free hand toward Anna and smiling at the man next to her. "Told you we'd be seeing more soon." She turned back to Anna and said, "We've been here waiting. What took you so long?" Her hand landed on her hip like a scolding mother.

The man next to her looked Anna over. He wore all black, which stood out strongly against his pale skin.

"Uh..." Anna's eyebrows rose at the woman. She was almost six feet tall and thick with muscle. Her brown hair was pulled away from her face into a messy, low bun. Her blue eyes sparkled with her smile. Her skin was tan from sun, and her face glowed with sweat. Anna blinked at her and said, "We left from Hillcrest four days—"

"Stop it, Merry." The young man gently swung an arm up to slap her shoulder. "She doesn't know you, yet. She has no idea you're joking."

"Right," Merry gave a sheepish smile, "Sorry, just messing you about. I'm

Merry, this is Will." She thumbed at herself and then pointed at the young man next to her.

Anna took in his lithe frame, fair skin, and long, dark hair. Half the dark strands were pulled back out of his face in a small knot. Long ears poked through and curved into a soft point. He rolled his eyes and looked down at the corner where the wall met the ground, the tops of his cheeks turning a pale, cool pink.

Realizing she was being extremely rude, Anna made herself look at the ceiling and then to Merry's eyes. The woman's eyebrows rose, waiting for a response.

"I'm Anna, Anna Hale. I came here with—"

"All right, I'm starving." The door to Pyran's room opened and he came out next to Anna. He had changed his clothes. "Let's find something to eat."

"Pyran, this is Merry and Will," Anna said, pointing to the others.

Pyran blinked at her, face going blank. "Hello, I'm Pyran, Pyran Taggert. Nice to meet you." He extended his hand and Merry took it, giving a solid shake. Her hand was as big as his.

"What do you say, Will?" Merry nudged him with a smirk on her face. "Why don't we get these two a proper welcome meal?"

Will sighed thoughtfully, looked between Anna and Pyran, and then shrugged, noncommittal. "Why not?"

"Yeah!" Merry cheered, then held a finger up to Anna and Pyran. "Give me one minute to get out of my armor and I'll be ready to go!" She walked into a room across the hall from Pyran's.

"I'll be right back." Will entered the room across from Anna's.

As the doors shut, Anna turned to Pyran, shaking her head as her cheeks heated. She put her hand to her forehead. "By the Mother... This is not going well."

"What do you mean? We just met them."

"You don't understand," Anna hissed through clenched teeth. "I was so awkward, and I *stared* at his *ears*."

"His ears?" Pyran asked.

Anna shushed him. "They're pointed. I've never seen a– I've never seen them before."

"Oh," Pyran carried out the note as he understood, "He's half-elven. Full blooded elves are more…angular." Pyran's face screwed up as he worked to find the right word to describe elves. "My dad did some work for an elf in Hillcrest who was 104. He didn't look older than forty."

"I have to apologize," Anna said. "Sons and daughters, I feel awful."

Pyran shrugged. "He's probably gotten it before."

"Wait," Anna froze and looked Pyran over. "You changed. I probably still smell like everything we walked through on the way here!" Anna rushed into her new room and flung the door shut. In a flurry, she threw off her clothes and grabbed a new set from her pack, one of the two clean outfits she had left. She smoothed her hair in the little mirror on the desk as best she could.

Merry was waiting with Pyran as she stepped out. He was inspecting her left arm, which ended a little further than her elbow with the rest missing.

"And you've got a custom shield?" Pyran was asking.

"Yeah, but I could make the everyman's shield work if I had to. That's how I started. Just have to adjust the far strap the right way."

"Oh," Anna said, surprised. When they looked up at her, she asked, "Have you been fighting that way for a long time?"

"I lost my hand almost twenty years ago. Been doing it this way ever since."

"I'm sorry," Anna said. "I don't mean to pry."

"No, no way!" Merry reassured her. "I was just telling your friend." Fought a bear on the farm." She smiled wickedly. "I won."

"Wow." Anna's eyebrows rose. "I can't imagine."

"Oh, it was all teeth and claws." Merry showed her teeth and formed her right hand into a claw and swiped at the air. "Heavy bastard, too. But we always kept our shovels sharp, and that came in handy."

Anna nodded with a small, nervous smile. She pictured Merry squaring off with a big, brown bear, the kind she had avoided in her own neck of the woods. A quiet moment passed before Anna felt the need to fill it. "We came from Hillcrest. Where are you from?"

"Originally I'm from around Tuvale, grew up on a small farm up there with my family. When I lost my hand, they decided I wasn't much use to them anymore, so I picked up a sword and a shield and went to Altumburg," Merry answered casually, as if she was talking about the weather.

"They– what, kicked you out?" Pyran asked. "That doesn't seem fair."

Merry shrugged. "I could've stayed, I suppose. They would've taken care of me, but they would've looked down on me the whole while. There's no place on a farm for someone who can't do their share. Besides, I'm happier here. Here, I can do things."

Will exited his room. He had changed as well, and he had let his hair down to cover most of his ears. He still wore the black leather gloves, but the rest of his leathers had been replaced with a gray shirt and black trousers.

"I can do things like take Will down in the training ring, right, Will?" Merry teased.

"Just once today, and you'll never let me forget," Will joked back, a small smile on his face. As he glanced at Pyran and then Anna, it fell slightly.

"We're all hungry," Merry said. "Let's get going already!" She took off towards the stairs, leading the way. Will followed behind while Pyran and Anna took up the rear. At the bottom of the stairs, Merry turned left and Will followed.

Pyran hesitated. "Isn't the cafeteria the other way?"

"We're taking you to get some real food!" Merry called back to him.

"Come on," Will nodded his head toward Merry as he spoke. "We'll show you around town a little."

Pyran shrugged and turned to follow. "As long as there's food."

"So much food!" Merry called back again.

They exited the Barracks and started walking downhill. Pyran jogged to catch up with Merry so that he could continue their conversation about her form with a sword and shield. Not wanting to be left behind and still feeling guilty for staring, Anna caught up to Will.

"Hey," she started as she approached, "I'm sorry about earlier. You're the first person I've met with– Well, it was rude of me to stare, anyway."

He kept his gaze ahead toward Merry as he pushed hair out of his face and over his ear. "Don't worry about it. You're not the first person to do it." His mouth formed a thin, pursed line.

"Oh, no, I don't think they're weird," Anna hurried to reassure him. "They suit you." His jaw clenched, and she realized she wasn't helping. "Even if I thought they were weird, I'm from a small town far from here. A lot of things are weird to me."

He looked over at her from the corner of his eye, his head lifting a little in interest. "I thought you said you're from Hillcrest."

"That's where we left from, but originally I'm from Wallset."

"Hm," he hummed, and his lower lip pushed up in appreciation. "You don't see many people from Wallset."

"So everyone tells me," Anna nodded. "There aren't many of us, I guess."

"I'm sure," Will said thoughtfully, "There aren't many people who want to live next to the wall."

"We're not—" Anna started to argue, then decided it wasn't worth it and let out a huff.

"I take it you've had this conversation before?" Will's eyebrows were high.

"Only a few times today," Anna answered, only half-joking.

They were quiet for a moment as they watched Pyran and Merry talk. Pyran paused in his stride to show his form and swung an imaginary blade. Merry nodded excitedly and then faked a shield bash.

Will jerked his chin at them, saying, "He's obviously a swordsman. What's your weapon of choice?"

"A bow," Anna answered. "You?"

"Daggers, mostly."

"Daggers? Just daggers?"

"*Just* daggers?" Will's face shifted into feigned offense before it fell into a smirk. "We'll see if they're *just* daggers tomorrow."

"I've told you I use a bow. Of course you'll beat me tomorrow when I've got a shortsword. Pyran has consistently."

Concern flashed briefly across his face before one of his eyebrows rose. "Are you hustling me?"

"What?"

"You're trying to play it like you'll be terrible tomorrow, then I'll take it easy and you'll smash me before I realize how good you are."

"No, I'm just being honest with you."

His eyes narrowed again. "You don't need to impress anyone. Besides the captain. Other than him, you don't need to impress anyone."

"I'm not trying to hustle you," Anna insisted. She looked around as they approached the first wall. "Wait, where are we going?"

Will's grin turned impish, and there was a glint in his eye as he answered, "You'll see."

Anna's brows drew together at the look on his face, but it was clear that he didn't want to give up more information than that. She decided to change the subject. "I've told you where I'm from. Now it's your turn."

"Here," he shrugged as they passed through a gate in the wall.

Anna watched Merry give an overenthusiastic salute to the guard stationed at the doors, and Will gave a silly little wave with a wiggle of his fingers. The guard looked irritated.

One of Anna's eyebrows rose in curiosity. "You're from Kastarus?"

"Yep."

Anna looked at his dark shirt and pants. Both were worn out and the pants were a little big. *I thought everyone from the capital was well-off.*

"What?" he asked, bristling at her look. "You saw the ears and figured I was from Salwell?"

"What?" Anna asked, confused. "No, I just didn't think you were from here."

"Oh." He relaxed, his chin lowering back down. "Well, there's all kinds in Kastarus."

"I think I'm beginning to understand that," Anna said, looking around.

Again, it was noisier on this side of the wall. Even though it was dinner time, people were hustling in every direction around them. Some people carried shopping bags, others wore dirty jumpsuits from working, and now and then, Anna spotted a pale green robe. The four of them wove through the crowd while they walked. She looked up and spotted a few people on a balcony above, watching the crowd with drinks in hand. A woman caught her gaze and waved coyly.

"Come on." Will put his hand on her shoulder and pushed her forward. "Don't fall behind." His hand was forceful, but it also helped her keep her balance as someone brushed shoulders on their way by.

"Sorry," Anna apologized, glancing at him before finding Merry and Pyran ahead and following them.

"That man is picking pockets," Will added. "Keep your things in front of you."

"My pockets are empty," Anna replied, but she lifted her bag and held it to her chest.

Merry stopped a few blocks down the road. Anna looked up at the sign over the door and found the shape of a calf and foot with toes pointed down. On it were the words *Left Leg*. Anna looked at Pyran.

"Isn't this one of the spots Jen said to avoid?" Pyran asked.

"Jen sounds like a priss," Will said as he passed by and walked inside.

"You wanted food," Merry said, "They've got food." She followed Will.

Anna took a deep breath and looked at Pyran. Her stomach was grumbling loudly. "They've been here before. It can't be that bad."

"Or it *is* that bad and this is all part of some sick initiation," Pyran muttered, but he walked forward.

"Thanks for that idea," Anna hissed from behind him.

The room was full of shouting and laughter and stomping. It smelled like a horde of sweaty people, which was exactly what they found inside. Anna suspected that most of the patrons had all just gotten off from a shift at a local factory, from the way they smelled.

She wrinkled her nose as she followed close behind Pyran, a hand on his shoulder so they wouldn't get separated. Pyran stopped somewhere in the middle of the room, and then sat at a table. Will and Merry sat next to each other across from him. Anna sat down next to Pyran, who shouted to Will and Merry over the noise, "I hope the food tastes better than this place smells!"

Merry laughed, then patted the table affectionately. "It does!"

Anna smiled at Merry's enthusiasm and softened. "What do you order?"

"We'll order for you!" Merry said.

"What?" Pyran asked.

"We'll order for you!" Merry said louder, assuming Pyran hadn't heard her.

Pyran, tired and hungry, let out a big sigh.

Anna patted him on the back and looked around the room.

Most of the tables were full of men and women in dirt-and-grease-spotted coveralls, celebrating the end of the work day, but two hooded figures sat at one table in the corner, and there were a few tables where small families sat.

A server came by and spotted Will and Merry. Her dress was low-cut in the front and her hair was twisted back and clipped on her head. She seemed as hot as everyone else, sweat glistening at her hairline. She grinned and asked, "What'll you have?"

"The usual," Will answered. "Four."

"Ah!" her eyebrows rose as she took in the others at the table. "And four it'll be, right out, toot sweet!" She hurried off.

Anna watched her go, and then another server came out of the back, his button-down shirt undone almost to his navel. It had to be twenty degrees hotter in here. *Mother, it's hot. I'd hate this job.* Anna rolled up her sleeves to cool down her arms.

One of the servers passed by and dropped off four full mugs. Will took a drink, set it down, then addressed Pyran, "So, Merry is from a little farm in the north, Anna's from a little town in the south. Where are you from?"

"Hillcrest," Pyran shrugged.

"What's the story with you two?" Will asked, pointing between Pyran and Anna.

"What do you mean?" Anna asked, confused.

"Why did Hillcrest send both of you? Are you married or something?"

Anna choked on the first sip of her ale. Sputtering, she set the mug down and looked at Pyran. He had wrinkled his nose in discomfort.

"No," Pyran told him. "Neither of us are married, and we're not together, either. I just met her."

"Not married," Anna agreed, once she had righted herself.

"So why'd they send two of you?" Will asked again.

"We're both very capable," Pyran answered, without missing a beat this time. "I'm one of our top fighters. I'm trained in strategy. And Anna has spent her life in the woods north of the wall with a bow in her hand. She could hit a deer in the eye from 300 feet."

Anna's ears heated. "That is a major exaggeration."

"Apparently, she can also do math," Pyran said in a flat tone.

Anna rolled her eyes.

"Is that...not normal?" Merry asked, eyebrows drawn together. "I'm not good with numbers, but I know a lot of people who do well enough."

"No, it's kind of an inside joke," Anna said, waving her hand dismissively. "Never mind."

Merry shrugged.

"Why did you join up?" Pyran asked Will. "You don't seem like the type."

Will was scanning the room, but he shrugged at Pyran as he answered. "It was the only option." It was clear he wouldn't give more of an answer, which was fine with Anna. *I don't want anyone prying, either.*

Pyran stared at Will for a moment, then sat up straight and brought his hands forward. He counted on his fingers as he said, "We've got myself with a sword, Anna with her bow, Merry with a sword and shield, and Will with his daggers. The captain's from Luminport. We're still missing Eysa, Lakoona, and Delphia. Who do you think they'll send?"

Will's eyes narrowed as he thought.

Merry was quick with a response. "No one knows till they get here."

"The obvious ones are a healer and a mage," Will said. "Eysa will most likely provide a mage. That should rattle Captain Heiser."

"What makes you say that?" Anna asked.

"What, he didn't give you the whole talk about how great Luminport mages are?" Merry asked with a laugh.

"Oh," Anna smiled as she recalled their conversation with the captain. "Yeah, kinda."

"Whoever Eysa sends is going to be up against that," Merry said.

"I'm sure the captain can put aside his favoritism for the mission," Pyran offered.

Will chuckled into his beer.

The server returned with four plates of food. The dishes were deep, but wider than a bowl. Inside was a large cut of some kind of pie, its innards cascading out and covered in gravy. It smelled like fresh lamb seasoned with garlic, coriander, mint, and pepper alongside something she couldn't make out.

"I'll be back with another round of drinks for you all," the server smiled.

Merry immediately picked up a spoon and dug in.

Will picked up his spoon, but looked at Pyran and Anna as he said, "This is a Capital Farmer's Pie. Remember it when you order for yourselves next time." Then he started eating.

Anna and Pyran picked up their own spoons and took their first bites. Pyran groaned in satisfaction, and Anna relaxed. As they quickly got through their bowls, Anna could feel herself grow tired, her body now allowing itself to feel exhausted as she rid herself of hunger. She sighed in satisfaction and set her empty spoon into her empty bowl.

"Jen has no idea what she's talking about," Pyran decided as he set his spoon down.

"She really doesn't," Anna agreed.

"There," Will said, sitting back with his arms crossed. "Welcome to Kastarus."

15

ANNA WOKE THE NEXT MORNING TO A HORN SOUNDING AND TO ACHING legs. The four of them hadn't stayed out late, but her body had wanted to give out the entire walk back to the Barracks. Her shower had felt amazing. Now, after a dead sleep in the same position all night, her legs twinged as she tried to rise. She groaned, but got up and stretched before pulling her hair into a tight braid, changing into her last set of clean clothes, and then layering her leathers on top. *I'll have to figure out where to do laundry tonight.*

There was a soft knock on the door. "Anna," Pyran called from the hall.

"Be right there," she called back. She met him in the hallway.

"Come on," he hurried her, "Merry and Will are already downstairs."

"Sorry," she said sarcastically, "I couldn't decide which gown to wear."

Pyran rolled his eyes right back and led her to the cafeteria. She nearly made a couple of wrong turns, but he corrected her.

The dining hall was expansive and full of people in matching gray armor. A neat array of tables and benches stood between them and a serving line at the back. Pyran hurried Anna into line, and then they spotted Will and Merry at a table by themselves in the corner. Anna yawned as she sat down with them. She rested her head in her free hand as she ate.

Merry was chattering at Will about something, but she stopped to greet the two of them. "Good morning!"

"Morning," Pyran replied.

Anna responded with a grunt of acknowledgement that she tried to make as polite as a grunt could sound.

"Not the morning kind?" Merry asked her.

Anna shook her head and ate a spoonful of food. "No, and my legs are killing me from walking for four days."

"Did you do your stretches?" Pyran asked her.

"Yes, commander," Anna mocked Pyran's serious tone and scrunched her eyebrows together.

"Just checking," Pyran grumbled.

"Took me a while to stretch the aches off my legs after I first got here," Merry offered. "Then Will put me through the grinder in training, and I ached all over again."

Anna glanced from her food to Will, who was still sitting quietly, eating. Apparently, he was also not a morning person. Anna briefly wondered how training would go before she drifted back into mindlessly staring at her food.

Breakfast ended too quickly, and then the four of them walked to the courtyard. Anna had never seen a space like it. It was sprawling, but on each side was a wall rising three stories. Small structures dotted the edge of the open area, and Anna could see the stables at the far end. People milled about, some of them set up in sparring circles and already training. She noted small targets set up in the middle of the open space. If she wanted to use her longbow, she'd need the length of the courtyard, though.

Anna's hand found each of her weapons where they were strapped to her, checking that she had them all.

"Ah, welcome!" Captain Heiser's voice greeted them cheerily. He walked into view with a smile almost as bright as his pale gold armor. A giant sun was embossed on his chest plate. He clinked a little as he approached.

He glanced from Merry to Will, then took a longer look at Anna and Pyran as he put his hands on his hips. "Let's start from the beginning, shall we? Show me what you've got. Pyran, you seem a good fit for Merry, and Anna will take on Will." He gestured to two nearby sparring circles. "Warm up, and then we'll get going."

Anna pursed her lips. She didn't know what she had been expecting, but she didn't want to spar with someone to start the day. She stayed near Pyran as they did some simple stretches and movements to get their blood pumping. Her friend was grinning.

"What?" she asked quietly as she reached for her toes.

"What do you mean, *what?*" Pyran answered. "This is exciting. I'm looking forward to seeing firsthand what Merry does with that shield."

"I forgot," Anna grumbled, "You love this stuff."

Pyran chuckled. "You'll be fine." He glanced over at Merry and Will.

Anna followed his gaze. She found Merry doing leg swings and Will stretching his arms from side to side. He held his daggers as he stretched, and she watched the blades twirl between his fingers.

"Uh," Pyran started a little nervously, then recovered. "He's not going to hurt you. You're just sparring."

"Right," Anna tried to make herself agree. "Sure."

When she couldn't delay it any longer, Anna took her shortsword in her hand and stepped into the ring with Will. He was rolling his shoulders and watching her nonchalantly.

"Anytime you're ready," the captain called out.

Anna took a deep breath. Behind her, she heard footsteps on the ground as Pyran and Merry moved.

"Ready?" Will asked her expectantly.

Anna nodded stiffly.

Will glanced at Captain Heiser briefly, then turned back to her. She caught an almost-imperceptible shake of his head before he said, "Loosen up. I won't hurt you."

And then he was moving. Anna only had enough time to spin to the side and out of his path, using her shortsword to block the blade that flew at her like a dart—only the *dart* was still in Will's hand.

Blinking, Anna shoved forward with her sword and broke contact, giving her more space. She reminded herself to regulate her breathing.

Will moved again. He was tall and his limbs were long. In a flash, he was a tornado of blades headed towards her. She parried two slicing swings as she dodged, blocking a third blow. Her sword and his dominant dagger were stuck at the hilts. Anna saw his other blade moving from her peripheral vision. If she dodged, he'd be able to swipe with the first, but if she stayed, he'd cut through her with the second.

Anna sucked in a short breath and felt a spark at her clavicle under her leathers and tunic. In one smooth motion, she turned her blade so that the dagger she had pinned at its hilt slid out and away, ducking and rolling toward the arcing blade in his second hand. The blade flew by, just inches over her rolling form. Unfamiliar with the movements she was making, Anna missed the continuation of the roll onto her feet and found herself on the ground on her back, looking up at Will from behind him.

"What was that?" Will spun to face her, surprise on his face.

She didn't give him an answer. Instead, breathlessly, she swept out a leg to knock him off his feet.

He frowned. Rather than letting her shin contact his and knock him off balance, he lifted his leg and hooked his foot around her ankle as it swung, then raised it. Anna cried out as she found herself spun face down in the dirt. In the next instant, Will kicked the sword from her right hand, knelt over her, and pinned her arm behind her back. She clenched her eyes shut as she saw his dagger moving toward her throat.

When nothing happened, she opened them again. The point of the dagger hung in the air in front of her face, until Will turned it around and tapped her on the forehead with its pommel, giving a mocking "Boop," as it made contact. Then he released her and stepped back.

Anna's face heated in embarrassment. The ringing in her hand subsided from the shock of her sword being knocked away, and she stood up.

"Hm," she heard Captain Heiser grunt thoughtfully from just outside the circle. "Good job, Will."

She turned, avoiding Will's gaze, and looked at the captain. He was crouched stiffly in his armor with a hand to his chin thoughtfully. He returned her gaze, saying, "A little rough around the edges… *interesting* form…"

Form went out the window. There was no time for form. Anna's jaw clenched as she waited for him to send her home.

"...but I haven't seen anyone slip past Will like that before. Well done."

Surprised, Anna's eyes widened.

The captain laughed at her reaction. "What? It's apparent that melee isn't your specialty, but that's not why you're here, is it?"

It took a moment for Anna to realize he was waiting for her to respond. "Uh, no," she agreed. "I'm not here for melee, sir."

"Right," the captain nodded. He stood. "It's important we understand our own strengths and weaknesses—and the strengths and weaknesses of the rest of this mishmash group—if we're going to work together. Before we set off, we need to become one graceful limb."

Anna nodded, mostly following his metaphor.

"You're the head of this supposed body, I take it?" Will asked.

"Correct." The captain nodded and swung his arms behind him, where he held them stiffly as he stood at attention, his salt-and-pepper covered chin lifting into the air.

Anna heard Will snicker. The captain ignored it.

"Okay." The captain stepped out of his stiff posture and towards Anna. "Let's work on this, and then later you can show me what you do with your bow. You seem a little tense, so we can start there."

The captain took Anna through a couple of simple movements to loosen her up. As she did them, she glanced at Pyran and Merry. They were moving together with their swords and Merry's shield, going over form. Anna returned her attention to her task and followed the captain's instructions.

"Much better," he praised. "You should never be tense during a battle. It only creates more room for error."

"You're never tense during battle?" Anna asked him.

He smiled under his trimmed mustache. "I was a long time ago."

"And what battles were these?" Will asked, pausing his movements to raise an eyebrow at the captain. "There hasn't been a war in centuries."

"I think you'll learn during our endeavors," the captain turned to Will, a smile on his face and a glint in his eye, "that there doesn't need to be a war for there to be battles."

Will wrinkled his nose at the answer and went back to his movements.

The captain checked in with Pyran and Merry, and then came back around to them.

"All right," he said to Anna, "now that you're loosened up, let's go back and fix what went wrong. I need both of you to move through the same motions you made during your sparring, but at half speed."

Anna had never done this before. Will didn't seem too keen on the idea either, but he moved to stand in his starting position. The captain stepped out of the ring.

"Whenever you're ready," he told them.

Will looked at Anna and nodded. She hopped from foot to foot once, twice, shaking her arms out as she did, and then nodded back. Will moved forward at a walking speed. Anna watched him move so fluidly that it seemed like time really had slowed down. Her brows furrowed as she tried to understand it.

"Now," the captain called out to her, "correct your mistakes. How should you react here?"

Anna took a breath and fixed her grip on the handle of her shortsword. She met Will's blade with her own. She found it awkward trying to move so slowly. Until this point, her training had all been aggressively fast-paced. Carefully, she parried, stepping aside as she swept his dagger in the other direction.

"Good," the captain praised. "Better."

She caught Will giving a little nod to her, a half-smirk, half-smile spreading across his lips. Something in her chest jumped at the expression.

Mother, I'm so nervous.

She continued her slow momentum and separated from him. She wobbled a little as she moved, but returned to a ready stance and waited for the movements she knew were coming next.

Will caught himself lightly on his foot and pushed off to turn his momentum. Anna watched him use that momentum to begin slowly spinning, daggers glinting in the sunlight as they approached her again. *I have no idea what to do next.*

Taking an educated guess, she put her sword between them, angling it so that his strikes would glance off. She also knew what was coming next, so after the second strike slid to the side and away—as Will spun completely around again—she adjusted her blade in front of her and began moving her back foot. His blade met her sword, and Anna turned her wrists. Will's blade spun down and away.

"Yes!" the captain cheered. "Well done!"

Will's second hand was coming, and the answer was no longer a haphazard dodge and roll. Anna's lips pressed together in focus. Will's blade arched upward. She hesitated, then wobbled with indecision, tripped, and fell down.

The captain chuckled as he said, "That's enough." He stepped into the ring. "Do you see how Will can move through those motions slowly, without stuttering his steps?" he asked Anna.

She nodded and glanced up at Will, whose face was blank except for the corner of his mouth lifted in the smallest of smirks.

"That comes from balance. This morning, we're going to work on your balance," the captain said. When Anna wrinkled her nose, he said, "After lunch, you can use your bows."

Anna nodded in acceptance.

"Will, why don't you take a turn with Pyran? Merry can referee." The captain nodded toward the other sparring ring.

Will nodded and walked by, glancing at Anna as he did.

Anna spent the rest of the morning working with the captain. He walked her through a lengthy run of slow movements designed to strengthen her core, and she ran through them too many times to count, shortsword in hand. Her abs and back were burning when a soldier caught Captain Heiser's attention, someone in blue following close behind.

Anna continued her movements, sweat dripping down her forehead, until the soldier walked away and the captain called for everyone's attention.

"Everyone, this is Roscoe Dixon, from Lakoona. They'll be joining our team."

"You can call me Ros," they said in a flat, raspy tone.

They had short blond hair, so fair that it looked like little wisps of gold cloud as it stuck out in different directions. A flick of dark eyeliner framed gray eyes behind their pale lashes as they looked around, sizing everyone up as their thin lips chewed something. There were freckles on their face and their exposed forearms.

They wore loose navy pants that tied at the waist and ankles, along with a pale blue tunic and a leather breastplate that was also dyed navy. A long, tangled creature with scales and sharp teeth was embossed on their breastplate. They shifted their feet, and Anna noted their boots were thin and soft. In one hand was a short metal staff, a little longer than their leg, carved in a twisting pattern at the ends, and with leather wrapped around the middle. Anna could tell Ros was a little shorter than her, even as they stood straight.

"Ros is a Lakoona Kraken, trained traditionally with a staff," the captain continued, then turned to Ros, "We'll get you situated into a room during the lunch break. Warm up, and then you can show us what you can do."

Ros nodded, stepping to the side and beginning their own version of a warmup.

"Thank you, carry on," the captain told the rest of them.

Anna huffed at the thought of returning to her strengthening movements, but started the dance from the beginning. Occasionally, she glanced over as Ros spun their staff around too fast to follow or jumped from a handstand to a cartwheel. Other soldiers around the courtyard were watching too, pretending to drink their water or finding a reason to walk nearby to get a look. When Ros finished, they walked over to the captain.

"Good!" the captain said loudly and clapped his hands together. "Clear the sparring ring!"

Will, Pyran, and Merry stepped back from the ring. Anna stopped her movements to turn and watch.

"Pyran," the captain called to him, "Let's see how you strategize *this.* You against Ros."

Pyran's eyebrows were sky-high, but he nodded. "Yes, sir," and he stepped into the ring. He stood in his ready stance, knees bent and sword extended forward as he held it with both hands.

Ros joined him across the ring, standing with their legs together and staff held out slightly to the side. They nodded to each other and then began circling slowly.

Pyran shuffled, his form strong, as Ros stepped lightly, almost without sound. Then Ros bent forward and ran at him. Anna watched them spin their staff and swing at Pyran. Pyran blocked with his sword, the clash of the metal giving a resounding clang. Anna was sure that Pyran's teeth were vibrating at the contact. Still, he moved to strike a blow. Ros was quick to jump back and out of his range. They continued this little dance, Ros jumping in to attack while Pyran blocked. Pyran would attack and Ros would dodge out of the way, as light as a feather.

Then Ros paused, not taking their turn to attack. They spun their staff in front of them and Anna heard a soft *snick* before the staff's ends jumped outwards to twice its length. Merry let out a little gasp of surprise. Ros smirked and moved in again. Their dance resumed, but this time, Ros had more reach than Pyran. They swatted him on the shoulder, on the back, once on the rear end. They were having fun with it. Pyran's face was red.

"All right," the captain stood from his crouch. "That's enough. You've made your point."

Still grinning, Ros jumped to the other side of the ring and returned to their starting position. They knocked their staff against the ground twice, and Anna heard another *snick* as the ends of the staff jumped inward again.

Pyran frowned at Ros from his position across the circle and rolled his shoulder.

"It wasn't really a fair fight," Ros told him in their airy voice. "A little more training with me, and you might have a chance."

"I look forward to it," Pyran said, sincerely.

Anna resisted the urge to roll her eyes at her friend's enthusiasm.

The sun was high overhead as the captain said, "With that, we'll break for lunch. Ros, you can follow me."

Ros bowed their head at Pyran appreciatively, and then followed the captain. When they exited the courtyard, Merry said, "I've never seen anything like that."

"I've heard of the Krakens," Pyran shrugged. "I thought they were made up to scare children into behaving."

"Looked real enough to me," Will said. "But real or not, we have a long way to go before we become *one graceful limb*." He mocked the captain in a snobby tone.

"You don't like the captain," Anna observed.

"Not really," Will agreed.

"Will doesn't like anyone too much," Merry said.

"So what is it about the captain, then?" Anna asked.

"The fact that you're already calling him *the captain* might have something to do with it," Will replied.

"That's what he is," Anna argued, annoyed with him.

"What happened when we were sparring earlier?" Will asked, changing the subject. His eyes narrowed at Anna.

"What do you mean?" Anna asked. "You very easily kicked my butt."

"When you evaded my last strike. What was that?" he pressed.

Anna's brows furrowed as she thought about it. Her hand fiddled with her leathers around her collar. "I was just trying to not get sliced," she answered defensively.

"No, it was different," Will shook his head. "With your speed and timing, that should've been the end of it."

"Thanks for that." Anna rolled her eyes.

"She got lucky," Merry jumped in. "Leave her alone, Will."

"Hm." Will let out a frustrated grunt, but let the conversation drop.

Frowning, Anna turned from Will to look at Pyran. She could see his mind working through his last fight.

"Oh, stop it," Anna told him. "They're going to train with you, and you'll have picked up the right strategy by the end of the day."

Pyran sighed. "Fine. What's for lunch?"

Lunch was very similar to breakfast, but Anna didn't mind because she had barely registered what breakfast was as she ate it. She talked with Merry about how the morning had gone, and Merry offered some pointers about balance. Anna understood that, for the others, working on balance had been part of their early days. She briefly remembered covering it, but it hadn't been highlighted as actual attacks or defensive stances. Begrudgingly, Anna agreed to run through the core strengthening movements every morning with Merry. Pyran agreed to join them.

Will ate quietly, staring down at his food.

Anna was still tired after lunch, but her mood had improved. Captain Heiser and Ros joined everyone back in the courtyard, where Ros began to show Pyran how to fight against a Kraken. Merry and Will stopped to watch as the captain approached Anna.

"Grab your bows," he told her. "I'm sure you've been looking forward to this."

Anna grinned as she collected her bows and quiver. She followed the captain across the courtyard, and they stopped in front of a row of targets.

"We don't have much space here, so these will have to do." Captain Heiser looked around, eyes landing on a short wooden tower across the courtyard.

"Why don't you go up there? That's about seventy-five feet. I'll clear the space for you."

"Yes, sir." Anna nodded and made her way over to the tower.

Haphazardly joined wooden boards made up the little structure. Here and there was a cleaner piece that replaced a broken board. Rickety stairs led up to the landing at the top. Anna thought the whole thing might blow over if it ever had to stand against a strong wind. From the top, she had a clear view of the courtyard. The captain was roping off the area between her and the targets.

The summer sunlight warmed the courtyard, and a soft breeze floated through, the bit of wind that could make it over the building and into the yard. Anna nocked an arrow and held her bow ready, pointing at the ground. There were five straw targets lined up against the courtyard wall. Silently, she ran through everything she'd been taught.

"Whenever you're ready," the captain called up to her.

Anna raised her bow and took a breath in. As she released her breath, she released her first arrow. It landed just high of the bullseye. She nocked another arrow and repeated her breathing and release. This one landed in the bullseye, barely to the left. Next, she steadied herself again, turned slightly toward the remaining targets, and she launched three arrows in quick succession, similar to what she had done when she was tested in Hillcrest. The first of these landed in the same spot as her second shot, the second was as centered as she had ever seen, and the third was slightly to the right of center.

"Well done," the captain praised from the bottom of the tower. "Can you do that on the move?"

Anna's brow furrowed as she contemplated the captain's question. "Uh, yeah, with my shortbow."

"Of course," the captain agreed. "Come down and let's see it."

Anna made her way down the creaking tower and met the captain at the bottom. "What do you want me to do?"

"Move down this wall," he gestured to the wall opposite the targets, "and hit the targets as you pass."

"Okay." Anna checked that her quiver was fastened correctly to her back and then readied an arrow. She glanced at the captain before doing as he had said, walking down the wall and pulling her bow up to aim. *Shunk.* The first arrow hit the bullseye.

"Faster," Captain Heiser told her.

Anna strode faster and shot the second arrow. It hit its mark.

"*Faster*," the captain urged, his tone forceful.

Anna broke into a jog. She shot at the third and fourth targets, almost missing the center of her last shot.

"Run," the captain pushed.

Anna sprinted past the last target and released an arrow. It landed to the left of center. *Dammit.*

She looked back at Captain Heiser and found him inspecting the targets. He turned to look at her again as she walked toward him, and he said, "Good. You shoot well, but you're going to be under pressure when we need you. Here's what you'll work on. I'm going to have someone spar with you over here. They'll start at a distance. I need you to hit a target before they reach you. You need to fight them off, and then hit a second target. Understood?"

Anna nodded, gripping her bow tightly to help hide her frustration. *This is going to be rough.*

"Maybe tomorrow, we'll work on shooting from horseback," the captain mentioned with a casual wave as he turned to find her someone to spar with.

Anna sighed, but she held her tongue. She looked around the courtyard as she waited for the captain to return. People were sparring in the numerous circles spread across the space. A few worked with wooden dummies stuck into the ground. Racks full of practice swords and padded armor stood at each end.

A guard came from the doors at the end of the courtyard with a man in violet robes in tow. Anna could tell they were headed for Captain Heiser as they crossed the yard.

When they reached him, the captain looked the man in the robes up and down, then crossed his arms. Anna watched him nod twice, and then he shook the man's hand. He said something to the guard, who hurried off. The captain waved Anna back over, and she complied and rejoined the group.

"This is Bennett Day," the captain introduced. "He's a mage from Eysa. Bennett, this is the team. Will Grey, Merry MacGill, Pyran Taggert, Ros Dixon, and Anna Hale." The captain pointed each team member out. Will gave a disinterested wave, Merry smiled, Pyran nodded, Ros looked Bennett over, and Anna smiled and nodded in acknowledgement.

Bennett looked nervous. He had dirty blonde hair and gray eyes. His robes were simple, but Anna could tell they were made from fine material.

"How is he going to train with us?" Will asked.

"You've never practiced with someone Mother-blessed?" Ros asked.

"He won't be training with us, mostly. One of Kastarus' mages has agreed to prepare him. We'll work with him on strategy and teamwork occasionally," the captain said.

"I'm looking forward to it," Bennett managed.

"Us, too," Ros answered with a smirk.

A woman approached wearing a pink dress that had long, trailing sleeves. Her thick, blonde hair was tied into a braid that hung down to her knees behind her and swung side to side as she walked, a contrast to her dark skin. Crow's feet crinkled at the edges of her eyes as she met Captain Heiser and Bennett with a smile. Outside of those small wrinkles, she seemed ageless.

"Hello," she greeted in a sonorous voice, "I'm Irene Brooks. They sent for me to work with your mage."

"Very good," Captain Heiser nodded. "Irene Brooks, this is Bennett Day. He comes from *Eysa.*"

Will snickered at the captain's tone as he gave Bennett's hometown. Anna caught Merry elbowing him as she glanced over.

"Nice to meet you," Irene said to Bennett. "That's a long journey. Are you ready to begin now, or do you need some time?"

"Oh, I'm ready now," Bennett answered quickly.

"Good," Irene told Bennett. She nodded to Captain Heiser and then led Bennett away. "Follow me."

Anna watched them pass by. Irene looked over at her, and then held her gaze. Her head seemed to turn to the side slightly in curiosity, but then her gaze slid away, and they were gone.

"Now that's settled," the captain turned back to the group, "we can resume our training." He asked Merry to assist Anna with her practice, instructed her on the goals, and then sent them back to the targets.

"This should be interesting," Anna told Merry. "Why do you think he picked you to help me?"

Merry smiled. "Because I'm big. Hard to shoot around. Oh, and if you misfire, I can use my shield to block any arrows."

Anna laughed. "I won't shoot you."

"I know," Merry agreed. "But better safe than sorry."

Merry stood at one end of the targets while Anna stood across from them. Then, Merry shouted *Go!* and took off running at Anna, who tried to get a shot away, fight Merry off, then fire another shot. Anna had thought the shooting part sounded easy, but when Merry began, she overestimated the time she had and failed to get her first arrow sufficiently nocked.

After that, it was an uphill battle. Merry wouldn't go easy on her because she wanted her to be fully and competently trained, but Anna wished that for once, they could start slow.

Still, she refused to let herself be embarrassed for long in front of the rest of the team and all the others training in the courtyard. After the third try, Merry reminded her she didn't need to beat her with her sword. She just needed to break away with enough time to get a shot off. It frustrated Anna that she hadn't connected those dots sooner, but after that, she could refocus herself and take out her frustration on her bowstring.

By the time training was over for the day, Anna could consistently shoot her first arrow with accuracy and fight Merry off long enough to shoot a second arrow, albeit one that missed the mark. Anna was sure Merry must be getting frustrated with her, but she never showed it. The first time Anna had shot off a second arrow, Merry cheered loudly enough to draw everyone's attention, and Anna had to tell her to stop shouting.

Anna felt beat. The pain brought her flashbacks to when she'd started training in Hillcrest. All she wanted to do was lie in bed, but she had to eat dinner, and if she didn't stretch, she knew she would regret it tomorrow. Merry told her she would stay with her and they would stretch together, saying, "I'm worried that if I'm not here, you'll fall over and not be able to get back up."

"Tell me you're at least a little sore," Anna groaned as she swung her arms in circles.

"Sure," Merry chuckled, stretching her shoulders from side to side. "I am a little sore. That was a lot of running."

"Thanks," Anna laughed lightly, not convinced.

After stretching, the only thing that motivated her was her empty stomach and Merry's threats to carry her if she stopped walking. When the two of them met up with the rest of the group on their way out of the courtyard, Pyran looked like he was in a similar state, and even Will looked worn out. Captain Heiser stood by, waiting to dismiss the group.

"Tough day?" Anna managed.

Pyran was rolling his right shoulder. "Lucy could learn a thing or two from Ros."

Anna smiled. "I bet."

"You liked it," Ros said from where they stood stretching. Anna was sure they were teasing, but their face remained straight.

Pyran sighed and looked at Anna wearily. Anna glanced curiously past Pyran at Ros, but when Ros sent her a wink, Anna immediately looked away, eyes widening.

"What?" Pyran asked as he watched Anna get flustered, and then glanced back at Ros, who was focusing on stretching.

"Where is our new magic friend?" Merry asked.

"Ah, yes," the captain looked around the yard.

Anna found Bennett in the courtyard's corner, talking with Irene. Irene left and Bennett looked around.

Merry raised an arm to wave enthusiastically. "Over here! Come on, we're starving!"

Anna saw Bennett's blush from across the courtyard. He ran a hand through his hair nervously, making his way over.

"All right," the captain began as Bennett joined the group. "This was a productive day, and I expect the same tomorrow. We're still waiting on someone from Amgen, but I think we've got a good crew here. I'll see you all in the morning."

"Thank you, captain," Merry told him. "Have a good night."

"Same to you," he nodded to her with a smile, and then made his way into the Barracks.

"Where to?" Merry turned to Will. "Back to Left Leg?"

"Sorry to say, but I won't be joining you tonight," Will told her, not sounding sorry at all. "You'll have to go on without me." He looked down at his hands, tugging at the edges of his black gloves.

"Oh," Merry said, a little surprised. She quickly recovered and turned to the rest of the group with a grin. "Looks like I'll be leading this *Merry* band to our meal!"

This got a smile and a fatigued sigh out of Will.

"We aren't going to eat in the cafeteria?" Bennett asked.

"Oh-ho-ho," Merry hooted excitedly. "I'm about to show you a much better meal than this sad cafeteria could ever provide!"

Anna grinned conspiratorially at Pyran.

"Right, well," Will said, "I'm off."

"See you tomorrow!" Merry told him.

He walked away with a small wave over his shoulder.

Merry turned back to the others. "No need to shower, but we'll head back to our rooms to change first, and then we'll be on our way." She marched toward the door into the Barracks as if leading an army.

"Shouldn't we shower for dinner, though?" Bennett asked, confusion across his face.

"You'll want to shower after dinner," Pyran told him.

Anna laughed with Pyran, and they both followed Merry. Ros joined next, and Bennett trailed behind. Anna glanced back at him and found him looking down, fiddling with a thread at the end of his sleeve.

For a mage he is extremely... normal.

As Ros caught up to Merry, Anna hung back and let Bennett catch up to her.

"How was training?" she asked.

She seemed to have startled him a little, but he responded with a smile. "It was good. Ms. Brooks is a master. It's Anna, right?"

"Yes, that's me," Anna agreed.

"You can call me Ben. Bennett sounds so formal." Bennett told her. "I saw you training with Merry. It all looked incredibly difficult."

Anna's face slid into a sarcastic smile. "It was difficult, but I'm sure your training is tough, too."

"In a different way," Bennett nodded. "It can be physically taxing, but it's mostly mentally tiring."

"Really? How do you mean?"

"It's hard to explain to someone who's never experienced it before," he said, pausing to think. "It's like… It's like trying to solve equations while running for miles."

Anna's brows furrowed. "Equations?"

"Hard math problems," Bennett explained.

Anna nodded in understanding. "Your body and mind have to work together."

"Right," Bennett agreed. "Your mind is doing the important part, but you need your body to support what your mind is doing, even though the two don't seem to go together at all."

Anna thought for a moment. "So it's like physical math?"

Bennett let out a sigh of a laugh. "Not exactly. Your focus is more important than your intelligence."

"It's like a willpower thing, then?"

"Yeah, that sounds right."

Anna hummed thoughtfully. *How much willpower does it take to start a fire or heat metal? How much willpower is there in a mage light? What determined if your willpower could make magic or if it was just that—the drive for something to happen and not the actual happening?*

16

BENNETT'S ROOM WAS NEXT TO PYRAN'S, AND ROS' WAS ACROSS THE HALL next to Merry's. Merry, Pyran, and Ros were in the hallway waiting in their street clothes by the time Anna changed and fixed her hair.

"So, where is this place we're going?" Ros asked. They had replaced what must have been a uniform with a pair of brown trousers and a loose, tan-striped shirt.

Merry smiled. "It's a little hole in the wall just outside the first ring."

"The food is great," Pyran assured them.

Bennett stepped out of his room next, wearing another set of robes. This one was a deep amber with dark green embellishments.

"Our Mother's child does not wear street clothes?" Ros commented to no one in particular.

Bennett's cheeks darkened. "I wear these all the time. Almost everyone does in Eysa."

"This will be interesting," Ros said, looking at Merry.

"He'll be fine," Merry waved a hand in front of her dismissively. "We're in Kastarus. There's all kinds here."

"Let's go already." Pyran's hands went to his stomach. "I think my gut is trying to eat itself."

Anna stuck close to Merry and Pyran as the group wove through the crowds. She remembered some landmarks from their last trip to the Left Leg, but not enough to find her way on her own. Being in this giant city was disorienting and completely threw off her sense of direction.

Once they were past the gate of the inner wall, Anna knew they weren't far. As they walked under the sign and into the restaurant, the smell hit her again, harder than she remembered. *Maybe I blocked it out with the memory of the food.* The place was just as busy as the previous night, and just as loud. Merry led everyone to a table at the back where there was just enough room for them all to squeeze in.

"Back so soon?" the server from yesterday greeted Merry.

"I'm back, and with more friends," Merry told her, gesturing at the rest of them.

"You and Will sure have some interesting friends," she said, looking around the group.

"That we do," Merry agreed. "The usual, five of them."

"Coming right up!" the server grinned, and then hurried to the kitchen.

Anna noticed a table of men eyeing Ben, speaking to each other with frowns. She nudged Pyran with her elbow and nodded her head at them.

Pyran looked up. "I see them."

Ros glanced at them, then turned back to their own table. "All kinds," they repeated what Merry had said earlier, "even the kinds that are still *superstitious*," they said, disgusted.

"What?" Ben asked, looking around.

"Don't worry about it," Pyran told him. "They wouldn't do anything."

"Who wouldn't do what?" Ben asked, confused.

"Those men over there don't like your clothes," Ros said plainly.

Ben's brows drew together and he frowned. "Are you sure they're looking at me? Maybe there's someone behind me they don't like or—"

"It's you," Anna confirmed.

"I heard some people were still wary of mages, but I thought that was only in the most secluded corners of Telluth," Ben said.

"I guess there are not-so-secluded corners of Kastarus that feel the same way," Pyran said.

"Hmm." Merry looked over at the table with a judgmental frown of her own. She caught one man's eye and crossed her arms, her eyes never leaving his. He frowned, spotted the arm without the hand, and then averted his gaze to his table. Merry turned back to the group.

"Simple, but effective." Ros grinned at Merry, bemused, and Merry smiled back.

The waitress returned with mugs for each of them and winked at Merry before hurrying away again.

"You really don't own a normal pair of pants and a shirt?" Pyran asked Ben.

"No," Ben shrugged. "I've worn proper robes since I started training in Eysa when I was five."

"That's a long time," Anna thought aloud.

"Says the girl who started shooting arrows at the same age," Pyran grumbled.

"Impressive," Ros said, looking at Anna. "How did your little, chubby child's fingers hold a bow?"

"Uh." It took a moment for Anna to process Ros' strange question. "My father made me a miniature one."

"Hm." Ros nodded, satisfied with that answer.

"How long have you been training with a staff?" Pyran asked Ros. "Since you were two?" he joked.

Ros grinned coyly. "I was selected to join the Krakens after primary school."

"Selected?" Merry asked.

They nodded. "It's a great honor. In Lakoona, when you are nearing the end of your primary education, you may choose to be tested. The results show what path your career will take, and you may not go against the results once they're decided."

"It's not just for the military, then?" Pyran asked.

"Most professions in Lakoona support the program."

"What if you wanted to be a blacksmith, but they told you to become a fisher?" Anna asked.

"Then that is the way of things," Ros answered. "You may either take up a fishing net or leave town."

"Harsh," Anna said.

"Most do not enter the test unless they are sure of their outcome, or they cannot decide what path to take," Ros told her. "A person must enter the test freely, or their judgment is undone."

"That's one way to do it," Merry said. "In Tuvale, most people do what their parents do."

"You knew you wanted to become a Kraken?" Ben asked Ros.

"Yes, but since so few pass into this path, there was still a chance I wouldn't succeed."

"That sounds incredibly stressful," Anna said.

"Mm," Ros hummed in agreement and nodded.

"Merry, you seem like you've always been into this *warrior thing*," Ben observed, waving a hand vaguely at the words. "Is this what your parents do?"

Merry grinned, excited to tell her story again. Ben and Ros listened intently as she gave all the graphic details, and then explained why she had left. Ben gasped at the violent parts and Ros snarled at her family's reaction to her lost hand. Anna and Pyran sipped on their drinks contentedly.

"I couldn't *begin* to imagine," Ben told her at the conclusion of the story.

"Yes," Ros agreed. "Your family should be ashamed."

Merry shrugged, grinning. "I'm happy with where I am. I honestly hope they are, too."

Ros thought on that for a moment, drinking from their mug, and then they looked at Pyran and asked, "And what of you, my pupil? How did you come to this vocation?"

"My dad's an accountant and I hate math," Pyran answered.

"Fair enough," Ros' eyes sparked in amusement as they grinned, and then they turned to Anna. "And you?"

"Uh, necessity," Anna responded, keeping her answer short and vague, taking a sip of her drink to give herself a moment to think. When she lowered the cup, she added, "The family business wasn't making enough."

Ros nodded, accepting this response.

"Ben," Merry turned to him with an excited smile, "I've been dying to ask. What's it like to do magic?"

At first Ben's upper lip rose at the question, as if he had found a fly in his drink, then he took a breath and straightened his face. "I don't know how to answer your question, because I have no comparison. I don't know what it's like to *not* be able to *do magic*." His hands raised to make air quotes.

Ros laughed, and then said through the laughter, "You're a proud one."

Ben frowned at Ros. "I didn't mean it that way." He looked back at Merry and let out a sigh before trying to explain. "I've always had my abilities, but they were erratic when I was little. Learning how to use them was like learning a language or a dance you had forgotten a century ago."

Merry let out a little, interested, "Oooh."

Ros held in a giggle.

"My father is a mage, too," he continued, "so it was a little like going into the family business." He glanced at Pyran. "He's a professor at the university."

"Let's see something," Merry encouraged. She licked her fingers and put out the candle in the middle of the table. "Can you light this candle?"

"Sure," Ben shrugged. He put his hand out, palm facing the candle, and swept his fingers in a smooth circle with a twist of his wrist. A flame sprung up from nowhere and fluttered at the wick.

Merry giggled and clapped excitedly.

That's not how Cricket did it.

"Here we are," the waitress announced herself, arms full of food. She had two bowls balanced on one side and three on the other. She set them down and Merry passed them on. "Enjoy!" she said cheerily.

"Finally," Pyran groaned as he picked up his spoon.

"Dig in!" Merry told Ben and Ros. She didn't need to tell Anna or Pyran.

THAT EVENING, ANNA WROTE TO HER MOTHER. SHE TOLD HER ABOUT Kastarus and the people she had met. She left out how disorienting the city was and anything about the mission, except that when she was done, their debt would be half paid off. When she reread it, she found it a little too concise, a little too cold. She added to the end:

As hard as this has been, I've had good moments too. People, in general, are kind. I miss you. I love you.

Anna

17

When the sun rose over the barracks and filtered into Anna's room for a second time, Anna once again found herself stiff and aching all over. The strengthening movements had worked muscles she didn't even know she had, and it felt as if she was going through conditioning all over again. Still, she had to get up to put her letter in the post before training. She strained into a sitting position, groaning as she worked her way onto her feet. She took a few minutes to stretch before she got ready, grabbed the letter, and then left her room. The hall was quiet as she made her way to the stairs.

Once down the stairs, Anna paused. She focused on remembering the orientation of the building compared to the sun and then figuring out which direction the sun was in, which was hard with so few windows. She knew she needed to be on the west side of the building. Finally, Anna pointed a finger and spun in the direction she thought she needed to go. She started walking.

She ended up doing a lap around the building, not because she had gone the wrong direction, but because she hadn't recognized the little entryway she was looking for. The second time around, she found the young man sitting at the desk just inside the doorway, but she couldn't recall his name.

"Hello," she greeted him.

"Morning," he responded, looking up from the desk with bleary eyes. Anna wasn't sure if he had been reading or sleeping.

She held up her letter. "Should I give this to you? Or is there somewhere for me to—"

"I can take that," he said. "They come to drop off and collect every afternoon from this door."

"Great!" Anna handed him her envelope. "Thank you."

"Sure," he said, taking it.

As Anna turned to walk away, the door swung open and a familiar figure walked in.

"Will?" Anna asked in greeting.

His warm brown eyes were red around the edges from exhaustion when they turned up to her in alarm. "What are you doing here?"

"I had a letter," Anna answered. "Were you…out all night?" Anna looked him over. He wasn't in his training clothes, but his long, straight hair—normally so sleek and put together—was coming out of the little knot he had tied the top half of it into.

"I wasn't here, if that's what you mean." He moved past her and started walking down the hall towards the stairs.

Anna hurried to follow. "Are you all right? Did something happen?"

"I'm fine," he answered without turning to look at her, his pace making it clear that he didn't care to be followed. "It was a planned absence."

"Oh, okay." Anna relented and slowed to her normal pace. Will disappeared around a corner in front of her.

When she reached their rooms, the hallway was empty. Frowning, she stepped into her room to do some more focused stretching before she grabbed her gear and met the others in the hallway.

Will had already gone to breakfast when Anna greeted the team. She found them waiting for her.

"Did you get up late today?" Pyran asked Anna.

"No, I've been stretching," Anna told him. "I think I'm going to be sore for a month."

"I know what you mean," Pyran said, looking at Ros, "but half of mine are bruises."

Ros smiled back, their thin lips stretched over their teeth coyly. "Bruises are teachers."

"Yeah," Ben sighed and looked between the two. "I think I'll stick to magic."

This put Merry to laughing as she led everyone down the hall.

The group found Will at the end of an empty table in the dining hall, eating by himself. When Anna asked Merry if they should let him be alone, Merry responded, "What? Never!" and took a seat right next to him. The others filled in around Will, though no one took the seat directly across from him.

"Good morning," Merry greeted him.

He nodded in acknowledgement.

"You missed a great supper," Merry told him. "Ros told us about their big test, and Ben told us about the university."

"Mm," Will nodded, pretending to be interested as he took another bite. "I'll have to catch up with the newbies."

"Why do you sound as though something crawled up your ass?" Ros asked him, their raspy tone sincere enough even if the question seemed aggressive.

Will grinned sarcastically at the bowl in front of him. "Didn't get much sleep last night." He picked up the steaming mug next to his bowl and took a drink, then wrinkled his nose. "The coffee here is awful. Merry, remind me next time that the coffee is awful."

"You don't listen when I do," she told him.

"No, I don't." He frowned into the mug, looking into it as if he saw a centipede crawling around inside. "At least it's caffeinated."

The table was quiet for a moment as people ate, and a question came to mind that Anna voiced out loud. "Where does Captain Heiser eat? I never see him in the cafeteria."

"He gets a tray delivered to his office," Merry said.

"Anyone with a rank of captain or above gets room service," Will added. It seemed like he was getting more comfortable, or awake, or both.

"Fancy," Ros remarked. "In the Krakens, we all eat together, regardless of rank."

"Anyone of authority at the university gets meal delivery," Ben said. "It gives them more time to complete their work."

Will looked over at Ben with a deadpan expression, and then pushed an invisible pair of glasses up his nose. Ben's brows drew together in confusion.

"He's calling you ink-nosed," Pyran clarified for him.

"Ah," Ben frowned lightly. "I'll take it as a compliment, then."

Ros chuckled.

Anna sighed, but a smile formed despite herself.

"Who were you sending your letter to?" Will asked her, putting her on the spot.

The smile fell. Anna had enough of Will's attitude this morning. "My mother, if you have to know."

Something flashed in Will's eyes at her response. "Telling mummy and daddy all about your trip to the big city?" he asked, a smirk on his face.

Anna realized then that she was most certainly the youngest member of the group. Besides Pyran, who was only a few years older, most of the other team members were around ten years her senior, if she had to guess. Will looked to be Pyran's age, but Anna had no idea how half-elves aged.

"Just my mother," Anna replied, with her face worked into a practiced, expressionless, blank slate. "My father died ten years ago."

Merry swatted Will on the arm hard.

"Ow!" Will rubbed where she had hit him. "How was I supposed to know?"

"It's fine," Anna told Merry.

"It is *not* fine," she argued indignantly. She turned back to Will, expression still cross. "Say you're sorry."

"I'm sorry!" Will held his hands up, palms out in surrender. "I didn't know!"

"You think the captain's going to drag a horse out of the stables for you today?" Pyran changed the subject, looking at Anna.

"Mother, I hope not." Anna shook her head at the bowl in front of her and worked on finishing her meal.

When the group assembled in the courtyard for training, Captain Heiser had everyone start with stretches and then strengthening movements—even Ben. By the end of warmups, Anna could see sweat rolling down his face. After that, he was permitted to train with Ms. Brooks while the rest sparred.

The captain matched Anna with Pyran at first, to *loosen her up.* She felt better after working with the familiarity of Pyran's movements, even if she didn't win. Will was matched with Ros. Anna and Pyran's match ended first, so they got to watch the end of it.

Anna felt like she was watching some kind of quick, graceful dance. Where Pyran had been stumped by Ros' movements the day before and only able to react, Will seemed to read them, able to see what they might do next and adjust before the move came. They looked like a bluebird and a bat spinning around the ring. In the end, Ros won, but it had been close. Will looked irritated.

When the captain announced that she would be the next person to go up against the staff user, Anna thought she had misheard. She looked at Pyran in confusion, who just shrugged back, his eyes showing a bit of concern.

"Take it easy," the captain told Ros. "This is just to gauge the two of you against each other. You're the only two who haven't sparred together."

Because they were the last two left, the others got to watch. Anna tried to keep herself calm, but she didn't like what was about to happen. She white-knuckled her shortsword as she took her spot across from Ros.

Anna noticed that Ros was not smirking, as they had been with Pyran or Will before the match started. Instead, they were looking Anna over with a tranquil expression. They had also shrunk their staff down to its shorter length. *Maybe after they beat me with it, I can ask them how it works.*

"Ready?" Ros asked her.

Anna nodded. "As I'll ever be."

"Let's begin." Ros spun the staff in their hand before stepping to Anna's right.

Anna readied her sword to parry and adjusted her feet to keep her opponent in front of her. She caught Ros' staff, and it glanced across her and away. Ros continued the movement, switching the staff to their other hand as it spun and turning their body with it. They transitioned into an upward swing as they came back around. Anna ducked back, almost losing balance but maintaining her footing. The staff whipped by overhead. Ros continued the movement again, turning it into another attack.

If I'm ever going to get a hit in, I need to stop their movement and make them falter somehow.

Anna took a breath and let her grip on her shortsword relax slightly as she considered what to do. She turned the sword, narrowly avoiding another swing of the staff as it glanced off. Ros was light on their feet, even lighter than Will. They could adjust and redirect in the blink of an eye. *What could I do that would startle them?*

Anna had a thought, but she didn't like it. After dodging and blocking another few attacks, she decided it was her only option.

The next time Ros swung, Anna stayed still, tensing her muscles to prepare for contact. The staff landed hard on Anna's side, and she couldn't help the grunt of pain that escaped—but it worked. Ros' eyes went wide as they watched Anna take the blow, and their movement paused. Somewhere outside of the ring, Merry let out a gasp.

Anna took the opportunity and swung her sword at her stilled opponent. Ros, of course, caught on and jumped back five feet, out of reach. Their eyes narrowed at Anna and the smirk they usually wore returned.

"There's a…unique choice," the captain commented. "I wouldn't normally recommend taking a hit from your opponent in order to get your own in, but it's an interesting thought."

Ros jumped back in with renewed energy. Anna could tell they were going a little harder now, and she struggled to keep up. Her breath came in hurried pants as she forced her body to move, to get out of the way, to block and parry. She felt a spark of heat just below her neck and dodged a swing that might've collided with her ear by moving faster than she had ever been able to. Soon she was overwhelmed, and Ros landed another hit, right where the first one had landed. The captain called the match.

"Ow," Anna winced and held her side. "You planned that."

"I did," Ros agreed, smirk growing wider. "A good opponent will use whatever weak points they know you have."

Anna smiled halfheartedly through the pain in her side. "Bruises are teachers, right?"

Ros' eyes sparked with joy as Anna quoted them, and they nodded.

"I had a trainer at Hillcrest that would've loved you," Anna said, moving out of the circle.

"Maybe one day you can introduce us," Ros replied.

Anna was paired with Will next so that he could show her how to stay light on her feet without losing her balance. Meanwhile, Merry and Pyran sparred against Ros. Anna was half-watching them as Will began instructing.

He bounced on his feet, saying, "You have to keep your weight on the balls of your feet. If your weight is at your heels, you're just anchoring yourself. Are you listening to me?"

Anna blinked and turned to look at him fully. "Yeah, weight on the balls of my feet."

Will was frowning, but the dark circles around his eyes had improved since this morning, and he had fixed his hair. He twirled a dagger in his hand as he looked thoughtfully at Anna. "Show me your usual ready stance."

Anna lowered herself into the athletic stance her trainers had taught her—legs spread just wider than her shoulders, right foot in front of her, knees somewhat bent, hand holding her sword out, pointy end up.

Will stuck a hand out and shoved her shoulder.

Anna lost her footing and stumbled back a step.

He let out an exasperated sigh. "I thought you were listening."

"I didn't know you were going to do that!" she said, annoyed. She lowered into her stance again, saying, "Do it again."

Will shoved her again.

Anna's feet stayed where they were as her upper body bent backward.

"You're trusting your feet to hold you in place when you should be trusting your feet to move you," Will told her. He sounded bored. "Here." He tucked his dagger into the little scabbard at his belt and then put both hands on the sides of her shoulders. He took hold of her and lifted her lightly, just a couple of inches, so that her heels left the ground. "Stay there."

Anna's eyes widened as he took hold of her, but he was quick to release her again. She was surprised at his touch, and then doubly surprised at how easy it was for him to lift her. She held herself on the balls of her feet, letting her heels float off the ground.

"Your stability comes from your core," Will told her, putting a hand over his stomach, "and your feet give your stability movement."

Anna sighed in frustration. *I'm not about to let this guy know he got to me.* She tensed her core muscles, which were basically all the areas where she was most sore, and she tensed her jaw. Then she adjusted her shoulders and her hold on her sword.

"Better," Will said, sounding unimpressed. He crossed his arms as he looked at her. "I just don't get it."

"Get what?" Anna asked him, even though she had told herself she wouldn't talk with him.

"There are rare, random moments when you're fighting," he told her, "when you can be as fast and as nimble as the best of us, but the rest of the time you're so clunky. It's like you get temporarily possessed by someone that can actually fight."

Anna frowned at him. *Gee, thanks.*

"What?" Will pursed his lips at her irritated expression. "You can't tell me you don't know what I'm talking about."

"I don't know," she told him. "I guess I get lucky and pull it all together now and then."

"No, I don't buy it," Will told her. "That doesn't make sense."

"I don't need you to *buy* anything," Anna grumbled. She rolled her shoulders and hopped from foot to foot a couple of times, trying to keep her movements light. It was difficult to focus on what her core was doing and what her feet were doing at the same time.

"Fine," Will relented with an irritated sigh. "You don't have to tell me. Show me a swing, but use your core and keep your feet light."

The rest of her training with Will focused on how to use the strength movements she had learned yesterday while moving with her sword. He kept his instructions brief, and Anna remained quiet.

It wasn't time for lunch until her body was burning with fatigue again. Pyran, Merry, and Ros talked excitedly over their food about their match, comparing with each other what they each could have done better and what the others might have missed. Anna listened as Pyran told the story of how he and Merry had landed a hit on Ros. He smiled with pride.

When everyone went back to the courtyard to train, they found Captain Heiser there with two young dwarven people wearing long red tunics and black pants underneath heavy metal armor. The light shone off the half-suns embossed on their shoulder pauldrons. They were short by human comparison, and not stout like Cricket. They had brown skin and dark hair, both with the same hazel eyes—the same features overall, actually. At first glance, the only difference Anna could see was that one wore their hair in two braids, one on each side, and the other wore theirs in one thick, long braid that hung down their back.

"Here's the rest of the team," Captain Heiser said as they walked up. "Will, Merry, Pyran, Anna, Ros, and Bennett." He pointed to each of them. "This is Callum and Clara Phaon from Amgen."

"We're originally from Delphia." A male voice came from the one with the single braid.

"Yes," the other agreed with a little higher, more feminine voice. "We're from Southside." When no one gave an indication of understanding, she continued, "Southside? South of the river, but still on the coast."

"Ah, right," Ben nodded.

They glanced at each other with worried expressions before turning back to the group.

"I'm Clara," the one with two braids said, putting a gauntleted hand on her breastplate. "He's Callum." She held a hand out to her counterpart.

"Twins, if it wasn't obvious," Callum said with a sigh.

"It's fairly obvious," Will said.

After an awkward, quiet moment, the captain said, "They're healers, but they're trained with weapons as well."

Clara held up a mace with a grin, saying, "I'm as good at closing up a cut as I am with Skullcrusher."

Callum lifted a heavy crossbow, adding, "I can stitch you up or make you bleed with Skullpiercer."

"The names are a nice touch," Will said flatly.

"Oh, I agree," Merry said enthusiastically.

After introductions were over, they dispersed again into training groups. Anna spent the rest of her day shooting her bow from horseback. It was a ridiculously challenging task, considering that Anna had never ridden a horse. Captain Heiser spent most of that time trying to teach Anna how to handle a horse while the others watched from afar more than they trained. Anna caught the new twins snickering to each other several times.

When training was finally over, the captain told Anna that they shouldn't require riding skills for this mission, and that today would be the last time Anna was required to try. He added that when they returned after the mission, it would benefit her to take some instruction if she ever hoped to further her career.

Anna didn't mention that after this mission, she was planning on running back home to Wallset as quickly as she could—on foot.

With the team assembled, the captain told them they would all start eating dinner together, including him. "We have about a month left to pull all of you into a functioning body, so we must maximize the time that we have."

"Not just a limb, then?" Will taunted.

The captain let a tensed jaw slip past his professional demeanor, but he otherwise ignored Will's question.

"We could all go to the Left Leg," Merry shrugged.

The captain raised a curious eyebrow at her, but said, "We'll meet at my apartment after training. The Council has afforded me a cook while I am in town. None of you will need to pay from your own pockets." He gave his address, then said, "I expect all of you there at seven."

Will sighed as he left, then mumbled, "I didn't think I'd be subjected to formal dinners."

"It's a cook hired by the Council," Merry told him. "I'm not going to complain about eating good."

"Eating well," Ben said casually. When they both looked at him, he said, "You mean eating *well*."

Merry shrugged, "Well and good."

Will shot Ben a short-lived, irritated look, then said, "It's the formal part I'm complaining about."

"How formal are we talking?" Pyran asked.

"I'm sure the captain will be in uniform," Will said. "We'll be expected to show up in something of similar *quality*."

Anna blinked, visualizing her tiny, worn-out wardrobe. "What do you mean by that?"

"I doubt he'll be enforcing some kind of dress code," Pyran said.

"He might not enforce anything, but those types always expect it," Will replied.

Ros picked up on Anna's concern and told her, "You could borrow one of my shirts. The sleeves may be short, but we could roll them up."

"I brought several outfits," Clara spoke up. "It's a shame you're so tall, or you could have borrowed some." It didn't sound like she really thought it was a shame at all.

"I'll, uh, see what I can pull together," Anna told Ros, offering a passing appreciative smile.

"Apart from dress, does anyone know how to get there?" Ben asked.

Most eyes turned to Will.

The half-elf huffed and shook his head, but said, "Fine, I'll lead the way. Everyone meet me in the hall at half-past six." Then he rushed off.

As the rest followed him to shower and prepare, Anna noticed Irene Brooks waiting by the door into the building. The mage smiled at her.

"Hello, Anna. Do you have a moment?"

Anna glanced at Pyran, who shot her a questioning look. Anna shrugged. "Sure."

The group carried on without her as she stopped with Irene. Her thick blonde hair was tied into a tall, intricate updo today, and Anna wondered if her neck ever got sore.

"Your name is Anna Hale, correct?"

Anna nodded.

Irene leaned in a little closer. "Are you Bren and David's daughter?"

Anna's eyebrows rose high. "I am. How do you know them?"

Irene's face lit up with a smile. "I knew them when we were young. I went to school with them in Wallset."

"You're from Wallset?" Anna asked, incredulous.

Irene nodded. "I know it must seem so strange, but I thought you looked familiar, and then I heard your last name. I had to find out for myself if you were their child."

"No, I—" Anna laughed once, joyful and confused. "I just never expected to meet anyone from Wallset outside of Wallset."

Irene laughed, and Anna found herself thinking how pretty the sound was. The mage said, "I haven't either, which is why I decided that I *must* speak to you. I see you are training with Captain Heiser. Are you in town for the mission he's preparing for?"

"Yes," Anna answered. "I came with Pyran. He's from Hillcrest. We're both representing Lord Woulfe."

"I see," she nodded in understanding. "How are your parents?"

Anna's face fell a little, but she answered. "My mother's doing all right. She runs a bakery. My father passed away ten years ago."

"Oh, I'm so sorry!" Irene said hurriedly. "I didn't know David had passed. He was a wonderful person when we were young—your mother, too. They were always kind to me when it was much easier not to be."

"My mom," Anna started, "I think she told me about you. I'm glad you're doing well."

Irene smiled again. "It's nice to see someone else with ambition from that little town." She glanced down at a watch she pulled out of a skirt pocket, then said, "I apologize, I have to go, but I want you to know that I'm here if you need me. Just have someone call for me, and make sure they say it's Anna Hale asking."

"Thank you," Anna told her. "I appreciate that."

She watched the mage walk away, her periwinkle satin dress shifting from pale blue to violet as she moved. She couldn't wait to write home about her. Her mother would be just as amazed as she was.

18

ANNA MADE HER WAY TO HER ROOM, SHOWERED, AND THEN LAID OUT her clothes on her bed. She stared daggers at the nicest shirt she had, as if it would suddenly turn into something appropriate for dinner. She heard a knock on her door.

"Just a moment!" she called, quickly slipping on the shirt and a pair of pants.

Pyran was on the other side. He wore the coat from his father, and he filled it out well.

"Did you find something to wear?" he asked her.

Frowning, Anna threw her arm out to one side in a little flourish to highlight her outfit, then mock curtsied with the hem of her shirt. When she stood up straight, she could see that Pyran looked concerned. "This is all I've got."

"Come on." Pyran took hold of her arm and pulled her out of the little room. Anna let him drag her to Ros' door and knock.

Ros opened, wearing a fitted shirt with gold brocade, unwrinkled tan pants, and dark boots. "Yes?" They took in Pyran and then Anna. "Ah, one moment." Ros shut the door to a crack, and then disappeared behind it.

When they returned, they held a collared shirt in their hands. It was a deep emerald green with thin, even stripes of shiny emerald thread. "I have no pants that would fit your length," Ros told Anna, holding the shirt out to her, "but this should suffice."

"Thank you." Pyran said, and they walked back to her room. "We're going to have to find time to get you something to wear if we're expected to do this every night."

Anna sighed and took the shirt. "Seems like it."

She went into her room and shut the door to change. She'd thought the shiny material woven into the shirt would be itchy, but when she slipped it on, she found it to be one of the softest things she'd ever worn.

There was a little mirror on the desk, and she leaned it up against the wall so that she could see herself. The shirt stood out in high contrast to her plain brown pants and boots, but it brought out her eyes. Anna wondered if Ros had planned that. She extended her arms in front of her and noted the distance between the sleeves and her wrists. She rolled them once, twice, and then looked in the mirror again.

The tails were long enough that Anna figured the shirt was meant to be tucked in. She tried to recall what Ros had looked like when they'd answered the door. She tucked the shirt all the way around. *A belt might help at the waist, if I had one.* She frowned and turned her attention to her hair, doing the only style she was sure of—a tight braid.

When Anna opened her door, she found Pyran waiting impatiently. "Have you been standing there the whole time?"

"Yes," Pyran looked up at her face, and then at her outfit. His eyes moved higher, and his nose wrinkled. "You could've done something different with your hair."

"Noted," she said flatly, looking past Pyran and out at the others.

Merry stood by Ros, wearing a mid-length black skirt with ruffles at the hem, shiny black boots, and what Anna decided was the definition of a *blouse.* It was made of a light material in a soft yellow with a flouncy bow that tied and then lay at her chest. Even her hair was coiffed just right, held out of her face with a headband. There were little embroidered flowers at the ends of her sleeves.

Ros was wearing the same gold shirt and brown pants they had been wearing when she had seen them before, and Ben was wearing a different set of robes. This one was a deep blue with light green leaves embroidered on all the hems. The fabric seemed to shimmer in the mage light of the hallway.

Callum had on black trousers and a red, collared shirt, which was intentionally left half-tucked. His sister wore a red dress with an A-line skirt and bell sleeves. The little faux flowers at her collar matched one that was pinned into her hair. Both siblings wore the same thick braids they had been wearing.

Anna played with the roll of one of her sleeves as she and Pyran joined the group, her cheeks flushed in frustration. "Thank you for letting me borrow this," she told Ros. "I'm going to try to find something for myself soon."

Ros smiled as they took her in. "You're welcome. It looks good on you."

"Thank you," Anna relented, not wanting to be rude. She wanted to say something like *this shirt is wearing me.*

"Don't you like dressing up?" Merry asked cheerily. "I've always enjoyed it, but there weren't many chances back home. I've gotten to wear more pretty things since I lost my hand than I ever had before."

Pyran smiled at her, amused. "You look great, Merry."

"Thank you," Merry beamed and gave a small curtsy.

"It is nice to get out the finery now and then," Ben agreed with her.

"Oh, these are your *nice* mage robes," Ros said to him, teasing. "I could not tell the difference."

Ben frowned at them, and they grinned back. Then, despite his irritation, the corner of Ben's mouth lifted and he huffed a laugh.

"We get to dress up all the time," Clara said. "Plenty of appearances at court in Amgen, considering Lady Cate is our aunt."

"And I dislike it every time," Callum added in a grumble.

"Oh, hush, Cal," Clara told her brother. "You look grand."

"You're just glad I let you dress me to match."

Clara let out a little high-pitched squeal, and she nodded.

"We're all ready, then?" Will's bored voice sounded behind Anna.

She turned and found that Will had entered the hallway and shut his door completely silently. He stood with his hands in his pockets, wearing a dark gray, collared shirt, black pants, and boots. A thick leather belt circled his waist, holding a scabbard with one of his daggers. His hair hung straight and loose over his ears and around his face.

"Yep, we're ready," Merry answered.

"Follow me, then." Will turned and led everyone down the hallway.

Rather than walk away from the center of the city after exiting the Barracks, as they had always done to get to the Left Leg, Will turned and walked further in. They made their way toward a third, smaller, interior wall. The gate here was open, and Will led everyone through as two guards looked on, one standing at each side.

Moments later, Anna was only a city block from the castle that dominated the center of the city, its turrets and spires looming overhead so high that her neck strained to see them. *I could see the whole city from up there.*

"Keep up," Clara said as she passed Anna. "We wouldn't want to lose you."

"Sorry." Anna pulled herself out of her thoughts and made herself look away from the massive structure. She hurried to catch up with the others.

"I think this is it," Will said, stopping in front of a row of tall, narrow homes built side by side. The number above the door matched the one the captain had given as his address.

Merry knocked on the door. A tall, thin man answered, dressed in a black suit with a white bow tie. "Captain Heiser is expecting you," he said. "Do come in."

Anna filed in with everyone else. They entered an extended hall that led past several closed doors before opening to the dining room at the back of the house. A long table took up the room with ten chairs, one on each end and four down each side. The table held nine settings that were laid out neatly, leaving the space on the closest end empty. She raised an eyebrow at the multiple plates stacked onto each other, the tiny fork sitting next to the normal fork, and the stemmed glassware sparkling under the mage light chandelier.

She was so preoccupied with assessing the settings that she didn't realize until too late that she was putting herself at the end of the table, next to Will and across from Pyran. The twins flanked the head chair across the table, followed by Merry on Will's side and Ben on the other. Ros found themself between Pyran and Ben. Everyone was sitting, so Anna followed suit.

The man in the suit reappeared and opened a door on the other end of the room, through which Captain Nathaniel Heiser walked in.

"Welcome!" the captain greeted everyone with a smile. "My home in Luminport is much more accommodating, but this will do." The brass buttons on his blue uniform sparkled.

The servant, Anna deduced, pulled out the chair at the other end of the table. The captain sat, and then the servant turned and left again.

The captain flapped his napkin open in front of him with a light *snap,* and then set it across his lap. "While he finishes our meal and brings it out, let's talk about why you are all here. What we discuss at dinner does not leave this group." He looked around the table and met everyone's eyes in turn. When it was clear everyone was listening and that they understood, he continued, "Good.

I'll begin with context. There have been Vasbrute sightings at the southern border, north of the wall, near Dore."

Ros quirked an eyebrow. "There have always been rumors of the Vasbrute sneaking in. What is different now?"

"These are not mere rumors," the captain answered. "There are confirmed sightings of a group of Vasbrute roaming the forest north of the wall. Lady Gratadia's forces have found their camps and their tracks. The question we seek to answer is not *if* they are there, but *why*."

Ros was silent, processing.

"They want another war," Callum said with a shrug. "It's the only reason for them to come topside of that wall."

Clara nodded.

"We can't jump to any conclusions," Captain Heiser said. "The Vasbrute are not as stupid as many of you have been led to believe. They'll have reasons for coming out, and if it is *war,* there will be a reason behind that as well." The captain took in a breath and let it out in a sigh. "We are to travel to the wall, investigate, and then bring an answer back to the Council."

"Excuse me, sir," Merry said.

"Merry," the captain acknowledged her.

"Maybe I'm wrong," she said, "but doesn't the Council have better people for investigations than a group of soldiers who've just met?"

The captain smiled easily, but there was something sharp in his eyes. "The Council has various agents for uncovering various kinds of mysteries. It was deemed that this mission would most likely require a use of force." The sharpness faded, and he added, "As for the reasoning behind gathering you all from different corners of our great nation, they felt that the shared responsibility would ensure the integrity of the mission. I see it as an opportunity to understand the strengths in each of our regions. To that point, I'd like to discuss roles.

Most of what we'll be doing is tracking, watching, and listening. For this, we'll need scouts steering us. Anna and Will, you'll fill this role."

Anna instinctively looked at Will, who looked back at her. Before she could read anything on his face, he turned away and returned his gaze to the head of the table.

"Next role, important on any mission, is that of the healers. Clara and Callum fill this role."

"Of course," Callum nodded and leaned back in his chair, satisfied.

"Happy to help," Clara agreed with her own nod.

"Next we have our fighters, those whose sole responsibility is defense of the group in combat or leading offensive strikes. Merry, Pyran, and Ros are our fighters."

"Goes without saying, really," Merry smiled at Pyran, who smiled back, and then at Ros, who grinned as they nodded in agreement.

"Finally, we have our mage." One of the captain's hands gestured toward Ben. "We all know who that is. He'll be supporting us with his abilities as we go. A mage is a versatile tool. You must be ready to be clever, Ben."

Ben nodded. "Whatever we need, I'll take care of it."

"Good," the captain nodded seriously.

The door opened and the servant walked in with steaming dishes full of food. Everyone got a healthy portion of fresh, grilled fish and vegetables with a citrus-based sauce, and then the man in the suit disappeared again.

"During your time off tomorrow," the captain said between bites, "I want you all to consider what areas you, or the others, need to work on. I've been paying close attention to each of you and I have my own shortlist, but I can't catch everything. We'll start fresh at the beginning of the week with squadron training—signals, code phrases, group work. Then we'll develop our roles. By the end, it should all come together."

"You said we have a month?" Ros asked.

"Yes," the captain said casually.

Next to Anna, Will almost choked on his food.

Eyes wide, Pyran said, "Uh, sir, that's rather quick to develop—"

The captain waved a hand in front of him dismissively, seeming unconcerned. "The time will pass quickly, but it will have to be enough. You are already well-trained professionals. I'm just stitching you together into a coordinated group."

Pyran turned to Anna, skeptical. Next to him, Ros' face was serious. The twins shot each other concerned looks, and Ben was looking down into his food with worry.

"Have faith!" Captain Heiser encouraged as he took in the feeling in the room. His face was set in a tense seriousness. "You are all young and inexperienced—certainly when it comes to military conflict—so I'll give you a piece of advice. You've been sent here because you have the abilities required. Your leadership knows you have what it takes, and you have all proven your abilities to me since your arrival. Do not," his closed fist met the table in a dull *thud*, "let your emotions regarding the difficulty of the mission ahead keep you from realizing that opportunity." His eyes lifted to pass over each of them at the table, as if asking anyone to argue.

As he met Anna's gaze, she felt herself hunch slightly, trying to make herself smaller. After his eyes made their way around the table, he said, "Do not get in the way of your own potential. Trust me as your captain to help you realize it."

THE GROUP WALKED BACK TO THE BARRACKS QUIETLY AFTER DINNER. THE captain's serious tone had put a damper on everyone's mood. Even Merry was silent. It wasn't until they'd made it past the short interior wall and into an isolated alley that Ben said, "That was..." and then trailed off sullenly.

"That felt like getting a lesson from Dad," Clara said, speaking to everyone, but mainly her brother.

"Yeah," Callum agreed.

Anna realized that was what she'd been feeling, too. It had been a long time since she'd had that kind of conversation with her father. Once, she'd tried to run away after she'd gotten irritated during an accounting lesson and argued with him. He caught her, but he didn't stop her. Instead, he gave her the tent. She had spent most of the night outside, but ran back home after hearing a wolf howl in the distance. That morning he'd explained that they needed to know how to keep the books so that they could pay for the house that kept them safe from wolves and bears and other predators, and told her she was doing great when she applied herself.

Soon, you won't need my help anymore, he'd said.

"He's a boss, not our father," Ros stated, glancing at the twins with a frown.

"Sure, but that's basically a work dad," Clara said with a sigh. "Unfortunate that we've upset him so early in the game."

"To be fair," Pyran said, "He is asking a lot. A month is almost nothing."

Will wove his fingers together behind his head casually as he walked out in front of everyone. Without turning, he said, "A month is all we've got. We either go along for the ride or find a way out."

"*Will,*" Merry frowned at him.

"What?" he turned to glance at her. "You think the captain wouldn't want more time if he could have it? I'm not his biggest fan—"

"You're not anyone's *biggest fan,*" Pyran cut in.

Will ignored him. "—but he has to take what he's given, and he's handling it rather well."

"What do you mean?" Pyran asked.

"Sure, he can't control timelines," Will shrugged, "but beyond that, he's an established captain from Luminport, nearing retirement age with a good amount of awards under his belt…"

"What are you saying?" Ros narrowed their eyes at him and crossed their arms, stopping.

The others stopped too, curious to hear what Will would say.

Will sighed and lowered his arms, then turned around to look at Ros. "As Merry pointed out, the capital has several specialized forces that would be more appropriate for this type of mission." When nobody responded, Will frowned and said, "The Council isn't sending them, and it's not because of *integrity*," he repeated snobbily. "They aren't sending them because they want the mission to fail."

"That's ridiculous!" Clara said in a high voice.

"Is it?" Will asked. "By recruiting people from each of the governances, they've ensured that each governance will be invested. The captain is honorable, but expendable. We'll all do our best and then be lauded as martyrs when the war begins." He looked across their astonished faces and added, "Half the Council has been itching to deal with the Vasbrute for hundreds of years. They've been the sad ending to the war story that Telluth would rather sweep under the rug. Plus, the undesirable land they were left with has some *very* desirable resources."

"How do you know all that?" Merry asked.

"I keep my sharp ears to the ground and I'm not an idiot."

"That can't be true," Anna found herself saying. "Surely there's some version of this where we come out on the other side alive."

Will's head nodded from side to side thoughtfully and then he said, "There might be, but the odds are stacked very intentionally against us."

"Is that why—" Ben started, then had to restart, "Is that why the captain was so intense tonight? Do you think he knows?"

"He must have an inkling," Will said. "He's not stupid, either."

"We could put a stop to it!" Clara said, taking a step toward Will. "We could notify our aunt of what's going on, and she would make them stop it."

Will was shaking his head. "Keep your voice down. That wouldn't work. Everyone on that Council is used to this kind of political game-playing. If it was allowed to pass, then they aren't going to appeal. My bet is that there's actual concern about the Vasbrute mixed in with all the political angles."

Clara looked at Callum, a little fear in her eyes.

Seeing his sister like this, Callum turned to Will with a frown. "So, what? You must be right because you *keep your ears to the ground?* You're just trying to scare us and you have no proof. Maybe *you* want the mission to fail."

"I just want to get paid," Will grumbled into the night air. "Believe me or don't believe me, that's on you. I've done my part. I'll do you all one better and let you know that when this all goes to shit, I'll be gone already." He turned toward a street opening on the left and stalked into the city, away from the Barracks.

19

THE NEXT FREE DAY ANNA HAD, SHE WENT LOOKING FOR IRENE BROOKS. One of the officers working in the Barracks led her into town, towards the castle, and then right up against it. There was a dark stone wall surrounding the giant feat of construction, and they led her along the outside until they came upon a line of townhomes stacked neatly in a row. They reminded her of the captain's apartment, but larger and grander. Intricate detailing marked the peak of the roofs and the corners of each porch. Large windows shone out from the back of the porches, but gauzy curtains obscured the views inside. He led her to the third home, marked simply by a metal three next to the door.

"She should be here," the officer told Anna. "I'll wait to make sure she lets you in, and then head back. You know your way back to the Barracks?"

"Uh," Anna glanced back the way they had come. *It couldn't be that hard, could it?* "Yeah, I've got it."

The officer nodded, and then waited expectantly. Anna made her way up the porch, and as she did, a light behind the window came on. She reached up and pulled the knocker back, then knocked three times. A moment passed, and then she heard a click. The door opened and Irene stood on the other side, smiling, not touching the door.

"Hello, Anna! I'm so glad you came!"

"Hi." Anna smiled back, glancing from Irene to the open door and back again. "I was hoping I could ask you a favor."

"Of course! Come in, come in," Irene walked into the foyer, and then around a corner.

The foyer was small, but magnificent. Shined black and white tile lay over the floor, set in a checker pattern diagonally to the doorway. Light wood paneling covered the walls and the coffered ceiling, where a crystal mage light chandelier hung, sparkling in the light from the small stained glass window on the wall to the right.

But that's not an outside wall. The other townhomes sat right up against either side of this one. Intrigued, Anna stepped inside. She turned to shut the door and found it closing on its own before it gave a soft click and latched shut.

"You like the entry?" Irene grinned from the doorway she had disappeared through a moment ago. She held two stemmed glasses in her hands, each filled with something pale and bubbly.

Anna nodded and glanced back at the little window. A female peacock was illustrated there in shining glass, colored in rich whites and creams of various textures that sparkled in the light beyond.

"Being a mage certainly has its perks."

Anna looked back at Irene, who held one glass out to her. When Anna hesitated, she added, "It's just a little bubbly to celebrate you being here. It's a good vintage from Yurrport that I think is impossible for anyone to dislike."

Anna took the glass, smelled it, and then took a drink. It tasted like sunshine over a valley full of tall, sweet-smelling grass. "Wow." Her eyes widened, and she looked at the glass again.

Irene's smile brightened to a full grin as she flashed white teeth. "I'll have to introduce you to the wines of Telluth. You won't find anything from Wallset here, thank the Mother." She turned and walked further in.

Her pale pink dress swished as she walked through the first room. There was a parlor in front of the window on one side, and a large stone fireplace on the other. It was the same dark stone that made up the castle and so many of the buildings, but intricately carved into feathers and swirls, and then polished to a high shine. A large mirror hung over the mantle. It must've been antique, because hazy gray spots bloomed from the edges of the glass and marked the reflection pictured in it. Anna looked up at her red hair, green eyes, and her old, oversized shirt framed in gold.

Irene continued, "Are the Wilcotts still running the Inn?"

Anna turned from her reflection and found the mage woman leaning on one of the high-backed dining chairs in the next room with her forearms. Her golden hair was piled beautifully on her head again today, and Anna wondered again if it strained her neck. "Yeah, Jo and his son run it." She followed her into the dining room.

"I suppose that's the way of things when you grow up in a small town," she sighed. "Unless you have a natural affinity for magic and most of them are scared of you." She took a drink.

Anna sucked in a breath. "I'm sorry that happened—"

"Oh, don't be!" Irene waved a hand between them dismissively and stood up. "Without that push, I might not be where I am now, Mage-Counselor to Lady Gratadia."

Anna's eyebrows rose. "You have a title?"

She nodded. "And all my living expenses paid for. Now, let me share the wealth. What was that favor you mentioned?"

"Well, I—" Anna started, then tugged nervously at her shirt. "We're going to have dinner at the captain's apartment every night, and I'm supposed to dress up."

"Ah," Irene nodded and finished her glass, then set it on the table. "Follow me!" With a sweep of her skirts, she turned and started up an ornate staircase on the right side of the room.

Anna started, then glanced at the glass in her hand. She'd barely drank any of it. *It would be rude to waste it.* She carried it with her.

The second floor of the home held a library and large living room full of comfortable-looking chairs and couches. The third floor was where Irene stopped. She led Anna down a hallway with three doors, and the third opened as she walked up to it.

"There we are." Irene moved aside to let Anna enter first. "Pick whatever you like!"

The room inside glittered. It was twice the size of Anna's room at the Barracks, and full of the finest clothes she had ever seen. Gowns covered two walls. A third held slightly more casual shirts, pants, and dresses. Shoes lined a shelf that circled the room above the clothes. At the center stood a four-sided chest of drawers with sparkling jewelry on top, matching the crystal chandelier that hung above. The room smelled floral and bright.

"Mother," Anna breathed out, taking it all in.

"Oh, I don't think she or her Well had anything to do with this," Irene chuckled. She put a hand between Anna's shoulder blades and gently pushed her into the room. "Go ahead, look around!"

Anna had never been girly. She hadn't owned a dress since grade school. But as she stared around this room, she suddenly believed that was more from practicality than what she wanted. There had been nothing this fine in Wallset. Her hands lightly grazed the fabric as she walked around the room, afraid that if she held something, she'd dirty or tear it. "I don't even know where to start," she said, turning back to look at Irene.

The mage grinned and gave a gentle nod before walking over to the wall that wasn't full of evening gowns. "Let's start here, then. We'll work our way over to the other side of the room. You'll have to pick out something for the ball."

"The ball?"

"Of course! The Council is throwing a ball to commemorate the country's 423rd anniversary. The governors haven't worked together this closely since..." Irene paused and blinked, thinking. "Well, since the reunification after the war, really."

"Oh."

"Come now, don't look so *scared*!" Irene chuckled and took Anna's shoulders in her hands. "Balls are great fun, if you know how to navigate them. I'll teach you!" Her warm, brown eyes matched her smile as she looked into Anna's green ones.

Anna took a deep breath and let the mage's contagious smile catch. "All right."

"Wonderful!" Irene pulled back, delighted. "Now, let's see. I think we'll start with this..."

Anna spent most of the day trying things on, sipping bubbly, and eating snacks from a little gold tray that had appeared while she was changing into the second outfit. Irene told her stories about her days at court, little lessons about who or what to avoid, as well as court manners. She left with two outfits, which the mage carefully packed into a trunk for her to carry back to the Barracks.

The first was a full suit in a soft navy color. It had comfortable straight-legged trousers, a shiny, pale blue button-down shirt with a collar and pearl buttons, and a jacket that matched the pants and pulled in flatteringly at her waist. When she had looked at herself in the mirror with it on, she had briefly felt like she could walk into the Council chambers and demand whatever she wanted.

The second was a dress made from a soft, stiffer material in a striped sage and cream pattern. It was sewn in such a way that the stripes came in at her waist, flared out with the skirt, and stood up and down at her shoulders and collarbones. The structure of it felt nice, too. It didn't feel loose and flouncy as she imagined Merry's yellow blouse did. It felt fitted and secure until the skirt, which came to a practical length just below her knees. It had little ivory buttons on the right side at the waist and up to her arm so that she could get into and out herself. It was like nothing she had ever seen, and she liked it all the more for it.

Feeling refreshed from her time with her new friend, Anna headed back to the Barracks. She made several wrong turns and it took her twice as long as it should have, but she was still smiling when she crossed the threshold.

THAT NIGHT, ANNA WROTE ANOTHER LETTER TO HER MOTHER. SHE ANswered her mother's questions about food in the city and told her about her meal at the captain's apartment. Then she wrote about Irene, and how happy she was to meet someone from home.

She says she remembers you and Dad, that you were nice to her. She's so friendly and charming—I can't imagine anyone being mean to her. She was excited to see me, too.

I think you'd die if you saw her closet. She's letting me borrow a couple of things. It's amazing what she's been able to do. She's Mage-Counselor to Lady Gratadia. I never thought I'd see anyone from Wallset, let alone someone with a title.

Maybe you'll get to meet her again too, someday.

Lynnie

20

ANNA LOOKED AT HERSELF IN THE LITTLE MIRROR THAT STOOD UP ON HER desk. She had decided on wearing the dress, but when she put on either outfit in this bare little room, it seemed like too much…*or not enough.* Her mind drifted to Irene Brooks and the little jewels the mage had worn around her neck, at her ears, on her hands. Anna reached into the collar of her dress and pulled out her necklace. The little blue teardrop sparkled in the low light coming in through her window. The silver chain was too long for it to sit correctly above the dress at her neck, but it looked nice falling over the hem and onto the fabric.

It's definitely better than nothing.

She wrinkled her nose at her boots—she had tried to clean them off, but they were so scuffed that it didn't matter—and left her room.

"I'm going to talk to him," Ben was saying indignantly as Anna pulled her door shut behind her. "If he doesn't know, he should, and if he does, then we deserve a discussion. A confirmation and a choice, *at least.*"

"We aren't supposed to know," Ros said in their low, breathy voice. "We could get into trouble." They didn't sound deterred.

"You think the captain would go to someone on the Council about it?" Pyran asked.

"No," Ros told him, "I think the Council is watching him. Surely they have ears trained on him."

"The butler," Clara said, eyebrows pulled together thoughtfully.

Ros nodded.

"Then we'll discuss it when the butler is away," Ben said.

"He'll have an ear pressed to the door," Ros said.

Ben frowned and looked down at his feet, thinking.

"Oh, Anna!" Merry greeted, happy surprise on her face. "You look wonderful." She was wearing a dress she'd bought that day, a shiny blue fabric with a loose skirt, stretchy sleeves that showed off the muscles on her arms, and a wide belt with a silver buckle.

All eyes turned to Anna.

"You *can* clean up," Clara announced in revelation. "Callum doubted you."

"I never said a thing!" Callum argued, "You're the one that said—"

"That looks good on you." Clara cut her brother off and continued speaking to Anna. "Good choice." Clara wore a pink shirt with puffy cap sleeves and a couple of decorative buttons and piping at the collar, and a mauve skirt...or not. As she shifted from one hip to the other, Anna saw that the skirt didn't connect at the middle. It was like a skirt on each leg, pants wanting to be a full skirt. Callum's mauve shirt matched the fabric, and he wore simple black pants and shiny black boots.

"Thank you," Anna told Clara. "What are you all talking about?"

Ben spoke up. "We're going to talk to the captain about all this suicide mission nonsense." He crossed his arms, a loose cream shirt covering them. His robe was a light tan color that started in a vest over the shirt and then swept down over his legs. Images of cranes in tall grasses were stitched into the fabric. It looked ridiculously luxurious to Anna.

"We're going to try," Pyran amended. He had on the same jacket he'd worn the previous night, the one from his father, but his shirt and pants were new.

"We're talking about talking," Ros said, "but if it's true, we are treading dangerous waters. Anyone could be listening in that house." They were wearing a black shirt with a sharp collar and sleeve cuffs with a pair of charcoal pants. The contrast of the deep black against their pale features was almost startling.

The hallway was quiet for a moment, then Pyran spoke up. "*In* his house. What if we get him out? What if we take a walk after dinner? We can claim it's team building."

"That could work," Ros said hesitantly, "but we'd want to get him away from the Council district."

"We could ask if he'd like to walk off dinner with us back towards the Barracks," Clara proposed. "That alley where we stopped last time seems like a good spot for private discussions."

Ros and Pyran nodded in agreement.

"That's settled," Ben said. "Let's go to dinner."

"What about Will?" Anna asked.

"I'm sure he'll meet us there," Merry told her, though Anna could tell she *wasn't* entirely sure.

WILL JOINED THEM AS EVERYONE WAS GETTING SEATED AT THE TABLE. THIS time, Anna paid enough attention to seat herself at the middle between Merry and Pyran. The twins took the same seats next to the captain. On her side were Clara, Merry, Anna, and Pyran, and on the other side were Callum, Ros, Ben, and an empty seat.

As Will took the empty seat next to Ben, the captain said, "Ah, so you have decided to join us."

"I'm sorry," Will said tensely. "I got caught up in some business."

"As long as you don't make it a habit," Captain Heiser told him. "These meals are important to our team dynamic." Then he addressed the rest of the table. "Welcome, everyone. I hope you've all had a chance to rest today and consider what we discussed yesterday."

The butler came out with the food, and the captain flipped his napkin again and laid it on his lap. "Now, I'd like this evening to be the official introduction of the team. We're going to start with a short summary from each of you—simply tell us who you are, where you are from, that kind of thing. I'll start.

"My name is Captain Nathaniel Heiser, age fifty-four. I was born and raised in Luminport and joined the military after my schooling was complete. I started in the infantry and eventually rose to officer, and then to captain. My service consists mostly of surveillance or convoy missions to the northern border, southern border, and to the East."

At the mention of the east, both of the twins' eyebrows rose in interest.

"You've been East?" Clara asked him.

"I have," he nodded. "It's similar to Telluth, but those humans are closed-minded. They fear everyone that isn't them. It's why they left, I suppose."

"You've *talked* with them?" Ros asked. They looked surprised and disgusted.

"Briefly," the captain said. "I was sent there as a young captain to discuss a loan of crop during a bad year. They were kind enough to share under the terms of an expensive contract. Anyway, enough about me. We'll move to our healers." He looked at Clara and Callum.

"All right," Clara sat up straight in her chair with her chin high, which still made her shorter than the others at the table. "My name is Clara Phaon, daughter of Aimar Phaon and niece of Lady Charlotte Cate. Age thirty-two. I am from Delphia, where my father is mayor. I've been trained as a healer since I was a child. During my primary schooling, I insisted on being trained with my mace, rather than the traditional healer's rapier."

"Why a mace?" Pyran asked her.

"Being a healer means I do very close physical work with brutal wounds. I wanted to inflict those kinds of wounds, not just heal them." Her brown eyes met Pyran's down the table.

Pyran didn't have a response to that.

"Your turn," Clara told Callum.

"Fine," Callum rested an arm on the table in front of him. "Callum Phaon, son of Aimar Phaon, nephew of Lady Charlotte Cate, from Delphia, thirty-two. You can call me Cal. Trained as a healer from the same age as my sister. When she insisted on the mace, I insisted on the crossbow, so that I could cover her."

Anna decided it was sweet how Callum chose to support his sister. It seemed he let her take the lead, and was content to fill the role left in her wake. She wondered what it might've been like to have a sibling growing up.

"You both trained as healers, though," Ros commented. "Why?"

"When we started training as healers, we were too young to make our own decisions," Clara said.

"Our parents decided that since we were the *same*, we would train the same." Callum's tone at the word *same* dropped mockingly into a low, nasal area of his voice. Then he said to Ros, "Your turn."

Ros straightened and addressed the table. In their low, somewhat raspy voice they said, "My full name is Roscoe Dixon. Age thirty-six. I'm from Lakoona, where I joined the Krakens after schooling, and I've been training with them ever since."

"Do all the Krakens use a staff?" Clara asked them.

"Every one of us trained with the staff. Some have other weapons they use as well," Ros answered with a shrug. They turned to Merry and gestured for her to take her turn.

"Merrit MacGill," Merry said with a nod. "I'm thirty-eight, and I come from a farm in Tuvale before I joined up and moved to Altumburg. Lost my hand in a bear fight, as most of you know." She waved her handless arm in front of her with a grin. "Happy to be here."

"A *bear* fight?" Callum asked with wide eyes and an appalled expression.

"A fight with a *bear*?" Clara echoed, also staring at the end of Merry's arm with wide eyes, though she looked more intrigued than scared.

"Yep," Merry nodded. "Ran the monster through with my shovel in the end."

Callum sucked in a shaky breath as Clara gasped.

"I'll have to tell you the tale after supper," she told them. "Enough about me. What about Ben?"

Ben looked up, not expecting to have been called next. "Uh, all right." He set his silverware down and rested his hands in his lap. "My name is Bennett Day, but Ben is fine. Age thirty-five. I have a wife and daughter back home. I was born and raised in Eysa, where my father has been a professor at the academy for years. I studied magic with him from an early age and joined the academy as soon as I was able."

"You have a family?" Anna asked, surprised.

He nodded. "They stayed in Eysa."

Anna pursed her lips and glanced at Pyran, who shared her concern.

"Show us something magic!" Merry urged enthusiastically.

Ben smiled nervously and glanced down the table at the captain, who was watching him. "It's not the time, Merry."

"No, no," the captain grinned, "I insist." There seemed to be a challenge in his eyes.

Ben took a deep breath. "Very well." He raised his arms and started moving his hands, looking up at the mage light chandelier over the table. The lights morphed together, opening like a flower into the shape of a bird the size of the chandelier. It looped around the ceiling, flying gracefully, before sweeping up, wings spread wide, and then bursting into its individual lights that reattached themselves to the chandelier.

Anna gasped at the silent explosion, and Merry cheered. The twins clapped politely. Ben looked down the table to see the captain considering the chandelier.

"Not bad," the captain said with half a grin. "You have a skill with illusion."

"Thank you," Ben said with a stiff nod, and then he turned to Anna across the table. "Your turn, I believe."

"Sure," Anna nodded and adjusted herself in her seat. "Anna Hale."

The captain cleared his throat.

Anna's cheeks flushed lightly. "Anna*lynn* Hale. Please don't call me that, call me Anna. Age twenty-four. I'm from Wallset." She paused, then added, "Daughter of a baker. I learned to hunt and gather, how to use my bow, for my mom's bakes before I joined up in Hillcrest. That's it."

"You know how to bake?" Merry asked.

Anna hadn't expected any questions. "Mostly, but I preferred the lessons from my dad."

"I'll go next," Pyran offered during the next quiet moment. "Pyran Taggert, age twenty-five. Born and raised in Hillcrest and joined up after school, but I've been training with a sword since I was young." The table was quiet a moment, so he added, "My dad's an accountant."

"It's good to know what you want from a young age," Callum told him, nodding his head. "Or what you *don't* want."

"Right," Pyran agreed. He turned across the table to Will. "Best for last?" he joked.

This got a smirk out of Will. "Flattery," the half-elf acknowledged, then turned to the table with one arm hooked around the back of his chair. "Will Grey."

"Full name," the captain called from the head of the table.

Will rolled his eyes. His cheeks flushed slightly as he said, "*Willard* Grey, but if any of you call me that, I'll cut you." He glanced pointedly at the captain, and then his gaze returned to address the whole table. "Born and raised in Kastarus. Age twenty-six. Joined up for the money." He gave a forced grin and then moved to pick up his silverware again. It was clear that he would not be continuing the discussion about himself.

Anna watched Will for a moment. He looked his age, and she had thought he wouldn't—that he was much older but looked young due to his heritage. He always acted so confident, too.

He caught her looking and raised a questioning eyebrow. She quickly turned back to her food.

After that, conversation turned to how different everyone's homes were to Kastarus. The captain's description of the sunrise on the Eastern coast set the twins off on a rant about how their sunsets in the west were better, which turned into the captain noting that where Luminport sat at the end of the peninsula, it also got amazing coastal sunsets.

Merry talked about how all the flat land around Tuvale and Thrupath had always seemed boring to her, and that someday she'd like to go north and see the mountains or west to the rolling hills. Ben told her about the cliffs at the ocean's edge in Eysa, and how the academy stood right at the edge of them. Ros talked about Lake Lakoona and how she would always prefer the freshwater to saltwater. Pyran agreed, telling her about his childhood next to Long Lake.

"What about you, Anna?" Merry asked her. "What was Wallset like? Did you like it?"

"Wallset is surrounded by forest," Anna told her. "I spent almost every day in the trees. I loved it."

Her sincere answer made Merry's smile brighten.

The conversation continued on until everyone's plates were empty. Most of them ate quickly, either in anticipation of the coming conversation with the captain, or because the food was delicious. They'd been served roast duck with a red wine demi-glace that melted in her mouth.

"Captain Heiser." Pyran addressed the head of the table as he set his napkin down in front of him. "Would you be interested in walking with us back to the Barracks? It might be nice to walk off some of this lovely meal."

Anna noticed that Will stopped playing with the bit of food left on his plate as he looked at Pyran.

The captain chuckled. "You're right, it would be a good idea to walk some of this off," he smiled, "but I need to prepare for training tomorrow, and it looked like it wanted to rain this evening."

"Oh, come on," Merry urged. "It would be good for team building."

"We'll get plenty of that tomorrow," the captain told her.

He wasn't budging. The captain's polite refusals made Anna's lips push together into a frustrated line. The captain caught her expression and lifted a curious eyebrow at her. Anna's face heated and she didn't know what to say, but she knew she had to say something.

She opened her mouth, starting with, "I'm sorry, sir, the real reason we'd like you to walk with us is..." She felt a little spark as she had an idea. "...we appreciated your advice yesterday, and a few of us were wondering if we could pick your brain. We didn't want to take up time at dinner with it, because we know this time is important, but..."

"Ah," the captain grinned and glanced around the group at the table, then returned his gaze to Anna, "I see." He thought for a moment, mumbled something about a tight training schedule, then said, "I suppose I could accompany you all part of the way back." He stood. "I'll grab my coat."

Anna let out a little sigh of relief. Everyone stood as the butler came out to clear the table. At the door, the captain grabbed a light jacket from the coat tree and slipped it on.

"Now, where would you like to start?" he asked them.

Pyran jumped in, asking the captain a strategy question about the roles they had discussed the day before and how they would work together. As everyone walked out, the captain fell into an explanation of how the fighters would be positioned in the group and each of their main tasks.

Merry made little comments and questions, all of which Anna was sure were genuine to what was being discussed. The captain had naturally moved on from the fighters to the healers by the time they got to the alley they were looking for. Clouds rolled over the sky as the sun was setting.

"Sir," Pyran told him during a pause, his nerves showing as he fiddled with the buttons on his jacket. "This isn't the only thing we wanted to discuss with you." He stopped walking, and everyone else followed suit.

The captain turned, eyebrows lifting. "Huh," he said as he looked at them all, "and here I was, ready to give an entire lecture on our team dynamic. Well, what were you all looking to discuss in an alley as night approaches?" He put his right hand to his hip casually, but Anna noted he had a dagger holstered there behind his jacket.

"Nothing like that," Ben said urgently. "No, we just didn't want any extra ears."

The captain hummed thoughtfully, and his shoulders relaxed a little. "The butler?"

"Sir, we think this might be a suicide mission," Merry stated bluntly.

The captain smiled humorlessly and looked down to his feet. He scratched his short beard a couple of times, then looked at the group again. "So you *have* caught on."

"Will was the one who caught on," Clara said. "We're all trying to figure out if it's true."

The captain turned to Will. He seemed to size him up, as if this was his first time seeing the half-elf. Will stood at the back of the group, watching quietly with a frown. Anna thought she saw his chin rise just slightly.

The captain turned to the group again and said, "I had hoped none of you would realize yet. There's nothing to be done about it."

"So it is true," Callum said quietly.

"Yes." The captain's shoulders deflated and he leaned onto one hip. "I've had to deal with my fair share of politics during my time in service, but this is the bleakest. This mission would be a catalyst to someone's grand designs, if we fail."

"What about our aunt?" Clara asked. "What about Lady Cate? She could stop it."

The captain's mouth lifted in a sad grin. "Either she couldn't stop it before, or she's in on it. Neither would change now. I'm sorry."

Clara let out a deflated huff.

"But," started the captain, "I believe what I told you all yesterday. If we're clever enough, we can still return home victorious. Whoever's scheme this is thinks they're sending in an assortment of grunts, but I'm looking at some intelligent warriors. We'll need to be clever, more clever than those who sent us—more clever than we've ever needed to be. I won't stop you if you choose to leave. I won't even report you for desertion. But if you all stay, we have a chance."

Anna could hear what he wasn't saying. *He* didn't have a choice. He would have to stay. Now that she thought about it, she didn't have much of a choice, either. If she left, she'd have to live the rest of her life in hiding and force her mother into it with her, or they'd need to escape to the west, which Anna decided sounded even more unpleasant.

Anna had been pressing her nails into her palms and then releasing them as she thought, pressing and releasing, pressing and releasing. Now, she fisted her hand and said quietly, "I'm staying." When the captain looked at her, she took a small step forward and repeated it. "I'll stay."

Pyran huffed a breath from beside her, and she realized the position she'd put him in. She turned to look at him and found him chewing on the inside of his cheek.

"Pyran," she told him, "you don't have to—not because of me."

"I'm in," Pyran stepped up next to her, looking at her with serious eyes, and then turning to the captain. "I'll stay, too."

"I'm staying," Merry said easily. "Gotta top the bear story somehow, right?"

Anna smiled as Merry stepped up next to her.

"Will?" Merry turned to the half-elf.

Will's eyebrows drew together.

"I'll stay," Ros stepped forward. "You'll need me."

Everyone turned to the twins.

Clara glanced at her brother, then stepped forward. "I'll stay." She turned and looked expectantly back at him.

Callum stared back for a long moment, then let out a little dismayed grumble and stepped forward. "I can't believe we're doing this."

"Fine," Will relented, but didn't move forward. "I'll stay."

21

THE CAPTAIN GAVE EVERYONE STRICT INSTRUCTIONS NOT TO DISCUSS WHAT they'd talked about in the alley and to carry on as normal. He also promised to push them hard in training. If they were going to get through this, they would need to be at their best. Then he left them to return to his apartment.

They walked back in quiet contemplation, until Ben stopped Anna in front of the Barracks. "Could I talk to you for a moment?"

She turned to him. "Sure."

The others continued into the building.

His eyes darted from hers down to the necklace she was wearing. "Have you had that necklace for a long time?"

Her eyebrows drew together and her lips pulled into a line. *Does he care if I was digging around in ruins? Should I lie to him?* "No, not very long."

This seemed to surprise him. "It's not, say, a family heirloom?"

"No," Anna shook her head and reached down to hold the little gem on the necklace between two fingers. She looked down at it, then back at Ben. "Why are you asking about my necklace?"

Ben considered her for a moment, his face serious and thoughtful. "Have you noticed that when you wear this necklace, sometimes you effortlessly make the right choice, even when you most likely wouldn't have?"

"What do you mean?" Anna asked.

"You might feel lucky wearing it, like sometimes things fall into place for you where they normally wouldn't."

Anna's head tilted to the side. "Sometimes..."

"I have a theory that what you've got there is some old magic—older than Telluth as we know it. Did you feel anything from it tonight when you convinced the captain to walk with us?"

Anna took in a deep breath and closed her fingers around the pendant. She hesitantly nodded. "Sometimes it feels like a little, warm shock, and then it's gone. Whatever comes next seems to work out. You're not going to take it from me, are you?"

Ben smiled. "No, I won't take it from you. But I think my theory is correct. Long ago, before the war, people would enchant items like that with good fortune, a little ray of power that would give them luck when they wore it. I'm almost certain that's what you've got. We need all the help we can get, so hold on tight to that. I just wanted to see if I was right, and to let you know what you've got. That's all."

"Oh," Anna relaxed the hand holding the pendant. "Thanks."

"Have a good night." Ben turned and walked into the Barracks.

"You, too," Anna replied. She twirled the pendant in her fingers briefly before tucking the necklace under the collar of her dress again. *I knew it was special.*

When she returned to their shared hallway, she found Pyran standing outside her door, waiting.

"Hey," he greeted her. "I wanted to talk to you."

"I'm suddenly so popular," she joked.

"What did Ben say?" he asked.

She waved a hand flippantly. "Nothing, really. Just thanked me for getting the captain to come along."

"Oh, well, come on." Pyran turned and led Anna into his room.

She followed and found he had set up the space similar to his tent in Hillcrest. His family portrait was on his nightstand and his sword lay on his desk, recently cleaned. The old shortsword sat next to it, polished to a high shine. "What do you want to talk about?"

"Could you shut the door?" he asked her.

"Sure." Anna turned and closed it behind her.

"Do you remember what Commander Lyon said? About sending him updates?"

"Yeah," Anna nodded. "I was letting you handle that." She took in a deep breath, crossing her arms. "Do you think we should tell him?"

Pyran sat on his bed and let out a thoughtful gust of breath through his nose. "I've always felt like I could trust him."

Anna sat down next to him. "I feel that way, too, but I'm not sure what to think anymore. Poor Cal and Clara, they're not even sure about their aunt."

"True," Pyran said. "But Commander Lyon puts his people first. He even works against Lord Woulfe when he has to. He's on the right side."

"Even if we knew we could trust him, what could he do to help?"

"I was thinking about that, actually," Pyran turned to her. "If he knew where we would be and when we would be there, he could send a small squad to help."

"Without telling Lord Woulfe or the Council?"

Pyran nodded.

Anna's brows drew together. "I don't know, Pyran. This is all just…*beyond* me." She shook her head. "I mean, we'd be stepping into some treasonous territory there."

"But what if—" Pyran put a hand on Anna's shoulder. "What if we could raise our chances? We could completely turn this thing around."

Anna stared down at her hands in her lap and realized she was fiddling with her fingers nervously. She stopped and let them rest in her lap. "What if our letters are found? What if we're found out?"

Pyran leaned toward her. "We'll write in some kind of code. We'll think of something he'll understand. And so what? If we're found out, we'd be cast out of service, maybe do a little time. Sounds better than being sent to die."

How did I get here? "I'll think about it. Maybe this is something the captain should be in on."

Pyran nodded and leaned back again. "We should talk to him, get the details of when and where. I doubt he'd be opposed to a little help."

THAT NIGHT, ANNA WROTE HER MOTHER ANOTHER LETTER. SHE KNEW SHE couldn't say much, and she didn't want to, but she felt the need to talk to her mom. She wanted badly to talk to her dad. So, when she was done telling her mother how much she loved her and missed her and had slipped it into an envelope, she grabbed a fresh sheet of paper and addressed it to her dad. She told him everything down to the finest detail. Everything she'd enjoyed and everything she was dreading, all the people she had met and the places she'd been, all of it filled the page with ink until she had to turn it over to keep going.

I miss you, she wrote. *I wish you could be here. I wish you could talk to me about bears and deer and birds again. I wish you could tell me it's going to be okay.*

When a tear stained the page and blurred the ink, she folded it roughly and shoved it into the bottom of her pack. Then she blew out the candle on her desk and tried to sleep.

THE NEXT DAY, EVERYONE STARTED THEIR TRAINING WITH SOME STRENGTHening movements, and, while they were busy physically, the captain made sure they were also busy mentally. He asked them simple math problems or easy questions about their life, like what their parents' names were or whether they had a pet. Anna did all right when they started, but began to lose balance more frequently as her body tired from the movements. While they rested, the captain went over codes and signals.

Next, the captain had them run through their own movements with their weapons at high speed while making them recite or show the code or signal he asked for, so that their codes and signals were as much muscle memory as the weapon movements. They were all worn out by lunch. When the captain freed them for their break, Pyran caught Anna's gaze and gestured at the captain with a nod of his head.

"Now?" she asked quietly.

"Yes, now," he told her. "Would you rather we wait and the letter doesn't make it in time?"

Anna huffed at him, not able to come up with a proper response. She let him lead the way to the captain, who was slowly making his way out of the courtyard.

"Captain Heiser," Pyran called.

The captain turned to them with his eyebrows raised in slight surprise. "Yes?"

"We have a question for you," Pyran said, "regarding that walk we were taking."

"Ah," the captain's thick brows came down in concern. He glanced around the courtyard, then told them, "Hold that thought and follow me."

The captain led them into the Barracks, and then to a corner of the busy cafeteria. "Now," he turned and stopped, "what is it you'd like to ask?"

"Do you know Commander Lyon, sir?" Pyran asked.

"I know he's the commanding officer who sent both of you," Heiser told him. "I know he's earned his position."

Pyran glanced at Anna, then back to the captain. "We think he can help. Before he sent us, he told us what the mission was about. He's had people watching, he knows what's been going on, and he hasn't been sharing that information with Lord Woulfe, which if you knew him, you'd know—"

"I'd know that's a good thing," the captain finished for him. "I'm aware of Lord Woulfe, and I would agree. The man is the definition of narcissistic, although he almost isn't smart enough to wield it." He put a hand to his face and scratched his beard thoughtfully. "But you trust your Commander Lyon?"

"With my life," Pyran told him. "He'd give over the lord's house for his people—or his life, if he had to."

Captain Heiser turned to Anna, a silent question in his gaze.

"Yes," Anna said. "I trust him."

The captain nodded, apparently convinced. "All right. How do you propose we make contact without being found out?"

"He's asked us to send him letters, to keep him informed. I'm sure I could code a letter asking for help, but I need to know where we'll be and when we'll be there," Pyran said.

"Fair enough." Captain Heiser squinted at the ground for a moment, thinking. "At the end of the month, we'll be called in front of the Council for our sendoff, and then travel to Dore will take four days. Is he familiar with the area?"

"Yes. He knew where the camps were, sir," Anna spoke up. "He had them marked on a map for us. He had sent his own people to investigate."

The captain's eyebrows rose. "I'd like to see this map."

AFTER TRAINING WAS OVER, CAPTAIN HEISER TOLD PYRAN AND ANNA THAT he would join them on their walk back to their rooms, "to inspect that they had everything they needed." This raised some eyebrows in the rest of the group, who followed closely behind. When they made it to their hallway, the captain gestured silently for everyone to join them in Pyran's room. After they had all squeezed in, Pyran reached for his pack and the captain addressed the room.

"Pyran and Anna came to me this afternoon with an idea," he told everyone. "Commander Lyon in Hillcrest is already accustomed to working around his governor. In fact, he has gone behind his lord's back and secured a map of Vassian camps so that he could prepare Pyran and Anna before they left."

Pyran rolled out the map from Commander Lyon on his bed. Everyone leaned in.

"They have proposed," the captain continued, "that they send a coded message to him asking for help, and he would send a small squad to meet us."

The captain bent over the map. He looked at it intensely for a moment, and then hummed thoughtfully. "Either the Council's spies missed a camp, or your Commander Lyon's spies are just that good," he grumbled quietly to himself, still staring at the map. "Honestly, I wouldn't be surprised if it was intentional."

There were seven camps marked with X's around the wall and near Dore. They were labeled A to G from left to right. The captain put a finger on the symbol closest to Dore. "E. That is our first mark. We'll be there nineteen days from now. Do you think you can get that across to him?" The captain turned to Pyran.

"Yes, sir."

"Hold up," Will said from the back. "How do we know Commander Lyon won't sell us out?"

"He's already working behind his own governor's back," Ros reasoned quietly. "What guarantees that he won't work behind ours?"

"We trust him," Pyran told them. "He's the commander of Hillcrest's forces because he worked his way up from the bottom, and because he would put his life on the line for any of his people."

Anna nodded. "I trust Lyon. What I'm not sure is how we're going to tell him where we'll be and when we'll be there *without* telling him."

"Leave it to me," Pyran said. "I've known the commander for years. He'll understand what I'm saying."

The room was quiet for a moment as most of them stared thoughtfully into the middle distance. The captain broke the quiet with a question.

"Are we in agreement? We'll send Commander Lyon a message to send us some extra hands?"

"Seems like it's the only chance we've got for help, and we need it." Merry said, then smirked. "I was ready to say we could do it on our own, but I'll always take more *hands.*"

"*Merry,*" Clara said, both amused and appalled by the joke.

"So you'll trust this Commander Lyon, but we can't trust our Aunt Charlotte?" Callum asked.

"The further we keep this from the Council, the better," the captain told him.

Clara let out a dramatic harumph, but then quieted.

AFTER DINNER THAT NIGHT, PYRAN AND ANNA STAYED UP CRAFTING A LETTER.

Commander Lyon,

Anna and I have arrived safely and are training under Captain Heiser in the capital. The mission we are being sent on will be challenging and take some time.

The risk is high, and the cost could be even greater. We'll stay and train for a month before being sent out.

My cousin in Dore is still upset with me, but I'll try to see her. I should be there 32 days from now. They're looking for people for a job, and they need the extra hands. They'll have to be smart and fast, too. Quiet, most importantly. Without the help, they'll be underwater. Let me know if you could recommend anyone.

"You're sure this'll work?" Anna asked, frowning at the letter.

"Positive."

"I wish we could speak more plainly," she said, "but then we could be found out..."

He shrugged. "I think we walked the line well. Ready?"

"Sure," she conceded.

He signed and dated the letter before sealing it shut.

22

THE NEXT DAY, ANNA SHOWED UP TO TRAINING TIRED FROM HER LACK OF sleep the night before. Pyran had put the letter in the post this morning. To say she wasn't in a great mood would be an understatement, so when the captain told her that she'd get to spend the next few days in the forest outside of the city, she was excited and relieved. However, he followed that up by telling her that she'd be showing Will how to scout and track, and her optimism dwindled.

Now, she waited for him by the southern entry of the Barracks. She wore her leathers and her shortbow along with her quiver, her satchel, her knife, and her shortsword at her belt. Will met her there with his leathers on, his daggers in their scabbards, and a scowl on his face.

Already tired of his attitude, she crossed her arms and told him, "You weren't exactly my first pick either, but it has to be done, *scout*."

"Easy, *scout*. It's not you, it's the woods," Will told her.

"You don't like...the woods?" Anna asked, confused and a little surprised.

"No." He answered as if it was the most obvious thing he'd ever had to say. "They're dirty and you can't tell where you're going. It all looks the same."

"Interesting." Anna started walking.

"Interesting? That's all you've got to say?" he asked, following after her.

Anna waited until they were outside of the city gates to respond again, which meant that the two of them trudged through the city in annoyed silence. They made their way through the tall grass surrounding the main wall, walking toward the forest to the west. Anna felt relieved as she spotted the trees in the distance. "The woods aren't dirty. The air is the cleanest there. You can tell where you're going by the sun and the stars, and each little grove is different from the last one. But you wouldn't know that, being a city boy."

"Okay, tree girl, go ahead and show me. I'm looking forward to walking around in the mud with you all day."

"Well, I see you're as positive about this as you are with anything," Anna grumbled.

Will scoffed. "Just because you see things as rainbows and cloud shapes doesn't mean that's the way things are. It's like you wake up each day and forget we're being sent to die."

Anna stopped, shoulders tensed. She whirled on Will. "I don't forget. I've just decided I'm going to *do* something about it. You could join me." He didn't respond, so she added, "I hope you won't leave us when we need you the most. Why don't you take off already, like you keep telling everyone you'll do?"

It was clear Will hadn't expected Anna's tone and proximity. His expression settled into a frown again quickly, his shoulders slumped. "I can't leave until the ship is going down."

"Why not?"

"Can't we do this some other time?" Will moved around her to walk again.

"I'd rather not spend all day teaching someone that doesn't care, so tell me why you care—why you can't leave—and then we'll carry on."

Will stopped with a sigh and turned back to her. Looking down to a spot on the ground, he said, "I owe the city a debt. The only way to pay it is to serve, so I joined the military. If this doesn't work out, I'm screwed either way."

Anna blinked and gave an intrigued, "Huh."

"What?"

She started walking towards the trees.

"What?" Will repeated, catching up. "What do you mean, *huh?*" He stood in front of her, not letting her pass.

Anna sighed and put her hands on her hips. Then she turned her head and stared at a bush off to the side. "It's familiar, that's all."

"What's familiar?"

She crossed her arms and glanced at him. "I'm here because of a debt."

Will's brows drew together in confusion and he blinked. "What is there to get into debt over in Wallset?"

"Taxes," Anna grumbled, "mostly."

"You couldn't pay your taxes?"

Anna huffed. "You know what? If you tell me why you've got debt, I'll return the favor."

Will's face went stony and his mouth shut.

"That's what I thought." Anna let her arms fall to her sides. "All right, these woods look pretty similar to the ones I know. What would you like to hunt first? Probably easier to start with rabbit, but we could start with deer."

"Hunt?" One of Will's eyebrows arched.

"Yes," Anna nodded. "As the other *scout*, you'll be obligated to help me catch dinner. Plus, it'll teach you how to track and how to sneak."

Will narrowed his eyes at her. "Fine, let's start with the rabbit."

Anna smirked. "Okay, I'll show you how to set up a snare."

As she led him through the trees, she pointed out various edible plants, inedible plants, and picked at the ones a rabbit would eat from.

Surprisingly, he paid attention. He stopped making snarky remarks, at least. They stepped into a little grove, and she pulled a short rope out of her pocket. She showed him how to tie the knot for the snare, attached the free end to a bush, then put some of the rabbit food down. The next one, she had him set. She had to help with his knot. He set up one more snare and managed it on his own.

"We'll check those at the end of the day," she told him. "And again tomorrow, if they're still untouched."

Will hummed in dissatisfaction. "I thought I'd at least get to shoot an arrow."

Anna rolled her eyes. "We're not shooting anything today. We'll go for deer next."

"We're just going to look at some deer?"

Anna huffed a little laugh. "Deer are observant. We have to be quiet and track them first. Once you see them, you have to stalk them until you're close enough for a shot, preferably downwind. We don't need meat, so there's no reason for us to kill anything today, unless we want fresh lunch."

"We could catch dinner for the team," Will proposed sarcastically.

"We'll have plenty of time to do that at the wall," Anna said. She looked around. "This time of day, they're probably bedded down somewhere. You'll have to be quiet now if you want to find them."

Will's hands flew up in a motion of surrender as he silently feigned offense. He gestured for her to lead the way.

Quietly, she told him what to look out for—what their tracks and feces looked like, what rutting might look like on the ground even though it was summer now and too early, what rubbing would look like on a tree. They both quietly made their way further in.

Anna was prepared to give a lesson on what to avoid when trying to be quiet, but she found Will watching her movements already. He was picking up on where she was walking, how she was moving, and what she was avoiding.

Eventually, they came to an old dirt trail, and Anna stopped. She showed Will the back of her hand with her fingers pressed together, their silent signal for *stop,* and then she pointed down at the ground.

Will spotted the hoofprints in the dirt, making their way diagonally across the trail.

In a whisper, Anna said, "We'll follow these to find where they're bedding down."

Will nodded.

Anna followed the tracks. As the ground turned to grass and leaves, the prints disappeared, but she could see where the deer had disturbed the leaves and moss. She pointed at each example of this. As they passed a sparse bush that had been heavily eaten from, she pointed at it for Will to take note. The grass turned into low bushes and shrubs with an obvious opening through which the deer traveled often, and Anna signaled for them to stop again. She leveled her hand horizontally and pushed it down twice. Will got the message and crouched down with her.

She leaned in close to whisper again. "They're most likely bedding down here. The wind is blowing at us, otherwise I'd say we might need to circle around. Let's go find them." She pulled away and looked onwards, cheeks heating slightly as she recognized he smelled like leather and sandalwood. Will nodded in her peripheral.

Carefully, they both crept forward into the deer trail. A little way in, Anna heard rustling leaves. She stopped. Will stopped with her. She turned her head a little to the left, towards the sound. There, about a hundred feet out through the shrubbery, was a cluster of deer. Anna smiled and glanced back at Will. He was staring ahead at them.

She mouthed quietly, "Do you want to get closer?"

Will stared for a moment, then nodded.

Anna put a finger to her lips, emphasizing the need to stay quiet, and Will rolled his eyes. They crouched lower still, moving forward almost on all fours, avoiding branches and dry leaves. They found a thick bush to hide behind and stopped to peer at the deer laying in the foliage or grazing nearby.

There were maybe thirty deer altogether. There were groupings of little ones curled up together, spots still showing on their backs. Anna's smile widened as she glanced at Will, who seemed completely engrossed. They sat there together for a long while before creeping out to move on to the next lesson.

As Anna was in the middle of a lecture on what berries here were safe to eat and which plants could help with healing, Will interrupted with a question.

"How do you know where you're going?"

"—important to look at leaf shape," she finished, eyes narrowed in annoyance at him. "I followed the deer's path back to the trail, and now I'm just curious where it goes, so I thought we could follow it for a little while."

"No, how do you know how to get *back*?"

"The sun, mostly," Anna said. "I can tell directions based on that, but when it's high overhead at midday, you can also use trees, moss, ant hills..."

When Anna glanced over at Will, he looked skeptical.

"Trees want sunlight, and they get the most by facing south, so there'll be more branches on the south side. Same with anthills at the base of trees, they want sun, too. Moss is the opposite. It hides in the shade on the north side of tree trunks and stones."

"All right," Will accepted her explanation. "Since we're missing lunch, what are we going to eat?"

"I was just getting to that." Anna jumped back into her lecture on berries, and soon she found them an abundant blackberry bush, and then a strawberry bush. She showed him how to identify a handful of different mushroom types, and they added some to their meal.

They made their way back to their snares and found a rabbit in one of them. Anna freed it, but held it tightly for a moment to explain to Will how to efficiently break its neck, then let it go.

By the end of the afternoon, Anna's boots and hands were dirty and her heart was light again. She smiled as she walked out of the trees and into the sunlight. She caught Will watching her and turned to look at him. "What?"

He shook his head. "Nothing."

She doubted it was nothing, but she let it go.

That night, as she showered and smelled the fresh air and the earth as it washed off her, she relived that quiet moment in the woods, watching the deer.

23

THE NEXT DAY, THEY CHECKED THE SNARES, FREED ANOTHER RABBIT AND reset the trap, and then moved further into the trees again. This time, Anna instructed him on the less friendly parts of a forest. She talked about how to spot and avoid snakes, what to do if you stumbled across a bear, and similarly, what to do about an encounter with wolves and wildcats.

"Moose, believe it or not, can also be very aggressive. Not sure what to do about that, but probably similar to everything else. Bottom line, get out without turning your back or showing weakness."

"You're saying we need to watch out for moose?"

"Probably not, but I'm trying to cover everything." She paused thoughtfully and then said, "Treecats are usually non-confrontational, but if you make one angry, it will attack you. Always look for kits, and avoid them if you find them. It doesn't matter how cute they are, mom will attack you, and mom is bigger."

There was a quiet moment before Will said, "You're…better here. Not so nervous."

Anna took a breath as she processed his statement. She felt a little heat in her cheeks as she said, "I'd rather be in the woods than anywhere else. I'm sure you feel that way about somewhere."

Will thought, and then answered uncertainly, "Maybe."

The conversation died after that, and they continued on. Anna was still curious about the old trail they'd come across yesterday, so she figured they could follow that a little further today. Casually, she began pointing out different birds and where they liked to nest. She named some of the bugs they came across. As they kept walking, the trees got taller and thicker.

"You know a lot about all of this," Will said as he flicked a beetle Anna had named from his arm.

"I spent almost every day in the woods, with my dad and after him," she said, tone softening. "Before he passed, he taught me everything I know."

Will glanced at Anna, a small frown on his face.

"Oh," Anna stopped, looking ahead. "Look at that."

Will stopped and looked. There was a clearing in the trees, maybe fifty feet around, and at the center was a half-fallen stone structure. "Some abandoned cabin?"

"Maybe." Anna walked toward it.

"Where are you going?" he asked.

"Where do you think I'm going?"

"You can't just walk in there," he said, hurrying to catch up.

"Why not?" she asked. "It's obviously abandoned, and we're scouts. I'm going to scout it out." She glanced back at him with a smirk.

He sighed through his nose in defeat and followed behind, watching the clearing warily.

They walked through the tall grass, making little swishing noises as their legs moved against the dense plants. The cabin was built from large fieldstones with a wood roof that had mostly fallen in. The chimney was holding up what was left of the structure. The rest of the building lay in heaps on the ground, which Anna carefully climbed over as she tried to get inside.

"What are you doing!?" Will hissed from the edge of the rubble.

Anna turned from the other side of the mess, her feet on wooden floorboards, and she smiled. "Have I finally found something you're not high and mighty about?"

Will sucked in an irritated breath through his nose. "You have to know what they say about these ruins. Nobody's supposed to mess with them. There could be old magic that—"

She cut him off. "They only say that because they're superstitious or they want whatever's inside for themselves." Her hand subconsciously traveled to where her necklace hung beneath her shirt, behind her leathers. "Don't tell me you're afraid of rumors."

Will looked around, then met her gaze again. "I take it you've done this before?"

Anna shrugged. "Maybe. Are you coming or not?"

Will frowned at her for a moment, then started climbing over the stones to get to her.

"That's the spirit!" Anna turned without waiting for him.

Inside the building, she found a lopsided table with a broken leg, ashes in the fireplace, and the frame of kitchen cabinets where the wall had come apart. She walked over to one cabinet that was still intact and opened the door. All it held was an abandoned rodent nest. Wrinkling her nose, she turned to look at the rest of the room again. She found Will standing in front of her with his arms crossed.

"Oh, yeah," Will commented, gesturing at the cabinet. "Great find."

"Oh, shut it." Anna waved a hand at him as she passed by him, inspecting the floor. There were scrape marks where the rest of the furniture must have been, chairs around the table and some kind of a sofa by the fireplace. The owner or someone who had found the place before her must've removed them. Her eyes traced the edges of the floorboards until she found what she was looking for.

"Aha!" Anna crouched and stuck her knife in the large crack between two planks.

"What is it now?" Will asked her unenthusiastically. "Did you find a pretty feather? Or a stone in the shape of a heart? Or—"

He stopped as Anna hooked her blade against something and pulled. A large patch of the floor next to the fireplace swung open. She turned to look at Will, grinning.

He blinked at her, eyes wide. "I'm not going down there."

"We're going down there," Anna said at the same time, then laughed at his reaction. "I can't uncover a secret room and not go inside!"

"I can!" Will argued, glancing into the dark hole. "It smells."

Anna rolled her eyes. She took an arrow out of her quiver and pulled an old strip of cloth out of her satchel. She wrapped the cloth around the arrowhead, tied a knot, and lit that end on fire. Then she threw it into the hole.

"What—"

Anna put a hand up toward Will, the universal sign to shut up. She watched the arrow fall and hit dirt more than ten feet down, where it stuck into the ground and illuminated about five feet around it. There were walls down below that matched the walls standing aboveground. *Good. It's probably the same size as the cabin is, built right below it.*

Anna looked back at Will. "It's too far down for me to get back up by myself."

Will looked at the hole, looked at her, and then looked at the hole again. He huffed a sigh and ran a gloved hand over his face as Anna continued to stare, silently wearing him down. "Mother, you are mad," he said finally, then, "Fine, but you're going first."

"Wow, tough guy," Anna teased. "Who knew your liver was so white?"

"Shut up," he said as he walked over.

"Lily white." Anna shook her head in mock disapproval. "Snow white."

"You're lucky I don't shove you into this dark pit," Will said. "That would show you."

Anna laughed lightly, lowering herself to sit at the edge and then twisting so that she held herself up by her locked arms. Will watched as she swung down, dangled briefly from her fingers, and then let go. She landed with a soft thud next to her burning arrow.

"Your turn," she said, looking up at him with a hand on her hip.

He narrowed his eyes determinedly and crouched by the opening. He lowered himself the same way she had, although he landed more softly than her. He frowned into the darkness as he stood up.

"All right." Anna plucked her arrow out of the ground and held it forward like a torch, clearing away the cobwebs in front of them.

As her eyes adjusted to the dim light, she could barely make out the edges of the big, open room. There were a few broken wooden chairs stacked against the wall, and then a pile of things covered in a shroud. She walked forward, and Will hesitantly followed.

Spiderwebs hung all over the space. Anna took her time with her small torch, burning through strands in front of her. Will stuck close behind, staying within her cleared path. When she reached the shroud, she walked around it, looking at its edges and high points.

"What are you doing?" Will asked, stopping in front of the hidden pile of stuff.

"Checking for traps."

Will huffed. "You *have* done this before."

"Ah," Anna said from the side of the pile. "There's a chain here. It's attached to something in the ceiling. I can't reach." Anna held her flame up toward the ceiling, where the chain came out of a small metal box.

"Wow," Will made his way over and looked up. "What would someone hide under such a contraption?"

"Only one way to find out. We have to disable it."

"We?"

"Yes, I need you to hold me up on your shoulders."

"It's always *Will, put me on your shoulders,* and never *Will, you can go up on my shoulders.*" Will mocked a high, feminine voice as he joked, but he kneeled down for Anna to climb up and pulled his hair out of the way. If she didn't know any better, she'd have thought he was enjoying this.

Anna stuck her arrow into the dirt nearby. She swung one leg over one shoulder, and then the other leg over his other shoulder. He rose and she lost her balance a little, frenzied hands landing on each side of his head.

"Easy," he told her, grabbing each of her legs with his hands and getting his footing. "I don't need you poking my eyes out."

"Sorry," she said quickly, moving her hands so that they were holding his shoulders on the outside of her legs. She hooked her feet behind his back. She felt flushed, and she was glad for the darkness. She looked up at the box, now almost within reach. "A little to the left."

Will took a careful step to the left and planted his feet.

"Perfect." Anna reached up and felt around the box, cautious of the chain. Her fingers found an edge that went all the way around, close up towards the ceiling. On one side was a hinge, and she thought she could feel a latch on the other, but her arms weren't quite long enough. She put her left hand atop his head for support and reached as far as she could with the right. As he grunted in annoyance, her fingertips grazed the edge of the clasp.

"Could you, uh, stand on your tiptoes?" she asked him.

He harrumphed, and she felt his shoulders tense. Then he lifted about six inches. She reached for the clasp, found the top side of it, and pulled it free. The metal lid swung open with a metallic creak of the old hinge. It swung back and forth loudly before settling.

She hummed thoughtfully as she tried to make out the mechanism in the darkness. "Could you hold up the light?"

"All Mother's Children," he grumbled. He stepped back and carefully crouched. Anna felt a hand leave her leg as he picked up the arrow and held it up before straightening again.

With the light directly underneath her, Anna could make out that the end of the chain was connected to a pin holding some kind of canister shut. "Probably gas," she muttered to herself.

"Gas?" Will asked, and she felt his head tilt up into her stomach as he tried to look at the ceiling. "Poisonous gas?"

"Most likely," she told him. She felt around the box with her fingers, trying to find how the canister was held in place.

"What are you doing?" Will asked, shoulders tense.

"I'm looking for a way to get the canister out. Once that's free, we can remove the canvas with it."

"If you get me killed out in the woods, *scout*, I'm going to find one of those old necromancers from the stories and I'm going to bring you back just to kill you again."

"Oh, calm down." Her fingers found a little bracket, attached with a couple of screws. She pulled the knife out of her belt again, put the thin end of it into the head of the screw, and turned. Will was quiet as she removed the screws, tensing when the first one fell free, and then again when she caught the canister and bracket with her free hand.

"There," she told him, slipping her knife back into its scabbard. "Easy! You can let me down now."

Will carefully knelt down on one knee, and Anna swung her legs off his shoulders. She held the canister and the chain close together, being very careful not to pull the pin in between them. "Pull the canvas this way, and then I can set these down."

He stuck the arrow into the dirt, then stood and moved to the pile. He took hold of the canvas, grimacing in the dark at the amount of dust that had settled onto it, and he pulled. The fabric shifted, sending dust clouds swirling. They were both coughing when the fabric landed on the ground.

Anna carefully set the canister and chain down on top of where they connected to the canvas. She pulled her arrow-torch out of the dirt, and then moved to inspect what they'd uncovered. There was a big, wooden trunk with a large metal lock on the front, a small, smooth wooden box sitting on it with no apparent lid, and a tall, delicately carved wooden wardrobe behind them, its doors shut.

Will crouched in front of the trunk, and Anna stepped in front of the wardrobe. She pulled at the double doors, and they came free with a stubborn *chink.* Anna waved her hands in front of her to clear some of the dancing dust that went spinning in the air. Inside, the main compartment held tatters of clothes, some still clinging to their hangers. Moths and mice had found and eaten most of it. There were three narrow drawers at the bottom of the compartment, which Anna opened one at a time.

The first was lined in blue velvet and held bits of stockings. The second, also lined in blue velvet, held some cufflinks, shining pins, and a few broaches. Anna fingered through the little ornamentations, picking out any of interest. She opened the third drawer and was surprised to find it empty except for its blue velvet lining. She ran her fingers over the interior to be sure. She felt a little spark at her collarbone as her fingertips pulled up an edge of the lining, and she gasped.

"What?" Will was next to her in an instant, looking her over, and then frantically into the wardrobe. "What happened?"

"I found something under the lining," she told him, pulling it back to reveal a paper packet underneath. "It just surprised me. That's all."

Will's worried expression fell into annoyance. "Well, what is it?"

Anna pulled out the paper packet and opened the end. "Letters. A bunch of letters." The folded papers were addressed in a curling, elegant script. They had been sealed with wax, but they were all unsealed now.

"Great," Will sighed and turned back to the chest.

Anna raised an eyebrow as he stuck two thin metal objects into the keyhole. "I take it you've done this before?" she mocked him.

Will smirked, still focused on unlocking the chest. "Maybe."

Anna looked through the letters while Will fiddled with his tools in front of the chest. She found seven letters in total, and they were all addressed to the same *Ms. Estella Meredith,* although the address itself was different on a couple of them. She didn't recognize any of the cities.

There was a soft click, and Will sat up triumphantly as the latch on the chest came free. He moved the wooden box onto the ground and pulled the lid of the chest open. Anna leaned in and held her torch over the top to see…a pile of moth-eaten fabric. Will let out a grunt of dissatisfaction before reaching in and pulling the fabric out. Anna leaned back.

After a moment of digging, Will pulled out a book and a small fabric bag, perhaps a coin purse.

"What did you find?" she asked, looking over the objects.

He opened the bag first and emptied the contents into his hand. Anna's assumption was correct. Coins spilled into his palm. They were varying metals and shapes. A few were hexagonal, a couple were square, and one of them had scalloped edges.

"Hm," Anna frowned. "Can't even spend that anywhere."

"These are ancient," Will told her. "Would probably go for a lot at one of the antique shops in the central district."

"What's the book?" Anna asked. It was bound in a fabric dyed in a marbled pattern. She couldn't see any lettering on it.

"Not sure." Will picked up the book from where he'd set it on the ground and flipped it open. There was a series of numbers handwritten at the top of each page, and underneath those, it was full of little notes in a quickly scrawled cursive.

"That's a diary," Anna realized.

Will grunted and rolled his eyes. "Some lady's ramblings about who she's having tea with." He made to toss it, but Anna grabbed it from him. He watched her flip through it for a moment, asking, "What? Curious about the life of a rich old dame?"

"These dates don't make any sense," she said. "Either it's in a different order than what I'm used to, or the year is…" She trailed off thoughtfully as she came to a realization.

"What?" Will asked.

"You're right," she told him. "Those coins are ancient. This is all from before *the War*."

"That's not possible."

"Why not?"

Will stood up with the coins in his hand. "Because there's no way it would still be here. Even if it had lasted all this time, how are we the first to find it?"

"There were signs of people camping out upstairs," Anna reasoned, "but that trap door could've been shut this whole time. I don't think anyone's been down here since it was closed up."

"That wardrobe should be eaten through by termites, or worms, or rats," Will waved an arm at the furniture. "Same with that trunk."

"The clothes inside are barely fabric anymore," Anna argued. She remembered her necklace and moved to touch the wardrobe. She couldn't tell if there was any magic there, but she hadn't been able to tell with her necklace, either. "Maybe the furniture is protected with some kind of enchantment. It would explain why they hid them away."

Will put the coins back into their little bag, then shoved the bag at Anna. "Here you go."

Her brows furrowed. "You don't want—"

"I don't need some ancient curse following me around."

Anna rolled her eyes.

"Take them," Will insisted, shoving them into her chest.

"Fine." Anna took the bag.

"You've probably got a handful of ghosts trailing you already, if this is what you do in your free time."

Anna smiled. She couldn't help but find it funny. "I don't, and you're overreacting."

"Let's get out of here." Will started walking back toward the trapdoor opening, swatting at spiderwebs in his way.

Anna shoved the coin purse and diary into her bag, grabbing the wooden box they'd set aside. Then she turned and caught up with Will.

"How are we getting out?" Will asked her.

"If you give me a boost, I can reach down and pull you up."

"*You're* going to pull *me* up?"

Anna sighed and shrugged. "I could manage, but I can try to boost you up if you'd prefer."

Will looked at her for a moment, worry flashing in his blue eyes. "You aren't going to get up there and then leave me here, are you?"

"No, I would never do that."

"Good," Will nodded awkwardly. "Right, well." He lowered to one knee, intertwined his fingers, and held his hands out for Anna to step into.

She stuck the torch into the ground, gently tossed the box onto the floorboards above, and then turned to him. "Ready?"

"Yep."

She put her hands on his shoulders, then one foot in his hands.

"One, two, *three*!" Will lifted her as she pushed off the ground with her other foot.

Anna reached up as she felt herself being lifted toward the opening. She grabbed the floorboards, swung forward once, and then back and up onto her locked arms. From there, she got a knee over the edge. "Whew." She rolled away from the hole before crawling back and looking down.

"What about your arrow?" Will asked, glancing at the little flame on the ground.

"It'll burn out eventually," Anna told him. She laid down at the edge, hooked her toes around the crack between two boards, and reached down with both arms. "Ready when you are."

Will nodded, rubbing his gloved hands on his pants nervously. He crouched back, swinging his arms down, then jumped as he swung them up, grabbing onto each of her forearms. Anna grunted as she pulled until his hands could grab onto the wood floor. From there, she grabbed his shoulders and helped him up into the room.

"There," Anna rolled onto her back, breathing heavily as Will got his feet under him. "Not so bad."

"I hope I never have to do that again." He started brushing off dust and spiderwebs and dirt.

Anna sat up and reached into her bag to pull out the coin purse. "I think you should take half. You've done half the work." When Will didn't answer, she added, "If ghosts haunt me, they're going to haunt you too, whether or not you've got anything. You might as well get something out of it."

Will looked over at her, then at the bag in her hand. "All right," he relented and stepped closer. She divided the coins as evenly as she could without knowing which ones were worth more, handing over half. Will took them, tucked them into a side pocket behind his leathers, and moved away.

"Wait," Anna told him, and he stopped. Anna dug back into her bag and pulled out the jewelry she'd found. She pushed them around in her open palm until she found a sizable brooch she assumed was made of gold, and a pair of silvery cuff links with little crows on them. She picked them out and held them out to him. "I found these in the wardrobe. You can have them." She didn't mention that the cufflinks seemed like something he would wear.

A little surprised, Will took them from her and inspected them, then tucked them away like he had the coins. "Thanks."

"It's the least I could do after your help." Her face grew into a teasing smile. "And now I don't need to tell anyone about your white liver."

"Yeah, yeah." Will turned to walk back toward the rubble, but Anna caught a smile at the corner of his mouth.

They both climbed out, finding themselves back on the old road they'd followed to get there. She looked up at the sun and then at the surrounding shadows to get a sense of the time. By her judgment, it was around lunchtime. "Have you ever had fresh rabbit?"

He had not, so she insisted they make their way back to their snares to get lunch. As they had the other times they checked, they had caught a rabbit. In no time, she had shown him how to set up a campfire, how to skin the animal and remove the unsavory bits, and then how to roast it. Will watched quietly. Anna figured he found the messy bits uncomfortable, so she handled it all. After the rabbit was cooked, she tore it in half and handed one half to Will, who took it hesitantly.

Anna bit into her piece. Juice ran down her chin, which she wiped at with her hand. She hummed in satisfaction. The meat was a little sweet, a little gamey, certainly not too dry. After she swallowed, she told Will, "It's hard not to dry them out, but I've had plenty of practice." She went back for another bite.

Will looked dubiously at the meat in his hand again, and then finally took a bite. He wiped at the juice rolling down his own chin. "That's...good."

"You don't have to sound so surprised," Anna told him with a smile, halfway done with hers already. "I've been wanting to get out and make my own meal for days. I'm over that cafeteria."

Will ate more quickly after his first bite. Between mouthfuls, he said, "I know we were joking around before, but it really seems like you break into places often enough to know what you're doing."

The corner of Anna's mouth lifted. "I never break into people's houses, if that's what you mean." There was a moment of quiet that made Anna doubt he believed her, so she explained, "A lot of the woods around Wallset are old and empty, like any of the woods by the wall. There are all kinds of abandoned buildings out there that most people avoid. The only danger I've ever seen are traps set by owners who are long gone, probably so dead that their grandchildren are also too dead to want anything they left."

"So you just wander around in the woods until you find ruins?" Will asked, incredulous.

Anna shook her head, smiling. "I would go out every day hunting and gathering for my mother's bake shop," she reminded him. "Most of the others would stay close to town, find what they need, then get back home. That's how my dad was too, unless we were camping." She paused, looking at the mostly eaten rabbit in her hands. She could hear her father's voice in her head, his instructions on how to roast a rabbit. "When it was just me, I found it easier to go farther out." *To get away.* She took a deep breath, let it out, and moved on. "One day, I fell into an old basement. The woods have pretty much overtaken anything that was built out there, so it can be hard to see unless you're looking for it, especially in the snow."

When she looked over, Will was watching her with an unreadable expression, his face set calmly while the fire and the sunlight reflected in his golden eyes. *Time to change the subject.* "Seemed like you handled that lock pretty easily. Do *you* go around breaking into people's houses?"

Will's expression shifted into wariness. "There was a time when I...found those particular skills useful. I haven't done that in a while."

Wrong subject. "I'm sorry. We don't have to talk about it."

"It's fine. We're all young and dumb for at least a little while."

"You say that like you're an old man," Anna teased with a smile, "but you're only, what? Twenty-six, was it?"

Will grinned back. "I might as well be an old man compared to you."

"Two years." Anna rolled her eyes and turned back to her food. She watched him as he looked into the flames. Finally, she asked, "Why do you always wear those gloves?"

Will looked down at his hands and the black leather gloves that covered them. He frowned. "Because I do."

One of Anna's eyebrows rose. "You even wear them at dinner."

Will didn't reply.

"All right, don't tell me. But it's a little weird."

Will rolled his eyes. He looked down at his boots.

"When—" he started, hesitated, and then started again. "When this mission fails, they won't let us come back. You'll need somewhere to go."

Anna frowned at him. "I can't run. It's not an option for me. I have to take care of my mother." She paused, then asked, "What makes you think this is still going to fail, anyway? Even now that we're getting help from Commander Lyon, you're convinced it won't work out."

"People far over our heads have decided that it should fail," Will argued. He hadn't raised his voice, but Anna still felt scolded. "They'll make sure we don't make it back. The Vasbrute aren't exactly known for asking questions before ripping people in half, either. They could already know we're coming." He leaned back and crossed his arms. "You have to agree there's a large possibility we'll still fail. You come across as a prepared sort of person. You need to think about what you'll do."

"*I'll* decide what I need to do. I don't need you to tell me."

"Sons and Daughters, you're stubborn."

Anna sighed, pushing the hair falling into her face behind her ear. "*If* we fail and *if* I somehow survive...I'd have to go get my mother and we'd leave. Maybe we'd make our way northeast past the border, to the humans there. Maybe west to Velles. I've never seen a palm tree." She thought for a moment. "That is, if I can get to her before they do. I've heard the Council has ways of finding you anywhere. What's your plan?"

"I can't go east with these ears. I'll have to go northwest."

Anna nodded in understanding, then shot him a hard look. "Even if the odds are against us, I'm betting on us. When all this is over, I want to be back home, helping my mom with the shop. If there's any chance of that, I have to try."

"I'm just being realistic," Will told her, frowning. His golden brown eyes pierced into hers as he said, "Sometimes your best isn't enough."

Anna wondered why she couldn't let herself acknowledge the inevitability of it all. If she stared too long at any of it, her chest felt like it was caving in. "You're right. But isn't there something, someone you'd like to come back to?"

Will looked at her for a long moment, something sad in his eyes, before he looked away without answering.

Her brows furrowed as she wondered what he wasn't saying. *Does he really have nothing to return to? Or does he still not trust me enough to share?*

They spent the afternoon tracking deer again. When they eventually walked back into the city, they talked about the animals they'd seen—the deer they visited, the pack of wolves they avoided, the patterned snake that slid its way across their path, and the family of foxes that had found them. Back at the Barracks, they separated to clean up before rejoining the group in the hallway for dinner.

Anna was silently pleased to see Will wearing the cuff links she'd found in the basement in the woods.

24

THAT NIGHT, ANNA PULLED OUT THE LETTERS SHE HAD FOUND AND read them.

She tried to read them, anyway. The cursive on some words was so ruffly that it was hard to make out. It seemed there were a couple of people writing to the same woman. They never included a return address or a name, only their initials at the end of the letter. One was M.T. and the other was P.K. From what she could make out, both people were keeping tabs on happenings in the city while Ms. Meredith was stuck out of town. Anna tried to match up the letters to the journal they had found, but couldn't work it out. She was tired after spending the past couple of days outside. She hid it all in her bag and set it aside before going to sleep.

A FEW DAYS LATER, THE CAPTAIN PAIRED ANNA AND CALLUM WITH BEN.

"You should all be out of the fray if all goes as planned," he'd told her and Callum. "Show him what he needs to know in case he gets pulled in."

Ben was given a shortsword and a dagger to train with and to carry through the course of the mission. They spent all day with him, starting with the basic movements before moving into sparring practice.

By lunch, Ben had tied the top of his robe around his waist and was sweating through his undershirt. Anna was sweating lightly in her leathers too. During breaks, they chatted about home. She found out that Ben's wife's name was Larrisa and their daughter's name was Idalia, after his wife's mother who had passed. They had a small, white, fluffy dog named Snip. Anna told him about her mother and her father, and about the neighborhood cats they gave treats in return for rodent hunting.

Later in the day, as they were taking a longer break than they probably should've, Anna asked, "You said your father is a professor at the academy. Do you get your magic from him?"

"Some people think it could be hereditary, but it's never been proven. It skips generations seemingly at random and appears in some bloodlines that were devoid of it before. Personally, I think it has to do with nurture more than with nature."

"What do you mean by that?"

Ben thought for a moment, and Anna could see his brain working as he tilted his head. "Like many things, I believe magic to be a skill. I think we all have the capacity for it, but some have a predisposed talent more than others. I think anyone, even you, could acquire the use of magic."

Anna knew he hadn't meant any offense by the *even you* comment, but it still stung her a little.

"The fact that you're able to use that necklace shows you have some capacity for it, even with no training," he continued.

Anna thought about this for a moment, then said, "But it's called the Well-Mother's blessing. Are you saying you don't believe it's something the Mother gives to particular people?"

Ben smiled wryly. "My personal belief is that there are no gods. But, if there is a Mother, I think it would be more likely that she allows certain people more talent with it than others, like physical skills or mental skills. Anyone can become trained with a sword or numbers, but not everyone comes to those skills easily."

Anna grunted thoughtfully. "I understand. It's an interesting way to look at things."

Ben's smile grew a little. "But you aren't entirely convinced?"

Anna's head tilted from side to side as she considered his question. "I'm indifferent to the existence of the gods. If they do exist, I don't care for them." She noticed his curiosity piqued and rushed ahead. "What I'm caught on is that if what you say is true, if we're all capable of magic, why don't we see more people using it?"

"Now we're stepping into a conversation to which those of authority at both academies like to ignore, including my father." Ben seemed excited about the discussion. He smiled and his gray eyes brightened, happily carrying on. As he talked, his hands worked their way into the conversation, he began motioning enthusiastically. "The root of the issue is *access*. Without access to knowledge, these people can't learn. And there are plenty of blockages. Cost is one large factor, location, belief." He listed them on his fingers. "Even here in our capital, there are people who think this power is a curse rather than a benefit. Put all three together, and you'll find that very few who live away from the academies can come so far to learn."

Anna smiled at his shift in mood. "It seems like you've thought about this a lot."

"Yes," he nodded. "I mentioned my father wasn't a proponent of such discussion. I made the connections about access shortly before I graduated, and I proposed to him a plan for a series of smaller, simpler schools positioned around Telluth. They'd be less expensive and closer to most than the academies. Students there could focus on the basics of training, and then those that could and wanted to could further their magical education at the Academy. I called them *lighthouses.*" He smiled at the name, and then it fell slightly. "While he agreed that access is sometimes an issue, he doesn't think it's our responsibility as the educators to concern ourselves with it."

Anna's brow furrowed. "Whose job does he think it is?"

Ben shrugged with a sigh. "The government, maybe. He didn't say. The conversation was over after that. I brought it up because with his position, the headmaster would listen to him, but he refused to carry it any further." He sighed sadly. "I think part of my father likes how the schools choose and control magic users. He likes that there is exclusion."

"I'm sorry," Anna told him. "I like your idea."

"Thank you," Ben's smile returned at full force. "I've been thinking about it more recently. With my daughter Idalia joining the Academy, I can't help but wonder what would have happened if we weren't in the position we are now."

Anna nodded. "You're right. Many people in Wallset are afraid of it, and those that aren't could never afford to send their kid to an academy. I don't think there was a single kid at school with the blessing while I was there."

"None that felt they could show anyone their abilities," Ben proposed.

I wonder if anyone in town is hiding it. She said thoughtfully, "Irene came from Wallset. She said she left as soon as she could, because people weren't kind to her when they found out."

Ben shook his head. "It's even more common than I thought."

"Maybe..." Anna spoke as she thought, and had to start over in her excitement, "Maybe you could talk with Irene about those schools, the lighthouses. She could be interested in helping."

Ben's eyebrows rose and his smile grew. "That's a good idea. When this is over, I'll talk with her about it." *When this is over.* Anna wondered what that would really mean for them.

25

ANNA STOOD IN HER ROOM, HANDS ON HER HIPS, STARING AT THE WOODEN box she'd found in the basement of the abandoned cottage in the woods. She picked it up and turned it all around in her hands. She couldn't find any cracks or hinges that might show where it opened. She ran her fingers over it, but all she found was smooth wood. It was like someone had carved it right out of a tree as one solid piece. She hummed thoughtfully and set it down again. She grabbed her little dagger and attempted to stick it in at each of the corners.

"What is this even made of?" she asked herself as she failed to get the blade to stick into the wood.

She picked it up and shook it. Nothing rattled around inside. She flipped through the old diary. There was no mention of a box, let alone how to open it.

With a sigh, she resigned herself to asking for help. She left everything in her room to cross the hall and knock quietly on Will's door. At first, she was afraid the knock was too quiet, but he answered after an anxious moment of her standing awkwardly in the hall. He was wearing the dress pants and the button-down shirt he'd had on for dinner, but the top couple of buttons on his shirt were undone. He seemed annoyed when he first opened the door, but that quickly shifted to intrigue when she spoke.

"Do you remember that box we found?" Anna asked.

"Yes." Will's eyebrow lifted.

"I've been trying to open it. I can't figure it out. I'm not sure the thing is even made of wood. Could you—"

Will was already shutting the door behind him and passing by her to enter her room. She followed and crossed her arms as he stood in front of the box on her desk.

He lifted it and looked around at every side, then shook it.

"It doesn't make any sound," Anna said.

Will hummed in contemplation, then took out one of his daggers.

"I tried that."

"I have a process," he told her, then attempted to jam the edge of his blade into the corners of the box just like she had.

Her shoulders slumped and she leaned on a hip, quietly letting him follow his *process.*

Will took the knife to the last edge and pushed against the box hard, his knuckles white and hands shaking with the force. Nothing budged. He stepped back, a little breathless from the effort, and stared at the box. "I've seen this one other time. There's only one possible explanation for this."

"What?" Anna's posture straightened with hope.

"This is closed with magic."

Anna's face fell again and she let her arms drop to her sides. "So we can't open it?"

"*We* can't, but..." He walked past her and out into the hall.

"Where are you going?" she asked in a hushed whisper-shout as she hurried after him.

Will stopped in front of Ben's door and knocked.

Ben answered in a blue and green paisley pajama set, looking like he had already been asleep. "What is it?" he asked, wiping at his face.

Will leaned in to speak in a quiet voice. "We've got something you should look at."

Ben looked confused as his hand fell away from his face to hang loosely at his side. "What do you mean?"

"I've got a box I can't open," Anna said. "We think it's magically locked shut."

"Mmf," Ben groaned in interest and waved an arm forward. "Lead the way, I suppose."

Anna and Will led Ben back to her room. The mage walked slowly behind them, padding barefoot down the hallway. Once in the room, Anna pointed out the box and Ben's expression turned speculative. He picked it up and turned it over in his hands, then set it down intentionally on a certain side. Anna watched curiously. Ben lifted a hand and waved it slowly over the top of the box. Something glowed, and Anna and Will stepped closer to get a better look. Some kind of rune or symbol had appeared, glowing a soft white light.

"This is a magic lock," Ben confirmed, but his brows furrowed. "It feels old. Where did you say you got this?"

Anna glanced at Will, who shrugged. She said, "I found it in the woods."

Ben's sleepy brain attempted to process what she'd said. "You found...this old, enchanted box just...sitting in the woods?"

Anna held in a laugh at how absurd Ben made it sound and looked at Will again, who shook his head and rolled his eyes. She answered, "It was in an abandoned cottage we saw when we were out training."

"Can you open it?" Will cut in, pointing an irritated hand at the box.

"I think so. I've seen the glyph before, in books." Ben lifted his hands, waved them over where the glyph had appeared, and mumbled some words that Anna couldn't make out. The glyph glowed, then seemed to dissolve into the air.

There was a soft click, and the top of the box sprung upward enough that someone could fit their fingers underneath.

"Thanks," Will said. He and Anna both pushed closer to the box and he started lifting the lid.

Inside, they found a small dagger with dark jewels on its hilt, a letter, and a ring. Will reached for the dagger as Anna pulled out the letter. Ben reached in and picked up the ring to inspect it.

Anna pulled the folded papers out of the envelope. The yellowing paper was old, but it was holding up well. There was nothing written on the envelope, but at the top of the page she found familiar initials—E. M. *Estella Meredith.* She skimmed the words below.

Ben hummed in interest as he looked the ring over, drawing Anna and Will's attention. It was a thick silver ring decorated with the relief of a five-petalled flower. "This is a first," the mage mumbled to himself.

"What?" Anna asked.

"This is a ring of protection," Ben said, showcasing the ring out in front of him for the others to see. "Against necromancy."

"Necromancy?" Will asked, surprised.

Ben nodded.

"I thought…" Anna stared at the ring, then turned her head to Ben. "I thought necromancy was made up to scare children from running off into the woods by themselves. Ghost stories and all that."

"Oh, no," Ben shook his head. "It is *very* real and *very* dangerous. Necromantic power is entirely illegal and has been since before the war, but ages ago, there were those few that thought it was worth it to cross that line. There were people raising the dead, using blood curses—all kinds of unethical magic. It is extremely rare to see anything like that today."

"This ring protects the wearer from necromancy?" Anna asked, pointing at the little band.

"Mm-hmm," Ben nodded. He held it out for someone to take.

Will wrinkled his nose. "Rings aren't really my style." Then he turned back to the dagger in his hands.

Ben pushed the ring toward Anna.

She took it, asking, "You don't want it?"

"Sure, I want it," Ben laughed, "but it's not mine. Besides, I have other ways to protect myself."

The ring seemed large for her, but when she slipped it over the middle finger of her left hand, it shrunk down to fit as it passed over the last knuckle. Terrified that it would never come off, she grabbed it and yanked. It pulled off easily.

Ben chuckled, watching her.

"What?" she asked, annoyed and flushed.

"Proper magical items are made so that anyone can wear them. It wouldn't do any good to forge a powerful ring that only fit one person. It will change to fit you if you put it on, and then only you willing it to come off will take it off, short of someone cutting it off."

"Oh, all right." Anna hesitantly put the ring back on. Again, it fit itself to her finger.

"I can have this, right?" Will asked Anna as he held the dagger in his hand, feigning a couple of slashes. "It's more my thing, anyway."

"Oh, uh, sure," Anna said, watching him move like the knife was already an extension of his arm. It was steel with a leather-wrapped handle, and there were two deep blue gems on the hilt, one on each side, and a third on the pommel. They were so dark that they were almost black until the light of the two candles on her desk hit them, and they sparked blue.

Ben noticed Will imitating throwing the dagger and said, "I'd be careful if I were you."

"What? Why?" Will asked. He threw the dagger and it stuck into the wood of Anna's bed frame with a *thunk*. There was a satisfied smirk on his face, until he evaporated into mist without warning.

"Oh!" Anna yelped.

Will materialized where the dagger had landed, seeming to appear out of thin air. With wide eyes, he turned to Ben and Anna. "What the *fuck*?" He focused his anger on Ben, "Why didn't you say anything?"

"I tried. You didn't give me a chance to look at it, so I could only make an assumption," Ben told him with a roll of his eyes. "You're fine. It's a jump blade. Some military carried them before the War, but they were destroyed. *Most* of them were destroyed, it seems. Fascinating." He turned to Anna. "What does that letter say?"

Anna shook off the shock of Will's momentary disappearance, lifting the letter so that she could read it. "E. M., I hope this letter finds you well and safe, though we both know that safety will not last. This ring and dagger should afford you protection and escape from our shared foe, if necessary. Wear both whenever possible. I look forward to the day that you and I can meet again, face to face, after all of this is over. Until then, P. K."

"You know these people?" Ben asked, an eyebrow lifted.

Anna smiled sheepishly. "No, but it's the same person who wrote the journal we found, and P. K. wrote her some other letters. I think it's all from before the war."

"It must be," Ben said, looking around at the items. He yawned and his body slouched again. "I don't know what the two of you have gotten into, but it could have serious value in the academic world. I know a few historians who would leap at the opportunity to study such things."

"We'll share when we're ready," Will gave a placating smile and ushered Ben to the door.

"I'd be interested in taking a look for myself during our free time," Ben said, before he was gently shoved into the hallway.

"Of course," Will agreed amicably, then shut the door on him. He turned to Anna, and a genuine smile stretched onto his face.

"What?" she asked.

"Did you see what I can do now?" he asked smugly. He threw the dagger again, this time at the little stool beside her and in front of her desk. It landed with a *thunk*, and Will disappeared before reappearing next to her, stumbling slightly.

"Be careful!" she said, putting a hand out to steady him.

He turned to her, smiling wide. "Ha-*ha*! Did you *see* that?"

"Yes," she said, laughing a little at his contagious mood. "I saw."

"This is amazing!" Will put both hands on her shoulders and shook her lightly. "Thank you!" Taking the dagger, he rushed out of her room.

26

THE REST OF THE MONTH WAS SPENT ON TEAM MANEUVERS. THEY FOUGHT as a group against some of Kastarus' soldiers to ensure that they understood all their signals and knew what to do as a team. Anna spent most of this time with Ben, Will, or Callum, because she would either begin a battle up front scouting, or at the perimeters, shooting arrows.

The first day was rough, everyone bumping into each other as they learned how to effectively communicate. Anna spent a lot of time learning how to get a good shot on the enemy when they were engaged in combat with a friend. She was given arrows with padded ends that made a silly *bonk* noise as they bounced off armor, but ensured that they wouldn't hurt anyone in training. There had been a couple of instances on the first day when Anna's padded arrows had hit Merry or Pyran. Ros had caught one in the air before it made contact and shot Anna a warning glare. Later, they scolded her during lunch in the tame tone that only Ros could use to tell someone they were very upset with them. Anna was much more conservative about shooting near her allies after that.

She wasn't the only one that was having issues. Merry had a bad habit of catching allies in the beginning or end of her massive swings if they got too close. The others learned to give her space. She rarely needed help, anyway.

Ros and Will learned their efforts were best spent in different areas. They were both the fastest on the team, and when they stuck close together they unbalanced the front. Instead, one would work in tandem with Pyran or one of the twins while the other took on those Merry couldn't reach. Occasionally, the two would share a signal and switch. Anna hadn't seen Will use his new knife, which she was glad for, as it would have looked incredibly suspicious.

The twins worked on staying in the center, so that they were within reach of most of their allies for healing in combat. Clara, driven as she was, tended toward the front, while Cal with his crossbow tended toward the back. Ben was also told to keep near the rear, where he would be mostly protected. He was also told to cast real spells, but to tone down their potency. Anna startled a little each time a soldier was lightly frozen to his spot or buffeted with wind.

At the end of those days, everyone was always exhausted and hurt. Before the captain would let them go, he'd have Clara and Cal tend to the team so that they were ready for the next day, and so the twins got some healing practice in.

Anna thought of Mr. Farney. What he had done was nothing like the twins' abilities. She was astonished at their healing magic. She couldn't help but stare as Clara healed over a cut on Pyran's neck from a sword that had gotten past his armor. Her hand glowed over the wound as she spoke so quietly that Anna couldn't make it out. When she pulled back her hand, the cut was a tiny scratch. Anna rarely required any healing, she avoided most direct conflict, but the few times it was needed, she wondered what the warm light could've done for her father.

The following days went a little more smoothly. It was becoming clearer to Anna when it was appropriate to shoot near her engaged allies, and she had less mishaps. The captain pulled her aside at lunch one day to remind her that as much as she should avoid hitting her teammates, her aim was good enough that she could be more active. Anna pushed herself to be a little less cautious.

She also worked with Cal on how they should split and direct their attacks. Using signals, they came up with a sort of language to communicate where they were focusing, if the other person should aim elsewhere, or warn of incoming soldiers.

Ben must have gotten a similar talk from the captain about withholding his abilities, because the battlefield began to fill with magic. Besides his ice and wind, he started shooting sparking balls of fire at the soldiers that ignited on impact and knocked down anyone nearby. Anna wondered how much stronger the attack would be if he wasn't holding back.

Now that Ros and Will were aligned, opposing soldiers didn't know what to do with them. The two moved so quickly that they couldn't be stopped. Pyran and Clara worked out a maneuver wherein they flanked Merry as she collected soldiers to her and forced their enemies to break up. Then Ros and Will would cut through, and any order on the opposing side fell apart. After lunch, the captain had to recruit more soldiers to fight them.

Things seemed to fall into place.

"That went much better than before!" Clara grinned as she worked on healing a large bruise on Merry's upper arm. Everyone was sitting sprawled out in various levels of armor, much of it removed to allow the healers to get to the worst spots.

"It helps that we're all recognizing the signals and remembering to give them," Pyran said as Cal tended to his hand. He had smashed it against a shield during training, and his fingers were swelling.

"Yes," Captain Heiser nodded, standing at the edge of the group. "I'm glad you're all seeing how critical communication is. You did well today." He crossed his arms and looked around at everyone.

"*But...?*" Will asked from his spot on the ground, leaning back against his elbows. "I hear a *but* coming."

"But," the captain continued, "These soldiers are not Vassian. The Vasbrute are going to be a different and more difficult challenge. They're bigger, stronger, and more organized. Remember that as we finish out our training this week. Consider coming up with clever solutions while we're here, playing in the sandbox. I like the maneuver that Pyran and Clara put together around Merry." He nodded to Pyran and Clara as he mentioned them. "As our biggest and strongest fighter, she's going to draw them in naturally. We can use that to our advantage instead of letting it overwhelm us."

The captain continued, "Ben, I'd like you to work on using your skills to direct our enemies where we want them, to scatter them, to confuse them. One thing the Vassians are unlikely to have is a fully trained mage."

Ben nodded, his expression turning serious as he considered these instructions. "Yes, sir."

"Good." The captain looked at Cal and Anna. "Same for you two. You can do more than take individuals down. Get disruptive."

"Yes, sir," they said in unison.

27

THE MORNING OF THE BALL, ANNA ATE BREAKFAST AS EARLY AS SHE DID on a training day. Ros found her in the cafeteria and sat next to her.

"Why are you up early?" they asked as they sat down.

Anna's cheeks darkened a little as she answered. "Irene wants me at her house by lunch to get ready, and I'd like to get in some movements and stretches before then."

"Ah," Ros nodded in understanding. "Does that embarrass you?" Their pale eyes narrowed as they read Anna's face.

Anna huffed a laugh. "It just feels silly, spending a day getting all dressed up when we're about to go on this mission."

"Maybe," Ros started with a shrug, "but maybe it is just as important. We are going to show them who they're sending out on their impossible task. Show them who we are, why we matter, and that we aren't shrinking back from the fight."

Anna sighed. "When you put it that way..."

"You're unfamiliar with the rules of court, but some would argue that more deals are made on a ballroom dance floor than during Council meetings."

"So I'm learning," Anna nodded, thinking of the lessons she was getting from Irene on her off days.

"It's good you have Ms. Brooks," Ros said, "She's showing you how to hold your own on that stage, how to not be used as a pawn."

"Right," Anna agreed. "I'd be lost without her. Do you know a lot about court?"

Ros grinned. "The Krakens are retained as security at any official event in Lakoona. I've learned much through observation."

"You're like a jack of all trades, you know that?" Anna said with a laugh.

"Of course!" Ros puffed up their chest. "It is the mark of a good Kraken to be versatile." They ate for a moment before they asked, "You will meet us there, then?"

Anna nodded.

"Ah," Ros grinned again. "It will be a grand reveal."

Anna's cheeks flushed again as she rolled her eyes.

ANNA SPENT THE AFTERNOON AT IRENE'S HOUSE, BEING FLUFFED AND coiffed for the ball. The mage had gifted her a navy gown unlike any Anna had ever seen. The material was like a waterfall at night. It shimmered when she moved, rustling as if announcing her presence. Its square neckline with wide straps rolled into a gathering at her waist that Irene called *ruching*. From there, it cascaded over her legs. The bottom was lined with a wide, stiff strip of something that made the hem meet the ground in waves.

Beneath the piece of art she wore was a structure of boning and padding that Anna had been nervous about at first, but she'd found that, similar to her leathers, it offered support and did not restrict movement. She wore low satin heels that clicked across the marble floor of Irene's home and down the cobbled streets of the inner city. Her pendant necklace hung between her collarbones, and a pair of borrowed silver tear drop earrings were clipped to her ears, revealed by her pinned-back hair that fell in waves behind her shoulders.

She was wearing more fabric than she ever had in her life, but she still felt exposed. The cool night air caressed her exposed clavicles and arms in a way that sent goose bumps over her shoulders as she hurried towards the castle with Irene.

"A lord or lady always moves quickly outside at night," Irene told her. "There's no respectable business to be done in dark alleys or street corners."

Anna glanced into the shadowy places they passed, wishing she had brought a strap to tuck her little knife against her leg. All she had were her bare hands, which were also her least effective weapons.

When they arrived at the castle, she could hear music drifting through the air, and the sound of waves in the distance. As she looked up at the towering spires, Anna wondered where the ball was taking place. A large balcony on the third floor was lit by warm light.

"Perfect night for a party," Irene smiled, glancing up at the stars. She pulled Anna through the two-story tall front gate, waving coyly at the guards stationed on either side.

They made their way across a carefully groomed yard that circled the main structure. Fireflies hung over perfectly square rows of hedges and around flowering trees. It was so peaceful that it felt like their clicking shoes and swishing dresses were intruding.

"Mesmerizing, isn't it?" Irene said and patted Anna's arm in hers. "A wonderful little enchantment."

"Enchantment?"

"Of course," the mage grinned with amusement. "To keep the lightning bugs organized. They're normally such erratic little things."

"Of course," Anna repeated, glancing around one more time before they stepped into the main hall of the castle. The sound of music dimmed inside the dark stone, but Anna could still make out the sound of the ocean. It sounded like the castle was breathing softly, sleeping.

A black rug and warm mage light sconces led them to a staircase on the right side of the wide hall. A man in a black suit with long coat tails stood at the bottom step, holding a small silver candelabra.

"This way, ladies," he said, inclining his head.

"Don't worry about us," Irene told him. "I know where we're going."

Anna let her lead them up two flights of broad, winding stairs, passing two more servants. At the third-floor landing, two women in black opened a pair of tall, ornate wooden doors.

The room they revealed was vast, an entire wing of the building full of dark marble, chatter, and music. An open balcony swept across the right side and the back of the room. It was dark outside compared to the light of a dozen crystal chandeliers, but Anna thought she could see the glittering sea in the distance. A row of tables full of food spanned from the doorway to the far balcony. To the left were rows of round tables where well-dressed guests sat and nibbled. To the right was a small band and an open dance floor where several couples moved in circles.

She only realized she had stopped when Irene pulled her gently into the room. A woman carrying a silver tray walked by and handed them each a sparkling drink in a stemmed glass.

"Wow," Anna breathed, looking around.

Irene held the glass close to her face, smelled it, and then shrugged. After a sip, she said, "All the governors are in the city for the meeting. Quite a night for your first ball."

"You think I'll attend more than one?" Anna asked.

"They'll hold a ball when you return victorious. Maybe even a parade."

She didn't respond. She was too busy processing the party in front of her to think about any in the future.

A handful of people came forward, greeting Irene.

"And who is this beautiful thing on your arm?" a woman cooed.

"This is Anna Hale," Irene grinned proudly. "She's part of that special team the Council put together, *but*," she sang the word for emphasis, "more importantly, she comes from my hometown."

"Wow," a woman said, giggling and turning to look at Anna. "What a change for you!"

"What do you think of the capital?" another woman asked. "How does it compare to home?"

Charming. Try to be charming. Irene's lessons raced through Anna's head as she tried to think of what to say. "It's very different, but I like it." *Vague, but it'll do.*

"Oh, good," the woman responded with a smile.

"You're probably learning so much," a man said.

Anna nodded politely.

"Are you a mage, like Ms. Brooks?"

"Oh—no, I—"

"What does your family do?"

"Uh, my mother is a baker."

"Fascinating! What were your local foods?"

Anna's face burned as she tried to keep up. "My mom made a lot of meat pies and sweet pies. She—"

"How homely. I'm sure they're delicious."

"I've never baked in my life! Can you bake?"

"All right, all right," Irene put her hands on Anna's shoulders and steered her away. "That's enough for now. We need to mingle!"

They walked away toward the food.

"Is it always like that?" Anna asked, a little breathless.

"Only until they find the next best thing. That's the game for you. Try to stay top of mind, but not so exciting that they can't leave you alone. It's a balancing act."

"What's exciting about being from Wallset?" Anna asked, picking up a small white plate and taking a couple of finger foods—bite-sized sweet peppers wrapped in bacon and little muffins, each stuck with toothpicks for easy handling.

"Nothing, but *different* is exciting, at least until you figure out it's not so different."

When her plate was empty, a servant in black collected it from her. "What's similar about Kastarus and Wallset?"

Irene's eyebrows rose as she looked at Anna. "Kastarus may be bigger, but it's all the same. Some people are going hungry, some people are more than comfortable. Preachers of the Creed shout at people in the streets. People sit in dark alleys, sunburnt out of their minds on solim and waste away as dealers prowl the same alleys, looking for anyone with something to give. Most people sit quietly at home, just trying to protect what they have from people that would take it."

Her chest rose and fell as she caught her breath. Before Anna could ask if she was okay, she was changing the subject. "But we're at a *ball*," she sang the last word with a grin. All of her vexation seemed to disappear. "We're here for drinks and dancing and fun while you get an eye on the court. Now, where's the rest of your team? I'd love to check in on Mr. Day and speak with the captain."

"All right," Anna responded with a weak smile, still feeling a little conversational vertigo.

They both turned toward the tables. The team was gathered around one table at the far end, most of them chatting with drinks in their hands. The captain wasn't with them.

"Hello!" Irene greeted brightly. All eyes lifted to the two of them. "Mr. Day, I hope you're enjoying the party."

"Certainly," he responded. "This is much better than the faculty dinners in Eysa." He was wearing a set of fine silk robes the color of barely-burning coals that made his grey eyes stand out. Deep red trim and a scrawling detail wove around the collar and at the end of the sleeves, offsetting the dark charcoal of the fabric.

"I can imagine," Irene chuckled sweetly. "Stuffy old professors aren't much fun."

"Have you been introduced to the team yet?" he asked.

"Briefly," she responded.

Ben started to the left. "The Phaon twins, Callum and Clara, from Delphia."

"Wonderful to meet you," Clara smiled. Callum nodded a silent greeting. Clara wore a slinky violet gown that showed off her fit figure, and there were thin golden chains woven into her braids. Cal wore a gray suit with a matching violet vest. A gold chain hung from a button and up into his vest pocket.

"Same to you, dear," Irene dipped her chin in a nod.

"Pyran Taggert from Hillcrest."

"Nice to meet you," he told her. "You might be the only person who could turn this woodswoman into a lady. Well done." He wore a green suit with a tan vest.

Anna rolled her eyes.

"Thank you," Irene laughed. "It's nice to see your hard work appreciated." She winked at Anna.

"Ros Dixon from Lakoona."

Irene's brows rose with interest. "The Kraken. I've been hearing about you. The other soldiers are mystified."

Ros grinned and shrugged. "Nothing to be mystified by. Just years of training." They wore a pale blue suit vest and matching pants, showing off their strong arms.

Irene nodded. "Quite right. That's what I always tell those curious about my powers."

"Merry McGill from Tuvale."

"Another small-town woman," Irene said. "That's always nice to see."

"Thank you," Merry smiled. "I like how busy the city is." She was wearing a periwinkle dress with a sweetheart neckline and thin straps at her strong shoulders. A lacy, see-through fabric laid over the skirt.

"Me too," Irene agreed.

"And Will Grey," Ben finished, "from Kastarus."

Will grinned stiffly and lifted his glass toward Irene in greeting. Anna noted that he was still wearing his black gloves, and she spotted the crow cuff links at the end of his sleeves. He looked well put-together with his black pants, black satin shirt, and satin-trimmed suit jacket. His hair hung down, hiding his ears.

"Pleasure to meet you," Irene said, turning back to Ben to ask, "Where's the captain? I was hoping to catch him for a moment."

Ben gestured to a group of people across the tables from them. Captain Heiser stood in his military finery with brass buttons and gold trim glittering. Anna didn't recognize the people he was talking to.

"Lovely to meet you all." Irene waved and walked off in their direction.

Anna sighed in relief and turned to her team. "You all look very nice. It took two stylists to turn me into this. I have no idea how the rest of you managed."

"*Two* stylists?" Clara asked, a dreamy look in her dark eyes. "Of course. I mean, you look so *expensive*."

Anna's cheeks heated. "Are you planning to buy me?"

Clara giggled. "No, silly! I only mean to say you look like you belong at court. Like your parents own the Marvista mines or something. *That dress!*" She fanned herself with one hand.

Anna rolled her eyes as her cheeks grew even warmer. "Don't get too excited. It's only for tonight."

"I can tell you love it, though," Clara said with a smug grin."She's right," Merry said. "It's the way you're carrying yourself."

"Besides," Ros chimed in, "anyone who says they don't like dressing up is lying. Especially in clothes made for them, and that dress was *made* for you."

Anna cleared her throat and turned her gaze to the polished floor. "I get it. We're all pretty."

"Cheers to being pretty," Pyran raised his glass jokingly.

Everyone joined in. "Hear, hear!" Clara offered.

"So," Pyran turned to the twins, "where are the governors?"

They both looked around the room discretely.

"Lord Moineau is over there," Ros nodded their head toward the far end of the buffet. A semicircle of people surrounded a tall, dark-skinned human man in a blue suit with a white satin vest and cummerbund. He had short, white hair and a matching beard trimmed with a kind of swirling, intricate pattern. He watched the dancers as they spun around the room.

"Our aunt is sitting at a table, speaking with Lord Inwood," Clara said, gesturing to a group of people gathered around a table. Most of them were standing, except for two.

Lady Cate wore a stiff red gown embellished with metallic cords tied into fancy knots that reminded Anna of the braids Clara and Callum wore. Lord Inwood was older, with pale blonde hair that fell like silk down his back and a matching mustache and beard. His deep purple robes and long pointed ears gave him away as an elven mage.

"Lord Woulfe and Lord Finke are by the food," Cal said, looking at the middle of the buffet. Two men stood together, conversing loudly about the quality of the food. Anna recognized Lord Woulfe immediately. All the rings on his hands could've paid her debt five times over, and his green plaid jacket was trimmed in silver thread. The other man had a dwarven stature. His tan skin and brown hair showed age, with wrinkles at his eyes and gray hair weaving through the intricate braids that started at his head and worked their way down into his beard.

"Lord Finke is the dwarf," Clara added, then pointed to where the captain stood with Irene next to him. "Lady Dato is speaking with the captain."

Lady Dato wore a cream shirt and vest with brass buttons similar to the captain's. Her gold-toned skirt gathered at the back, giving her a simple silhouette, and her blonde hair was gathered into a chignon. Even in the short moment she watched her, Anna could tell she had a habit of pushing her glasses up her pink nose as she talked.

"Who's everyone else?" Anna wondered aloud.

"Advisors, merchants, well-connected families," Clara said. "Military leaders, too. Anyone with a stake in the politics of it all."

"Doesn't all of Telluth have a stake?" Anna asked.

"Sure," Clara said, "but these people all have the money or means to affect things."

"The blood of any nation," Ros said with a flat tone, "money."

Anna narrowed her eyes at Lord Woulfe. *Would he even notice a missing ring? If I got hold of one, it would probably be enough to go home and pay off that loan.*

As if he could feel her looking, Woulfe's eyes turned to meet hers. He smirked in recognition before turning back to respond to something Finke said.

Anna shivered.

"I don't see Lady Gratadia," Clara commented, looking around. "Oh, wait. There she is, by the band."

Anna looked and found a young woman with tan skin and dark hair curled and pinned around her head. She wore a glittering silver gown with a flowing skirt and high collar. The sound of the band dimmed and then stopped, and she smiled. Then Anna heard her voice across the ballroom as if she was standing next to her.

"Welcome," Lady Gratadia said. "It has been some time since the Council has convened wholly in person, and I'm glad to see you all here."

A woman next to her was holding her hands out in front of herself as she spoke, and Anna realized that she must be a mage enhancing the volume of the governor's voice.

"We gather today to celebrate this great country and all we have accomplished, to remind ourselves what we are capable of when we work together for a better Telluth, for *all* its people. As we face the challenges to come, I ask that we all hold that idea close and continue to foster our relationships with each other."

The room filled with light applause and Lady Gratadia paused. When it faded, she continued.

"Now I'll let you all return to the party. Enjoy the food and dancing. May Noctis be with us under their stars."

More applause sounded as the band started up again, and a large group of people convened on her.

"How long do these things normally last?" Pyran asked.

"All night," Clara answered. At Pyran's surprised expression, she added, "People usually start leaving at midnight, though."

Pyran sighed and tugged at the ends of his sleeves.

"This is our chance to observe the governors," Ros said, "and anyone else of interest."

"Right," Cal nodded.

"What do we know already?" Pyran asked. "Who should we pay attention to?"

"Lady Cate is on our side," Clara said sternly, "I'm positive."

"And I doubt Lord Moineau supports a suicide mission. He holds all life sacred," Ros said.

"Even if he's making a choice for *the greater good*?" Pyran asked. "I'm sure the opposing side would make that argument."

"He would see through such a thin argument," Ros insisted.

"I don't trust Woulfe as far as I can throw him," Anna said.

"Which wouldn't be very far," Merry chuckled. "I don't think you could pick him up."

Anna huffed a laugh.

"I don't know much about Finke," Clara said, looking at the pair of lords. "He's reclusive—doesn't travel much from Altumberg. My aunt jokes that he's not the brightest candle in the chandelier."

"What about Inwood?" Pyran asked, looking at Ben.

The mage shrugged. "He's the tie-breaking vote on the University's board. He's...conservative and values tradition."

"Probably hates Vasbrute, then," Pyran said.

"Probably," Ben agreed.

"I think the captain's got Dato covered," Cal said.

The two were chatting, occasionally laughing together.

"I think you're right," Pyran said.

Will laughed quietly.

"What?" Merry asked him.

"It's just funny watching all of you play *espionage*."

"Not helpful." Pyran rolled his eyes.

"And what's your plan, strategist?" Will asked, his brown eyes bright with amusement.

Pyran shrugged. "Listen, I guess. If we can get a sense of who we can trust—or who we can't—we may be able to work something out."

"It's easy to get vain people to talk," Cal added.

Clara side-eyed him. "Why do I feel like that was directed at me?"

"If the shoe fits," her brother grinned cheekily.

She swatted his chest, and he laughed.

"I'm going to dance," Clara announced. "It's amazing what people will tell a pretty girl. Are you coming, Anna?"

Anna stiffened. "What? No!"

"Those shoes were made for dancing," Clara urged.

Anna shook her head. "Then they should probably find someone else's feet."

The shorter girl sighed and pulled her braids back behind her shoulder. "Fine. Let me know if you change your mind." She wiggled her fingers in a wave and walked away. Anna watched her approach a circle of younger people, and then a moment later, a man was leading her to the dance floor.

"Huh." Will sounded impressed.

"If anyone's going to pull information from someone, it's Clara." Cal somehow sounded both annoyed and proud. "You should see her fish for the name of a new designer."

"What about Ms. Brooks?" Pyran asked.

"She seems kind enough," Ben shrugged.

"I think so," Anna agreed. "She wouldn't be so kind to me if she thought I was going to die in a week, right?"

"You'd be surprised," Will murmured.

Anna frowned at him. "What do you know? You don't like anyone."

"I like Merry," Will protested.

"Thanks!" Merry smiled.

"I'm going to talk with my aunt," Cal announced. "See if she knows anything, or if Inwood will give anything away."

As he walked off, Anna moved closer to the remaining group.

"I'm going to *mingle*," Ros said, their face set in determination.

Anna grinned at Pyran. "That'll be interesting."

"No kidding," he said, watching them walk off. "I'm going to get some food. Maybe I can pick up something from Woulfe or Finke. Anyone else?"

"I could eat." Merry followed him.

That left Anna with Will.

"Going to wander off, too?" he asked, looking down at the drink in his hand. "Surely you've had enough of me."

Anna huffed a laugh. "Maybe if I were any good at *espionage*," she said the word in a snobby tone, "but there *is* one thing I'd like to find out."

Will's eyebrows rose, but he still didn't look at her. "And what's that?"

"You put on a suit, and yet you still wear those gloves?"

"This again." Will sighed and took a drink. "I wear them because I want to."

"Are your hands ugly? Covered in scars or warts or—"

"No!" Will looked at her now. His cheeks reddened as he held her gaze. "My hands are fine."

Anna's eyes narrowed as she tried to read his response, a skill she usually thought she was good at. Her mother was an open book to her, even in letters, but this man challenged her.

Will's brows drew together and he pulled his gaze from hers. "It's none of your business, anyway."

Anna looked at the gloves again. The hand holding the glass slowly turned it between his fingers. "Fine," she sighed.

After a quiet moment passed, Will asked, "What do you think of all this?"

Anna considered the question, looking around the room. "I think it takes a lot of work and a lot of people to throw a party for the Council." She watched a servant rush by and gently take her empty glass. "It's amazing how they all seem so used to it."

Will nodded and a half-grin crossed his face. "Money breeds a different kind of person."

"Surely they can't *all* be from wealthy families."

"Maybe a small portion of them aren't, but they're still making more money working with the Council than some people would see in a lifetime." He glanced at her. "That kind of money changes a person, and not for the better."

Anna hummed thoughtfully. Now and then, she'd see a story in print about someone's philanthropic endeavors. This governor had gifted so much to build shelters for the homeless, or that merchant gave funds to feed the hungry on Winter Solstice. What little she knew of the wealthy, however, was Lord Woulfe. *Vain and selfish. Guided by greed.*

Then again, the twins spoke highly of their aunt, and many of the common people liked Lady Gratadia. Were those people blinded by their hope for change? Were the twins blinded by their own privilege? She looked across the room at Irene. Finally, she answered. "Maybe. I'd like to think that some keep straight heads."

Will grunted noncommittally in response.

The music slowed and the dancers slowed with it. Clara moved off the dance floor to chat with another group her dance partner had introduced her to.

The remaining dancers held each other close and swayed gently.

"Don't say anything to Ms. Brooks," Will said, startling Anna out of the trance the dance floor had lulled her into.

"What? Why not?"

Will took a deep breath. "I don't trust her."

Anna rolled her eyes. "Thank you for your input, but unless you have some kind of reasoning behind that, I'll stick to what I know."

Will was watching Irene across the room as the sparkling woman told a joke, and even Lord Inwood cracked a smile. "She's too good with people. She could talk a fish out of water. People that good usually have a reason for it."

"Perhaps it's a developed skill, honed after leaving home and rising to become one of the most important mages in Telluth. Confidence and social skills are not inherently evil."

"It's more than confidence," Will argued.

Anna's frown deepened. "I thought we agreed that you wouldn't tell me what to do."

Will clenched his jaw. "I'm only trying to help."

"This particular help is unnecessary," she told him, wondering why he was being so obstinate about this.

"Fine."

"Fine."

Anna fiddled with the ruched fabric over her stomach for a moment, and then said, "I'm going to get another plate."

"Fine."

"Fine," Anna huffed, and she walked away.

28

All Merry and Pyran had learned was what food the lords preferred at feasts and what they preferred in their women. After she was done eating, Clara pulled Anna into a conversation with a group of young merchants. They mostly asked about what it was like living so close to the wall, as much as Clara tried to steer the conversation another direction. They also learned that Woulfe controlled a steel foundry, which would naturally benefit from a war.

Irene introduced Anna to Veronica Sico, Lady Gratadia's closest advisor. She was friendly, but busy. After a short conversation about their accommodations at the Barracks, she was off to speak to someone else.

Anna spent some time accompanying the captain, who introduced her to Lady Dato and the head of the navy, which was based in Luminport. The governor seemed intelligent, especially in military history and strategy. She also seemed to be good friends with Captain Heiser. They spoke informally, more like colleagues than two officers of the military.

Avoiding being pulled into another introduction by Irene, Anna slipped out onto the balcony. On one side, the gardens and fireflies stretched out below, and on the other, ocean waves crashed against the rocky cliff the castle was built onto. It was so far away that the sound of waves was quiet still. She found a spot near the corner on the garden side. She could taste salt in the air as she leaned against the thick stone railing that came up to her ribs. She watched the fireflies and sipped her drink. A full moon hung over everything like a dim, pale sun.

Time passed. How much, she didn't know, but her drink was empty by the time she heard a voice behind her.

"Did you come to jump, too?"

Will.

He came up to her and matched her relaxed posture, his forearms resting against the top of the short wall. He looked out at the trees. "Do you want to go first, or should I?"

Anna looked at him, unamused. "Go ahead."

"All right." Will took hold of the stone and prepared to pull himself over.

"Stop! Stop!" Anna hissed, pulling at his shoulders and looking around in embarrassment.

Will chuckled and turned to look at her, crossing his arms and resting a hip against the stone.

"You are impossible," she told him, flushing. Nobody seemed to pay attention, though. The balcony was full of couples in hushed conversations and a group of people smoking cigars at the far end, staring out at the ocean.

"I try," he grinned, watching her.

She swallowed, taking in his smug expression and letting her heart slow again. She turned back to the garden, unable to think of a smart retort.

"I thought Clara might get you to dance," he said.

"That would be as impossible as it is for you to be happy about anything."

"Really? Seems like you enjoyed watching."

Anna swallowed again, heat rising back to her cheeks. She hoped he couldn't tell in the darkness, but the moon was so bright. "I can't dance."

When he didn't respond, she looked at him and found him watching her again. His eyes were golden in the moonlight. "What? No jokes?"

He grinned and shrugged, saying, "Everyone starts out not knowing how to dance." He paused, then added, "And I'm not surprised with how you move when we spar."

"There it is." She smiled, despite her irritation.

He chuckled. Then he turned and rested his arms against the stone again, his hands folded together over the open air. "My mother taught me how to dance. Said every respectable young man should know how."

"Respectable?" she raised an eyebrow at him.

"Hilarious." He rolled his eyes this time. "I could teach you. You'd learn balance."

Briefly, a thought invaded her mind. She imagined him holding her close the way the dancers had when the music slowed. Her heart fluttered, and she shoved the feeling down in bewilderment, but when she looked at him staring at her, it did it again. Her breath caught inside his deep, golden gaze, but she shoved at the feeling again and cleared her throat. "You came out here to talk about dancing?"

"I came out here to apologize." His intense gaze turned to his hands and he frowned shallowly. "I shouldn't tell you what to do. I just want you to be careful."

"You don't tell Merry to be careful," Anna said, eyes narrowing a little. "Or Clara."

Will sighed. "Merry killed a bear with a shovel. And I'm pretty sure Clara has used Skullcrusher to actually crush a skull."

True. Anna blinked. "I know I'm not as strong as the others—"

"No, you're not."

"—but I know who I can trust as well as anyone. Irene grew up with my parents."

"All right," Will put his hands up. "I'll back off."

"Good. Thank you."

They stood quietly again.

"You look nice," Anna told him. "I like the cuff links."

"Thanks, I almost died getting them out of some gods-forgotten basement in the woods."

Anna laughed.

He smiled.

Then he left, saying something about getting some food, and dodging the little force in violet moving their way as he did.

"Anna!" Clara called. "There you are!"

Clara dragged her into a conversation with some of the younger merchants. Anna mostly stood there quietly as Clara subtly asked them what they thought of the governors. One of them asked Clara to dance and Anna excused herself before any of them got any ideas about asking her onto the dance floor.

It was almost midnight when Anna ran into Irene as she stepped out of the toilet room.

"Oh, Anna!" Irene smiled and caught her shoulder to steady her. "I hope you're having fun."

"Yes," she answered, finding her bearings again. She looked down into the dark hall her friend had come from, and then at Lady Dato, who stood wide-eyed and frazzled behind Irene.

"Oh," Irene glanced from Anna to Lady Dato and back again. "I was just complimenting Lady Dato on her attire. We had to step outside the room to get a bit of quiet. Isn't that dress so understated and elegant? I could never pull it off, but it simply *shines* on her!"

“Thank you,” the governor nodded at Irene with an uncertain smile and then turned to Anna. “Excuse me.” She rushed off back into the party.

“There’s someone I’d like you to meet,” Irene said, pulling Anna back inside and into a crowd.

THE LETTER ANNA WROTE TO HER MOTHER ABOUT THE BALL SPREAD across two pages. She tried to relay every detail about the outfits and the room and the music. She especially tried to provide detail on her favorite foods across the buffet tables. She couldn’t write about the research the team was doing, but she could write about the governors.

And the dancing. She tried to explain the dancing. When she got to her time on the balcony, she considered telling her mother about the moment with Will, but her embarrassment won, and she left it out.

Thinking about it now, it reminded her of scenes from her mother’s novels. Hearts skipping a beat and a character caught in someone’s eyes.

But that thought made her wrinkle her nose, and she frowned at the idea. It was clear that Will only tolerated her, and whatever she felt had been brought on by the dress and the music and the drinks. He had still been difficult—argumentative and unserious. All he’d done was apologize for being rude.

I was confused by all of it. It was only natural. The whole night was engineered to be charming and enjoyable. My subconscious built it up into something it wasn’t.

She thought of Will’s golden eyes.

Right?

29

ANOTHER FULL DAY OF TRAINING FOLLOWED. AS EVERYONE WAS RETURNING to their rooms to get ready for dinner, Anna heard Pyran call to her. Halfway into her room, she stopped and leaned back into the hall to see what he wanted.

He appeared with a broad smile on his face and a letter in his hand. "Commander Lyon."

Anna's eyes widened. "Come here!" She grabbed her friend by his armor and pulled him into her room, quickly shutting the door.

Pyran ripped open the letter, tearing the wolf seal, and started reading out loud. "Pyran, I'm happy to have received your letter. I wish you and Anna the best on your mission. As for your cousin, I think I have a few people in mind. Tell your cousin to expect them on time. Regards, First Commander under Governor Wolfe, Thomas Lyon."

"He's sending people," Anna smiled, a sudden relief washing over her.

"Yes," Pyran nodded, breathless from reading too fast and smiling back at her.

"Hurry up and get ready for dinner," she told him. "I think we need to take another *walk* with the captain."

The dinners at Captain Heiser's apartment sometimes turned into veiled affairs where all the participants shared a secret but couldn't discuss it. Unless the captain was talking about the mission or giving direction, the conversation always felt shallow to Anna, and she noticed that Will usually refused to take part. The twins, seemingly skilled at such things, held up most of the conversation, along with Ben and Merry. This dinner was no different.

Tonight, in her impatience, Anna had seated herself in the middle of the table. During a lull in the conversation, she stared silently at one of the crow cufflinks on Will's sleeve until his head lifted and he caught her. She looked down and away, ignoring the heat that rose to her face.

The captain finished his plate and set his silverware down, then pulled his napkin from his lap and set it on the table. "There is something important we should discuss."

All eyes turned to him.

He looked around at each of them, a serious expression on his face. "At the end of this week, we will meet with the Council. They want to give a personal sendoff," his face turned down and his eyes darkened a little, "for a mission like this. They'll also go over more details on timing and travel. I'll introduce each of you, as I'm sure some didn't have the chance during the ball. You should all be dressed appropriately. We'll meet with them in the morning, and then you'll have the rest of the day to prepare. We leave the following morning."

Pyran cleared his throat. "Captain, we'd appreciate it if you could walk with us again."

The captain's eyebrows rose. "Ah, yes, I suppose it would do me good after such a large meal."

It was a warm summer night as the sun set over the rooftops of the city. Their novelty had faded each time they walked to and from the captain's apartment, and Anna felt closed in. The only building that she still marveled at was the castle.

When they were in the alley, the captain asked, "Am I right to assume you've gotten word back from Commander Lyon?"

"Yes," Pyran smiled. "He's sending a few people to Dore. They should meet us there."

"Good, good." The captain's tense shoulders fell a little in relief. He put a hand on Pyran's shoulder. "They'll be of great help. Do you know the people he's sending?"

Pyran shook his head. "All he said was that he would send a few. I'm sure Anna and I will recognize them when we get into town."

The captain nodded. "We'll be staying one night at the local inn. I'm sure they'll know to meet us there." He looked at the wall next to them thoughtfully, then looked the group over. "There's more to be said about this meeting with the Council. We'll all need to be wary."

He thought for a moment, scratching his bearded chin, then said, "I want you all to watch the governors. We've got a general idea of them from the ball. Do your best to read them. While we travel, we can discuss what we see. We've run out of time to do anything before we leave, but there may be opportunities we can take advantage of." His expression turned melancholy. "I must ask you all one more time. Do any of you wish to leave? There are ways of getting out of Telluth."

"No, sir," Pyran responded first. "I'll see this through."

"Me, too," Anna agreed.

"I'm with you," Ros added.

"Like I said," Merry grinned, "have to top the bear story somehow."

"Us, too!" Clara took her brother's hand.

Cal sighed, but he nodded. "We're with you."

"Yeah, yeah," Will rolled his eyes. "I would've left already, wouldn't I?"

ANNA WOKE THE MORNING OF THE COUNCIL MEETING WITH HER THOUGHTS racing. As she put on her dress and prepared for the day, she worried that the help Commander Lyon was sending would get delayed in their journey to Dore, or a pack of hungry wolves would attack while in the unfamiliar woods, or bears would raid their supplies. As she braided her hair, she imagined the Vasbrute as hulking monsters, tearing each of them limb from limb before cooking them over a fire. Tense and unable to shake her feeling of impending doom, Anna met her team in the hall.

As the captain had directed them, everyone was in their best outfit. They said little as they made their way out of the Barracks and into the center of the city.

Anna remained stuck in her head the entire walk to the castle. Only when the high walls loomed over her did she rejoin her surroundings.

It was an entirely different sight during the day. The seat of the Council was a huge stone building with many parapets and towers. It was built with dark stone. It seemed an opposing force to the old structures in Hillcrest made of shining white. Large blocks held the weight of its peaked roofs as they scraped the sky. The shingles were a deep blue shale. Its exterior glistened from each tall, thin window, like the night sky.

There was one entrance on this side of the wall, a gate two stories tall made of woven wrought iron. The arched opening held the relief of a waterfall carved into stone at its peak, pouring out and turning to a winding river. Anna squinted up at it as the sun shone down and warmed her face.

A messenger greeted them at the gate and then stepped up to a small window in the stone wall, speaking with someone on the other side. A moment later, the giant iron gate swung inward. The messenger rejoined them to lead them inside.

The courtyard was about a hundred feet wide and spanned the perimeter of the castle in front of them. Paved paths wove across and around a well-trimmed lawn, along which ran short shrubbery trimmed squarely at a foot tall. Anna noted the handful of soldiers positioned at balconies and bridges along the upper levels of the exterior. Their dark armor almost disappeared into the stone behind them until the sun's rays hit them at the right angle, bouncing off brightly into her eyes.

Straight ahead stood a set of double doors as tall as the iron gate outside. They had been open for the ball, and now she saw they were stained dark and covered in iron rivets. As the group neared, both doors began to swing open silently, revealing a dark interior.

As Anna stepped inside and out of the sun, she shivered and blinked into the shadow. Her eyes adjusted, and they were met with a long, wide hallway lit at regular intervals by mage lights similar to the ones at the Barracks, but with their glass coverings cut or carved to resemble suns. The effect was a brighter light that shone farther, and on the wall underneath and above each light, they cast faint rainbows that streaked out from the light for a couple of feet.

Their boots slapped against the stone floor as they traversed the hall. There was the faint smell of flowers, as if turning down the right corridor would lead to a garden in full bloom, but there were no corridors.

There were seven tapestries on the walls. On the top of each was the name that a state and their capital shared. First was Amgen, with pale cliffs rising in the distance as a wave crashed against the rocks far below. Next, Anna saw Hillcrest. Treed hills were woven in the background, and in the foreground was a giant, dark gray wolf leaping at a white hart, jaw spread and fangs showing. The hart was graceful even as it was frozen mid-stride, bounding away. Anna couldn't tell if the wolf was about to latch onto the deer with its teeth, or if the deer was fast enough that it was escaping the wolf's gnashing jaw.

After Hillcrest was Kastarus, with a river winding through trees and spilling out into the sea. Eysa was on the other side of the hall. It showed a tall gray tower on a high cliff, its windows painted with gold thread. Then came

Lakoona, with a water dragon spinning beneath the waves of the lake, alongside a variety of fish. This was followed by Altumburg, with mountains rising across the horizon. Last was Luminport, with a large sailboat cutting through rough water and a distant lighthouse standing in the background.

The messenger stopped in front of a set of double doors, a matching relief of a waterfall above its peak as well. It was so high Anna could barely make out a cobweb that fell from the ceiling and stuck to the base of the waterfall. It waved in an unfelt breeze.

"Wait here," the messenger told them before disappearing through a normal-sized door to their right. The door latched behind him, and then there was silence.

Anna hugged her goose-bumped arms to herself. She wondered how they kept this space warm in the winter.

"You all right?" Pyran leaned over and asked her quietly.

She nodded. "Just cold."

"Good," Pyran sighed before a teasing smile spread across his lips. "I thought maybe you were nervous to look Lord Woulfe in the face."

Anna grunted a laugh, and a small portion of the tension fell from her shoulders. "I couldn't care less about that. Actually, I'm glad he'll finally have to see me."

"Your glares are powerful," Pyran said, "but I don't think any glare would make that man feel shame."

"Hush," Captain Heiser told them with a warning glance.

Pyran and Anna straightened themselves. Anna didn't know what sort of signal the captain had received, but just then, the doors in front of them swung open and into the next room.

Captain Heiser stood at the front of the group, but he made no move forward. Anna looked past him and inside.

It was a large, square space. A wide, oval rug made of rich blue fabric covered the center of the open area in front of them. Past that stood a sprawling table in a half circle where seven people sat. Above the rug hung a bright, sparkling mage light chandelier. The glass at the top of the chandelier was built to resemble sea birds. Behind the half-circular table were various smaller tables with more people. Everyone was facing the open doors. Behind them all was a wall of windows that rose to the high ceiling and looked out onto the ocean in the distance.

"Captain Heiser," the woman standing at the center of the half-circular table greeted, "Welcome! Please come forward with your team." Lady Gratadia stood with her left hand standing on its fingertips on the table in front of her. She wore a dark linen dress and vest with shining gold buttons, under which was a gold silk shirt with billowy sleeves and ruffles at the end. Her warm brown eyes passed over the group observantly and her dark brown hair was pulled back out of her face.

The captain gave a respectful bow of his head in reply before walking forward. Anna and the others followed. They stopped in the center of the oval rug.

"Please," she spoke again, "introduce yourselves. We didn't all have time to chat during the party."

It was then that Anna spotted Irene. The mage sat at a table directly behind Lady Gratadia, in a satin lavender dress. When their eyes met, Irene smiled at Anna, who smiled back.

"Thank you, Lady Gratadia." The captain spoke directly to her, and then shifted to address everyone at the frontmost table. "I am Captain Nathaniel Heiser of Luminport." He spread an arm and pointed an open hand at Will. "This is Will Gray of Kastarus, one of our scouts. Next is Merry Macgill, our lead fighter from Altumberg. Clara and Callum Phaon, our healers from Amgen. Pyran Taggert, another fighter, and Anna Hale, another scout, both from Hillcrest. Then Ros Dixon, a fighter from Lakoona. Finally, our mage, Ben Day from Eysa."

As the captain introduced the team, Anna looked at each of the people at the table in front of her. At the leftmost seat was Lady Cate. She was short and tan-skinned with intricate braids woven through her dark hair, pulling it out of her face before they cascaded down her shoulders. Her gray dress was trimmed in gold braids, and a golden knot pendant hung at her chest. For the first time, Anna had a direct view of her. Her nose reminded Anna of the twins' noses.

Next was Lord Woulfe in a maroon jacket with silvery trim. His double chin was pronounced as he looked out from under his brow at the group assembled before him. His hands rested one on top of the other on top of his belly. His eyes glanced over her casually, as if she was a lamp in the corner of the room.

Following Woulfe was a half-elven man in exquisite mages' robes, Lord Inwood. He looked about sixty, though Anna still wasn't sure how half-elves aged. His robes were purple with pale blue and silver accents. He had long, straight white hair and a long, white mustache and beard. He sat with a straight back, and his fingers were steepled against each other at his chest. His green eyes inspected the group, but his expression gave nothing away.

On the other side of Lady Gratadia sat an older human man, Lord Moineau. His bright blue eyes matched his blue linen button-down shirt. His face was set into an even expression as he looked over the group in front of him. Next was Lord Finke. Gray peeked through his hair here and there as it wove together with his beard in an intricate pattern of braids within braids. His hazel eyes looked out over everyone with an openness that the others were lacking.

Finally, at the rightmost seat of the table was Lady Dato. Her blonde hair was pulled up into a large, smooth bun and her light brown eyes looked through a pair of wire-rimmed glasses. She wore a navy blue vest with a double row of bright gold buttons, a sharp pressed collar, and a gold chain that was pinned to her vest and then disappeared into a breast pocket. She wore a pale blue shirt underneath in a similar style to Gratadia's.

"It's an honor to meet all of you," Lady Gratadia said. "I'm sure you're aware of the mandate of this mission, but it's time we paint the full picture."

Anna monitored Lord Woulfe as Lady Gratadia spoke. He looked bored. He glanced around the people gathered as if waiting for someone to hurry the meeting along or end it. When his eyes met hers, they passed just as quickly to the next person. His nonchalance infuriated her, as she clenched her jaw and pushed her fingernails into her palms.

Lady Gratadia continued, "In recent months, there have been a handful of credible Vasbrute sightings in the forest outside of Dore. I'm sure we're all well aware that this directly violates the treaty."

Lord Woulfe's hand moved to lie on the table, a visible sign he was inserting himself into the conversation. "There was a murder," he interjected as the lady paused briefly.

Lady Gratadia sighed, her eyes closing in quiet annoyance as her hand moved from the table to press flat against her lower ribs. When her eyes opened, she was again the picture of politeness. "Lord Woulfe is partially correct. A man died from a serious injury during a run-in with the Vassians, one Bill Blakely. He owned a small orchard outside of Dore. The circumstances of how this occurred have not yet been determined.

"We are tasking all of you to investigate *why* the Vassians are breaking the treaty. If you can, keep yourselves and your intentions hidden from them. We're unsure of their state of mind or their numbers. Start at the Blakely's orchard, and then follow their trail into the forest. Then, depending on what you find, we can assess our path forward. That is, if a show of military force is necessary."

Woulfe grunted, and Lord Inwood spoke in a smooth voice, "I'd say that a reminder of who they are up against is past due. It is clear they think they can gallivant across the wall and do as they please."

"Hear, hear," Lord Woulfe agreed enthusiastically, with a couple of knocks on the table of his fist.

"We understand your concern, Lord Inwood," Lady Gratadia told the half-elf. "However, it is imperative that we investigate before we act, and I would hope to receive the same from them were the situation reversed. The Vassians have adhered to the treaty laws for centuries. There is surely a reason for their breaking them now."

"Ah, yes." A malicious smile formed on Lord Woulfe's mouth. "I'm sure they were being *quite* reasonable when they killed your countryman."

Lady Gratadia ignored Woulfe's comment, instead staring ahead at the people in front of her with a slight frown on her face.

"It may not be a reason we *like*, Lord Woulfe," Lady Dato took a turn to speak, "but we can't judge until we've got the full story. We can't incite wars based on misunderstandings."

Lord Woulfe harrumphed and settled his hands onto his belly again.

Lady Gratadia spoke to the captain and his team, "I am sure you're all beginning to understand how *delicate* the situation is. I cannot offer any advice or warning as to the state of the Vassians currently present north of the wall except to say that you should be cautious, as I'm sure you're already prepared to be.

"As for what I know, you will sail tomorrow morning. You'll stay a night in Osborough, before stopping in Dore. Supplies for your journey into the forest will be ready for you there. From then on, it is up to you, but know that if we do not receive word after two weeks of your arrival to Dore, we will need to take more… *extreme* measures, so we ask that you send word by then. Ben Day," she addressed the mage, "Irene has told me that the two of you can communicate rapidly over great distances."

"Yes, Lady," Ben flushed as she put him on the spot. "Similar to teleportation circles, it is possible, with the right resources, to send letters across space rather than through it. In this way, I could—"

Ben's ramble was cut off as Lady Gratadia offered him a gracious smile and said, "Thank you. You will be supplied with whatever you need for this endeavor. Time is of the utmost value in this, and so we encourage these otherwise extraneous magics. I've set up a time for you to meet with Irene this afternoon to create a list of supplies you need to be prepared for tomorrow. If you think of anything else, any other enchantments or conjurings you would find helpful, don't hesitate to add the necessary items to that list."

Ben's eyes were as big as saucers. "Yes, Lady. Thank you."

She nodded respectfully in reply and turned back to the captain. "I know we've put together a list already, but you will go through it again with my counselor Veronica, to ensure that nothing is missing and that you are ready for your departure."

The captain nodded in response. Lady Gratadia took a deep breath in and let it out as she looked over at the entire group in front of her again. Her brown eyes shone with sincerity as she said, "I could not imagine a more difficult task than what lies before you. Not only are you stepping into an unknown climate, you are being asked to do so discreetly. There are an abundance of lines that only you can decide in the moment to keep or to cross. The path this assemblage takes rests solely on the outcomes *you* provide. Know that our faith in you travels with you. May your journey be swift, your instincts keen, and your blades sharp, should it come to it."

Lady Cate spoke up, "May Sollis light your path, Noctis grant you rest each night, Viterra give you strength, and Morterra hold close your fate. Well-

Mother's blessings upon all of you."

Anna noticed Lord Woulfe roll his eyes at her prayer.

"Thank you, Lady Cate." The captain bowed his head respectfully.

"May we see you all safely back again," Lady Gratadia said, as a farewell.

"Thank you." The captain bowed, and the others followed suit. Anna gave a quick, awkward curtsy before the messenger reappeared to lead them out again.

ANNA SPENT THE AFTERNOON WORKING ON ONE LAST LETTER TO HER mother before they left, something she had procrastinated doing for days. She wasn't allowed to discuss the mission, and she didn't want to put her mother in any danger, so she kept the message brief and vague.

Mom,

We leave tomorrow. I can't tell you much, but what we'll be doing is dangerous. I trust the people I'm with. If things work out, we'll all be all right.

Don't forget that when you're updating the books, you need to account for the cost of materials. I know sometimes you forget that. Also, if you need help with gathering, I know Alvin is always looking for a way to make a little money. If you throw him a couple of coins, he'll get you what you need. If the house becomes too expensive to maintain, or if you get lonely, talk to Jo. He'd let you move into the Inn and run your shop from there, as much as he grumbles about your overcomplicated baking.

I love you. After this, I'm coming home.

Lynnie

30

THEY SET OUT THE NEXT MORNING, AFTER THE HORN. ANNA HAD PACKED almost everything the night before, so she only needed to put on her gear and throw in what little was left.

Everyone met in the hall, as had become habit, but the mood was serious. They were quiet, except for quick greetings as each person joined them. Ros was the last in the hall. A large, deep blue-stained leather pack hung off their shoulder. As they looked around, Merry greeted them with a *Good morning*, and the others looked at each other anxiously.

"Come now," Ros said, looking around at everyone after they shut their door. "We're getting to the *fun* bit. We finally get to go and *do*! Let's lose all the worry. It'll do us no good."

"Right." Merry nodded before taking a deep, cleansing breath and putting on a smile. "Let's show the Council that we won't fail that easily!"

A corner of Ros' lips lifted at Merry's attempt at reassurance, though it didn't seem to do much for the rest of the team. "That's the spirit! Besides, even if we are to meet our end, we'll be spending a day on the waves and two nights at well-kept taverns on the country's coin. Surely that is something to look forward to."

"That's enough for me," Will spoke up, surprising everyone. His hands were on his hips, and he shrugged as everyone turned to him. "What? As much ale as I want each night doesn't sound so bad."

"It's a positive," Cal agreed reluctantly.

"The best meals available along the coast," added Pyran. "Doesn't sound like a bad deal."

"It's the days on horses I'm dreading the most," said Clara. "Each of us staring at the horse's ass in front of us for hours on end."

That got a laugh out of most of them.

"Hey, Ben," Ros called out to him, "Is there any magic to improve the smell of a horse's rear end?"

"Nothing sustainable for days," Ben answered. "You would be better off tying a bunch of roses to their tails."

"That would be a strange parade," Anna said.

"And a poor use of roses," Clara added.

As everyone chuckled, they made their way down to the first floor and out of the Barracks. They walked across town, their nervous energy now focused on telling travel jokes. The city passed by quickly, and soon they found themselves at the docks on the east side of town, an area Anna had never seen.

She had heard the gulls and tasted the salt in the air in other, quieter parts of the city, but here, it was like she was stepping into another world. A breeze rolled off the water, carrying the briny smell of the ocean as it tugged at the strands of hair that had loosened themselves from her braid.

The sound of organized chaos filled her ears as people rushed about back and forth, calling out to crewmates or haggling over shipping costs, and the waves tumbled against the shore, washing over and crashing through all other noise. The call of a gull cut high through everything as they moved about. The white birds dotted the docks like wildflowers in a grove. Some flew right overhead, checking the newcomers for food or danger. Many walked along the streets or perched on piles of cargo. Anna watched one bird waddle by, joining the traffic that moved along in front of them.

A wide walkway moved traffic along the shore and butted up to a boardwalk that split like limbs into docks, reaching out over the water. Anna's eyes followed from the planks in front of her out over the sand, and eventually, on the ships docked in the distance.

"Oy!" an old man's voice called from nearby. A man with white hair and a short, scraggly red beard peppered with white squinted through the sunlight at the group, which deepened the crow's feet around his eyes. An array of other, lighter wrinkles spread over his suntanned skin. He wore a simple shirt and pants with sturdy boots. "In all that armor, you must be the crew the Council wants sending to Osborough. I's told to meet you here."

"That's us! Merry MacGill, nice to meet you!" She held out her hand for him to shake.

He took it and gave a firm wag before releasing it and thumbing to himself, "Name's Torgeir. Follow me. I'll get the rest of your names as we go." He turned and started walking down the boardwalk. He had a bit of a limp on his left side. Everyone followed as he bobbed through the crowd.

Torgeir led them around a maze of cargo and down to one of the longer docks. He stopped near the end of it, in front of one of the bigger ships. Anna stared up at it with the same wonder she'd had when she stared up at the castle in Kastarus for the first time.

It was a bigger ship than she had ever seen outside of a line illustration in her schoolbooks. A long ramp led the people loading it up and on board. Three large sails were gathered up onto their masts, waiting to be released to pull the ship out to sea. The masts, which must have been thirty feet high, were topped with little green flags. A carving of a white horse with a golden horn in its forehead rose out of the front of the ship. Its long mane flowed behind it as it leaped forward with its front hooves in the air. The ship bobbed with the waves, like a giant, upside-down house that was drowning.

Anna froze as she realized she'd be spending the day on board this swaying monstrosity.

"Your names now, please," Torgeir said as he stopped to the side of the ramp, "so's I can properly introduce you all."

Merry looked at Will standing next to her.

"Will Grey," he said plainly.

"I'm Clara Phaon," the first twin offered, "and this is Callum Phaon, of Delphia. Nice to meet you."

"Ros Dixon," Ros said with a nod of their head.

Pyran, who was also staring wide-eyed at the ship, took an elbow to the ribs from Ros when he didn't respond. "Pyran Taggert," he said quickly, before looking up at the ship again.

"Bennett Day," Ben said with a smile.

"Anna Hale," Anna responded lastly. Her hands fisted at her sides, and her nails were digging into her palms nervously. She tried to focus on Torgeir, but the ship's movement behind him made that difficult.

"Very good," Torgeir grinned. He opened his mouth to speak again, but was cut off as Captain Heiser walked over. His butler walked with him, carrying his bag.

"Thank you. That'll be far enough. I can take it from here."

The butler handed over the bag, and then said, "I wish you luck, sir."

"Well, thank you. I'm looking forward to another of your marvelous meals when I return."

"Certainly." The butler bowed before walking off the way he had come.

The captain turned, noticed everyone arranged in front of Torgeir, and introduced himself. "I am Captain Nathaniel Heiser." A realization came across his face, and he quickly added, "Not a ship captain, of course, a military captain."

"Hello, sir," Torgeir greeted with a businesslike nod. He turned back to the group and swept an arm out toward the ship behind him. His eyes lit up. "This is our lady, the *Empress.* She's smooth and swift. Held by her, we'll reach Osborough by the high moon." A romantic sigh left his lungs. "As I said, I am Torgeir, the first mate. Captain Crawford will likely introduce herself once you're all on board. They should be finished loading the heavy cargo in a moment, then we'll get you settled. Wait here, if you would."

The older man turned and made his way up the ramp with more energy than they had seen from him so far.

Captain Heiser turned to the group with a smile on his face. "Look at all of you, bright-eyed and bushy-tailed. Good morning."

"Good morning, captain," Merry greeted. "It's a great day for traveling."

"Indeed, it is." His eyes crinkled with his smile. He glanced at the blue sky, then turned back to the group. "I wasn't expecting you all to be so eager, to be frank."

"Of course we are eager," Ros told him. "Our moment has finally arrived—our catalyst to whatever our future may be. We wish to meet it."

"Well said," the captain agreed. "I hope that eagerness lasts. We have a long trip ahead before we can truly begin."

He leaned over toward his luggage, opened the lid, and pulled out a handful of scrolls. "These are Writs of Duty. There is one for each of you. I don't expect to use them, but if we are asked to show proof of our employment, that is what we'll need." He handed them out to each of them. "I have the coin we'll be using, and we'll get to keep whatever we don't spend, divided evenly between us, so perhaps we can try to be more frugal on the trip back."

The unspoken words, *if there is a trip back*, seemed to hang in the air. The captain cleared his throat. "I hope some of you know some traveling games, or these two days are going to pass painfully slowly."

"I've got a few," Merry said cheerfully. "It used to take ages to ride the cart into town from the farm, so me and my siblings had to do *something.*"

"Great," Will teased. "We're going to spend three days playing *I Spy.*" He looked out at the water and added, "And there won't be anything but waves to look at today."

Torgeir returned, coming down the ramp with his unusual gait. "We are ready for you now," he called, and he waved a hand to motion for them to join him.

Anna held the straps of her bag tightly and gritted her teeth as she followed the others.

Pyran fell into step beside her and eyed her grip. "You doing okay?"

"Mm-hmm," Anna nodded stiffly, staring at Ben's back as she followed him closely and tried to avoid looking at the ship.

"You sure?" Pyran asked.

Anna took another step and her foot landed on the ramp, which bounced slightly from the others walking on it, swaying a little with the ship. A small squeak escaped her and she stopped.

Pyran sighed, then said quietly, "It's my first time on a big ship, too. Here." He held out an arm for her to take.

Anna pursed her lips and looked at Pyran. She decided she was less worried about looking silly than she was about falling off the ramp and into the blue water below. She put an arm through his and held on tight. They took the next step onto the ramp together, and Anna squeaked again as she left the stability of the dock. Her grip on Pyran's arm tightened, and Pyran put his free hand over hers, holding tight. Anna looked over and found his face flushing and eyes wide. *He's just as scared as I am.*

"You big dummy," Anna said under her breath.

"What?" Pyran turned to her.

She clenched her jaw and glared at the end of the ramp. "Just hold on, okay?" Then she took a deep breath in.

"All ri—"

Anna stormed forward, refusing to look down or to the side or anywhere but the very edge of the ramp. Pyran's steps joined hers as she dragged him forward. Her feet landed on the deck, and then Pyran's. She didn't let go, but she let her arm relax a little. She released the lungful of air she had taken at the other end of the ramp. Pyran chuckled, then let out a full laugh. He let Anna keep holding his arm, but let go with his other hand.

He looked over at Anna. "I thought you were scared."

"You were, too," Anna told him. The ship rocked and she stepped one of her feet back to better stabilize herself as her eyes widened. When she recovered, she told him, "I didn't want to drag it out."

"This way!" Torgeir called from further down the deck of the ship.

Anna, stance wide and solid, looked around. There was one main level of the deck of the ship, which she was standing on now. At the back, there was one more, taller level. Several doors lined the front wall of that upper level, one on each side that went below deck, and a large set of double doors that led straight through. Stairs on each of the far sides led to the upper deck, where the rearmost mast climbed out of the ship.

Anna noticed the wheel of the ship at the front railing of the upper level. A woman stood there, conversing with several crew members. She was striking in a long, blue coat that glimmered with brass buttons and polished black boots. She had tanned skin and brown hair cropped at her neck. Her thin, pointed nose and brows made her serious expression even more severe.

Torgeir led the group through a side door and down to the lower level. A tight hallway brought them to a moderately sized room with four beds stacked two on each side.

"Seeings as you're not with us for a full night, we've set you up here. There are beds for those that would like a nap, and anyone is welcome on deck so long as you don't get in the way."

Everyone shuffled through the door to set down their things. As Clara squeezed into the space, she gave a little, disapproving hum. Cal held to a bed frame as though the ship would turn completely sideways at any moment.

When everyone's bags were settled, Torgeir said, "Very good. Now I'll take you up to meet Captain Crawford."

He led everyone onto the main deck, then up the stairs to the next level. He walked toward the woman in the blue coat who Anna had noticed earlier. She dismissed the person she'd been talking to as she saw the group approaching and turned to face them with a polite grin, her posture straight and hands clasped behind her.

"Captain,"Torgeir greeted, "this is the group from the Council headed for Osborough."

Her eyes flickered over everyone before reaching Captain Heiser. Her smile reached her eyes as their eyes met.

"As I live and sail," she said. "Is this really Nate Heiser?"

Captain Heiser smiled and chuckled, saying, "I've collected my own title of captain since you've last seen me. I'm more gray than before, but time will do that to a man, though it doesn't seem to have made its mark on you, Ivette."

Anna thought she saw Captain Crawford blush, though her expression remained unchanged. "Still brimming with compliments while on dangerous missions across Telluth, I see." She turned to address the whole group. "I am Captain Ivette Crawford, master of the *Empress*. You may call me Captain Crawford. Our home dock is in Luminport, but we've accepted the Council's contract to transport you through to Osborough as we make our way south. Torgeir has shown you to your quarters, I presume? Good," she said, on confirmation from her mate.

"I apologize that we could not be more accommodating, but the ship is full, and such is the way of things with last-minute requests. You're welcome to enjoy the view on deck as long as you aren't underfoot.

"We expect clear skies through to your destination. It should be smooth sailing, as we are not going far from the coastline. Meals are served from the galley down below. Torgeir will find you when lunch is ready and then dinner. If, while on board, you find the waves upsetting your stomach, as it seems it may be for some of you," she looked pointedly at Cal with a smile, "we ask that you go to the galley and ask for ginger. If the ginger doesn't settle you, try to keep anything that comes up off the boat and into the waves. Any questions?"

When no one responded, she said, "If you think of anything pressing, you can find me in my quarters." She turned to Torgeir. "We're ready for departure. Please prepare the crew."

"Yes, Captain," Torgeir nodded, then turned to Captain Heiser and the team. "I recommend the view from the starboard side as we leave port." He pointed to the side the dock was on, and then he gave a nod and left. The captain had already turned to speak with someone else.

"Come on!" Merry started moving toward the position Torgeir had pointed out. "I want to get a good spot on the railing."

"...I'm going to go find some of that ginger," Cal said, breaking away from the group to go down the stairs.

Clara rolled her eyes at her brother. "He's never liked boats."

As everyone else followed Merry, Ros asked, "How do you know this captain, captain?"

Captain Heiser smiled thoughtfully, then leaned against the railing as he answered, "Do you remember when I talked about the negotiations with the East?"

Ros nodded.

"Captain Crawford was my transport. She, like me, was out to prove herself to her peers and the Council. Now, from my understanding, her ship is the most trusted on the Eastern coast."

"Come on, captain," Merry urged. "That was more than a friendly greeting."

The captain shook his head. "It was a long time ago. I'll let the past stay in the past."

"Boring," Merry teased as she joined him at the railing.

The boat suddenly jolted, and Anna grabbed for the railing.

"We're taking off!" Clara said excitedly, a bright smile spreading across her face as she moved to get a better view off the side of the ship. "This is my favorite part."

The crew bustled around the ship with ropes and chains and tools that Anna didn't recognize. She was caught between watching them and watching the boat slip away from the dock. Long oars emerged from the side of the ship closer to the waterline. They dove in unison and pushed the ship through the water.

When the dock was a good distance away, there was a shout from Captain Crawford. Each sail fell open, one at a time, with a great rustle of fabric. As they unfurled, they revealed their colors. Wide stripes of yellow and blue filled with air and pulled the ship forward into the wind. Now that the ship was in motion, it seemed to push back at the waves rather than letting them roll against it.

The people on the dock became smaller and smaller, until they were indistinguishable in the distance. Now they were slicing through the waves as if they weren't there.

Anna let herself relax a little more.

"I realize now that I should have asked, do any of you have experience with sailing?" Captain Heiser said.

"Callum and I take ships when we travel to Amgen, or on the rare occasion to Yurrport or Eysa," Clara said casually. "Callum will most likely spend the day in bed in our quarters. The waves don't...agree with him."

"Hmm," Ben hummed thoughtfully, "Your healing abilities don't offer some kind of mechanism to ease the sea sickness?"

"On shorter trips, he can calm most of it, but long trips like this would require a lot of energy, so he will usually just put himself to sleep."

"And you don't get this sea sickness?" Ros asked her.

Clara smiled. "No, I've never felt that way. I enjoy being out on the water."

"Lake Lakoona is large enough for some tall ships," Ros said. "I have been on a few of them, but this is my first time on the sea."

"Like Clara, I've sailed from Eysa along the west coast," Ben said.

"Have you ever been to Velles?" Clara asked excitedly after he spoke up.

Ben's eyebrows rose at her enthusiasm. "No, I haven't."

"Damn," she let out. "I've heard it's like paradise, but I've never been allowed to go."

"I should think not," Ben told her.

She scoffed.

"What?" Anna asked. "Why shouldn't you go to Velles?"

"The islands of Velles are where most of the solim in Telluth comes from," the captain explained with a frown. "As beautiful as the islands are, it is a very dangerous place."

Anna's mind returned her to the cathedral in Wallset and the people being cared for, sick from their withdrawals from the drug. Even if they could make it to sobriety, they almost always went right back to solim. They'd show up in a few months or weeks, sunburnt all over again. Anna's mother had taught her about addiction from a young age, when she'd help deliver leftovers to the Creed. She pitied the people she saw, painfully recovering, and had vowed to never touch the stuff.

"Well, I've never sailed," Pyran said, bringing the topic of discussion back around, "but I'm sure that's obvious."

"I apologize," the captain sighed, "I could have done more to prepare you."

Pyran shrugged. "I'm getting used to it."

"And how are you doing, Anna?" Captain Heiser asked her.

"I'm all right," she answered, still holding the railing. "It's better now that we're moving."

The captain nodded. "Any queasiness?"

"No," Anna said with a little relief in her voice. "Thank the Mother. Just working on my balance."

"I didn't know you could get seasick," Merry said. "This is my first time on a boat, but I feel fine."

"It's your great constitution," Will told her. "The same reason you can drink me under the table."

"Will, you haven't sailed before, have you?" Merry asked him.

He shook his head, his dark eyes squinting in the sunlight. "It's not so bad." He looked as confident as if her were still standing on the dock, easily following the sway of the ship.

Anna was jealous.

She turned back to the coast and found Kastarus disappearing. The tall peaks of the city and its crowning castle were fading into the horizon. The ship moved south now, the green coastline a distant marker off this side of the ship.

"Oh, Anna!" Clara took hold of her arm and pointed with her other hand. "Look at the dolphins!"

Anna followed the shorter woman's finger down the side of the ship toward its rear, where there were fins weaving in and out of the waves around the ship's wake.

"They like to chase the ships and jump out of the water," Clara told her. "They're smooth and gray like they're made of sea glass, with a fin on their back that you'll see come out of the water first." Her free hand reached for Pyran's arm on her other side, and she said, "You too, Pyran! Look!"

Pyran let her pull him to the railing and leaned over it. His eyes caught the movement in the water, and he watched closely.

"Me, too," Merry said, making her way back to the railing and leaning over the edge.

"I'd like to see these dolphins," Ros agreed.

"I'm going to get my book," Ben said. "I've seen my fair share of dolphins."

"Boring!" Clara and Merry said at the same time, before breaking into laughter.

Anna gasped as one dolphin leaped out of the water and over the wake of the ship.

Will appeared next to Merry, drawn in like everyone else. They all watched the creatures play in the water for a moment, a few more of them taking a turn to jump out of the waves. The captain watched them all with a grin on his face. Then Will stepped back, saying, "I'm going to find something to drink."

Merry picked her head up from where she was leaning over the railing to tell him, "Would you grab one for me?"

"Sure," Will waved a hand in the air as he walked away.

Anna was mesmerized by the creatures in the water. They made some kind of squeaking noise, and Clara giggled. She wasn't sure how much time had passed before Will returned. He handed one cold mug to Merry, who shifted over so that Will could fit into the space between herself and Pyran.

The sun was higher in the sky when the dolphins finally split away from the ship. Anna realized the animals had distracted her so well that the tension from being on a big, floating compilation of wood out on the ocean had faded. She noticed that the crew on deck had settled in as well, and the ship was steadily moving forward with full sails.

While she found the open water and almost cloudless sky nerve-racking, she was enjoying the sea breeze and the sunshine.

"We'll probably see more before we make land in Osborough, though they'll be hard to see in the dark," Clara said, stepping away from the railing. "I'm going to go check on Callum."

Anna looked at Pyran and found that he had calmed down as well. He was leaning casually against the railing of the ship and grinning at the waves. Briefly, she forgot where she was and what she was really doing here. For the moment, she was just a young woman experiencing a beautiful day on the ocean for the first time.

Pyran turned and noticed her looking at him. "What?"

"Hm?" Anna hummed in response as she pulled out of her own head. After processing the question, she replied, "Oh, nothing. Just…thinking about how nice this is. I didn't think it would be like this."

"Ah, yes," the captain grinned from his place at the railing. "I've found there is a rule when it comes to any journey. There will always be at least some small part you find beautiful." He looked around the ship briefly, then said, "Speaking of which, excuse me." He stood up from the railing and walked away.

Merry grunted a laugh. "Never seen the captain like that. Not while any of us are around, anyway."

"He doesn't want to bed any of us," Will said in his flat, wry tone.

Ros eyed Will with a tilt of their head, asking, "You do not find Captain Crawford attractive?"

Surprised by the question, Will's head pulled back on his neck and Anna could see the tips of his ears turning pink. "Well, I… sure, but—"

Ros cut him off with a shrug and said, "Her physicality, combined with their shared history, would make many interested in bedding. It's a natural progression, one I'm sure you are not above."

Anna, seeing Will struggling, tried to help him out. "I think Will was just pointing out that it may not have much to do with affection. Anyway, it's not exactly appropriate while we're actively on a mission."

"Yes, thank you," Will nodded in relief.

"Appropriate," Ros scoffed and rolled their eyes. "Why is this not appropriate?"

"It could be distracting," Pyran offered with a half-shrug.

Ros shook their head, a small grin forming on their lips. "What work is to be done now? We sit and wait for this ship to deliver us south. We will all need distractions by the end of the day."

Anna looked at Pyran, Will, and Merry, who all seemed to accept Ros' logic. She found she couldn't argue against it, either.

Merry started laughing at Will's thoughtful expression. "Since we're all looking for distractions, who wants to play cards?"

There was a unanimous agreement, and they all joined her in finding a good place to play. Anna found herself next to Will as they followed behind. He said under his breath to her, "One of these days, I'll get Ros to understand that I'm usually joking."

Anna laughed. "I think it's your tone. Ros is too much of a straight-talker to understand that your *serious* tone is anything but."

"At least you understand me," he sighed theatrically, and then said more sincerely, "Even Pyran has trouble with it. The other day, I had him halfway through explaining how someone might throw a greatsword before he realized I was being sarcastic."

Anna laughed again. "That's just how he is. Pyran could talk swords until an elf babe gets wrinkles."

Will chuckled.

The group found a spot in the rear corner of the upper deck. Merry found a low table and carried it over before anyone could tell her she should ask the crew before rearranging the furniture. It was only after they had all settled on the deck around it that she told them she'd had to remove an assortment of boating equipment from its top before she claimed it.

When Pyran grunted his surprise and disapproval, she said, "What? I left it all there where it's supposed to be. Would you rather I brought it all with me?"

Though it was usually better to play cards with a group of four than five, their larger group size worked in Anna's favor, as she was unfamiliar with most of the games that Merry and the others knew. Anna got the feeling that the simple games she played with her mother after dinner would be childish to those that played cards frequently.

Anna sighed in annoyance after one particularly long round of Jack and tossed her cards onto the table. She leaned back on the heels of her hands.

Merry laughed at her, tossing her own cards on the table too.

"It's just that those aren't even the same suit!" Anna complained, gesturing a hand angrily at the little pile of jacks they had each thrown in.

"That is why it's called Jacks," Ros told her. "The jacks overrule the other cards."

"Okay, okay," Anna leaned forward again. "Let's try again."

"Here," Will walked around the table from his spot at the railing to take a seat near her. "I'll help you. Anna Hale is going to learn how to play Jacks today or my ears aren't pointed." He positioned himself next to and slightly behind her.

Pyran dealt the cards with a sigh, obviously annoyed at playing the same game over and over. Anna picked up her cards and fanned them in front of her so that Will could see.

She felt him lean in to get a good look, and then he said quietly by her ear, "Ah, you've gotten a lucky hand." He pointed at the two jacks she was holding. "If the two of us can't win this one, there's no hope for you."

Anna smelled leather and sandalwood again. She felt heat rise to her cheeks and ears. She told herself it was from his proximity, but there was a flutter in her chest that she did her best to ignore. "I've got little hope by myself, regardless of what's in my hand," she replied. "Let's see what you can do."

The game started with Ros, who threw in a lower card. Merry followed with a queen of the same suit. Anna knew that right now, Merry was winning, but also that Ros had most likely played her low card to draw out any cards of that suit so that they might win a hand later with a higher card.

"You have options here," Will said in a low voice. "You can play your king and hope Pyran doesn't have the ace, or you can toss a jack and ensure you win the round."

Anna stared at her cards, then at Pyran. After a moment, his blue eyes rolled and he said, "Play a card!"

Anna pursed her lips, and then said, "This is what I don't understand. Shouldn't I just play the best card?"

"If you do," Will replied, "you might lose the chance to take a hand later in the game."

Anna huffed. She grabbed her king and threw it on the table.

Pyran grinned, obviously pleased, and set his ace down slowly while staring at Anna. "All that deliberation and you still came out at a loss."

Anna gave Pyran's leg a shove.

"Calm down, children," Ros said, though the half smile on their lips belied their amusement. "No need for jabs."

Pyran started the next round with a king of a different suit. Ros followed with a queen of the same suit.

"Ros must have no jacks, or they would have played one to win the round," Will told her.

Merry laid a jack of a different suit. Currently, the hand was hers.

Anna put her fingers on the jack of the suit Pyran had laid and waited to see what Will would say. He nodded, his head still close to hers. Anna laid the card down with a triumphant grin, and then drew the hand into a small pile in front of her to count it as hers.

"Well done." Anna could hear the grin in Will's voice. "If you had played that jack earlier, you would've lost that hand."

"True," Anna said, "but I would have won the first one."

"The game is all about calculated risk," Will told her. "Sometimes the highest risks pay off, sometimes the lowest risks don't."

Anna started the next round with a king. The others were forced to match suit, and so Pyran laid a queen, Ros laid a nine, and Merry played an ace. Merry started the next hand with another ace.

"Mother," Will said, "Merry got a fine hand as well."

Anna laid her last jack, hoping to take the hand. Pyran scoffed and laid a ten. Ros sighed and laid a king. Merry played a ten.

With two hands for Anna, one for Pyran, and one for Merry, what Anna needed to win was to either take this hand or give it to Ros. She laid the only card she had left, a hopeless ten. Pyran played off-suit with a grumble. Ros smiled and played an on-suit queen. Merry laid a nine.

"And that's one game of Jacks to Anna," Will said, leaning back. He clapped a hand against her shoulder proudly and stood up.

"Could we play again?" Anna said, gathering up the cards. "I think I'm catching on."

"We've played Jacks seven times," Pyran groaned. "Let's play a different game."

"You lot know how to play Anchor?" A member of the crew joined the conversation, stepping over to see the cards on the table.

"Sure!" Merry grinned.

"I do," Ros agreed.

"What d'ya say we put a little money down?" another crew member joined his friend with a grin on his face. Where the first man was tall and thin, the second man was of average height and fairly muscular build. They both had dark hair and a shadow of stubble on their faces.

"I'm out," Pyran said, moving away from the table before standing up.

"I don't even know how to play," Anna said, rising to stand too.

Will stood leaning against the railing behind Merry, his arms and ankles crossed. He watched the crew members with a skeptical eyebrow raised. Anna made her way around the table to lean next to him, and then Pyran joined her on the other side.

"Name's Skinnerd," the tall man stepped forward and held a hand out to shake. Merry and Ros each took it in turn. "That there's Sam." He thumbed back at his friend.

Sam gave Ros and Merry a nod.

"Are you, like, a strong-woman?" Skinnerd asked Merry, looking her over as he took the open seat next to her.

Merry grinned. "Strength is certainly one of my strongest features, although…" She lifted her hand-less arm and waved it with a smile.

Both of the men's eyebrows shot up.

"How'd a lady like you lose a hand?" Sam asked, taking the open spot between his friend and Ros.

Merry jumped into her story, and Ros gathered up the cards to shuffle. Will smirked as he watched his friend tell her favorite tale.

"A *shovel?*" Skinnerd asked, looking at his friend skeptically. "No shovel

I've ever used has had an edge capable of cutting into a bear."

"You've never worked on a MacGill farm," Merry said. "We keep our spades sharp."

"Speaking of spades..." Ros cut in, having had enough of Merry's tale. "Shall we?" They shuffled the cards on the table with a flourish before they began dealing them out.

"So, what do we say?" Sam looked around the table. "Five gold apiece. Winner takes the pot?"

"Sounds reasonable," Ros said.

"I'm in." Merry grinned, refocusing her energy on the cards.

"All right," Skinnerd leaned forward and started gathering his hand.

Sam set his handful of coins next to him on the table, and the others did the same. The game began, and Anna watched with no understanding of what the rules were or what the goal was. It was like Jacks in that each person took a turn around the table playing a card, and whoever won that hand got to go first for the next hand.

She watched them track points as they finished each hand, then prepare for the next. The high cards seemed to win each hand, unless someone laid an ace, which then completely changed the rules. Anna wasn't sure, but she thought it might be reversing the value of the cards. With each hand its own round, if someone laid an ace, they couldn't win. Aces didn't seem to be worth any actual points.

The game continued. Ros played an ace, then Merry triumphantly played a second one. Merry won the hand. *So the first ace changes the rules, then the next ace is worth points?*

Merry won the game, mostly because of her hand with the second ace. She tried to push the money back to everyone, claiming she was just having fun, but they insisted.

"Let's raise the stakes this time," Sam urged. "Doubles?"

Ros rolled their eyes, but their grin gave away that they weren't truly bothered. "Fine." They set ten coins on the table.

Sam did the same, and then Skinnerd.

"You're sure?" Merry asked with a little laugh. When Sam and Skinnerd agreed, she shrugged. "All right." She put her coins on the table, half of the pot she had just won.

"Do you know how to play Anchors?" Anna asked Pyran.

"No, not really," Pyran said. "I tried to learn once, but my friend wasn't very good at explaining."

"Hmm," Anna hummed in dissatisfaction, then turned to Will. "What about you? Do you know how to play?"

Will nodded, watching the game closely as it started. He didn't voice any explanations, so Anna let it drop with a sigh and turned to watch the game.

The game started strongly in Skinnerd's favor before it swung in Ros' direction. As they were in the middle of it, Anna watched their faces, trying to discern what was going on. As the hand was moving around the table, Anna saw Skinnerd play an ace. She watched Sam laugh and tease his friend. His hand with the cards swung down and then back up, but Anna thought she saw extra movement in between, under the table. He happily played a second ace and the hand was his. As he pulled his arm back, Anna noticed a bit of white peeking out from in his sleeve.

"That was lucky," Skinnerd said. "That was the last ace!"

"Right!" Sam grinned.

Ros frowned.

"Wait, wait." Anna stepped forward and waved a hand in front of her to get their attention. "What's in your sleeve?" she asked Sam.

Sam turned to her in surprise, which he quickly covered with offense. "What do you mean? You don't think I can win a hand?"

Anna crossed her arms and stared at the man with a frown. "There shouldn't be a problem showing us what's up your sleeve if you weren't cheating."

Sam threw his hands up in aggravation. "What? I—"

He was cut off by Ros grabbing his wrist and pulling back his sleeve. Sure enough, a card was stuck to his forearm. "Lying sailor," Ros said, pulling the card free and throwing it on the table. "You stowed that ace from earlier and switched it."

"Sam!" Skinnerd seemed wholly upset. "I've told you about cheating. I won't stand for it. Certainly not with new friends!"

"It's basically a rite of passage with sailors!" Sam argued. "They should know better!"

"We're trying to give sailors a better name, remember?" Skinnerd said, looking disappointed. "Our nice new friends Merry and Ros here were expectin' a fair game. Leave the cheatin' for below deck when the whole table is underhanded agreeably." He turned to Merry and Ros. "I apologize for my friend. Far as I'm concerned..." he stood, clapped his hand down on top of the gold Sam had laid out, and slid it to the middle of the table while his friend protested, "his gold is forfeit, and he won't be playin' another game." He grabbed Sam by the collar, hauled him to his feet, and shoved him away.

Sam sputtered and tried to argue, red in the face.

"Sam," his friend scolded. "Now, that's enough! We're supposed to be makin' friends. This nice lady lost her hand and you've tried to cheat her out of a fair game, too. Go on! I'm sure there's work for you to be gettin' to."

Sam gave up and walked away.

Skinnerd turned around to look at the group. "I apologize. He shouldn't be bothering you again."

"He can have his money back," Merry told him. "We don't need it. I'd feel bad if we took it without winning it."

"Well," Skinnerd sighed, looking down at his friend's coins, "I think he owes the crew a round at the next dock, anyway." He grinned mischievously and pocketed the coins.

"I'll say," Will agreed.

"Anyway," Ros said, clearly ready to move on as they gathered up the cards in front of them. "Who wants to play again?"

"Could you teach me to play?" Anna asked, stepping away from the railing.

"Sure!" Skinnerd smiled. "You'll be the best Anchors player on your team if you stick by me! Here, you sit and I'll sit to the side here, show you what to do."

"We need a fourth, then," Ros said, looking over their shoulder at Will and Pyran.

"I'll play." Will stepped forward and sat in the open spot next to Ros.

Merry dealt the round. When Anna had all her cards, Skinnerd showed her how to organize them in her hands, according to his personal strategy. He was taller than her even as they sat on the deck, so it was easy for him to watch over her shoulder. He guided her card picks with either a shake of his head or by pointing at the card she should play. She won one hand, but the rest went to the others. When the game was over, she felt she understood the rules and could try to navigate the next one on her own.

"Not too bad for a first-timer!" Skinnerd congratulated her with a strong pat on her shoulder, standing up. "Unfortunately, I've got work to do, and I'm going to see that Sam isn't getting into more trouble. Thank you for the game." He nodded his head in a bow before turning on his heel and walking away.

"Interesting fella," Merry said as she waved at him.

"He must get tired of keeping watch on his friend," Ros commented.

"Sounds like he's used to it," Will said with a shrug. "Are we playing again?"

31

Lunch came along quickly after that, and Anna offered to help Clara bring Cal some food. The two of them made their way down the skinny hallway and found him sleeping. Clara gently woke him up, and they sat with him while he ate. He thanked them for thinking of him and then sent them away so that he could return to what he called a self-induced coma. Anna giggled at that as Clara rolled her eyes, and they left the room. Anna offered to return the dishes to the galley, and Clara let her.

When Anna returned to the main deck, she smiled into the bright sunlight. She squinted as she looked around, waiting for her eyes to adjust. She found Ben sitting on a stool in a corner near the front of the captain's quarters. His brow was furrowed as he read, concentrating. The book he held was thick and wide. Anna bent down at the waist so she could get a look at the title without pulling his attention away. It was bound in emerald green cloth with white lettering. *Underman's Guide to Ley Lines*, she read.

"What is a *lee* line?" she thought aloud to herself.

Ben jumped at her question, and the book fell flat in his lap as he looked across it at her with an unamused expression. "It's pronounced *lay*. They're strong currents of magic that flow through the world."

One of Anna's eyebrows rose in curiosity. "Are they like the lights they say you can see in the sky at night in the northern mountains? They say they're magic overflowing from the Well and dancing across the stars."

"Not quite," Ben said, placing a bookmark onto his open page and shutting the book. He leaned forward toward Anna with a gleam in his eyes. "Those are within our own atmosphere. Ley lines are..." He looked at Anna and then his gaze shifted to his hands. He splayed the fingers of his left hand and held it palm up. "You have to think of it as outside of dimension."

"Dimension?" Anna wrinkled her nose.

"Yes, outside of physical space. So, say this is our world. Telluth is somewhere on it."

"I thought the world was a sphere? That looks flat."

He chuckled. "That's right. I'm glad you know that, but, for the purposes of my demonstration, I'll keep it like this and we'll forget about shapes for a moment."

"All right."

"So this is where we are. On a separate plane entirely are the ley lines. They sit in consecutive space with our plane." He splayed the fingers of his right hand and put it on top. "It would be more accurate if they were in the same physical space, but you get the idea."

"Separate planes, in the same space," Anna repeated, brow furrowed like the mage's had been when he was reading.

Ben nodded and lifted his right hand off his left. "The plane the ley lines are on comprises a weave of magical energy that's always moving and changing. The ley lines are like the strongest threads in the weave. A mage uses the weave to craft and power their magic."

"I…see." *At least, I think I do.*

"That's how Will's dagger works, the one you found in that box. It transports its user through planes. It uses the weave to travel, rather than power."

"But necromancers are different, right?"

He nodded, his expression turning serious. "Rather than pulling power from the weave, they reach through it, taking energy from life itself and twisting the weave out of its destined array."

"So the weave is like the fabric of life? Or like a shield, protecting life?"

He grinned, tilting his head from side to side. "Sort of. Don't worry, there are entire courses dedicated to studying the weave at the university. I don't expect you to be an expert now, but that's the basics." He lowered his hands, and the gleam in his eyes fell away. "Those that believe in the gods also believe the weave acts as a sort of barrier between us and them."

"And you?"

"I don't think there's anything but energy beyond the weave. It's just the fabric of the universe." He sighed and picked up his book. "Anyway, Underman believes that ley line convergences allow a mage to do powerful things they would otherwise be unable to achieve. Instead of pulling on one ley line, you could pull on two or even three at a time. There was a better understanding of it all before the War, but much of that knowledge has been lost."

"Hm," Anna hummed thoughtfully. "Is there something powerful you'd like to do?"

"Doesn't everyone have something powerful they'd like to accomplish?" Ben raised an eyebrow, then looked down at the book's pages again. "I missed a lecture by one of Underman's grandsons while we've been training, so I borrowed this book before I left to reacquaint myself with the words from the man himself."

"Such a scholar," Anna wrinkled her nose. "Reading the same stuffy book twice is very much an ink-nosed thing to do."

"Then *ink-nosed* I shall be," Ben said with a grin. He opened the book and began reading again.

Anna sighed and walked away. She found Merry, Ros, Pyran, and Will in the same area where they'd been playing cards, but there was a handful of deck crew with them now. They stood in a tight circle, and Anna couldn't see what they were doing.

"What's going on over here?" Anna asked as she joined the group.

"Anna!" Merry greeted with a smile, turning to let her into the circle. "These sailors are also mages!"

"What, really?" Anna asked, looking around. There were four deckhands across from her, and they all had rope in their hands in various states of tying and untying. Ros had grabbed a bit of rope and was practicing with them and Will was braiding some rope together boredly. Pyran stood next to one of the deckhands and was following along closely, step by step.

"I don't think this is magic," Anna said to Merry. "I think they're just really good at knots."

"But look!" Merry held something up. "They made me this little man out of rope, and he *walks*!" She held up a bundle of rope that was knotted into the shape of a man. He had a small knot for a head, two loops for legs, and his arms were the ends of the rope. Merry tugged on an arm, and the legs wiggled back and forth as the head bobbed up and down.

Anna laughed, saying, "All right, maybe they *are* magic."

They spent the afternoon learning knots from the crew and sharing stories. The sailors talked about legendary creatures they swore they'd seen in the ocean—huge gulls that sang instead of screeched, giant turtles the size of ships, swarms of glowing jellyfish, and sea dragons. Ros shared the legend of the kraken of Lakoona Lake, and how it had been said to have disappeared with the elves. A crewman told the story of traveling upriver to trade with the dwarves. He talked about their massive marble halls and statues the size of mountains.

"I travelled south to trade with the Vasbrute," one of them began. "I saw an entire clan of 'em."

"Trade with the vermin?" one of the other men asked. "Your mind's confused from too much sun, you gaffer."

"What are they like?" Pyran asked, ignoring the skeptic.

"Tall, hulking things," the man said, throwing a wrinkled hand up high to show their size. "Their skin is almost gray, and tough as hardwood. Their teeth are all sharp, like wolves. I've no doubt they could rip a man apart with their bare hands."

"We've heard all of that before," one of the crew said. "Tell us something about them we don't know!"

The man scratched at his white beard thoughtfully. "Well, they wore clothes, full-on like you or me. But they were all bald. You can tell the higher ranks by the gold they wear." He traced rings above his own head to show them, over the top of his hat. "And they know how to follow manners, when they have to." He nodded appreciatively.

"That's it?" the other crew member asked, disappointed.

The older man shrugged. "I was on the ship the whole time. I could only see those that came on board or got close. It was so many years ago."

"Maybe you dreamed it," the skeptical man told him. "Sounds like your imagination to me."

"Bah." The storyteller waved a dismissive hand at his crew mate.

Anna caught Pyran's eye, and the two shared a look of curiosity. Before either of them could ask any questions, Merry proceeded again with her favorite story about her hand. Now it was her turn to entertain the crew. By the time she had exhausted their questions, the sun was hanging much lower in the sky.

As they made their way to the galley for dinner, Pyran commented, "I haven't seen the captain since this morning."

No one responded. Ros' smirk said it all.

EVERYONE GATHERED ON DECK FOR THE SUNSET. EVEN CALLUM MADE HIS way up, though the captain was still missing.

The red sun slipped behind the land to the west, painting everything in warm colors. Anna looked on with a mug of ale in her hand. She took a sip as she watched the dancing orange waves in front of her. She tasted something a little fruity and spicy in the beer. A breeze rolled through, and Anna shivered. Without the sun's bright rays, the open air of the ocean was cool. She heard gulls call in the distance and waves crashing against the boat. Eventually, the only light left was a purple glow on the distant horizon.

"That's enough for me," Cal said, rubbing his sleep-bleary eyes. "Let me know when we dock."

Book still in his hand, Ben said, "I'll follow you down."

Clara sighed and rested her back against the railing to look up at the sky. Anna followed her eyeline and saw all the stars that the sky could hold, the moon hanging in their midst.

"Isn't it amazing?" Clara asked her.

"Yes," was all Anna could say.

Clara hummed happily to herself, then pushed off the railing. "I think I'm going to get in a nap before we have to walk around town in the middle of the night."

"That's not a bad idea," Merry said, and walked away with her.

"And then there were four," Pyran said, to the little group still gathered.

Ros raised their eyebrows. "I think I saw a cask of wine down in the galley."

Pyran perked up at this. "I thought all we were going to get on this ship was ale."

Half of Ros' mouth twitched in a grin. "I don't imagine they want to share, but..."

"You're not suggesting..." Pyran started with a small laugh. "I mean, we're not going to steal it, right?"

Ros rolled their eyes. "I saw some of the crew partaking during dinner. I'm sure they wouldn't mind if we aren't too loud about it. Or do you have trouble being discreet?"

"I can be discreet," Pyran assured them, as they turned to make their way back to the galley. He hurried after them quietly.

Anna took a sip and looked over the rim at the only other person left. Will looked back, his own mug in his hands.

"Not a wine person?" he asked her.

She shrugged. "I've already got a drink. And I like their ale."

"I'm more a *what's available* kind of person myself," he joked, then leaned against the railing.

Anna huffed a small laugh. Another breeze rolled through, and she shivered again, bringing her arms in closer to her body.

"Cold?" Will asked her.

"It's fine." She took another drink, then rubbed her hands up and down her arms. "It's worth it to see the sky like this."

"Mm," Will hummed with a nod and looked at the stars. "There's always been a building in view when I look up."

"Really?" Anna asked, glancing over at him before looking to the sky as well. "There are a couple of clearings near Wallset where you can see almost the whole sky, though you'll still see some branches. Unless you climb the tree." She smiled fondly as she thought of the places her family used to camp in the summer, when she was small. She remembered laying in the cool grass as her dad taught her the constellations. "But it's like the emptiness out here makes it all brighter somehow."

"Maybe it does," Will said thoughtfully.

They stared up silently for a few breaths.

"I, uh," Will started and shifted his feet, "I'm sorry about your dad. Your mom's doing well?"

Anna's grin turned sad. "Yeah. From what I can tell in her letters, she's doing fine, if a little lonely." Hesitantly, she added, "It's been just her and me for so long now."

Will nodded in understanding.

"What about you? I haven't heard you talk about your family. Or anything personal, really."

Will laughed quietly, and then looked at Anna as if deliberating. Finally, he said, "My parents are gone. My dad buggered off before I was born and I lost my mom when I was little, though she was wonderful while I had her."

"Oh." Instinctively, her hand reached forward to touch his arm, "I'm sorry. No wonder you haven't said anything."

Will smiled, and it was so warm and genuine that Anna felt something inside her chest melt a little. Suddenly conscious of her hand on his arm, she pulled it back and put it on the other side of her mug.

"It's all right, I've made peace with it," he said. He watched her pensively. "Would you want to hear about my mom? And then you can tell me about yours."

"Sure."

"She was the human one," he started. "I used to get picked on for my ears, and I'd come running home to her asking her to cut them off so I could look more like her and the other kids. She'd sit me down and brush my hair and tell me she loved my ears. When I asked why, she always said, *because they're yours, and everything about you is perfect.* Silly things a mother says. I knew I was far from perfect, but it worked every time."

Anna smiled. "She sounds lovely. My mom's language was baking, so I got a special treat after a bad day. After we lost my dad, I tried to get her to stop and put the resources towards the shop, but she wouldn't. I think it's the best way she knows to tell me she loves me." Anna took another drink to hide her expression as she remembered the times her mother had attempted to show love in other ways, and she'd pushed her away. "I'm not really one for that kind of thing."

"Right, too much of a rugged woodswoman," Will teased.

Anna rolled her eyes.

"You know, I didn't pin you as someone that fell for the soldier type, but I suppose everyone enjoys feeling protected by a big, strong man like *Pyran*." Will's golden eyes were sharp and bright in the moonlight.

"P-Pyran!?" Anna spat, then broke into laughter. "You think that—?" another bout of laughs cut her question short.

Will's eyebrows rose. "I know you've said you're not matched, but you two always seem to be together, chatting like two of a kind. And I've seen you disappear into each other's rooms."

Anna froze, her face flaring with heat. "What? You've got it all wrong. Pyran is like—like a brother. He's just a friend. I shouldn't be telling you this, because he obviously isn't sharing the information himself, but he has a boyfriend back home."

Will's eyebrows rose into his hairline. "A boyfriend?"

"Yes, and he's the only person in the group I've known for longer than a month, so I think it's only fair if I'm a little chattier with him."

"And those disappearances into each other's rooms?" His eyebrows were still high, though they had fallen from their peak.

Anna shook her head. "We were talking about Commander Lyon, or he was probably helping me..."

"Helping you...?"

Anna huffed a sigh. "Helping me figure out what to wear to the first team dinner."

Will's eyebrows finally fell, and the corner of his mouth lifted into an amused smile. "You needed help picking out an outfit? I thought you looked nice in that green shirt that night."

Anna blinked, "It's Ros' shirt. That's why I had to roll up the sleeves. They were too short."

Will laughed, "I see. So dressing you up is always a group effort, then."

"Oh, stop it," Anna turned so that she was facing the railing. "It must not be hard when all of your options are *black*."

Will laughed again. "Fair point."

Anna smiled despite herself. His laugh something bound tightly in her chest. She felt another breeze, and she itched her head. Much of her hair had fallen out of the braid and into her face from the wind through the day, so she pulled the tie off the end and let her hair down. She shook it out with her free hand and let it fall onto her shoulders, wavy from the tight braid it had been confined to. Her neck, at least, was a little warmer.

"How do you wear your hair down all the time?" she asked Will. "Mine always ends up in my face."

"They say elvish hair has a magic to it that—"

"Okay," she said with a sarcastic laugh, cutting him off. "Never mind."

"What? You don't want to hear about my perfect elvish hair? Probably the one good thing I got from my dad."

Anna rolled her eyes. "You like the hair, but not the ears?"

"Hands down," he said.

"There must be some positive to them. Do you hear better than me?"

He shrugged. "I have good hearing, but I've never tested it."

"And there's more room for jewelry."

"Not really my thing."

Anna hummed thoughtfully. "Cool knives, that's more your thing."

"Right, you're catching on," Will grinned. "You won't see me stabbing with any old kitchen knife."

They heard a door creak open below and then the sound of laughter. They turned toward the noise to find Captain Heiser and Captain Crawford making their way out of the captain's quarters and over to the railing, wine glasses in hand.

Anna turned to Will with an amused smile.

"Should we sneak down to the galley and try some of that wine?" Will asked her.

Her mug was nearly empty, so she nodded.

They found Pyran and Ros in the middle of an arm-wrestling match, two bottles of wine sitting empty next to them. Apparently, this was Pyran's fourth attempt at a win, and Ros was teaching him proper form. As Will and Anna joined them, Will shared their gossip about the two captains, and even Ros gave an amused giggle.

32

EVERYONE GATHERED AGAIN AT THE RAILING AS THE SHIP DOCKED IN Osborough. Waves crashed against the nearby shore and docked ships creaked as they bobbed in the water. Captain Crawford's crew shouted back and forth to each other across the deck about getting the ship into the right position and securing their lines.

In contrast, the docks themselves were quiet. Gas lanterns lit the boardwalk over the sand with a warm glow. Occasionally, Anna saw a dark figure on a nearby ship moving closer to watch the *Empress* come in. All the gulls were asleep.

The crew shouted confirmation that the ship was secure, and then she watched some of them walk by with the team's packs, setting them on the dock, ready to be carried to the next stop.

"It's been a pleasure having you all on board," Captain Crawford said to the group. "Even if you found our wine," she smiled knowingly at Pyran, Ros, Anna, and Will.

Pyran held in a drunken giggle, his cheeks red even in the darkness.

Captain Heiser turned with a smile to Captain Crawford. "Thank you for carrying us safely across the waves. Perhaps we'll have need of your services again."

"Perhaps..." Crawford smiled coyly back, "we'd be willing to assist again."

Heiser carried on smiling dumbly at her until Cal cleared his throat. Broken out of his thoughts, the captain glanced around at his team. "All right, everyone. Time to disembark."

Callum led the way, happy to be getting off the water. His sister followed, talking animatedly with Merry about the docks at Delphia. Ben followed, holding his book at his side. Anna let Pyran and Ros walk ahead of her. Pyran was doing his best to walk straight, and it helped that he had his arm hooked with Ros'. Anna had watched Ros drink as much wine as Pyran, so she knew they must be inebriated, but their balance and manner seemed completely unaffected as they walked down the gangway.

Anna followed behind, hoping to catch them if the ship shifted and they stumbled. She and Will had shared a couple of glasses with them before the ship made its way into Osborough, but nowhere near what Pyran and Ros had consumed. Will walked beside her, watching the two in front of them with amusement. Captain Heiser was the last off. He took a moment to speak quietly with the ship's captain before following.

Torgeir met them by their things. When everyone stood waiting, he said, "The crew of the *Empress* wishes you luck on your mission. May the Mother watch over you."

"Thank you," the captain nodded. "May she watch over you all as well."

The first mate nodded with stiff politeness, and then made his way with his singular walk back onto the ship.

Clara yawned and then reached for her pack. "I'm ready for a warm bed."

"There won't be much drinking away the Council's gold tonight," the captain agreed, picking up his own things.

"Someone's already done enough drinking," Will commented with a chuckle, grabbing Pyran by the shoulder hard enough to make him stumble.

"Hey!" Pyran protested, brushing Will's hand off his shoulder. "I'm fine! Got no idea what you're talking about."

Will rolled his eyes and moved to pick up his pack.

Ros reached for theirs. As they did, Anna asked them, "How are you not as drunk as Pyran?"

Ros grinned mischievously. "Part of training with the krakens is teaching your body to break down a variety of known toxins."

Anna blinked. "You can't get drunk?"

Ros laughed and swung their bag onto their shoulder. "It is possible, yes, but it is much more difficult than it is for you or..." they waved a hand at Pyran, who hiccupped.

Anna sighed, but let a smile slip onto her face as she looked at her intoxicated friend. "You never told us that," she said to Ros.

Ros shrugged. "It is common knowledge in Lakoona."

"I'll have to remember never to get into a drinking contest with you," Will said.

Anna picked up her own bag and swung it over her shoulders.

When everyone had their things, the captain led the way into town. Several of them yawned as they made their way toward the gas lanterns at the end of the dock. Anna eyed the looming ships they passed. They creaked as they rocked with the waves, occasionally bumping the dock. To her they looked like giant, prowling monsters in the dark, waiting for the right moment to attack them.

"Boo," Will said quietly after creeping up noiselessly behind her.

Anna's shoulders tensed, but she kept herself from jumping. "Don't do that."

Will grinned to himself and stepped up to walk next to her.

"You can't say this isn't creepy. It's so quiet, and you can't see anything." She motioned a hand toward the giant, bobbing shadows.

Will shrugged and looked around. "Darkness doesn't always mean *creepy.*"

"What about the dark shapes that sometimes move around on the decks?" Anna said quietly, looking up at the top deck of the ship next to them with narrowed, searching eyes. She thought she saw a hunched shape move, and her hair stood on end.

"Just a night watchman." Will laced his fingers behind his head in a relaxed posture. "Watching for pirates who've come to steal their ships."

"Hm," Anna pursed her lips and looked ahead, the grip of each hand tight on the straps of her pack.

"There's almost always a reasonable explanation for the things we see in the dark."

"Almost always?"

Will nodded, and did not reassure her further.

The group fell into a quiet cadence as they left the docks behind, and the landscape shifted to wood and stucco buildings, many of them sitting three stories tall near the docks. The gas lanterns continued to guide them as the streets shifted to cobblestone.

Fortunately, the district they were searching for wasn't far from the shore. The sound of chatter and snippets of music broke the quiet as they entered the square where they would find their inn. Several taverns were still bright with commotion and firelight in this late hour. The captain led them to a building tucked neatly between two others, with a tavern on one side and a tailor's shop on the other. It was wood and stucco, like almost every other building around them, and had a large window at the front of the ground floor framed by muntins that broke the large piece of glass into a hundred small diamonds. The room inside was dark. The sign hanging over the door showed a fireplace and read *Hearthlight Inn.*

The door opened for them, and they moved inside. There was a couch under the window and stairs leading up to the left. In front of them was a counter that held a single, burning candle, and behind it sat a young woman on a stool. She was looking down at a book that she held close to the candle as she read. Her brows furrowed as the group filed in before she found a spot to stop, smacked the book shut, and let it fall onto the counter. "Hello. Captain Heiser and crew, I assume?"

"Yes." The captain stepped up to the counter. "We appreciate you waiting up for us."

She shrugged. "No problem. We've got four rooms ready for you." She paused expectantly.

The captain set a small coin pouch on the counter.

She nodded at it and hopped off the tall stool she'd been sitting on. "Follow me."

She led them up a flight of stairs, down a hallway, and then up another flight of stairs. She handed the captain four keys, gesturing at the four doorways down the hall. "These rooms are yours. Bathroom's at the end of the hall. Is there anything else you need?" Her crossed arms showed that she wasn't keen on receiving further tasks, but would help if she needed to.

"No, thank you. That's all," the captain nodded.

"All right. My father will be at the counter in the morning." She turned and left down the stairs.

The captain turned and addressed the group. "Merry and Ros, you'll room together. Clara and Anna. Will, Ben, and Callum. Pyran, you'll share with me." He held out three room keys.

Anna let Clara grab a key, and then Clara led her to the door with the number six hanging off its front. Clara unlocked the door and then entered with a yawn and a stretch. The short woman let the pack fall from her shoulders, and then fell face first onto the bed at the right side of the room.

"I can't wait to be asleep," her muffled voice said.

Anna grinned. "I feel the same."

There were two small beds, one on each side of the room. At the center of the far wall, there was a window that looked out across the dark city. Speckles of gas lanterns were the only thing she could make out. A chest of drawers sat under the window. Anna set her pack down beside the other bed and began to take her leathers off. "I'm sure you'll be more comfortable without your armor on."

Clara groaned loudly before she rolled over and sat up. She unbuckled the straps of her pauldrons and then her breastplate, heaving a sigh of relief. "You and Will seem to be getting along better."

Anna glanced across the room at her as her fingers worked the attachments of her own armor and said simply, "He's all right."

"Just all right?" Clara asked slyly.

Anna rolled her eyes. "We can talk now without getting into arguments. I'd say that's all right."

Clara let out a short, high-pitched hum meant to entice Anna to say more, but she was too tired. She changed her shirt and slipped under the covers. The sheets were clean and the bed wasn't uncomfortable. Quickly, she fell asleep.

SUNLIGHT FILTERED IN THROUGH ANNA'S EYELIDS AS SHE RETURNED TO consciousness. The first thing she did was pull the blankets more tightly to her and tuck her chin in and shoulders up under them. The smell of the sheets surprised her—she had been expecting the smell of her mother's baking—

She opened her eyes.

Clara was stretched out on the bed across the room. One of her arms lay above her head on her pillow, framing her face, the other was falling off the side of the bed. One corner of the sheets hid, coiled beneath and around one of the woman's legs. Her hair splayed around her face in a dark halo. Her breathing was slow and deep.

Anna stretched and let the sheets fall away from her face. Then she rubbed her eyes and scratched her scalp.

Two knocks sounded on the door. Pyran's voice called, "Get up! We're going for breakfast!"

Clara jumped in her sleep, then looked around with bleary eyes. "Breakfast already?" she whined.

Anna smiled with amusement, and she looked out the window. "I think the captain let us sleep in a little. It's later than the horn."

Clara hummed in acknowledgement, scrubbing at her eyes and then collecting her hair away from her face.

Anna got up and stretched. As she ran through one round of strengthening movements, Clara finally sat up and crawled to the end of the bed by her pack. She pulled out a hairbrush, comb, and a couple of hair ties. The brush was made of intricately carved metal, as was the comb. The ties were both black velvet. She started brushing her hair, and Anna watched her eyes clear.

Clara let the brush fall into her lap with a contented sigh and said, "A good hair brushing always makes you feel better, don't you think?"

"Mm. Mm-hmm," Anna grunted as she moved through one of the more difficult forms.

Clara gasped, and Anna jumped.

"We should braid each other's hair!" the healer exclaimed with a bright smile. "It's always easier on another person!"

"Uh," Anna turned to her pack and pulled out her own hairbrush. The handle was wood, carved simply into a comfortable shape for a hand. She tried to cover most of it with her palm before she started running it through her auburn strands. "I don't think so."

"Aw," Clara pouted, "Why not?"

"I've never braided someone else's hair," Anna told her, looking out the window. Heat rose to her face.

"You do a wonderful job with your own hair," Clara told her, jumping up to stand. "You just need to pretend that my head is yours."

Anna's brows drew together in befuddlement as the shorter woman approached.

"Sit on the bed and I'll show you," Clara ordered with a smile.

Anna complied. Clara sat next to her and turned her away.

"Tilt your head back. Good. Now, as you know, the basis of a good braid is how tightly you can get it woven." Clara ran her hands through Anna's hair, brushing it back, then she took a nail and slid it gently behind a small front section. From there, she tugged and started braiding.

Anna's eyes widened as Clara pulled on her scalp. It didn't hurt, but Clara ensured each weave was tight. At the end, she tied it off with one of her own ties and sat back to inspect her work.

"There," she said, satisfied. "Not so bad. My turn!" She spun and waited for Anna to do the same.

Anna felt at her head, running a finger gently over the braid. Not a strand was out of place, and Clara had inverted the weave from how Anna usually did it herself. The weave sat on top of her head, rather than disappearing into itself. Anna turned to face the back of Clara, who waited patiently. She raised her hands and ran her fingers through Clara's thick, black strands. Her hair smelled like saltwater and almond blossoms. Anna sectioned off some at the front, as she had felt Clara do, and then she braided.

"Don't worry about hurting me," Clara told her. "A good braid stings a little while it's being woven." Her dark hand fidgeted with the small necklace she wore. It had a small purple gem set in silver that flashed in the sunlight.

"All right." Anna tugged carefully on the sections she held in her fingers, tightening the short row of braid she had accomplished. She was braiding the way her mother had taught her—a section from the outside crossed over the middle to become the new middle, then repeated from the other side. It took her about twice as long as Clara had taken for hers, but Anna's hands weren't used to the motions of her fingers in front of her head. There were several moments when she had to stop and smooth a few strands into the weave, tug tightly, and then continue. "That's pretty," she told Clara, pointing at the necklace.

Clara hummed in agreement. "It's part of an enchanted pair. Cal has the other half. Some kind of finding spell. I use it when he tries to hide at parties."

"I'm sure he loves that," Anna smiled with sarcasm.

"He sure doesn't!" Anna could hear her grin. "Callum and I learned to braid each other's hair when we were little. He's very good."

"So are you."

"Thank you," Clara said, satisfied.

"Do you have a tie for me to use?"

"Yes, of course!" Clara held her other tie over her shoulder.

Anna took it. She braided it into the bottom third of the braid, tied a solid knot, and then took a moment to tie a pretty bow—the kind she would've put on a special-order box at the bakery.

"Done," Anna said, then leaned back.

Clara stood from the bed and rushed over to her pack to grab a little mirror. She looked at the front. A couple of shorter sections near her temples fell softly in front of her ears. Anna narrowed her eyes in disappointment, but Clara curled each around her finger, training them to roll away from her face, and kept grinning. Then she pulled her long braid over her shoulder and inspected it. Her grin grew into a toothy smile as she ran her fingers over the spots the ribbon was braided into, then stopped at the bow.

"And a pretty little bow!" Clara glanced at Anna. "I never see you give yourself a bow!"

Anna shrugged. "It felt right."

Clara smiled in return, then held out the little mirror. "Here."

Anna took it and looked at herself. At the edges of her face, where the hair normally would fall out and into her eyes, only the shortest hairs fell free. The rest was smoothly pulled back. When she pulled her braid forward over her shoulder, she found the end wrapped tightly by the tie. It was knotted, and the two ends hung down a little longer than her hair. "Thank you, it's perfect. You'll have to show me how you do it sometime."

"You're welcome!" Clara took her mirror back and then shoved everything into her pack again. "Let's get dressed so they can't blame any tardiness on us."

"Right," Anna nodded with a laugh, and she turned to her own pack. She changed into another of her oversized shirts, a simple pair of trousers, and then put on her armor. The leathers were so familiar now that she felt almost as comfortable in them as she did with her clothes.

When they both exited their room to freshen up in the bathroom, they found Ben walking back towards his room with wet hair, still in his pajamas.

"Good morning, Ben," Clara greeted. "Will you be wearing your sleepwear to breakfast?"

"Of course not," he told her.

"Best to get a move on, then," she teased. "We're hungry!"

Ben grumbled an incoherent response before disappearing into his room.

Clara turned back to Anna with the back of her hand by her mouth, as if to gossip. "Leave it to a snooty mage to need a daily bath."

Anna smiled, knowing Clara only meant it as a joke. Ben had proven too bookish and introverted to ever be seen as *snooty*.

Clara washed her face and her hands, and then moved aside to let Anna do the same. As Anna did, the shorter woman leaned in the doorway and crossed her arms with a *clu-clunk* of bracers against breastplate, lamenting her decision to not bring her own soap with her when she'd left Delphia.

"I thought it would be nice to try something new, but all of this cheap soap is drying me out." She picked at something under her fingernails.

"I hear they imported soaps and lotions from Salwell for our camp supplies once we get to Dore," Will said, moving past her into the room to take his turn at the sink.

"Really?" Clara smiled and looked up at him.

"No," Will laughed.

Anna snorted a laugh, which she hid by drying her face with a towel.

Clara sighed. "Figures." When Anna was done drying off, Clara asked her, "What about you? Is there anything you miss from home?"

Anna shrugged. "My mom made our soap. Other than that..." she thought for a moment, shifting to lean her weight on her other hip. "My mom's apple turnovers, I guess. She made them fresh every morning."

"Mmm," Clara hummed at the mention of the baked treat. "Maybe we'll get something like that for breakfast."

"Maybe." *It won't be the same, though.*

33

EVERYONE GATHERED IN THE HALL WHEN THEY WERE READY, AND THE captain led them to the tavern next door for breakfast. There were no apple turnovers, but there was sausage, eggs, and warm, buttered bread.

After that, they made their way to the stables on the south side of town. They were met with stable workers excited for the Council's coin and strong, well-groomed horses. It didn't take long to find a mount for each of them.

After all the baggage was settled, Anna could procrastinate getting on her horse no longer. She made an attempt, but couldn't get her leg over and stumbled back. The horse snorted and shuffled its feet slightly.

"I'm sorry," she said quietly to the bay stallion. His name was Bailey. "You're going to have to be patient with me."

The horse snorted again, as if in response, and Anna sighed.

"Here," Pyran was behind her. "Need a leg up?"

"Thank you," Anna said gratefully. "I think he's already annoyed with me."

"No problem," Pyran said, looking between Anna and her horse with an amused smile. He held out his interlocked hands, palms up. Anna put a foot in and jumped with the other one. With the boost, she could get her leg up and over and seat herself in the saddle.

"You might have to do that every time," Anna said, only half joking.

Ros brought their horse over to see what was going on. "You are the last. Are you ready?"

"Yes," Anna's cheeks heated at the realization that she was holding everyone up.

"All ready," Ros called to the captain.

"Then we go," the captain called back, turning his horse toward the gate. "I'll lead for now."

The morning passed by quickly enough. Bailey did well in the middle of the pack, and Anna found she didn't need to do much to keep him going with the group. The summer sun was warm on her head, and she was glad when they stopped beneath the shade of some trees to rest and water the horses before carrying on again. As much as they joked about horses' rear ends, the air mostly smelled like grass and saltwater. Gulls called in the distance now and then. She couldn't see the ocean, but they were still close. They would travel the coastline for a short time, until they came to a bridge where the path turned west and went over the Long Lake River.

The bridge was long and built in a bright, familiar stone. Somewhere in the middle of it, Anna realized it was the same material that made up most of Hillcrest and its bridge, and that if she followed this river northwest, she would eventually run right into them.

When they stopped for lunch, they were all sweaty from riding in the hot sun. Anna's legs were sore as she stumbled off the horse. They gathered on the south side of the road, where a thick forest gave them shade. Pyran pulled the map from Commander Lyon out of his pack and looked it over. Anna ate quickly and then joined him.

The map was just big enough to see the path from Osborough onward. Pyran pointed out that they were about halfway.

Anna looked at the little X's that marked where Lyon's spies had found Vassian camps. They were scattered around the wood they were at the edge of now. The one that wasn't in the Council's report was southwest of Dore. Anna turned and scanned through the trees behind them.

"Looking for a rabbit to add to your lunch?" Will asked, walking over to join them.

"They multiply like mushrooms in the shade after a rain. I would be doing the forest a favor. But no." Anna sighed. "I'm trying to gauge the distance between us and these marked camps." She pointed at the two X's south of them.

"There's been no Vasbrute sightings on the roads," the captain said from his seat on a nearby log. "We should be safe here. I would think they've moved on from these camps by now as well."

"Exactly," Anna put her hands on her hips. "If we were to go investigate these empty camps, we might find something useful, and the risk would be low."

Anna saw the captain's jaw clench. He looked out into the trees, and then glanced back at the rest of his team. Merry sat with Clara and Cal, telling an enthusiastic story. Ben sat next to Ros, both of them quietly eating.

"I wasn't planning to investigate until we had established supplies in Dore," the captain told Anna. After a pause, he continued. "However, I see the logic behind what you suggest."

Anna waited patiently as he thought for a moment. He called for Ros and Callum, who hurried over. Then he said, "Anna, I want you and Ros to find Camp A. Will, you'll take Callum and find Camp B. If you see any Vasbrute, turn and come back. If the camps are deserted as we suspect they are, look around. We were sent to find out why they're here, but we'll take whatever information we can. Anything could be useful. Understood?"

"Yes, sir," Anna nodded in agreement with the others.

"Good. The priority right now is your safety. Stay quiet. Stay safe. No risks."

The group nodded again.

"Meet us back here," the captain finished.

"Yes, sir," Anna nodded. Will caught her eye and gave a stiff nod, his lips stretched into a tight line, before he and Cal walked away.

Ros checked that their staff was secured to their back before nodding to Anna. "You lead. I'll follow."

Anna grabbed her shortbow and a quiver of arrows from her saddlebags. She checked that her hunting knife was still at her waist. Pyran looked up as she walked by, and they held each other's gaze for a moment before she turned to walk into the forest.

I'll see you later.

At first, her movements were stiff. She was jarred by the thought that they might actually run into a group of angry Vasbrute. Panicked questions crowded her head, leaving little space for clear thought.

What if we don't make it out? How will my mom know? Will she be okay? Where would she run?

"It would be great if the bugs would bugger off."

The mundanity of Ros' whispered complaint snapped Anna back into the present. A handful of gnats hovered around them, attracted to them for their smell as they quietly made their way through the shorter growing things that thrived at the feet of the tall, old trees. Ros silently shooed the tiny bugs away with a wave of their hand.

They were already damp with sweat from riding horses in the sun all morning, but there was a humidity in the air that was intensified within the canopy of the trees. This kind of weather wasn't unusual for midsummer in Telluth, at least for Wallset. Anna had spent many hot, humid summer days in the woods around her home, and she felt comfortable in the trees. It was almost like those days when she had explored further from Wallset than she had before, expanding her known territory. The same trees stood out to her here, the same birds chatted back and forth above her, and her goal was the same—locate an abandoned inhabitance and see what she could find there.

As they walked, Anna felt her coiled muscles loosen. The pungent smell of dirt and plants soothed her jangling nerves.

We're sure to hear Vasbrute before they ever see us.

She turned her focus to their path, making sure they were moving in the right direction based on the image of the map in her memory. She led Ros through the grass and shrubbery, avoiding anything that would make excessive noise. Unsurprisingly, Ros was light on their feet, and Anna often turned to check that they were still behind her.

The sun hung a little lower in the sky by the time they found a quiet clearing. It wasn't quiet the way an area away from civilization was normally quiet, though. It was almost silent because it was free of any animals. Something had scared them off, and Anna had a strong idea what that had been.

Sunlight shone down brightly from the gap in the woods where someone had cut every tree within a thirty-foot circle into stumps close to the ground. It was clear the area had once been as densely packed with trees as the surrounding forest. Anna stopped Ros at the edge of the trees with a silent hand signal and surveyed the area.

There was no movement, no noise to suggest there was anything at all nearby, let alone a group of Vasbrute. Some stumps sat tall and sharp with splinters of wood. Broken branches were scattered around the camp. Crude wooden fences circled the clearing, some logs pointing up and out with sharpened ends. It wasn't a completely enclosed perimeter, but it would be enough to control who came in and out.

Those trees were cut in a hurry. They needed every one of them for their fence.

At the center of the clearing was a wide, shallow pit full of ash. It was near six feet wide, but its depth was difficult to make out from a distance. There was a mass of ashes within. The grass inside the circle of the camp lay flat, trampled by the camp's inhabitants.

"Okay," Anna turned to Ros and spoke quietly. "There's no one here, but be careful. They could have laid traps."

Ros nodded.

The two of them stepped carefully past the fence and into the open space.

"There's no subtlety here," Ros observed. "They did not care if they were found."

Anna approached the firepit, walking over the stamped dirt. She had been right about the size of it. She found two branches that ended in pronged forks shoved into the ground across from each other. The smell confirmed that they had used a spit to roast a large animal.

Venison, maybe.

"You're right," Anna told Ros. "With a fire this size, I'd guess they wanted to be found. And why not? What's a group of humans, elves, or dwarves going to do against a full camp of Vasbrute?"

"I think they'd be surprised."

Anna assumed Ros meant to be encouraging, but their cool tone, in combination with their raspy voice, sent a shiver down her spine.

Anna moved to the other edge of camp, to another opening in the fence. She found a trail of dried blood. She guessed it was from whatever animal they had roasted. She confirmed her guess when she found a dried pool of blood swarming with flies and a rope hanging from a branch above. Her nose wrinkled at the smell. She took a small stick and poked at the sludge. It clung to the stick in rotten, coagulated strands, and Anna held back a gag. She let the stick fall, stood up, and turned away.

This is clearly where they hung their catch to drain the blood.

"They've been gone days, if not a couple weeks," Anna announced, holding the back of her hand in front of her mouth and nose.

"Mm." Ros grunted in confirmation that they were listening. They were crouched by a stump that sat near the fire. Anna walked over, curious about what they were looking at.

On top of the flat surface of the stump, which had presumably been used as a stool, were the words FOR BRANIK. A dark red stain saturated the carved-out letters. Ros leaned in closely and sniffed.

"Some kind of strange spiced wine, perhaps," they said as they pulled back.

Anna's eyebrows rose. "Not blood?"

Ros looked up at her with a mischievous smile. "Would you have preferred it to be blood?"

"No."

Ros hummed thoughtfully. "We must be careful with our assumptions. If we let them cloud our observations, we'll likely miss something important."

Anna nodded, taking the words to heart. Then she said, "I'm going to memorize the layout of the camp. If they went to this much trouble in a space they left again so easily, they probably set up like this every time."

"Good idea," Ros stood. "I'll help."

The two walked the entire camp, noting the size and placement of each tent and its stakes. They had brought nothing to write with, so they repeated each note back to each other to make them stick until they made it back to record them.

"I don't see any hoof prints," Ros commented as they were finishing.

"No horses," Anna agreed. "Are horses even strong enough to carry them? They're supposed to be built like statues."

Ros shrugged.

"All right," Anna sighed and looked up at the sun. Searching the camp had taken them almost as long as finding it. "I think we've seen all there is to see. Let's head back."

"I'll follow you," Ros nodded toward the opening in the fence they had come through.

WHEN THEY REJOINED THEIR GROUP AT THE EDGE OF THE FOREST, WILL and Cal were already back and relaying what they'd seen. The whole team was clustered together to listen, but they all turned to look as Anna and Ros walked out of the trees.

"Hello," the captain greeted, calling them over with a wave of his arm. "What did you find?"

Ros approached, putting their hands on their hips as they joined the circle. They looked down to where Cal was drawing in the dirt.

Anna saw a large circle filled with squares and a large X at the center. She recognized it as the layout of the camp. "Our camp was laid out the same way. I'll bet the larger tent near the middle is for whoever is in charge."

Callum nodded. "That's what we thought, too. Didn't see much else. The whole space was cleared out."

"You saw the fences and the giant firepit?" Ros asked them.

Will nodded. "Fences as tall as me and topped with spikes. A pit large enough to roast a bear."

"They roasted a deer at Camp A," Anna said. "Seems like they're pretty comfortable living off the land. That camp had been abandoned for maybe a couple of weeks, though."

The captain turned to Will and Cal. "Were you able to tell how long ago they left Camp B?"

Will pursed his lips and shook his head.

"No. Sorry, sir," Cal answered.

"That's all right." The captain sat back and crossed his arms. He squinted up at the sky thoughtfully.

"There was something else we saw," Ros said. "On one stump, they carved the words *for Branik.*"

The captain's eyes narrowed. "Was there any indication as to what it meant? Name? Place?"

Ros and Anna shook their heads.

"Well," the captain placed his hands on his knees and pushed himself to stand, "good job, the four of you. Sit and get some water while the rest of us ready the horses. We should arrive at *Dore's door* just in time to share a late supper with our new friends."

"Dore's door," Will muttered in exaggerated annoyance, before taking a seat and lifting his flask of water to his lips.

The captain smiled mischievously. "You didn't like it? I thought it was clever."

"It's a fairly obvious play on words," Ros told him with a shrug.

"Bah." The captain waved a dismissive hand at them. "None of you are in the mood for a joke."

"Not in the mood for a *bad* joke," Clara said with a laugh.

34

ANNA SPENT THE AFTERNOON DISCUSSING ROAD GAMES WITH MERRY and Clara. Merry told them that her siblings would count the carts and carriages they passed while hauling crops to sales booths in Tuvale, Thrupath, and Altumberg, or challenge each other to pick the most wildflowers while they stopped for a meal. Clara had killed time on ships to Amgen or Eysa or in carriages to Lakoona or Hillcrest by playing Hot Hands, Digits, and Odds and Evens with her brother.

"My dad and I used to count birds when we were sitting out hunting," Anna told them. She felt a painful twinge in her chest as she remembered sitting with him in the woods for hours, watching everything around them. "Woodpeckers, blue jays, sparrows, goldfinches. Cardinals were worth more points because he liked them the best, even though they were one of the easiest to find."

They counted birds together until they saw Dore in the distance.

The town rose out of the horizon like a dense grove of leafless trees. A tall wooden wall surrounded it, built from whole trunks, trimmed of branches and standing side by side, and stained dark to blend into the woods surrounding town. The gate was made the same way, but held together on the exterior by thick, iron straps. As they got closer, Anna could see the rooftops of taller buildings rising just over the wall, and the two people positioned above the gate, watching them approach.

"Hello!" one of them shouted from atop the wall. "What is your business here?"

Anna turned to the captain, who was shouting back, "I am Captain Nathaniel Heiser. The Council sent my team and I to investigate recent happenings around Dore."

One of the guards turned around to look somewhere on the other side of the wall, then turned back to them. "Very well," they called out. The gate opened slowly into the town. "Come through the gate to provide your papers to the guard there!"

The captain nodded exaggeratedly so that the men on top of the wall could see it before urging his horse forward.

The gates halted their motion when they offered enough space for two riders to pass through together. The captain led everyone inside. Wide, packed dirt roads filled the spaces between buildings, which were built similarly to the surrounding wall, though the logs used in these structures were turned and laid on top of each other horizontally. The other main difference was that each of the buildings were covered in solid color, some of them bright and others more subdued. People milled about from place to place in between them.

"Papers, please." A man in studded leather armor and a shining helmet stood between the captain and the town. He looked irritated as he gave the horse riders a once-over and scratched his stubbled chin.

Captain Heiser reached into a saddlebag and procured his Writ of Duty, holding it out to the man. The guard took it and unrolled it to look it over.

"Has Dore always kept such...strong defenses?" the captain asked him.

Without looking up from the scroll, he said, "Can't be too careful when you're this close to the wall."

"Of course," the captain nodded agreeably.

"Here you go." The guard handed the scroll back. "The inn's down Main Street on the left." He moved to the side and out of their way.

"Thank you." The captain tucked the scroll back into his bag and sat up straight again. "We appreciate your hospitality. Good day!"

"You as well." He didn't even attempt a polite smile.

As they all entered town, the gate behind them shut with a low *boom*.

"A friendly people," Will said, looking around. "Very happy to see us, obviously."

Cal laughed.

"Small towns tend to be tight-knit and defensive," the captain said. "That's all right. Most of our work is out of town."

People stared as they rode by. A child playing in the street with their friends stopped to point, and then they all watched as the group passed by. A woman hauled a child out of their path by the hand, the kid stumbling as they watched the riders instead of where they were going. A group of men outside a storefront watched them with crossed arms and hard eyes.

Clara smiled and waved at a couple of children. The little girl smiled back, but her older companion only stared.

Anna ignored them, mostly, as she had done when hurrying through Wallset.

This area of town appeared to be mostly business. A couple of fabric shops, a dried goods supply, general store, the butcher, the blacksmith, and a candle shop lined Main Street. The inn appeared on the left side of the road as they'd been told, just past the butcher. It was a two-story structure painted rusty red. A sign hung over the door, painted with the image of a cabin between two tall pines. It read, *Woodsgate Inn.* There was a long hitching post at the front, and a path around the side led to a horse barn built against the back of the building.

Before they could dismount, a boy rushed out of the inn and up to Captain Heiser, his blonde hair fluffing up in the air as he ran. "Hello! Welcome to Dore! We have your rooms ready for you, and I-I can take your horses!"

"Thank you, my boy!" the captain greeted with a grin before dismounting. "And what is your name?"

"I'm John, innkeeper's son," he said, looking up at the captain with wide eyes and thumbing back at the building behind him. "And you're Captain Heiser, sent by the Council!" He bowed his head in a quick signal of respect.

"That's right," the captain smiled back. "It sounds like you're prepared for us."

The boy nodded and looked down at his hands in front of him as he fidgeted with his fingers. "It's not often we get important people from the capital in town."

Heiser grinned down at him. "We come from all over Telluth. Perhaps we'll share some stories while we eat dinner."

John's eyes widened and he glanced past the captain at the rest of them. Clara smiled and fluttered a wave. Merry nodded and smiled, and Anna did the same. Ben gave a wave and a grin with Pyran.

"Wow." John turned back to the captain as he dismounted. "Really?"

"As long as the horses are cared for, and we have full plates in front of us."

"Of course!" John's expression turned serious as he accepted his mission, taking the horse's reins.

Anna dismounted with the rest, and Bailey shook his head and whinnied as if glad to be free of her. She sighed, handing over the reins to a man that came from the stables to help little John bring in the horses.

Anna noticed someone leaning against the porch railing, watching them. She could see leather armor under the person's travel cloak, along with thick boots and a brimmed hat. The person caught Anna looking and picked their chin up, allowing sunlight to shine on their face and reveal a familiar, thin smile.

With a gasp, Anna ran over and embraced her. "Lucy!"

Lucy wrapped her arms around Anna and squeezed before releasing. "You've gotten stronger since I last saw you. Good! I thought maybe we'd put as much muscle on you as you were ever going to get."

A moment later, Pyran was taking his turn to embrace their mentor. She squeezed him, patted him on the back, and then pulled away, saying, "That's enough. I've gotta create some kinda reputation with the rest of your team here, and I don't want them to think I'm sappy."

"I don't think anyone could ever take you for sappy," Pyran told her.

"Is it just you?" Anna asked, concerned as she looked around Lucy and saw an empty porch.

"Just me," Lucy nodded, her grin faltering briefly. "I'm all Commander Lyon could get away without provoking more attention. Apparently, teams of two or more require written permission from Lord Woulfe. I'm meant to be a *scout* checking out the wall." She shrugged nonchalantly. "Makes sense, what with all the rumors flying around the city."

"They're not just rumors," Pyran said. After Lucy quirked an eyebrow at him, he added, "We'll fill you in."

Behind them, the captain cleared his throat.

Anna jumped. She had all but forgotten where they were. She spun, saying, "Captain! This is Lucy Brighton. Lucy, this is Captain Nathaniel Heiser."

Briefly, Lucy's eyes widened. She blinked, and her face transformed into a mask of professionalism. "It's an honor to meet you, captain."

"A pleasure." He wore a stiff grin and gave her hand a solid shake. "I suggest we move our conversation indoors, and perhaps save discussion for when there are no curious, open ears."

Lucy nodded in agreement.

Double doors led them from the porch to the interior of the inn. To the left was a staircase that led up and turned right. Underneath it was a hallway that led further in. There was a large dining room full of long, heavy wood tables and matching benches. A family sat at one end of the room, eating together, and another group of people took up an entire table near the middle of the room. Judging by their similar attire, all covered in sawdust and wood shavings, Anna guessed that these people worked with wood. There was a bar lined with stools at the far end of the room. A couple of men sat together there, each with a mug. A woman stood at the end, folding napkins. The man behind the bar was wiping mugs with a towel. All their eyes turned to the strangers as they walked in.

Captain Heiser made his way to the bar, giving a nod in greeting to the table full of woodworkers as he passed. Pyran followed him. Anna led everyone to an open table, and then everyone sat down.

Merry speculated about what kind of food they served. Will wondered if the plates themselves would be wooden. They were discussing the quality of the ale as a man stood up from the full table and approached.

He was average height, and lean except for a small potbelly that was made more obvious by the way he pulled at the waist of his pants to keep them from sagging. He had light brown hair and a matching beard, which he scratched at thoughtfully when he was done adjusting his pants.

"Ale's all right here. If you're looking for a good drink, I'd recommend the brew house over west about a block," he said. He gave everyone at the table a once-over before asking, "You lot the ones supposed to be comin' to deal with them Vasbrute?"

"Vermin!" one of the men from the table threw out. They were clearly listening.

The man waved a hand dismissively over his shoulder at his friend.

Will leaned back and crossed his arms, disengaging.

"Yep!" Merry told him.

Ben said, "We're here to look into it, yes."

The man nodded. "It's about time we got some help from them governors. Though, I would've assumed they'd send more of ya. There aren't more of ya waiting outside, is there?" He glanced out the large front window next to the entry.

"No," Ben said, "but we're quite capable."

The man nodded casually, then said, "My name's Wes Kent. We're working a new house at the end of the street. I don't know much about these Vasbrute outside of the rumors and gossip, but I'd be happy to answer questions ya might have about the town."

"Do you know where the orchard is?" Merry asked.

Wes' eyebrows rose, and he said, "The Blakelys are just southwest of town, about half a day out. You'll see the house before you see the apple trees. Just follow the only road that runs that way."

"Thanks," Merry said.

"I heard about what happened out there," Wes continued. "Poor Millie and the kids are struggling with Bill unable to work. He's a hard-ass, but he didn't deserve that. It's good someone's lookin' into it."

"We'll get to the bottom of it," Clara nodded, determined and reassuring.

Wes grinned and nodded before making his way back to his table. The captain turned from the bar and walked over to the rest of the team. His face was set in such a serious frown that Wes and his colleagues put their heads down as he passed. Pyran followed closely behind with a look of confusion on his face.

Anna glanced back at the bar. The bartender was having a hushed but aggravated conversation with the woman folding napkins.

"What's wrong, captain?" Merry asked, the only one brave enough to ask. "Are they all out of beds?" she joked.

"Beds they have," Heiser sighed, and took a seat at the end of the table. "Our supplies, on the other hand..."

"What do you mean?" Cal asked him, then impatiently turned to Pyran and asked, "What does he mean?"

Pyran shook his head, "The man behind the bar owns the place, and he said that they were expecting us to bring supplies. He said that's what their communications told them. Nothing was received from Kastarus."

"Nothing?" Clara's brows drew down. "No food, no camp supplies... *nothing?*"

"The components for the sending spell," Ben said suddenly. "How are we supposed to get word back to the Council?"

Captain Heiser shook his head and stared down at the grain in the tabletop, thinking.

"How could this have happened?" Pyran's hands flew out to his sides. "This would have to be the most ridiculous miscommunication."

"Either a most egregious error has been made," Ben said quietly, "or this was the intended result of someone's tampering."

"My assumption is the latter," Heiser responded.

"I *agree*," Will said, feigning a high-city accent. "Question is, what do we do now?"

"Surely the city has supplies," Clara laughed nervously.

"And we have the Council's coin," Cal added.

"The sum we have was intended only to supplement the supplies we were supposed to have ready for us here. We may have enough for some of what we need, but by no means would we be able to purchase it all," the captain told them.

Pyran tapped his chin thoughtfully. "What if we prioritize?"

"Hold on," Anna stood from the bench and went to her pack, pulling out a piece of paper and a pen. She sat back down and set them out in front of herself. "What we need to do is to budget."

Clara scoffed. "Really, it's like that time father saw my wardrobe when we were teens. Do you remember that?" she asked her brother.

"This is serious, Clara," he brushed her off.

"So was that. I had to attend two balls in a dress I'd already worn out. Don't you remember the scandal!?"

"Yes, and then Jennifer Landon had to cut her hair ridiculously short because of something her little brother did a week later, and everyone forgot about your dresses."

"Dress," Clara glared at him. "That was the point."

Cal rolled his eyes.

"Enough bickering about parties," Ros said coolly. "How much money do we have?"

"200 gold," Heiser sighed.

Anna withered a little, but she wrote the number at the top of the page.

"And what is our top priority?" Ros asked.

Clara declared, "Comfortable tents!"

Ben called out, "The supplies for my spell."

Captain Heiser gave Clara a pointed look and said, "I would agree that the spell and *moderate* tents are at the top of the list. Without the tents, we cannot track anything out of town if the weather turns. Without the spell, the Council will assume us lost or dead, and after this whole fiasco, I wouldn't be surprised if those behind this sent someone to make sure of it."

Anna wrote *4 large tents* at the top of the page with an estimate of cost next to it. Then she had Ben list what the spell required, along with his own estimates of cost. The quality of materials Ben required consumed most of their budget, and he questioned what would even be available in a small border town.

Anna tightened her lips and stared down at the paper.

"What?" Merry asked her, concerned.

"We have enough for the spell and...tents. Might have enough for a little food, depending what tents go for." Anna swallowed, trying not to look discouraged.

"We may be here for a week or two," Ros said. "*A little food* will not be enough."

"Then we'll have to find our own food." Anna told them, tugging at her shirt to straighten it and sitting up a little taller. "I taught Will how to trap rabbits and forage, how to track deer. I can teach the rest of you."

Lucy leaned forward onto the tabletop and said, "Don't worry about me. I've got my own tent, and I can share some of my supplies. It's not much, but I'm sure Pyran and Anna can attest to the amount of food Hillcrest provides."

Captain Heiser nodded. "We'll manage with what we have. We'll have to. Tomorrow, I'll send some of you out to gather supplies first thing in the morning. For now, we'll get some dinner."

The owner, also frustrated by the miscommunication and repeating his gratitude that they had come all this way to help the town, gave them dinner for free and told them that breakfast would be the same.

After the meal, which went by quickly as everyone was starving after the journey, Anna and Pyran were tasked with bringing Lucy up to speed. The three of them gathered in Lucy's room.

"You could've told me you're working with *the* Captain Nathaniel Heiser!" Lucy said. She had been irritated before they even walked into the room, but Anna had mistakenly assumed that it was because of the situation she was now in.

"What do you mean?" Pyran asked. He and Anna shared a confused glance.

"That man led the infiltration into the West, and then facilitated the negotiations between us and those isolated weirdos. He's probably the most accomplished military officer of our time."

Anna's brows scrunched together. Captain Heiser had briefly mentioned his experience in the West, but had not included anything about how important or infamous it was. "If he's so important, why haven't we heard about him before?"

"He acts like it was just his job and he did it," Pyran added.

Lucy's palm flew to her face, irritation escalating. She took a deep breath, then her hand whipped away from her face to cuff them both on the side of the head.

"Ow!" Anna's hand jumped to her face reflexively to guard against another attack.

"What was that for?" Pyran cried out.

"That is because you two oblivious *children* have no idea how lucky you are. Everyone on the team must be as oblivious as the two of you, if they don't know what Captain Heiser has done. While he's apparently far more humble than I'd be in his shoes, that's no excuse for your lack of knowledge of current affairs."

"Current affairs?" Pyran scoffed. "That was like twenty years ago! We're not all constantly keeping up with political history like you."

Lucy rolled her eyes. "Just because I keep up with the papers..."

Anna and Pyran went over everything they knew, their meeting with the Council, and all their theories about what was going on behind the political curtain. Lucy sat at the edge of the bed, leaned forward with her elbows on her knees and her hands steepled over the bottom half of her face as she processed the information.

Her eyes narrowed, and she spoke into her hands. "Yeah, this is pretty shitty."

Anna snorted a laugh.

"Thank you for that helpful insight," Pyran said in a flat tone.

"Well," Lucy sat up straighter and put her hands on her thighs. "I knew we'd have to deal with Vasbrute, so that's what I came prepared for. We'll have to deal with the politics after the fact. What's the plan?"

"After we gather supplies tomorrow morning, we're heading out of town to the orchard where a man was assaulted. We'll find out what we can, and then go after the Vasbrute. We don't need to kill them, but that's what it might come down to," Pyran explained. "We've got a better chance with you."

Lucy nodded. "Anything can be killed. We'll just have to figure this one out as we go."

ANNA SPENT THE MORNING WITH MERRY, SHOPPING FOR CAMPING SUPPLIES. The captain had decided she would be most familiar with what they needed and that Merry could help her carry it all back to the group. Merry spent the time entertaining the woman behind the counter at the general store while Anna attempted to gather as much as she could with the budget she had.

Tents were first. The store had two options, but she could only afford the smaller tents if she wanted to have any gold left over for dried foods and first aid supplies.

After doing the math and then redoing it, Anna set three tents, two packs full of food, a length of rope, bandages, and healing salve on the wood counter between Merry and the woman.

One of Merry's brows lifted at the chosen items, then she looked at Anna. "Three tents? You remember there's nine of us, right?"

Anna frowned. "If we want other supplies, we need to sleep three to a tent. We can't afford another one."

Merry turned back to her new friend behind the counter. "Is there any kind of discount here? We need more tents."

"Well," the woman sighed and blinked her dark eyes down at the goods on the counter, "I can't give you a free tent. My father would kill me. But, since you're here about the Vasbrute, and after that whole mess with your supplies...I could loan you a couple of tents."

Anna's brows rose and she looked at Merry, who mirrored her expression. *I guess if we die, it won't matter if we can't return a couple of tents.* She held out her hand. "Deal."

The woman grinned and shook her hand.

Merry carried a pack of food, the pack of supplies, and three tents back to the inn without breaking a sweat. Ben and Pyran were the only ones missing when they rejoined the group, but it didn't take them long to come walking down the road.

"Hey, Ben!" Merry called once he and Pyran were fully in earshot. "What's that face for? You look like someone pissed in your oatmeal."

"In my gem dust, maybe," Ben grumbled.

"What is it?" Captain Heiser asked.

Ben frowned stiffly before he answered. "The jeweler was—"

"A prick," Pyran finished for him.

"Did you get what you needed?" the captain followed up.

"I believe so," Ben lifted the velvet bag to show the evidence. "At quite the upcharge. The gem dust seemed genuine, though."

"I assume that's an integral component," the captain said.

Ben nodded. "The most integral, along with the parchment and ink."

"So this could all be for nothing," Will released an arm from where it crossed over his chest to gesture at them. "If the gem dust isn't right, or if the parchment is crappy or the ink is old, the spell wouldn't work?"

"If the quality of the components is not what it needs to be, yes, it could compromise the spell," Ben said.

"And the Council doesn't get our message, and whoever *reorganized* our supplies sends people to hunt us down..." Pyran laid out the consequences.

"That all?" Will joked darkly.

"No wonder you asked for help." Lucy said, quietly enough that only Anna could hear. When she leaned back, she added for the whole group, "Precarious."

"I have a small supply of parchment and ink I brought with me, though it's most likely not enough for the entirety of the spell. I'll save it in case it's needed," Ben said.

"Leave it to a mage to pack parchment and ink on a hunting trip," Will teased.

"It's a good thing I did," Ben argued. "I was hoping to record our learnings about the Vasbrute. We'll be closer than any Tellan has been in decades, ever since trade broke down. But it will serve better for the spell in our current circumstances."

"How long do we have until these mysterious agents come for you?" Lucy asked.

"Two weeks after our arrival here," Pyran answered.

"Ben," the captain addressed the mage. "If the spell fails, will you receive any sign that it did?"

Ben shook his head solemnly. "The only sign would be that the Council receives a garbled message, or no message at all."

Captain Heiser nodded thoughtfully, then he squared his shoulders and put his hands on his hips, the pose he often took when it was time to stop talking and give orders. "We have two weeks to finish our business here and start our journey back to the capital. I suggest we get started."

There was a chorus of *yes, sir,* before the team began to gather their things strategically into packs. They needed to stay light on their feet as they approached the orchard. For all they knew, the Vasbrute could be lying in wait between the apple trees.

35

OUTSIDE THE CITY WALLS, IT WAS MUCH EASIER TO REMEMBER WHY THEY were there.

In a way, Dore reminded Anna of Wallset. It was a place where everyone knew everyone, and the biggest news was almost always who had married or who had grown old enough to meet Morterra. The sickness that had made its way through Wallset and killed her father had been the headline for weeks, and it had carried on in conversation for months. She'd been happy when it had finally left local discourse after one of the sheep farmers had twins.

Now that they were outside the walls of Dore, though, Anna kept her eyes and ears alert. The southwest gate led directly into a dense pine forest, and it took all afternoon to reach the orchard. During that time, they came across all kinds of normal wildlife, even a set of wolf tracks, but saw no sign of Vasbrute on the road.

Wes' directions were correct. The first sign they saw of the orchard was the house at the edge of an opening in the pines. It was a large two-story farmhouse, constructed similarly to the homes in town and painted sky blue with a faded white trim that was now mostly a soft cream color. The sun ducked behind the surrounding pines, and it covered the acres of apple trees past the house in its soft light.

Anna heard the sound of children shouting and laughing. A handful of them ran out of the trees, then froze as they noticed the small squadron coming up the road toward them. A couple of teenagers followed after them, and then a woman with dark, graying hair tied back out of her face. The woman gestured toward the house and said something to the kids. They hurried inside in the same way they had hurried out of the trees.

"Hello!" Captain Heiser called out to the woman, who started walking toward the road.

"Hello," she responded warily, stopping several yards away from the group of armored people approaching her home.

"Are you Mrs. Blakely?" the captain asked.

"Who is it that's asking?" Her eyes swept over everyone, a mixture of standoffishness and weariness underneath her sharp gaze.

"My name is Captain Nathaniel Heiser, and this is my team. The Council has sent us to investigate the death of Mr. Bill Blakely."

Her eyebrows rose at the mention of the Council, and then her squared shoulders drooped. "Yes, I'm Sandra Blakely."

"Do you have time to answer some questions?"

She nodded. "Why don't you come inside?"

The woman turned to lead everyone to the house. The captain gestured for those on horses to dismount, and then everyone followed her up onto the wraparound porch.

As the woman opened the large front door, the captain turned and said, "Ben, Anna, Pyran, Ros, with me. The rest of you, wait here."

Anna followed Pyran inside, and Ben followed her. The first room was a large living space. There was a long wooden bench along the wall by the door, lined with various sizes of boots. A little girl sat on the floor at the end of it, struggling to get a boot off. The rest of the room held an eclectic assortment of furniture, and a fireplace that opened up between this room and the next. The stone chimney dominated the room as much as the huge hearth.

The woman stopped in the doorway to tell the girl, "Lizbeth, get your brothers and sisters and play outside until dinner's ready."

"But you told us to get *inside,* Mama," Lizbeth protested, still struggling with her boot.

The woman smiled apologetically at the captain, then said to the girl, "I did, Lizbeth, but now I'm telling you all to go outside until I call you in for dinner. Then I'll help you with that boot you've tied in knots."

The little girl let out a heavy sigh, then relented. "Yes, Mama." She stood, stuck her socked foot into her other boot, then ran to a second doorway at the end of the house.

She shouted, "Mama says we're goin' back outside 'til dinner!" then took off running further into the house.

The woman turned to the five strangers in her doorway. "Come on in and have a seat. Would you like some tea?"

"That sounds lovely," the captain said, and followed her inside.

The back end of the house was dedicated entirely to the kitchen. The back wall was half pantry, half counter-topped cupboards, with tall windows that touched the ceiling and let in all the late afternoon light. Between the doorway and the far wall was the largest dining table Anna had ever seen in a home. It was made from pine, like most things around Dore. It was scratched and burnt, and there were little bits of color where a pencil might have left a page and landed on the tabletop. It was beautiful, filling the room all the way across.

Mrs. Blakely hung a tea kettle over the fire as the captain and his team chose seats at the table. They favored one side of the end closest to the large hearth.

Mrs. Blakely took the chair at the head of the table nearest to them. She sat stiffly and said, "What would you like to know?"

"I apologize that we need to bring this back up for you, but we need to know what happened to your husband," Captain Heiser asked gently.

She nodded and swallowed, then tried to settle her hands on the table in front of herself. She was still looking down at them when she started talking.

"About a month ago, my husband discovered that someone—or something—had been taking our apples off the trees. Of course, we lose some of what we grow to the local animals, deer, bear, and whatnot, but this was different. Entire trees were missing fruit.

"He put a couple of men out at night to watch who was stealing from us. That first night, they saw them..." She swallowed again, staring into the wood grain of the table.

"Them?" the captain encouraged her to explain.

She pursed her lips and checked all the doorways, then said, "They said that they were shaped like us, mostly, but they're two times the size. Thick as old tree trunks, but a dull gray color. They were...shaking the trees so hard that the fruit fell off, then collecting them. Our men ran after they saw them shaking the trees like that. Some of them were almost uprooted!" She pulled her arms in close and rubbed them up and down with her hands as if she felt a chill.

Anna glanced around the team, her back stiffening at the thought of running into even one of those things. Ros sat stoically, listening carefully, not taking their eyes off the woman. Pyran fidgeted in his seat nervously. Ben's mouth was set into an unnerved frown.

Ever professional, Captain Nathaniel Heiser sat with one arm resting on the table, angled to face the woman. If the woman's words surprised or frightened him, he didn't show it. His face the definition of calm and seriousness, he asked, "Did they say how many there were?"

She shook her head and met his eyes. "They didn't stop to count, but it was a whole pack of them."

Pack. Like wolves. Giant, built-from-stone, able-to-pull-trees-out-of-the-ground wolves.

The captain nodded in understanding. "What happened after that?"

"My husband—" Her breath hitched, and she looked down and away as she collected herself. Her eyes went glassy before she continued. "He was a stubborn man. An angry man, at times. He couldn't stand that we were being stolen from. I begged him to tell the guards in town, send for help. He wouldn't listen—said we'd lose everything if he let them take our livelihood."

Her hands shook as she clasped them in front of her on the table. "He pulled together a few people from the farm, as many as would agree to go, and they planned an attack the next night." A lone tear escaped and she swiped it away, taking a shaky breath. She shook her head. "Only two of them came back that night, and they only made it because they ran as soon as they saw them. We had to go back for my husband and the others."

A sob hitched in her throat, and Anna thought she could feel it jolt through her own body. Her vision blurred with her own tears. Quickly, she wiped them away with the end of her sleeve.

"Did they see what weapons the Vasbrute carried?"

She swallowed, then said, "They thought a few of them had swords strapped to their backs...and shields, but...they didn't use them. They said that-that..." She clenched her jaw as she focused on getting the words out. "They said that they ripped them apart with their claws."

Her jaw worked and her red-rimmed eyes dropped to the table again. "The monsters were gone by the time we got there. We brought everyone here. They were in bad shape, but we called the healer and it helped. Bill had...lost an arm, among other injuries. The healer stopped the bleeding and said he was going to be all right, but Bill just couldn't *stand* it." Her eyes shut tight and tears streaked down her cheeks.

"He said, how could he run the orchard without his arms? Without two good hands and two strong legs? What kind of father couldn't pick up his children or show them how to put in a day's work?" A sob escaped again, and she took a shaky breath. Her eyes opened and stared down at her knotted hands, the knuckles white. "I argued with him. He wouldn't listen to me. I found him the next morning, out in the orchard. The kids don't know, they *can't* know. They think the injuries killed him."

Anna sucked in a shaky breath. *What a terrible way to die.*

"I am so sorry for your loss," the captain told her, his voice low and gentle.

She nodded, wiping at her face.

The captain asked for the location of the attack, and she explained what part of the orchard they'd been in.

"Thank you," the captain told her. "That is a tragedy no one should have to relive, but what you've told us will help bring justice to your family and the families of the others. May Morterra give your husband peace."

She nodded solemnly. The kettle boiled over, hissing and sputtering over the fire, and she started, rushing to remove it from the heat. "I'm so sorry! I forgot about the tea!"

"That's all right." Captain Heiser stood and pushed his chair in. Anna and the others followed suit. "You have been beyond accommodating, and it's time we stop imposing in your home. I'd like to wait until we've got the light back to look at that spot. Is it all right if we camp in the orchard? We'll stay away from the house and be packed up again at sunrise."

"That's just fine," she nodded. "I'd feel safer for it."

As Anna walked outside, she found Merry running around with a handful of children. The little girl that had been struggling with her boot was on her shoulders. They shrieked and laughed as Merry chased them. Anna was surprised to see Will swoop in and scoop up a child, put them on his shoulders, and then walk up to Merry to have a mock battle.

A couple of older children, a boy and a girl, stood by the horses with Clara and Callum. It sounded like they were admiring the twins' armor. Lucy stood to the side, telling a story to a child that *oohed* and *aahed*.

A cord tugged at Anna's heart as she realized what she now shared with these kids. Suddenly, her throat burned and her eyes blurred with tears. She took a deep breath and tried to blink them away. She was stuck on the edge of the porch for a moment, lost in thought.

"You all right?" Will's voice said softly.

Startled, she glanced at him, and then quickly looked away to hide the water in her eyes. "Yeah, fine," she sniffled and then cleared her throat. Her face burned as she recognized what a terrible job she was doing.

Will said nothing, but he stood quietly beside her. She had the thought of leaning into him, of letting him wrap his arms around her. Her face got hotter, and she shoved the thought so far she was sure it would land in another governance.

"We'll find them and bring them to justice," Pyran said to the widow as she stood in the doorway.

She nodded, but didn't look too sure. "Be careful, please. I don't want any of you to be hurt. That wouldn't bring back my Bill."

"Of course," Captain Heiser nodded. "Well-Mother's blessings upon you all."

"And on you," she nodded.

That night, after Anna had shown Clara how to set up their tent, everyone listened as those who'd been at the table retold the story. The night was quiet after that until everyone went to bed, preparing to rise with the sun.

The next morning, they made their way to the spot in the orchard where the attack had occurred. Anna spun the ring on her finger. The five-petaled paxmortium flower flashed each time it saw the sun. She hoped it protected against more than necromancy, but she knew that Ben would've mentioned it if it did.

"She actually said they *ripped* them apart?" Clara asked, eyes wide in disbelief.

"Yes," Ros answered, matter-of-fact. "Even Merry won't have enough reach to stay away from their claws. If we get into it with them, we'll need to lean on our ranged attacks and hope those of us fighting up close are fast enough to avoid a grapple."

"Uh-huh, totally," Clara's voice came out in a squeak. She reached behind her to where Skullcrusher was strapped to her back, reassuring herself it was there.

"It's been a while," the captain said, "so we may not see much here, but anything we learn could prove useful."

"Mother and all her children," Pyran swore under his breath as he looked at the opening in the apple trees.

The morning sun was just peeking over the branches. The apple trees cast long, overlapping shadows. Two of the neatly planted trees stood crooked, some of their roots sticking out like a leafless bush. A small sword stuck out of one trunk. The ground was torn in places, and patches of grass lay scattered. It was as if a tornado had touched down in this one spot. As Anna took a sharp breath in through her nose, she could faintly smell the remains of viscera.

"Look around, but try not to trample anything that could tell us something useful," the captain ordered.

Anna squatted to inspect the ground. It was dark and soft in the shade of the apple trees. She recognized the boot prints that led into the space. *They're far apart. They were running. They scatter when they reach the new clearing in the trees.*

"The farmers thought they could catch them by surprise," she told the team.

Now she saw the tracks from the Vasbrute. They wore boots, but the tread differed from that of the farmers, different from any tread she'd seen before. *They're also more than twice the size of the farmers.* She blanched a little at the mental image of just how giant these things were, now that she had a foot to compare. She followed a set of tracks behind a berry bush.

With a gasp, she jumped back and covered her mouth with the back of her hand. Sitting under the bush was a chunk of human hand, three fingers still attached. Maggots had eaten through half the tissue.

"Woah." Cal caught her before she could collide with him, then followed her eyeline. "Yeah," he said, the words a little choked. "That's gross."

"They thought they were going to stick some Vasbrute with rusty old swords," Lucy said, swatting the sword sticking out of the tree trunk so that it made a *twaaang.* "Seriously, this thing could be pre-War, with the way it's never been taken care of."

"I'd argue that running headfirst at a bunch of Vasbrute is foolish, regardless of what you carry," Ben said. He stood in the middle of the open space with his brows furrowed.

"The wooden shields didn't help them any, either," Ros said, holding up two splintered pieces of a shield.

"They're strong," Merry said, then continued with a shrug, "but we used to hold a log-throwing contest at the county festival every year, and Lucas Fetterman could throw them pretty far. He could've maybe pulled a tree out of the ground."

"Merry," Pyran scolded.

"What? I'm just saying. You all have your unders in a twist, but they're just big, with claws and teeth, like most anything dangerous you find in the woods."

"Are you saying you want us to find you a sharp shovel?" Will joked, arms crossed as he paused his search.

"No, thanks. I'll stick with my sword and shield and keep my last hand."

As they chattered, Anna circled the space and found the large boot prints that showed which way the Vasbrute had gone. "They left this way," she called to the team.

Captain Heiser looked over at her and at the ground, then nodded. "We'll follow the tracks and try to get a sense of where they are once we've finished here."

Lucy picked up another sword and looked at it. As she turned it over in her hand, Anna saw that it was bent in half. "Do we think they have stone skin, or are we betting on that being a myth?"

"We can't count anything as myth unless it's clearly disproven," the captain responded. "We should overestimate here, not under."

"Right." Lucy dropped the sword and brushed her hands off on her legs.

"Judging by the smell and *chunks* of *people*," Will said, "I think we can say that those farmers really were torn apart. It's amazing that none of them died right here."

Ros stood in the middle, looking down at the ground. They mimed picking up something big and then swinging it around. "I think they used that branch as a club."

"Why go to that effort if you have a sword like we were told they did? Why pull people apart?" Pyran asked.

"Intimidation?" Merry suggested.

"They're already twelve feet tall and made of stone. Why would they need to be more intimidating?" Callum asked in frustration.

Merry shrugged.

"Maybe they didn't think it was worth grabbing their weapons," Pyran said, a sour look on his face.

"I don't think they were thinking rationally," Ben said, eyebrows still furrowed but eyes closed. He held his hands out in front of himself, palms down. Anna noticed that the tips of his fingers glowed.

"No, really? A bunch of hulking monsters not acting rationally?" Will responded sarcastically.

Ben pursed his lips, then said, "They have the capacity for rational thought. They're not driveling beasts. Telluth has made a handful of well-negotiated agreements with them over the years."

"And now they're breaking the biggest one," Ros thought aloud.

"We've confirmed that it's Vasbrute," Clara said. "Can't we just report our findings here and go back to the capital?"

"We were sent to find out *why* they're here," the captain reminded her. "Until we can answer that question, our mission is incomplete."

Clara assented with a heavy sigh.

A quiet moment passed before Anna said, "Ben? What did you mean, they weren't thinking rationally?"

Ben sighed and lowered his hands. He opened his eyes and looked at Anna. "I can sense...something, but it's too faint for me to understand it."

"Sense what?" Lucy glanced at his hands. "Battle frenzy or something?"

Ben shook his head. "I can't sense emotion—"

"Glad we're being honest with ourselves," Will teased.

"—but I can get a sense of magics. They leave a sort of stain on the area," Ben finished, ignoring Will.

"What kind of stain are you sensing?" the captain asked.

Ben shook his head as he searched for the right words. "It's...dark and unfamiliar. Not the kind of thing I'm used to at the Academy. And it's too faint to learn anything more from it."

"Great," Clara threw her hands up. "The giant monsters wield mysterious dark magic!"

"Can Vasbrute be mages?" Ros asked Ben.

The mage shrugged. "I don't know why they couldn't."

36

THEY HAD LEARNED LITTLE AT THE SITE OF THE ATTACK, BUT THEY'D confirmed the nature of what they were tracking. With renewed terror, Anna joined Will in leading the group into the woods.

Her hair raised at every little sound, and she had to trace the movement of every squirrel and bird to check that it wasn't a monster. Fortunately, the tracks were easy to follow. Just as with the abandoned Vassian campsites, they didn't seem to care if they were found. Bushes lay trampled, branches broken, and at one point, they found the remains of dead wolves. Anna couldn't tell if the forest or the Vasbrute had picked the bones clean.

They were quiet as they went. It was what the job required, but it left Anna with a lot of room in her head for her anxieties to fill. To stay focused, she ran through her internal library of medicinal and edible plants and gathered them as she went. The familiarity of the task settled her nerves, and she was able to free herself from her jumpiness.

As they set up camp that night under the branches, Anna shared what she had gathered with the team. Most of them snacked on the berries as they set up their tents and settled in.

"How did you gather so much?" Will asked her, after his tent was set up.

Anna shrugged. Gathering had been her only job for years. "It's easy to do as you go."

After another day of tracking, he approached Anna as they were setting up camp again.

"Here." He held out a small bag. "You can add this to your stock."

She took it from him curiously, and she found berries and mushrooms inside. She pulled some out to inspect them. "Good job on the blueberries, but there are a couple of false morels in here. You wouldn't want to eat those. The true morels have hollow stems."

Disappointment flashed across his face, but a sharp smirk quickly replaced it. "Just testing you."

"Uh-huh." Anna rolled her eyes, but her amused smile gave her away.

"Have to keep you on your toes." He turned and walked back to his tent.

"Who is that guy?" Lucy's elbow bumped Anna as she watched Will walk off.

Anna jumped in surprise. "What do you mean? That's Will. We introduced you to everyone when we were in Dore."

"I don't mean his *name*," Lucy said, irritated. "I mean, *who* is he?"

Anna shrugged. "He's from Kastarus. Fights with daggers. Light on his feet, fast, quiet. He's sarcastic most of the time. Why?"

"Just curious what's going on there," the woman smirked, and wiggled a finger between Anna and Will.

Anna snorted. "I didn't think you had an imagination, Lucy."

"I don't." Her smirk grew. "There's some tension there."

"Yeah, he's annoyed that I'm a wimp at melee and he had to teach me. That's it."

"Hm." She put a hand to her lips. "Maybe. Or there's something else going on."

"Go put up your own tent." Anna shooed her away.

Lucy laughed as she walked away, popping a berry into her mouth.

Anna watched Will help Cal with their tent for a moment, until he turned back and caught her staring. Then she quickly turned around to her own tent, avoiding meeting his eyes.

Each night was a similar routine. After putting up their tents, Anna and Will left camp to set up snares. When they came back, Merry and Pyran would be cooking what they had caught the day. The sun would disappear, and the stars would peek from behind the branches above them. Then, when they woke up, Anna and Will would check their snares before they started walking again. The routine kept her grounded. It was an echo of her time in the trees around Wallset that chased away the anxiety and fear biting at her heels.

THEY FOUND A CROW STUCK IN ONE OF THEIR SNARES THE NEXT MORNING. It cawed loudly when they appeared, and then louder as they approached. It tried to fly, tugging at the rope wrapped around its ankle and pulling at the bush it was attached to, sending feathers flying.

Will stepped forward to free it, dagger in hand. "Hold still," he said through gritted teeth as he tried to grab the bird. It didn't listen. He settled for grabbing the rope as high up as he could and cutting it free. In a cacophony of wings, the crow flew up into the canopy and disappeared. They could still hear it shouting as they moved to the next snare.

They walked further into the woods that day. Anna's nerves calmed as time passed. Now, on their third day in the trees, she made her way with careful ease. They had seen a couple of treecats that scurried off as they walked, but they saw nothing unusual except for the signs they followed through the trees.

Until that afternoon.

Anna signaled to Will to stop as she heard movement in the greenery ahead. He stopped, crouching thirty feet to her left.

A squirrel ran from the base of a dense bush ahead. Anna let out a sigh of relief.

Guess I'm still jumpy.

As she stood up, a hedgebear the size of Merry crashed through the bush and into the open space. It stared at her from twenty feet ahead, lifted its snout into the air to smell, and then bared its teeth and growled. Anna's breath caught as it lowered its head at her, and the spines across its body raised defensively.

"Anna." Will's hissed call came from her left, where he was still hiding.

He was probably waiting for a signal. She dared not look away from the bear, but she held her left hand out, telling him to *stay put*. Then she lifted both arms in the air to make herself appear as tall as possible.

The hedgebear continued its growl. It stepped toward her slowly.

"Shit," she breathed.

"Anna!" Will hissed again.

She waved her left hand at him, telling him to stay put. The bear's eyes snapped to the movement, and then it charged.

She yelled at the top of her lungs. The bear snarled. Will jumped up, a blade in each hand.

The hedgebear turned suddenly and ran away. It looked back at her before disappearing into the pine trees to her right.

Anna panted, listening as the sounds of its running faded away. *I just beat a hedgebear at a game of chicken.* Her pulse thundered in her ears.

"Mother's Children," Will swore, walking up to her. "That thing wanted to kill you."

Anna shook her head. "Hedgebears don't eat people. They hardly even eat meat."

"It still wanted you dead." He put a hand to his chest. He was catching his breath, too. He leaned forward to look her over for any injury.

"It was scared. It shouldn't have wanted anything to do with us."

"I can't believe yelling at it worked. And your hands in the air like that." He straightened and raised his eyebrows. "You looked ridiculous."

"Better than looking dead," she argued. A grin pulled at the corner of her mouth. "You were scared."

"Of course I was! That thing was coming for *me* after it got you."

Anna laughed, relief bubbling up like the head on a fresh pint of ale. "Mother, that was close." She looked down at her shaking hands.

Will eyed her as if she'd tried to dance with the bear. "Why are you laughing?"

"I don't know." She shook her head and giggled. "I wasn't sure that would work."

"You are unhinged."

"You had your daggers out. Why didn't you throw them?"

"I was trying to follow your lead, *woodswoman*."

"Hm," she hummed to herself. "I'm glad you did. It didn't really want to hurt us. I think it was displaced. We might be close to the Vasbrute camp. When they came in, they must have kicked the hedgebear out."

"And you just screamed loud enough that the whole forest knows our position."

Anna's eyes widened.

Will let out a deep sigh, looking pensive. His dark eyes scanned the trees in front of him.

"What is it?"

"What's *what*?" His eyes found hers, confused.

"What are you thinking about?" Anna clarified her question.

"We're about to spring the trap that we've been sent to spring." He looked at her with concern on his brow.

"We've been in the trap ever since we left," Anna argued.

Will nodded his head from side to side as he considered that. "You're not wrong."

"The Vasbrute scare you, though," Anna prodded.

"Don't they scare you?" he asked.

"Of course!" Anna shrugged her shoulders. "I just thought you were comfortable with your...*plan*."

Will leaned back and crossed his arms, his muscles rippling as they moved. His deep brown eyes narrowed slightly as he looked at Anna. "Maybe I'm not the one I'm scared for."

Anna stared at him, confused. He seemed irritated by her comment on his escape, but his words threw her off guard. She couldn't make sense of what he actually meant. Just as she began to lean forward in response, someone rushed through the trees behind them.

Ros, panting slightly, looked between the two of them and then they crossed their freckled arms. "And here the two of you are having a picnic. I suppose you wanted to have a screaming match, and that was the commotion we heard?"

Anna turned around. "There was a hedgebear," she explained. "We had to scare it off, but hedgebears usually stick around their dens. I think the Vasbrute are close."

Ros raised a skeptical eyebrow, then shrugged and dropped their arms. "I'll listen to the woodswoman. What do you propose we do, then?"

Anna glanced at Will, who was brushing the dirt from his hands, then she turned back to Ros. "We'll find a spot to set up a base...far from here. After we establish our camp, we can look for the Vasbrute camp, do some surveillance."

Ros looked at Will, who shot them a grin that didn't meet his eyes. "All right. I'll tell the others. We won't go any further than this."

Anna nodded, and then Ros disappeared the way they'd come.

37

WILL WAS QUIET AS THEY LOOKED FOR A SPOT WITH ENOUGH CLEAR ground to set up camp. Anna glanced at him occasionally.

He's probably scared for the whole team. You don't have to be best friends with people to care about them.

Anna thought about the others dying. She didn't know if she could bear it. *None of them deserve this. That's why it's all or nothing. That, and mom.*

They found a clearing underneath a canopy of the tallest fir trees Anna had ever seen. The lowermost branches of the oldest trees were thirty feet in the air, and she couldn't stop staring at them as she helped Clara with their tent. After they raised their shelters, the team paused for a quick snack. Anna guessed they could supplement a couple more meals with the food they had been rationing, and the rest would have to be gathered from the forest.

Captain Heiser didn't eat. He stayed in his tent instead. Just as she was finishing, he came out, finding a patch of grass to spread out their map, keeping the edges from rolling by placing rocks or sticks at the corners. Everyone gathered around him as he crouched by the hand-marked parchment Commander

Lyon had given Pyran and Anna. As Anna looked at it, she guessed they were somewhere between marks D and E, the last Council-confirmed camp and the camp found by Commander Lyon's spies.

The captain poked a point closer to D than E, and he said, "We're here. Anna thinks the Vasbrute are nearby, and our location would suggest that's probable." He nodded at Anna. "It looks like they've been moving west along the northern side of the wall, but they aren't moving in a clear pattern, and they aren't moving quickly. Their camps bounce from north to south along that route, seemingly at random. We're here to find out why."

He looked up from the map and into the faces of his team. "Why did they cross the wall? What are they looking for? What do they want?"

Anna nodded.

"Remember what we've learned so far. Look for connections."

The captain's words called to mind what she had seen at the abandoned camp. The layout of the structures and the large campfire. *For Branik* carved into a crude stool, stained into the wood as if left as a warning. Then she thought of the signs of violence in the apple orchard.

"I'm going to send out four of you to look for them," Captain Heiser continued. "Anna and Will. *Don't* run into any more hedgebears. Shout like that again, and we'll be sitting ducks." He looked at both of them seriously, but Anna knew the comment was meant to lighten the heavy mood.

"No more hedgebears," she nodded. "Got it."

"Ros, Callum, you'll join them. Stay quiet, use your signals, and be careful. If you find nothing, return by sundown. If you see them, come back immediately to report their location. We can begin surveillance later." His voice softened. "If you're compromised, do your best not to lead them back here." He looked at the others. "The rest of you will wait here with me. Merry, it might be a good time for you to catch some dinner, and we can have it ready for them when they get back."

"Sure thing, sir," Merry nodded.

"All right." The captain glanced back down at the map, then looked over his team again. "Double check all of your gear. We'll see you when you return."

Anna walked back to her shared tent. She would leave her pack here, but she needed something out of it.

She pulled out the last letter from her mother, folded it small, and tucked it into her armor between two pieces of leather. She checked that her necklace was still tucked into the collar of her shirt, her hunting knife and sword were still at her belt, and then pulled her quiver over her shoulder and strapped her shortbow to her back. She came out of her tent, hesitated, and then retied the lace of her left boot.

"Ready?" Will approached from the tent he shared with Cal. He had three daggers at his belt and a shortsword strapped to his back. The frontmost dagger at his waist was the jump dagger they had pulled from the ruins of the cottage, lost to time in the woods outside of Kastarus. Its pommel sparked blue in the sunlight as he walked, the only part of his gear that didn't blend into his dark, almost black leathers.

She double-checked the tightness of the knot at her laces, then stood. "Ready."

Will started walking, and Anna followed. Ros and Cal met them at the edge of the camp.

Cal gave a stiff, pale-faced nod in greeting. Ros watched them approach with their serious brows pulled low and their pale blue eyes icy as they looked them over.

"You two are fully prepared?" Ros asked. "I've already reminded Callum of the consequences we face if we fail to stay unseen and unheard."

"Ros was very descriptive," Cal added.

"No wonder you look like you're about to lose your lunch," Will told him.

"We're aware, Ros," Anna said. "And we're ready."

"Good," came Ros' simple reply.

"Let's go over hand signals one more time," Cal said, glancing between them nervously.

"I think you know them, but we might as well," Anna said. "I'll go through the signals, and you tell me what each means."

Anna cycled through their sign language and Callum named each one. "There, feel better?" she asked sincerely.

"No," he said quietly. He glanced past them at the group left by the fire. Anna followed his gaze and found Clara smiling and waving. Anna's eyes met Pyran's, and he sent her a nod, his face tight. Lucy slapped him on the shoulder, sending Anna a reassuring smile before pulling Pyran's attention.

Anna led them back to where they had seen the hedgebear, and then they paused.

"He came from that direction," Anna nodded towards the bushes the creature had burst through.

Cal nodded.

Anna looked at Ros and Will.

"You've brought us this far," Ros told her. "Time to finish the job."

Will nodded in agreement, his face drawn and serious.

It was encouraging. She realized, suddenly, how much they trusted her.

Anna nodded back, and then turned and led them further on.

They heard the Vasbrute first. It only took an hour of walking before they could hear the sounds of chopping wood, metal clanging, and gruff chatter. The voices were distant and they could only hear the loudest of them, but Anna was sure. The tones were deep and gravelly. Half an hour further, and they could see the spiky tops of the camp's fence, yellow and orange tents peeking over the top. Anna made the motion for them to stop, looking through the gaps in the bush in front of her.

"There are many deer here for roasting," a rough voice carried through the trees. "No wonder the humans and dwarves have such round bellies."

Laughter followed. There was more metal on metal, like two people sparring with swords.

From this angle, the rough fence that circled the camp and the tents just past them blocked Anna's view. She could only just make out a break in the fence on the left side of the camp, and she could see a full opening on the right side.

The sound of an axe splitting wood echoed off the trees, but she couldn't make out where the person chopping was. The sound paused and another voice, a little higher than the first, said, "There is too much shade here. We should take their deer and clear their forests for our own building if we're going to stay."

Log splitting began again, but through it, Anna heard someone respond. "They need the shade. Their skin is too soft for the full light of Sollis. They are burnt by it."

More laughter.

"Holy shit."

Anna froze as Cal swore under his breath, so quietly that she barely heard.

A figure stepped out into the opening in the fence, and Anna instinctively stopped breathing. *They must be seven feet tall, at least!* Their head and shoulders rose above the top of the fence. They had a bald head—in fact, Anna saw no hair on them at all—and pointed ears, not just at the peak of their ear, but the lobe also ended in a point.

Her attention was quickly pulled from their ears to their frame. They looked like a walking marble statue of Telluth's strongest person. They wore no shirt, their gray pecs and strong abdominal muscles exposed. Anna guessed that this was a male by the shape of their chest. His waist was at least double hers, and yet his shoulders widened into two rippling arms. He wore brown leather pants and dark, thick boots. He turned his head as he stepped into the break in the fence, scanning the trees. His dark eyes flashed red in the sunlight.

The hair on the back of Anna's neck prickled, and she felt cold sweat on her back, but he made no sign that he saw them.

He crossed his arms and angrily bared his teeth, exposing pointed white teeth that fit together like a dog's. His head turned away as he said into the camp, "We will take their deer and their trees, and it will still not be enough to cover the debt they owe for Branik. We will take that payment in blood."

There was no laughter.

The camp stayed quiet except for wood splitting and the sounds of metal on metal.

After a moment, the Vasbrute scanned the forest with one more red glare before turning and walking back into camp.

There was a tap on Anna's shoulder. She turned to see Will giving the signal for retreat, and she nodded in response.

She watched every step of her feet as they moved away.

38

WITH THEIR OWN CAMP IN SIGHT AGAIN, ANNA FINALLY ALLOWED HERself to breathe normally. Her neck and jaw were tight from how tensely she carried herself up to that point, each movement measured and overthought.

"Viterra give us strength," Cal breathed.

"Even the gods wouldn't be able to give us enough strength to equal *that*," Will said.

Anna shook her head, frowning. "Not *that*. They're people."

Will raised an irritated eyebrow at her.

"She's right," Ros said. "We cannot let ourselves forget their intelligence or reasoning. Their reasoning is the purpose of our mission."

"You're back!" Clara appeared around a tent. Her smile fell as she took in her brother's sour face. "Did you find them?"

"Yes," Cal answered, his dark brows pushing together in concern.

Clara was quiet as she walked with them into camp. They found most of their crew at the center, around the small fire there. A buck hung from a tree at the edge of camp.

Captain Heiser saw them first. He rose abruptly from his seat by the fire and took a few steps toward them, which drew the attention of the others.

"You found them," he said. It wasn't a question.

"Yes, sir," Anna answered as they stopped by the fire. The captain's tension brought hers back, and she stood stiffly at the edge of the circle.

Ros crossed their arms next to her. Will rested a hand on his hip, and Cal shifted his weight uncomfortably from foot to foot.

Merry, Ben, and Lucy sat by the fire. Ben's book was in his lap, and it looked like Merry had been drawing in the dirt with the stick she was using to stir the fire. Lucy leaned forward, resting her elbows on her knees.

"What did they look like?" Merry asked.

"How many were there?" Lucy threw in.

"Could you distinguish a leader?" Ben added.

Captain Heiser put up a hand, irritated. "Let them tell us what they know."

All eyes were on the four of them.

"The camp is set up identically to the others. They have someone watching each of the entrances at all times," Ros told them. "We couldn't tell how many there were, but I think our estimate of ten is still appropriate."

"Eight feet tall, more muscles than is possible on any other kind of *person*," Will glanced at Ros as he said the word *person*.

They nodded at him appreciatively.

"I wouldn't be surprised if they were made of stone." Will turned back to the others around the fire. "The one we saw wasn't wearing any armor. They don't have hair, either. Red eyes."

"They were talking," Anna started, "about a debt that they're owed. *A debt of blood* for Branik." She paused for a moment in thought. "It sounded like Branik was one of them who was killed. They blame everyone north of the wall."

Everyone was quiet for a moment as they took in the information. The captain crossed his left arm over his chest to hold his right elbow, and his right hand moved to his chin. He looked into the fire as he thought, and then asked, "Was there any sign that they were ready to move camp again?"

"No," Ros answered. "They were still cutting wood for the camp."

"They could pick up and move at any time, though," Callum said. "We don't know why they move camp or where they're going."

The captain nodded. "All right, here's the plan." He had Anna mark the approximate location of the Vasbrute camp on their map. "We'll run surveillance with the four of you. You'll take shifts in groups of two. You'll go close enough that you can hear, but stay far enough that you're easily out of sight. *Listen.* Try to find out who Branik was and how they died. Try to figure out how many of them there are. Look for weaknesses in their watches. Perhaps we can slip someone into camp if a large group leaves, or if they fall asleep at night. Hopefully, we'll find out what we need before it comes to that."

The fire popped, and Anna's heart stuttered. "No more fires at night," she said quickly, heart beating hard against the cage of her ribs. "And any fires during daylight should be small. No wet wood or leaves."

"Anna's right." Captain Heiser looked at each of the others. "We can't give ourselves away now that we're this close. Keep noise to a minimum. Hunt and set traps away from their camp. Ben will start the fires and put them out. No more chopping wood." He took a breath. "Be ready for anything. Sleep with your armor on and your weapons close. If you're going to piss in the middle of the night—"

Will's hand shot forward and grabbed the captain's arm. Everyone stilled. When Anna looked at Will, his jaw was tense, and he was looking intently into the trees. He tapped his ear twice and then pointed in the direction he was looking.

The direction they had come back into camp.

Anna's hair stood up, and a wave of nausea filled her gut. She listened for a few seconds that would turn into hours in her memory.

The fire crackled. A squirrel chittered and birds chirped. A crow landed on a branch at the edge of camp in a cacophony of wings flapping.

"Caw! Caw!" it eyed them and tilted its head. "Careful! Careful!"

Anna's stomach plummeted.

"They're coming," Will breathed.

"FUCK," CAPTAIN NATHANIEL HEISER CURSED.

"I thought you said they didn't see you!" Clara half-whined, half-scolded in a hiss.

"They didn't!" Callum whisper-shouted back.

Had he just pretended not to see them?

The crow cawed again and ruffled its feathers.

"Your orders, captain?" Lucy asked.

The captain turned to Will. "How far are they?"

Will's jaw flexed as he listened carefully. "Maybe ten minutes."

Anna marveled at his hearing.

Captain Heiser turned to the rest of them. "If you do not have your weapons, grab them *now*."

Lucy, Pyran, Clara, and Merry hurried to their tents.

"Will, Anna, Cal, hide yourselves. Not in the tents. Make them walk past you to get into camp. We want to surround them. If you can climb a tree, do it. Wait for my signal."

"Yes, sir," Anna blurted out of habit before turning. She almost ran into Will, who grabbed her shoulder with one hand and squeezed it.

"Remember what we talked about."

She nodded stiffly.

He leaned down to her ear and said quietly, "Stay out of sight, even after they pass." Then he turned, and on his light, fast feet, he found a tree to climb.

Suddenly, all Anna could hear was the breath she forced in and out of her lungs. Looking around, she saw a thick pine at the edge of camp. The branches were spaced well enough, and pine needles wouldn't make the rustling that leaves would. She grabbed the longbow from her tent and buried it in the leaves at the base of a nearby maple. She wouldn't be able to use it in the tree, but she could save it for later.

She jumped for the closest branch of the pine that could support her weight. The rough bark scratched at her hands, but the feeling was numbed now along with most of her senses. She was vaguely aware of the captain talking with Ben in the middle of camp. Those that had gone for weapons scattered again.

Anna inhaled and exhaled as she climbed higher, higher, high enough that they couldn't reach her, but that if she fell, she might have a chance of not breaking her legs or her back if she rolled right. She settled onto a thick branch, straddling it tightly between her legs so that her arms were free to shoot her bow.

The captain took a seat at the fire, and Ben circled his arms in front of him, and then made a motion like he was laying an invisible blanket over the air there. His mouth moved, but Anna couldn't hear his words. Forms grew around the campfire, taking shape to look like most of the team, sitting with Captain Heiser.

He's drawing them in. The captain is our frontline, our bait.

"Caw, caw!"

Anna's head swiveled. The crow was perched in the tree next to her, looking at her. *Had he been there before, or did he switch trees?* She made a shooing motion at him. He blinked back. She pushed her lips together in frustration.

But she had heard the crow clearly. Her ears were working again. Anna turned away from the bird and readied her bow. She nocked an arrow.

A storm of footsteps grew in the distance. They would come in behind her.

Good. The less I see them, the less time I have to grow a white liver.

Stay hidden, Will had told her. She thought of her mother, who would probably be closing up shop soon. She thought of her father. The briefest moment of comfort passed as she realized that no matter the outcome, she'd be with one of them when this was over.

The thunder of their boots on the ground slowed and quieted. Anna looked down. Below her, massive gray people were walking into camp. At the front was the one they had seen at the fence. She recognized his scar.

She blinked as she saw three of the heads marked with a gold circle. It shone too brightly to be a trick of the sunlight through the trees. She noted that these Vasbrute had their chests wrapped tightly in leather.

The leader of the pack walked slowly into the camp, his red eyes focused on the people around the fire. He stopped at the edge of the nearest tent. The captain and the images turned to look at him.

"You do not run, or raise your weapons and charge stupidly against us?" the leader called out to Captain Heiser, his voice full of sharp stones.

"No," the captain replied in an unbothered tone. "We know it wouldn't do any good." Still seated, and wearing a face of practiced calm, he continued. "Tell me, did you see them, or did you discover some sign of them after they left?"

Anna could hear a grin in the leader's voice. "Vassians are the best hunters that walk two legs. I smelled them before I saw them, and we knew you were near even before you knew we were."

A few of the Vasbrute split off quietly to circle the camp. One of them came to the base of Anna's tree. She hoped they wouldn't discover her longbow—or step on it and snap it like a twig. She felt a spark at her chest, and there was a rustling near the closest tent. The Vasbrute's head swiveled, and they turned to investigate.

"Stand," the Vassian leader demanded, "and meet your death with honor."

The captain's face broke into a cool smile. "I had hoped we might try to talk this out."

"I have no patience for talking with murderers," the leader growled, baring his teeth.

The captain sighed. "Very well." He stood and lifted an arm. He grabbed it with his other hand, stretching.

Anna stiffened, recognizing the beginning of the signal.

"With honor," Captain Heiser said, then dropped his arm down.

In that moment, Anna knew she couldn't hide. She loosed her arrow.

It sung through the air and buried itself in the soft spot between a Vasbrute shoulder and shoulder blade, although it wasn't as soft as she hoped. It barely stuck in. The *crack* of Callum's crossbow sounded, and a bolt buried itself into the ribs of another Vasbrute with a sound like grinding. Will's dagger flashed through the air and caught the back of a Vasbrute thigh with a scraping sound. Two darts stuck a Vasbrute, one sticking into an eye, the other scratching, but bouncing off a cheekbone. A roaring ball of flame fell from the sky and exploded at the center of the group.

They let out a collective roar, half in pain and half in rage.

The leader and the three closest to him charged forward, their skin blackened from the explosion. The images of the people around the fire dissipated, and Captain Heiser was left exposed. His face set into a grim focus and he drew the blade at his hip. The others charged from the surrounding tents and joined the battle.

The Vassian that Anna had shot turned to locate his assailant before the ball of fire struck. The earth shook from the blast, and Anna turned all of her energy to clinging to the branch she was on, almost dropping her bow as she did. Fire covered the ground and licked at the nearby tents. When she looked up, her mark was no longer where she'd last seen him.

The tree shook again, this time creaking as it swayed violently. She cursed and clung to the branch, legs and arms wrapped around the rough bark. Looking straight down, she saw the Vasbrute standing at the base of her tree, hugging the trunk and shaking it back and forth. His sharp, toothy grin told her he was unaffected by the arrow sticking out of his shoulder. He wasn't going to stop until she came out of the tree.

She had to do something. Anna let go with her right arm and her left held harder onto the branch, straining. Her fingers reached for another arrow, feeling around the opening of her quiver. They found the fletching and she yanked it out. Nocking the arrow was its own challenge. Her muscles ached as she fought to stay attached to the branch. Then she pulled the string taut, pressing her cheek against the bark underneath her to line up her shot. She saw the Vasbrute's eyes flash red, and she released. The arrow drove into his bicep and he howled, letting go of the tree.

With the release of the bowstring, the circle of Anna's arms was broken, and she fell sideways. Her face scraped against the branch as she spun, and she squeezed her eyes shut. She locked her legs together, and her calves cut short the sensation of falling, holding her to the branch. She cried out in pain as her ankles slammed together. She hung there long enough to open her eyes before the force of her body weight pulled her legs apart.

Branches flew by, and she tried to grab at them. They sliced at her exposed arms until her right arm found one thick enough. Her fingers wrapped around the branch, and it tore into her hand as she spun upright. Her weight pulled her fingers from the branch again, but it slowed her. She spun until her back hit the ground. The hard dirt knocked the air out of her lungs and her vision flared with stars.

Will 39

WILL DANCED AROUND THE VASBRUTE IN FRONT OF HIM. SHE WAS FAST FOR a creature of her size, but not as fast as Will. Still, he wasn't used to the reach of her massive arms, so he was glad that his thrown dagger had cut into her hamstrings. She held no sword, but her nails were hard and sharp. His forearm stung where the sweat made its way into the three cuts she'd slashed there.

The camp had erupted into chaos after Ben's magical explosive went off. Will had been watching as Ben set the trap, but only realized what the mage was doing as it happened.

They barely had numbers on the pack. If they kept the Vasbrute separated and distracted, they *might* have a chance.

In the distance, Will heard someone scream. The sound was abruptly cut off.

Maybe not.

He heard Anna cry out, and his eyes snapped in her direction. If he could get to her, they could fight their way out and make an escape. He couldn't tell what was happening past the tent between them. The Vasbrute woman used the opportunity to claw at him, but he caught the movement in his peripheral vision and spun in the direction of the attack. While the Vasbrute was committed to the motion, he slashed his dagger across her forearm. She cried out in pain, a deep, rasping sound, but the cut wasn't as deep as he hoped.

"Lucky little elf," she growled.

"*Not* an elf," Will countered through clenched teeth.

She pulled back. At his reply, Will thought he saw the red fire in her eyes dim. It was as if her anger had dulled, and with it her drive to fight.

Will didn't stop to ponder what had happened. Instead, he lunged, hoping to force her off balance so he could catch her with his blades as she tried to right herself. Instead, she took one step back and let him slice at her abdomen. It did no more damage than his previous hits. The fire in her eyes ignited again. She grabbed the wrist he slashed at her with and crushed it with her hand.

Will cried out in pain, but turned to drive his other knife at her. She knocked the attack aside, but in doing so, she let go of his other hand.

Will got what he wanted—space. He pulled his injured hand into his chest. It pulsed with pain, and he couldn't tell if she'd broken it. He tried moving it, and the pain flared hotter. Thankfully, it wasn't his dominant hand, but he could not use it now.

A blast sounded. They both looked toward the middle of camp. Another explosion of flame slammed into a group of Vasbrute gathered near the Captain, Merry, Pyran, and Clara. His squadmates stood in a loose V, most of the Vassians inside the formation.

"Get the mage!" The leader of the pack extended a gray, clawed finger toward Ben, who stood at the edge of a tent. Ben's hands were locked into the last form of his spell, and he panted and then paled at the finger pointed in his direction. He was about thirty feet from Will.

The Vasbrute in front of Will growled and turned to charge at Ben.

"No, you don't!" Will swung at her with his uninjured hand.

Blood swelled in the cut he dragged through her skin, but she ignored him. She closed the distance in a few long strides.

The mage's gray eyes widened with fear. "No, please!" He threw his hands up in defense.

The Vassian woman paused, standing stiffly with her claws raised.

As Will got closer, he watched Ben blink, seemingly stunned. He didn't move, but his fingertips glowed softly. *He sees something in her eyes.* Will saw Ben's mouth move, forming the words, "That's it, isn't it?" but the words were lost to the clamor of the battlefield.

The Vassian woman jumped as if struck by something, and then her claws were flying towards Ben and Will was racing to stop her.

40

ANNA CROUCHED UNDER THE BRANCHES OF THE SPRAWLING PINE SHE had fallen from. The Vasbrute man pushed her slowly into camp with each attack. Her chest heaved as she wheezed through each intake and release of her lungs. Her shortbow lay on the ground further back. She had dropped it when she fell and pulled her sword from her belt to defend herself.

Her longbow was out of reach. Her arms were covered in cuts from the Vasbrute's claws as she guarded and parried. She knew she wouldn't last long with the sword. She didn't have the skill, speed, nor the strength to match even Pyran, let alone a Vasbrute, but she had yet to think of a way to get out from under his claws. It seemed like he was playing with her, flaying her arms until he shredded her skin or he got bored. Meanwhile, it was all she could do to pull air into her lungs and let herself be forced further back.

She tried to remember her training, but each attack jarred her and left her thoughts incomplete.

Balance on the balls of my feet, then— Parry to the side, swing back with— Don't hold the sword too tightly—

She let out a grunt of pain and frustration as his claws swiped again and again. With no time for proper thought, Anna fell back into instinct. She needed room to breathe. Maybe the Vasbrute was like a bear or wild cat. Maybe she could trick him.

When his claws swung this time, she didn't try to parry or dodge. She stood her ground, sword finding a position below the attack. As the claws sliced into her arms again, she thrust her sword forward at his stomach. The Vasbrute was surprised. His eyes flared as her shortsword cut into his abdomen, then veered to his hip.

Red blood welled into the cut and spilled over, but it hadn't been enough. It was as if his skin was armor itself and the blade could only bite so deep before it was redirected. Even as he snarled in pain, she knew she'd only made him angrier.

It was clear she couldn't win.

Crack! Clara yelled in agony somewhere behind Anna, and she felt the heat leave her body and her hair stand on end. The Vasbrute in front of her caught the change, and he pulled the sword from his back.

"You know you'll lose," he said in his gravelly voice. "They always know before the end."

He swung his blade in an upward arc, catching hers. Anna's hands stung as her sword flew from her grasp. In her peripheral, the blade pinwheeled in the air before sticking its point down into the dirt.

His eyes flashed red as he swung again, saying, "The Son of Death can have you now."

His sword slashed down in the opposite arc of its first path. The sharp edge caught her armor just below her right shoulder, cut through the leather to slice into her chest, and glided through her flesh like it was bacon fat before exiting above her left hip.

All coherent thought left her mind, replaced by pain and fear. She saw the underside of the branches above her, and then the Vasbrute stepped over her. It felt like the sky and ground switched places, and she was hovering precipitously in between.

Will 41

WILL HAD REGAINED THE VASSIAN WOMAN'S ATTENTION AND BEN HAD escaped when he heard Anna's second, bloodcurdling scream. He turned in time to see the sword leave her body. He was already throwing the jump dagger. With a *thunk,* it landed in the tree nearest Anna, and the world shifted. Anna lay on the ground, staring into the sky as if seeing nothing, and bleeding badly from the wound across her middle. He rushed over and knelt, glancing at the Vasbrute who was still stepping away, oblivious to Will's arrival. He threw his hands at the center of the opening through her chest and pushed, trying to close what he could. Blood seeped past the edges of his hands and between his fingers, and Anna made a wet, gurgling sound.

Will's hair stood on end and his gut turned to ice. He pushed away what he knew was happening. "I told you to stay hidden," he said quietly, more to himself than to Anna. "I told you not to come out. Why did you do it? *Why?*"

Everyone was looking away from them. He turned, looking for someone in particular.

"Cal!" Will shouted. Anna was already so pale, and the surrounding ground was drenched in crimson. "Fuck, fuck, fuck," he breathed as more blood pulsed past his hands.

"Will... Will..." Anna's eyes rolled up.

"Shh, shh," he told her.

Will glanced up. On the other side of the battle, the Vasbrute woman lunged for Ben again. He shouted something in mage tongue as the hulking woman descended upon him, his hands circling each other and then flying toward the woman and the rest of the camp. She reacted as if struck by something invisible, flying back. As she did, an inky red cloud leaked out of her. A wave of energy rippled from Ben's hands and through the battle, and the Vassians all were struck in turn. As the red mass was forced from the leader of the pack, the clouds of energy writhed and vibrated.

Hands still outstretched, Ben spoke another word in the mage tongue, and closed his fists. A scream ripped through the space, not from any of the people there, but from the red mass. It seemed to shatter, bursting into nothing and leaving empty air behind.

42

ANNA FELT BOOTS ON THE GROUND NEAR HER. CALLUM STOOD OVER BOTH her and Will. “Mother—Will—”

“Help. Her,” Will demanded through clenched teeth.

A scream ripped through the space, so loud that her eardrums ached. Anna saw Cal throw his hands over his ears. When it stopped, he looked around. The Vasbrute were quiet.

“All right,” the healer bent over and reached for Anna’s arms. “Help me get her over here, out of view. Try to keep her flat.”

She felt Will take hold of her legs, and they carried her into the bushes. More stars danced around her vision as she watched the pine tree pass by, and Anna groaned. They set her down.

She had seen the blood on Will’s hands. It covered them like he had dipped his hands into a bucket of paint. Her heart skipped and jumped, but it felt dampened, like layers of furs buried it.

Her mind raced through every decision she’d ever made. Everything she’d ever said to her father. Why hadn’t she made the most of every moment with him? Every interaction with her mother. She should've opened up more. They'd both lost someone. Why couldn't she have hidden her disappointment, her frustration better? Every letter since she'd left had been so shallow. Why couldn't she say what she needed to? She should've made sure Pyran knew how much she appreciated him. The things she felt for Will, but never had the courage to say, raced through her.

She was barely aware of Cal leaning over her. She felt so hot, and her head ached. The healer's eyes glowed golden, and he pressed his hands to her chest. He pulled them back, his expression stunned, and leaned back to look her over. "It's not working." It sounded like they were surrounded by bees.

"What do you mean?" Will's voice was distressed through the hive in Anna's head. "Try harder!"

Callum shook his head, and his voice broke as he said, "I can't heal death, Will. She's dying."

"No, no!" Will's hands reached forward and grabbed Cal's wrists, putting them back on Anna's chest. "Try harder."

"There's nothing I can do," Cal said softly, almost too quietly for Anna to hear past the vibrating ache in her head. It was crescendoing. Her mouth was so dry.

"Anna. Anna," Will's red hands released Callum's and held her face. She could barely feel him. His brown eyes came into view, shining with tears. "Stay here, stay with me," he begged.

She wanted to. She would have loved more than anything to stay here, being held by him, and to say what she couldn't before, to him and everyone else. But the buzzing grew stronger until it consumed everything. Her vision faded to black.

The feel of his touch left her.

"Lynnie." Her father's voice called so softly that she thought she imagined it in the nothing that surrounded her. "It's all right, Lynnie."

Ben 43

BEN RAN FROM THE VASBRUTE WOMAN AS WILL SWUNG AT HER WITH HIS daggers, almost slipping on the ashen ground. The mage was shaking from the power he had registered inside of her. He wished he had more time to investigate, but her attempt at his life had left him with none.

He found most of his team gathered with the rest of the Vasbrute in the center of the field. As he watched, the Vassians broke through the formation, surrounding the captain, Merry, Pyran, Ros, and Clara. The dwarf woman struck out with Skullcrusher, swinging high for the head of the Vasbrute woman in front of her. The Vasbrute woman swung her sword for Clara's legs. Neither could defend or parry. The sword cut through Clara's left boot, through her flesh, and into her tibia. Clara screamed in agony at the impact, but drove her spiked mace up against the woman's gold-painted skull.

Crack!

Clara let out a wail unlike any Ben had ever heard. He felt his stomach turn as he saw the sword stuck most of the way through her shin. The Vassian woman stumbled, dazed, as blood dripped from her head. Another Vasbrute was quick to fill her place.

Ben peeled his eyes away, looking for the others. He saw the newcomer from Hillcrest, Lucy, fighting off a Vasbrute man on her own. Her shield lay yards away. She thrust forward and her sword cut into the Vasbrute's wrist, hacking into the joint. The Vassian man cried out and pulled his hand back. It sprayed hot blood over both of them before he shouted a growl and lunged, eyes and teeth flashing. His claws found purchase at the side of her breastplate, ripping it off.

The woman cried out in pain as he tore her abdomen open. Even as she stumbled, she drove her sword forward. The blade cut into his middle, and then she released it, slumping to the ground.

If she wasn't dead, she would be soon.

I have to do *something.*

Ben racked his brain for the spells he had studied and never thought he'd actually use—the spells for breaking blood curses and clearing evil spirits. When he'd taken up the research of necromancy and the like, it had felt as if he were learning a dead language, but if he couldn't recall now what he needed to, he and his team would be the dead ones.

Something from Flessey's Articles on Undoing*? No, he didn't cover blood curses. Cornelius Lyle's* Efforts Against the Necromantic, *maybe? Yes, there was an entire*

on blood curse-based possession and how to shatter it.

He caught movement from the corner of his eye. The Vasbrute woman he had broken away from was charging at him again. Will had disappeared. As quickly as he could, he ran through the words of the spells from the

he was thinking of, combing through them for the right one.

That one!

Ben shouted the recitation and thrust his hands into the movements, feeling the familiar thrum within him that came from casting. After the first verse, the air pulsed and the woman paused. He moved on quickly, finishing the words as his hands finished their circle and then throwing the spell out across the camp, toward the Vassian woman, toward the rest of the Vassians.

She flew back, struck by the force of the spell. The curse he had sensed separated from her, pulled from her very pores by the invocation Ben had worked. It hung in the air like a floating mass of fetid jam, the color of old blood. As the spell struck the other Vassians, they reacted likewise. Hands taut in front of him, Ben commanded the curse to stay, even as it pulled and writhed toward the nearest host. He could feel its will pressing against his spell, seething and malicious.

He needed to get this right. If he faltered and the spirit broke free, it would claim whoever was closest and drive them to come after him. If he miscast his spell, he could create the equivalent of a magical black hole, destroying them all. He centered himself, then shouted the closing of the spell and fisted his hands.

Be undone.

The curse screamed as he extinguished it, attempting to pierce his focus and keep him from finishing the casting, but it was for naught. The mass disintegrated violently.

Sweat beaded on his brow as he caught his breath. *If only Cornelius Lyle could see me now.*

"What—" The Vassian woman began to sit up, red eyes staring at him in shock, "What did you do?"

"You were cursed," Ben started to explain, "I—"

"Enough!" the Vassian leader called from where he stood in the midst of the paused battle. He had hold of Captain Heiser's neck and the man was held aloft, clutching at the Vasbrute arm trapping him.

"You have lost," the Vasbrute told the captain's team. "Lay down your weapons." He nodded his head toward them. "Gather them, and anything of value here. We take them with us to Vassa."

Ben yelped as the woman grappled him.

44

Something burned on Anna's left hand.

She twitched, then opened her eyes. Impenetrable blackness greeted her. There was no up or down, no ground or sky. She hung in a blank space.

She lifted her hand into her line of vision. The silver ring on her middle finger glowed white. It burned the same way her cheeks and ears did when she was embarrassed, or the way her muscles burned during strength training. It burned, she realized, with life.

"Annalynn Ivy Hale," a deep, unfamiliar voice called.

When Anna looked away from her hand, she found a dark figure in front of her, illuminated only by the light from her ring. The voice was masculine, as was the figure's face. Just barely visible were dark eyes, a square jaw, a prominent nose, and thin lips, all covered in tan skin. His dark hair, lost to her vision except for the pieces at the front that caught the light, gently fell over his forehead.

"Welcome."

He wore a black suit so dark that she could barely distinguish it from the void around them.

"Who are you? Where am I?" She felt calm. The void enveloped her in a softness. It took her worry, her fear, her excitement at the appearance of this strange figure, and it devoured them, leaving only her curiosity.

He gently smiled. "It is my ring you wear."

The petalled flower carved delicately into the metal on her finger shone back at her as she looked at it again. The flowers were a symbol of the peace one found after death, and they often grew on gravesites. The symbol of—

"Morterra." A pit deepened in her gut. An old hate, nearly forgotten in this dampening void.

"Yes." The god's deep voice filled the surrounding vacuum. His dark eyes flashed in the light. "I am the browning of leaves and the graying of hair. I am blood draining and wells drying, and I am lungs flooding and waves breaking. I am the end."

"I…am dead," Anna concluded.

"Not quite." The lift at the corner of his mouth fell again as he grew sober. "In order to explain, I must answer your second question. We are in what is called Intervallum, the space between. You might call it limbo. Each soul passes through this gate before reaching their infinite end." He gave her a moment to understand, and then continued, "I do not offer all a personal welcome. Though there are some that I greet personally, that is not why I am here. I come to you to make a deal."

"A deal?" Anna looked at him with furrowed brows. Her mind turned to the fables read to children, meant to teach them life lessons. One of them involved giving up your soul to Morterra—the lesson being that it was important to stay true to yourself, rather than give yourself up. Jokingly, she added, "Do you want my soul?"

The corner of his mouth turned up into another smirk. "Each soul is mine already. It is my responsibility to guide that energy back to the Well, where it can be forged into something new. No, I am not asking to take your soul, but rather that you hold onto it a little longer."

She frowned, not understanding.

"You have two options," he told her. "The first is simple; you let go of your soul, your self, and you find the everlasting peace that waits for everyone." His arm swung to gesture at the comfortable emptiness around them, and Anna felt the motion was as momentous as a mountain bending to point in a direction. "The second is more complicated. I will send you back to your life. You will get a second chance, but in exchange, you will be my champion.

"There are powers at work the likes of which have not been seen in hundreds of years, powers contrary to the Well and the Mother," he told her. "It is difficult for me to take action in the world. You would be my voice and hand. I have seen that our interests align, and the boons that I grant you would serve you well in our joint mission."

Anna's lungs expanded, even though there was no air. The pit in her gut shuddered. "Why me? If you are a god, as you say, you must know the way I feel."

"I do." Morterra seemed to shrink until he became a man, standing on invisible ground in front of her. "The ring you wear, in combination with the direction of the weave, has allowed me to reach through and choose you. I think you'll find there is more to me than what I take."

Anna contemplated his words. Distracted, she asked, "Was that my dad?"

His face softened to a smile that made her feel warm. "Yes. Souls are never truly lost. Sometimes, their energy finds the familiar energy of someone close to them, often when that person is coming to the gate here."

Anna returned to her contemplation. She could still feel that kernel of hate in her gut, but this space enveloped her in something gentle, something she hadn't felt since she was a child. It was like falling asleep in her father's lap, or eating a fresh birthday breakfast roll from her mother.

She asked, "I would still make my own choices, be in control?"

He nodded. "You would have your autonomy. You would also have my gifts and guidance. All you would give me is the chance to use them."

There was a part of her that was tempted toward the first option. Eternal peace sounded like the better choice on its face. But as soon as she thought about the people she would leave behind and the things she would leave undone, the answer was clear.

"I choose the second." She met his stolid gaze with conviction. "I want to go back."

A wide smile crossed his face, and the ring on her hand burned brighter. Warmth pulsed through her as he said, "Very well."

Will 45

WILL WAS CURLED INTO A TIGHT KNOT IN THE NEST OF BUSHES WHERE he and Callum had carried Anna. After her green eyes had dimmed and her pulse was gone, he started planning. He'd convinced the healer to hide with him as the Vasbrute had captured the rest of their team, before ultimately deciding to take them south across the wall. There had been an angry conversation between the Vassians and their new captives, predominantly Ben rambling something about dispelling a spirit. The pack leader had needed to be subdued by his own people, but they'deventually left without more bloodshed. They didn't bother looking for other survivors.

Will knew that he would have no trouble slipping away. What he was stuck considering was whether he could convince Cal to leave his sister. The chances were slim, probably slimmer now due to whatever injury had caused Clara to cry out in so much pain. Will was familiar with her pain tolerance from their weeks of training, and that kind of sound from her was new. She might have lost a limb.

No, Callum leaving isn't likely. I'd have to convince him to lie, tell them that I died, and go on without him.

"We should follow them," Callum said quietly, from where he was sitting on the other side of Anna's body. The bright sun filtering through the leaves was a stark contrast to the sad, defeated look on his face.

Will frowned. "Cal, I—"

Anna's chest heaved with a gasp. Both men jumped away as the body breathed again, slow and labored. The fingers curled against the damp grass, and then the feet kicked, knees bending and unbending as if relearning the movement.

"What the fuck?" Cal shouted, from ten feet away.

"Aah," Anna's voice came, and her face crinkled in pain. "Ow..."

"Anna!?" Will shouted at the body, looking frantically to the half-dwarf.

"Oh, *Mother*," Anna groaned, and her right hand grabbed at her chest. Her green eyes searched until her head turned and she found Will. He could've sworn that they pulsed brighter. "Will?"

"Anna!" He rushed to kneel next to her.

"Mother, *fuck*!" Callum got down on her other side. "You stopped breathing! We thought you were *dead*!"

"I—" she grimaced in pain and spoke between breaths, "was. Almost. He sent...me back."

"Shh, shh," Will took her other hand in both of his. It was warm. The ring on her hand felt like it had been sitting out in the sunshine.

"You should *not* be alive," the healer insisted. He gently pulled apart the hole in her leathers to look at the wound.

"He...sent me back," she insisted through the pain.

As Cal felt for the gaping hole in her chest, his fingers traced a rigid scab. "What? I..."

"Bandages," Will announced. "I'll get bandages!" He leapt up and and hurried into what remained of their camp.

He could hear Anna try to talk again, but Callum quieted her. "We can chat after we get you fixed up."

When Will returned with the medical supplies, Cal was focused on healing the slashes along her arms and the cuts across her face, but nothing happened under the glow of his hands. Together, they carefully took her leathers off, then Cal started to peel off her shirt.

Embarrassed, Will offered to get water while the healer cleaned her up. When he returned with a rag and a flask, he handed them to the healer. He did his best to avert his gaze as Cal cleaned around the wound, but his attention was drawn back when Cal began to mutter concerns.

"What?" Will asked him.

The half-dwarf shook his head. "I can't heal her, but it's like the wound is already mostly healed shut, like there are invisible stitches."

Will glanced at the wound. A long, thick scab crossed Anna's front, surrounded by silvery skin that had already scarred. He quickly looked away again, until Cal asked for help with the bandages.

46

"How do you feel?" Callum asked Anna.

She took a slow, deep breath, mouth tight and brow twitching through the pain. "Tired and sore, but better. Thank you." She glanced between him and Will, before asking, "What happened to the others?"

"They took everyone else," Will answered. "They said something about holding a tribunal once they got past the wall."

"We'll have to go after them," she said.

"You're in no state to do anything," Will told her with a small, disbelieving laugh.

"I'll get better, but we have to follow them."

Both men stared at her incredulously.

"You should be dead," Callum repeated. "The last thing you need to do is go charging over the wall. I don't know how you're *not* dead."

"That's what I was trying to tell you," Anna said, adjusting herself with difficulty so that she was sitting up. She was so tired, but she had to get this out. Will shifted to help prop her up on his lap.

"I should have died—would have died—but Morterra brought me back."

"Morterra? The god of death?" Cal asked in shock.

"You just came to," Will told her. "It's all right if your head's not on straight yet."

"I *talked* to him!" Anna insisted with a wince. The frustrated tension in her muscles seemed to stop Will from arguing again. "He told me that there's something going on here—a power working against the Well. He can't be here, so he needed a champion."

Callum was quiet when Will glanced at him.

"You're saying," the half-elf repeated back to Anna, "that the god of death needs your help."

Anna pushed her lips together as she thought about her response. "Kind of? More like we need his. He said he'd grant me boons."

Will looked at Callum again. He pulled his dark brow together in thought, lifted a hand to wipe across his face, and then let it drop after seeing all the dried blood on it.

"It would explain why I can't heal her. I can't heal fatal wounds, Will."

"This is ridiculous," Will replied, though she heard some doubt in his voice. "You don't even care about the gods."

"Morterra recognized his ring." Anna lifted her left hand to show them the silver band on her middle finger.

"All right, let's..." Will looked around. "Let's get you into one of these tents. Maybe you can eat something." In one smooth motion, he picked her up and stood, one arm under her knees, the other under her shoulders.

THEY DECIDED THAT ONE OF THE LADIES' TENTS WOULD BE THE BEST OPtion. They were among the few undamaged by Ben's fireballs. Cal offered to cook some of the venison Merry had hunted before the battle, but it was missing. Apparently the Vasbrute had taken that, too.

As Cal moved about camp, Will sat with Anna. He left the tent open so he could see the half-dwarf and vice versa for safety, but he was focused on Anna.

"He should rest, too," Anna said of Callum, her eyes still closed.

"He's worried about his sister."

A quiet moment passed, and then Anna asked, "Why didn't you run?"

When he turned back to Anna, her green eyes were on him. They were greener than grass in her pale face.

"...I couldn't."

"Why not?"

"I couldn't leave you to die." The tightness in his throat and the tears that burned behind his eyes surprised him.

Her green eyes softened. "I'm sorry."

"Don't be sorry," Will told her, wiping dried blood from her cheek. "Don't ever be sorry for that."

A weak grin formed on her lips at his touch. "Thank you. For staying."

Will shook his head. "Yeah. Same to you."

47

ANNA AWOKE THE NEXT DAY TO FIND THE TENT EMPTY. SHE GROANED IN pain as she sat up, but tried to keep herself quiet.

Don't want them to think I'm dying again.

She was still sore, but the pain didn't debilitate her like it had the day before. She crawled over to her pack and pulled out her hairbrush. She cringed as it caught in the blood dried in the auburn strands. She clenched her jaw and pushed through the stiffness in her shoulders.

Mother, I need a bath.

After brushing her hair, she knotted it on top of her head and tied it tight. It was looser than she liked, but her arms and shoulders were aching. Then she grabbed one of her oversized shirts and threw it on over the bandages that swathed her entire middle. She looked through her pack, before realizing where she had put the last letter she received from her mother. It had probably been soaked through with blood and then left to the side with her shirt when Callum bandaged her up. She'd look for it later.

Her lungs expanded in a deep breath, and she felt her skin tug at the scarring and scabbing across her front. The pain was uncomfortable, but not intolerable. If she could find some white willow bark, she'd take the little relief that it offered.

Then, she stood. The motion tugged at her wound again, and each flex of her muscles repeated it as she walked, but she pushed her way out of the tent.

Will and Cal sat by the fire in their armor, cooking rabbit. They both looked at her with surprise.

"You're standing," Cal said in disbelief.

"Woah, woah, woah." Will got up and made to walk over to her, but she shot him a hard look and he froze.

"I'm fine." She walked toward them stiffly, but she was proud of her pace. She looked theatrically at the rabbits they were holding over the fire and added, "I could eat, though."

They watched her approach, and then Will silently held out his stick to her. She took it, blew on it, and took a bite. It was good. A little overcooked, but not so dry that she was disappointed.

"Overcooked," she told him with a straight face, and then smirked, "but pretty good."

"Sit down!" Cal ordered.

Anna obliged, sitting on the stump between the two of them.

Will sat down and grabbed another stick with a rabbit prepared for roasting, sticking it into the fire.

"There's something we have to tell you," Cal said.

His lips were pulled back in a sad grimace, and he glanced at Will. She looked back and forth between them and asked, "What is it?"

Cal took in a shaky breath, opened his mouth, and then closed it again. He rubbed at the back of his neck nervously.

She turned to Will. The half-elf frowned, but he met her eyes as he said, "Lucy's dead."

She stopped breathing. She felt the blood in her face drain and her stomach fall. "No," she said, eyes no longer able to focus on anything. "No."

"I'm sorry," Will added.

She shook her head. "Where? Where is she?"

She stood, and Will stood with her. He took the stick from her and set it down before taking her arm and walking her to the edge of camp.

Lucy's body was on the ground. They had pulled her here from somewhere else. There was a trail of trampled grass and blood beside her. Her hazel eyes stared up at nothing, clouded, and her face was pale and colorless. They had placed her shield over her chest. Her sword was gone.

As Anna stared at the body, she felt lightheaded. Briefly, she thought she saw her mentor's eyes roll to look at her, but then she blinked and they were aimed at the sky again. Anna sank to her knees, her hands hovering over the shield.

"I don't think you want to—"

Before Will could stop her, she pulled the shield away. Claw marks raked across the woman's abdomen, messy tears of drying blood and torn flesh.

"*Gods.*" The shield fell from her hands as Anna gagged and fell back. Will reached for her arm and tried to pull her up and away, but she leaned back in. Her forehead met the dirt as she knelt next to her friend, tears rushing from her eyes. Pain pulsed at the front of her body as she sobbed, but she didn't care.

"Anna," Will said gently.

She shook her head against the grass.

The half-elf lowered himself to sit next to her. She felt a hand on her back as she cried.

She stayed there like that for a while. She couldn't tell how long. When the sobs finally stopped, she took in a heavy breath and slowly sat up. She looked at Lucy. She hadn't moved.

"We have to bury her." Anna wiped at her face with her sleeve.

"Cal and I will bury her." Will's hand rubbed her back.

"She needs her sword."

"I'll find it."

"Fuck." Her throat tightened again, and she glanced at Will. *He should've chosen Lucy. Why did he choose me?*

"Do you want to try to eat something?"

Anna sighed. She was starving. She nodded, her eyes on the dirt.

Will helped her up and back over to the campfire, and she let him this time. He handed her the rabbit she had taken a bite from. Her stomach rumbled painfully, and she didn't need any other push to eat. It took her longer than usual, but she ate it all.

Cal watched her like she'd grown a second head.

"What did the god of death tell you, exactly?" Will asked. He set his stick down so that the skewered rabbit was elevated over the coals, and he crossed his arms. His dark eyes fixed on Anna.

She wiped her mouth with her hand, which she then wiped on her blood-stained pants. "He said I'm still in control, but I've got his gifts and guidance."

"What does that mean?" Cal asked.

"I don't know," Anna admitted. "He wasn't specific."

"You're sure this wasn't just some near-death hallucination?" Will asked. "You believe in gods now?"

Anna huffed. "It wasn't a hallucination." Her right hand absentmindedly moved to twirl the ring around her finger. "It was just like you're talking to me right now, but in the space between life and death, and it was the god of death I was talking to..." Her eyes moved down to the fire, "And I heard my dad. I *know* that was real."

"She should be dead," Callum shrugged. "What other explanation do we have?"

"Fine," said Will. "I believe you."

"And," Anna started, ready to move on to another topic, "thanks to my god-given quick recovery, I'm ready to head for the wall."

Will laughed. He let out a full round of guffaws with his head tilted to the sky before he caught his breath. "You're not going anywhere near the wall."

She frowned at him. "We have to go after the others. They need us." She tried to relive the moments after she had fallen. She remembered a cry of pain from Clara, and then an awful shriek she couldn't place. *Was that Lucy?* "You saw what happened to Lucy. I won't let that happen to anyone else."

"I'm not leaving without my sister," Callum said with certainty.

"It happened to you, too," Will told Anna. He looked between the two of them. "Somehow, we survived. We cross that wall," he gestured to the south, "and we're walking right back into certain death."

"*This* was supposed to be certain death." Cal gestured around at the camp, at the burnt tents and the bloodstains on the ground. Anna noticed a familiar sword sticking out of the dirt by one tree, and the ground around it was covered in blood.

My blood.

"If we don't try, it's most likely certain death for them," the healer added. He had dark circles under his dark eyes, and he was glaring at Will.

They've already argued about this.

"I don't think we should count anything as certain death anymore," Anna said, looking at Will.

His jaw set, and he turned his head to stare out at the trees as he thought over his response. After a moment, he shook his head and turned his gaze back to them. "You want to track them all the way over the wall, find their camp, somehow sneak in—even though we've proven that's not possible—free the rest of our squad, and sneak them out? If we're seen, we're dead."

A red eyebrow lifted as Will said *we.* She knew they had him.

"Yes," she said.

Cal nodded sternly. He lifted the pendant he wore around his neck. "The necklace I share with my sister will tell us what direction we need to go to find their camp, and where they'll be in the camp itself."

Will dragged a hand over his face in exasperation. "There had *better* be gods, and they better all be watching over us."

"You're sneaky. You'll be fine," she told him. "And if we need a lock picked..."

"The estates in the city are a little different from a Vasbrute camp," he grumbled.

"Wait." Callum narrowed his eyes across the fire at the half-elf.

Will stiffened. "What?"

"Estates in the city?"

Will shrugged. "Some of those houses in the inner city sit empty for years at a time."

"And the Black Hand just let you in on their territory?"

Will shrugged, and his right hand moved to cover his left on his lap.

Cal stared at him, and then his eyes suddenly widened. "Take off your gloves," he demanded.

They stared at each other, each throwing daggers with their eyes. Anna stared between them in confusion. She wanted to ask a question, but she didn't want to put herself in between them.

"Fine," Will huffed. He reached down and pulled his left glove off, finger by finger. Anna stared as the black leather pulled back, revealing black skin from his wrist to his fingertips.

A tattoo.

The color faded on his palm, and his wrist was swollen and bruised.

Cal's lip curled in disgust. "You're one of them."

Will's eyes flashed across the fire in anger, but he didn't speak.

"One of who?" Anna asked. "Why is your hand black?"

Will glanced at her, and shame replaced his anger.

"That's how the Black Hand marks its members," Cal answered. "Telluth's largest criminal organization."

Anna's eyebrows rose, and she looked sharply back to Will.

He worked his jaw as he looked at the half-dwarf, and then he turned his gaze to his own hand. He took his right glove off and rubbed his wrist. That hand was as pale as the rest of him.

"Will?" Anna urged him to respond.

He sighed. "After my mom died, I couldn't find a job that paid me enough to keep the apartment. No one wanted to hire a kid for a man's job. So I took up thieving. Figured if I took from people that weren't around to care, I wasn't hurting anyone. But Cal's right." He nodded his head toward the healer. "That's Black Hand territory, and they don't like anyone worming onto property they've been paid to watch, or taking their marks, let alone a dirty little half-elf." He turned his left hand over, slowly. "The first time, they let me go. Gave me to the city watch and told me if they saw me again, they'd kill me. The city watch gave me to an orphanage in the outer city, but I was in the same situation as before. They had too many mouths to feed, not enough beds."

Cal's expression softened, but the frown still hung under his dark eyes.

"Anyway, when they caught me the next time, they gave me two options—they would gut me, or..." He held up his black hand.

"Why are you part of this team?" Cal asked quietly.

"A job went south. They set me up so that I took the fall." Will looked across the fire. "My sentence was this team. They told me that if I made it out alive, I'd earned a second chance. They figured they'd be rid of me, most likely."

Anna took in a long breath.

Will glanced at her, then began to put his gloves back on. "Now you know."

"We know that you worked for the most underhanded crime boss in Telluth."

"Don't be cruel, Cal," Anna frowned at him. "He didn't have a choice."

"You don't know who the Black Hand is," Cal argued, his eyes like granite. "The damage they've done. They steal, they burn, they kill, all for money and power."

"You're leaving out the work that the Hand does for the Council." Will straightened. "Or has your aunt not told you?"

Surprise flashed across Cal's face.

"You didn't know," Will read his expression aloud. "When the Council or one of its members needs something done—something they can't be connected to—they call on the Hand."

"And I suppose you know all this because you were so *high* within the ranks," Cal scoffed.

"I had connections," Will said, "but it's common knowledge in most back alleys that the Council needs the Hand more than the Hand needs the Council. The Hand has as much of a seat at that table as any of the governors." Will narrowed his eyes at the mayor's son. "It's incredible what people miss when they're busy partying, bellies full."

Cal's jaw tensed as he stared back across the flames at Will.

Anna shook her head, trying to understand the influx of information. "Both of you need to calm down."

They looked at her.

"What are you going to do? Fight about it? We're all on the same side here, remember?" Anna waved a hand between them. "Punch it out if you have to, but that won't get us anywhere, and I don't think we can afford either of you getting seriously injured."

Cal scoffed.

Will shook his head.

Seeing their irritation, Anna pushed on. "It doesn't matter how we got here, does it? We all traveled *very* different roads, but we're here now. None of us abandoned each other, and we won't start now. Right?"

"Right," Cal agreed, throwing his roasting stick into the fire.

Will nodded tersely.

"Good," Anna nodded herself. "I can forgive Will for stealing to survive. Can you, Cal?"

Cal raised an eyebrow at Anna, frown deepening, and then he turned the expression on Will. "I"m sorry you had to go through that." He sounded sincere, and very tired.

"Thanks," Will grumbled, rolling his shoulders uncomfortably.

"And I can forgive Cal for being ignorant and judgmental," Anna said, turning to Will.

Cal bristled.

"Will?" she pushed.

"Yeah." He cut a glance at Cal. "Don't worry about it."

"Gee, thanks," Cal replied, but the corner of his mouth quirked.

"That's settled." Anna threw her stick into the fire, wincing at the pain near her shoulder. "Now we can come up with a plan for our journey south."

"I don't care how you say you feel," the healer told her. "I'm not letting you walk all day tomorrow."

"Not happening," Will agreed.

At least they're getting along again. "We should at least try to get to the river," she told them. "I need to wash the blood out of my hair before I really start to smell."

Cal sighed, leaned back, and looked her over in the low light. His brows pushed together in concern.

"Fine," Will agreed. "But we're taking our time, and you're not going to carry anything, not even your armor."

"I need armor! What if—"

"If you *need* armor, we'll be in more trouble than we can manage," Will told her.

"Besides," Cal added. "You can't even put it on, or you'll open that wound."

Anna frowned and looked down at her chest. The area around her right shoulder was oozing again. She curled her lip at it, and then sat back more carefully than before.

48

CAL AND WILL SPENT THE DAY BURYING LUCY, GATHERING WHAT THEY could from the camp, and stowing the rest of their supplies in a tent they'd left standing. There were only a few that hadn't been toasted by Ben's fire magic.

Hopefully we have two tents to return to Dore when we get back. Anna knew it was trivial at this point, but she didn't want to add to her debt.

While they prepared, she napped on and off. She tried to fight it, to show them she was all right, but her body was exhausted.

Between strange dreams about unfamiliar people, she tried to feel if there was a change in her body. All she felt was the pain of her many wounds. Cal tried to heal her again—even just the cuts along her arms or on her face—but his magic did nothing. Instead, he took the salve from their first aid supplies and covered her in it.

She hadn't spent their money on painkillers, so she chewed willow bark when she was awake. The day passed in small chunks of awareness, and then the sun was setting and they were making sure she ate dinner. She didn't need much encouragement. She was hungry most of the time.

After her meal, she asked where they'd buried Lucy. They took her to a thick oak tree. Lucy's sword was stuck into the ground at its base like a marker, her shield resting against it. Anna told them she needed a minute alone.

When they had left, she sat on the ground by the sword. Her fingers traced the edge of the round shield, catching on the places the metal came together. Her mouth twisted, and she put her hand on the ground.

"It should be you," she said quietly. "I don't know what I'll be able to do as champion. I'm sure you would've been amazing." Her fingertips dug into the fresh dirt. She shut her eyes and breathed.

The leaves of the oak tree rustled with a breeze. A chickadee called somewhere in the distance. She felt something tickle her palm. When she looked down and pulled her hand away, a paxmortium vine had pushed up out of the dirt, a single white bud on its stem. Her mind flashed to the vines growing over her father's grave, the constellation of flowers that blanketed his remains, and then to the ring on her finger.

She wrinkled her nose and pulled her hand back to her chest.

"I'm going to find them," she told Lucy. "And I'll get them back, or die trying. I hope that'll bring you some peace."

Then she got up to find the others.

Cal told her that he needed to change her bandages. They went back into the tent together.

"Show me how," Anna said to him as he started peeling off the old wrappings, "so I can do it myself."

"You'll hurt yourself. If this is about modesty—"

"We're past that," Anna agreed, wincing as the bandage got stuck on scabs. "I just want to be able to do it myself."

"All right," he sighed. "But only because I know you'd try without me anyway."

Anna grinned smugly through her discomfort.

Cal rolled his eyes and started his lesson.

That night, they slept in a row in one tent, one of them at each of Anna's shoulders. She'd told them she would be fine on her own, but Cal was worried she might bust open the long scab across her chest if she rolled over, and Will was worried she'd spontaneously die again. So she laid stiffly between them until Cal started softly snoring, and her exhaustion took over again.

WHEN ANNA WOKE UP THE NEXT MORNING, WILL WAS SITTING UP NEXT TO her and Callum was gone. She'd managed to sleep through the night this time, and she woke up confused. A strange woman had filled her dream, calling out for help. Anna could still see the woman's eyes, even after she opened hers. Will looked down as she stirred.

"What?" she asked him. "Why do you look like that?"

He shook his head, still staring. "Like what?"

"Like my eyeballs are falling out or something."

"It's just— I think it's because you're so pale, but your eyes almost look like they're glowing green."

Anna blinked. "Pale, huh?" She tried to sit up and groaned. Will reached out to help, and she let him.

"You lost *a lot* of blood," he told her, glancing at the bandages under her shirt.

"Enough to kill me. I know."

Will let out a huff.

"You have to let me joke about it. I'm the one who died," she teased.

"Anna," Will's tone was serious as he looked down and away. "I know you're coping, but—" He looked back at her again. "Your blood...it was all over my hands. I watched the light *leave your eyes*."

She froze.

"I'd rather not joke about that," he said. "Please."

"Of course. I'm sorry." She shook her head as heat creeped up her neck.

He nodded, one of his hands raising to rub the back of his neck. "I'll go get Cal." He stood and left the tent.

Anna cleared her throat. She tried to push down the visual of her dying, out of her head. Her hands were shaking when Cal crawled into the tent. To keep them busy, she started to pull her shirt off.

"Hey!" the healer scolded, kneeling next to her. "Slow down or you're going to hurt yourself."

Anna huffed in irritation and let her hands rest back in her lap.

"What's your problem?" he asked. "I don't mind helping."

"I know," Anna sighed. "But I'm less of a burden if I do it myself."

"Burden?" Cal asked, incredulous. "Anna Hale, you rise from the dead and then worry about being a burden? Really?"

"If not for me, you might be at the wall already."

"By myself, maybe." He pulled the last of the bandages away. "We both know Will wouldn't have hung around just for me."

Anna felt the heat at her neck climb to her face. "Maybe, but I'm slowing you down."

He sighed as he applied more salve. At this rate, it would be used up in a couple of days.

"You are not a burden," he said earnestly, emphasizing each word. "*You* are the reason we still have a chance at a rescue."

She considered this. She couldn't think of an argument, so she let it drop. Her mind took her back to the previous conversation. She looked up at Cal's face, bent over her in concentration as he started wrapping.

"Was it...awful? Seeing me die. Are you okay?"

"Terrible." He didn't look away from his work. "One of the worst things

I've ever experienced. There was *nothing* I could do."

She blinked at him, stunned by his candid response. "I think I might've had it easier. Once I died...that space between life and death is comfortable, in a way."

"Maybe." He helped her with her shirt. "What was Morterra like?"

"He was..." She thought for a moment. Everything she wanted to say was contradictory. "He was everywhere. He knew who I was. He was massive, but—" she shook her head, "I should've been scared, or angry, but I wasn't. I just felt warm."

"Warm?"

Anna nodded.

"Not quite what I would've imagined for the god of death."

"Me either," she grumbled.

"You believe now?"

She nodded.

"And do you feel any different?"

"Nope. Just a lot of pain from the—" She gestured down at her chest and arms.

"Right." He nodded to the backpack. "I'll carry your stuff today. Will can carry the tent," he smirked.

"Thanks, Cal."

"You just focus on getting better. We might need you."

CALLUM LED THEM THROUGH THE WOODS, FOLLOWING HIS NECKLACE AND Anna's directions as she tracked. A short beam of red light pointed from the pendant toward his sister.

Will spent the first hour next to Anna, ready to catch her if she tripped on a rock or fainted. It took Cal telling him that he was only making everyone nervous to get him to calm down. After that was settled, they progressed steadily.

They made her stop for lunch and lie down when she was done eating. Anna wouldn't admit it, but she was thankful. The willow bark was barely cutting through the pain. Each step jolted the wound across her chest, and if she wasn't careful when she was pushing past branches and shrubs, they would scrape the cuts on her arms. The pain would've been enough to slow her down on its own, but her exhaustion slowed her further.

Now, laying on a blanket they'd spread out with sunlight warming her face, she was fighting sleep. She opened her eyes and turned her head toward where Will sat with one of his elbows resting on a raised knee. His other hand played with a dagger, tossing it in the air and catching it as it spun. Cal sat with his back to a tree, his own eyes drifting shut.

"Did it hurt?" Anna asked, glancing at his left hand.

He followed her gaze, then returned to tossing his blade. "Yes."

"Do you have any other tattoos?" she asked him.

"No."

"Is it true that there's an initiation?" Cal spoke up.

Will caught the dagger at its tip between two fingers. "Your first job is a trial. If you fail, they get rid of you."

"You must be good at breaking and entering," the healer said, opening his eyes to look at Will. "What got you caught?"

Will's head rolled over lazily to look at Cal. "It was a setup."

"All right." Anna sat up. She let herself wince, but held in the groan. "We can get going." *I'd rather start walking than have those two start arguing.*

Will jumped up to help her stand. Both men grabbed their bags, and they started moving southeast again.

That night, Anna found Mother's Hand in the night sky. This time, she looked up and wondered if its name was literal or metaphorical.

Is the Mother really up there, holding her hand behind the stars, behind the weave? Why do her fingers point south? Why can't the gods intervene? Am I the only one wearing a god's ring?

She twirled the band around her finger.

"What are you thinking about?" the half-dwarf asked her.

She looked over at him. "Did you believe in the gods? Before this."

He took a deep breath and his eyebrows rose. He pulled his legs into himself so that he was sitting cross-legged. "Our parents raised Clara and I in the church. I've always believed."

"I've never seen you pray the Following."

He smiled wryly. "Why would you? I'm not praying to you. Although, I might start now."

She rolled her eyes, then said, "Even now, though. I haven't seen you pray."

He looked at the coals that were left glowing in the middle of their little campfire. "A prayer is between the person praying and the god they're praying to. Anyone putting on a show isn't doing it for faith."

"And Clara? Does she believe?"

He nodded.

Anna turned to Will.

"No way." His hand cut through the air in dismissal where it hung over his raised knee. "I want nothing to do with them."

"Fair," Anna looked at the coals.

"Why?" Cal asked, bewildered.

Will scoffed. "They've never looked out for me. Never helped me out. Why should I care about them?"

They sat quietly with that for a moment.

"What about now, Anna?" Cal broke the silence. "I know you said you believe now, but..."

She let out a small, dry laugh. "I believe, sure. I still don't like them."

"Morterra saved your life," the healer argued. "Or gave you another one. Either way—"

Anna shook her head. "I'm thankful for that. Mostly. But where are the gods when people die from disease, or solim withdrawals? Where were they when those predators sold my mother a loan that could've—would've cost us everything? *Where were they* when my father was dying slowly, painfully from a sickness that took everything from him? Morterra couldn't even grant him the mercy of a quick death." Anna could feel her heart pounding, and she realized she'd raised her voice.

She looked down at the ring on her hand. "This time, *he* needed something. I'm glad that my mother's not going to get a letter in the post telling her she's alone in the world and, oh yeah, that she's going to prison because I didn't live long enough to pay off a *stupid fucking loan.*" She tried to stand, and hissed in pain.

"Anna." Cal tried to reach for her, eyes wide and face ashen.

"Give her a minute." Will stopped him. "She's not going to run off, but if she does, she's the only one of us that can find their way back."

Anna walked until the faint crackle of the coals faded, and she was staring out into the dark forest. She could still hear their voices softly behind her.

"Dammit." Leaves rustled as Cal sat back down.

"Yeah, that was a pretty shit thing to do."

"What? How was I supposed to know?" Cal hissed. "We were all talking about it. She's the one that brought it up!"

Will chuckled.

He's right. I brought it up. Anna wiped furiously at her eyes. *It's okay. I'm okay, and Mom's okay.* She let herself breathe for a moment, looking down at the scabs on her forearms. They itched. So did the edges of the wound across her chest.

"You're gonna have to apologize."

"I know that!"

A quiet moment passed, and then Cal asked, "Is everyone missing a parent or two? Are Clara and I the only ones that have both parents and actually like them?"

"Ros too, maybe."

"Damn."

An amused grin crossed Anna's face. She turned to walk back to the fire as Will said, "There's probably some correlation between broken families and throwing yourself into danger."

"Makes sense."

They both looked up as Anna appeared in the low light.

"I'm so sorry," Cal started, "I had no idea."

"*I'm* sorry," Anna interrupted, "I shouldn't have gotten upset with you."

"I get it, though." He winced.

"Who's ready for bed?" Will stood, looking expectantly at Cal.

"Sure." Cal followed him, walking toward the tent. "I'll fluff the pillows."

Anna felt a hand land gently between her shoulder blades and glanced behind her to find Will steering her toward the tent. Her eyebrows rose.

"Huh? Oh." His hand fell away. "Sorry." It was faint in the dim light, but she could see color in his cheeks, and then her own face heated.

"We should get some sleep." He cleared his throat and scratched the back of his neck as he let her walk herself toward the tent, trailing behind her.

Anna tried to decipher his touch and following embarrassment. *Clearly, he cares, but is it because I'm injured or is it more?*

49

That night, Anna dreamed of a vasbrute man bleeding in the grass. His red eyes drilled into hers as he said, "Help me." Pain filled his rough voice. A band around his head flashed gold. "Help. Me," he repeated. His bloody hands reached for her and his claws dug into her neck as he growled, "Help me!"

She woke with a start, her own fingers on her neck, gasping.

Will jolted up, looking around frantically. "What? What is it?"

She took in another unsteady breath. "Nightmare. It's nothing, I'm sorry."

He let out his breath and slumped back. He looked at Cal, still sound asleep at Anna's other side, and then rubbed his face with his hands.

She sat up. The morning sun peeked through the slit at the front of the tent, which shifted with a slight breeze. Her nose wrinkled at the smell of their sweaty bodies in the small space. "We should reach the river today."

"Thank the Mother," Will responded.

Cal stirred and started to wake.

Anna scooched herself to the entry and then climbed out. She stood and carefully stretched. If she let herself move as much as her muscles wanted, she'd pull at the fragile skin and scabs on her chest. She could feel the bandages sticking to her again, but it was better than the day before, and she wasn't quite as itchy. Gently, she let her hand slide over her shirt, over the bandages. The wound was sensitive, but she felt more whole than yesterday.

She convinced Cal to let her keep those bandages on until they found the river. Once there, she also convinced him to let her deal with them herself.

"Fine," he'd said as they came up to a wide, deep spot in the water, "but I'm going to check them once you're done."

Anna shrugged. "Sure."

Then they undressed.

Will had slipped his gloves off while she and Cal talked. Then they started with their shirts, pulling them up and over their heads. Anna abruptly turned around when she saw their muscular chests. Her ears grew red-hot.

Cal started laughing. "We're all getting in the same river."

"I'm...going over here to undress," Anna decided after spotting a large, full lilac bush at the riverside. She grabbed her supplies and hid behind it. Then she pulled off her shirt and slowly peeled away her bandages.

The wound had filled in. There was no longer a bloody divot running through it. The scarring around it was uneven. Eventually, the whole thing would be the same, uneven texture.

Her shirts would mostly hide it. She chewed gently on the inside of her cheek as she remembered the dress she'd worn to the ball, and then she wrinkled her nose at the mental image of her new scar climbing up from her cleavage and across to her shoulder.

Beyond the bush, the men splashed into the water.

Anna finished undressing and then slipped into the water with her bar of soap. The water felt shockingly cold on this hot summer day. It was fantastic.

She ducked under and came up in the middle of the river about thirty feet from the men, where it was deeper than her toes could reach. The sunlight filtering through the trees reflected off the water and hid anything underneath. Her necklace sparkled at her collarbone, pulled away from her body by the current.

Cal's eyebrows lifted at her as her head appeared, his own necklace shining through the water. Will turned to see what the other man was looking at. His eyes jumped from Anna's face to the top of her scar.

Anna turned away, her face reddening again, and she started scrubbing at her hair. She had swam and bathed in a stream before, but never with an audience.

"You don't need to be embarrassed," Cal told her. "I've already seen it."

Anna huffed a breath and glanced at the healer with a frown, suds covering her head. She ducked under again to rinse her hair. When she came back up, she felt lighter. She scrubbed her hair again, and then swam over to a spot on the rocky riverbed where her feet could touch and gently scrubbed her arms. The other two chatted about their desire to never camp again as she cleaned around her scabs. Some of them came free, revealing pink, healing skin. The scab on her face fell away, and half the scabs across her forearms. The salve had worked wonders. She was sure that the scars on her arms would be thin and light.

The scar on her chest was silvery in the water, almost metallic.

Cal and Will moved on to cleaning their laundry, and Anna followed suit. The outfit she'd worn during the fight was ruined, sliced up and covered in blood. Cal had said they'd burned it. That left her with three outfits. She put on the cleanest pair of pants and wrapped her chest. Then she washed the other two outfits, leaving her cleanest shirt dry so that she could put it on after Cal had checked her work. She laid the wet clothes over the lilac bush and then walked around it towards the others.

The men sat topless in the grass, their own clothes hanging from nearby branches.

"Bandages, Cal," she said, face growing warm for the umpteenth time.

They both turned at the sound of her voice. Will saw that she wasn't wearing her shirt, noticed her embarrassment, and then stared intently at a pair of pants hanging nearby, pink lighting his pointed ears to match her.

Cal laughed at their blushing and stood. "Are *my* nipples shameful?"

She scoffed and scraped together enough wits to retort, "You've seen mine. I guess it's only fair." She made herself look only at his face, but she couldn't help noting how muscular both men were.

The half-dwarf walked over with a smile in his dark eyes. He tugged at a loose wrap of bandaging near her waist and then tucked it in tighter. "Pretty good."

"Thanks," Anna rolled her eyes. "Does that mean you'll let me do it myself now?"

"It's stable enough, so sure," he shrugged.

"We should eat lunch before we move on." She looked up at the sky to judge the time.

Cal turned the charm on his necklace between his fingers. "All right." He looked over his shoulder at Will. "Lunch!"

Anna grinned with relief as she retrieved her shirt near the lilac bush and put it on, clean fabric sliding over her skin. She'd washed off the crust of her death. *Now I can move forward.*

When she rejoined them, Will had put his shirt on, and they'd laid out food.

Between bites, Cal said to her, "So, you've never seen a naked man."

Will slapped him in the ribs hard, a disapproving frown on his face.

Cal choked on the bite he had taken, then said, "What? Just stating the obvious."

"What about you, then?" Will asked him, challenging.

"I prefer the fairer sex," Cal shrugged. " I've had a couple of girlfriends. You? Have you seen a naked woman?"

The half-elf's frown returned. "Yes."

Cal waited for more, then relented. He turned to Anna, who had pretended to disappear. "So?"

She frowned at him in irritation. "No."

"Slim pickings in a small town, I suppose. I've had to meet more people than I'd like to at all my family's parties."

"There were a lot of parties?" Anna asked, glad the subject had changed. *Clara made it sound like there wasn't enough, but she loves parties.*

He nodded. "A party for the new year, a ball at summer and winter solstice, birthdays, weddings, anniversaries. We probably averaged one or two a month."

"Dreadful," Will said sarcastically.

Cal rolled his eyes.

They finished eating and stood. Anna packed her half-dry clothes into her bag, wondering what a life full of parties would have been like. Will walked over when she was done.

"I'll take that." He moved to pick it up.

"I've got it," she told him, putting her hand on the strap.

He put his hand over hers. "There's no reason for you to strain yourself."

"I feel good. I can do it."

They stared at each other for a moment, neither willing to give in, until Will let go. "Fine, but if you get tired—*at all*—you hand it off."

Anna nodded.

"This is the real reason you came back from the dead," he told her as he walked away. "You're too stubborn for your own good."

IT WAS LATE AFTERNOON WHEN THEY REACHED THE WALL. STONE BLOCK over stone block stretched up toward the treetops, three stories high. It still fell short of the old trees surrounding it.

Cal's necklace led them to a long stretch of blank wall, too smooth to climb. They walked east a little further and found the manned gate. A grown-over dirt road led to a set of heavy wood doors, firmly shut. A handful of armed guards in dark leather and armor stood around them. From their position in the brush, they could hear the guards talking about what was for dinner.

There's no way we're getting through the gate, even with our Writ of Duty. The Vasbrute that took the others wouldn't have come this way, either.

"We'll have to go around, find some other way through," Will said quietly.

"How?" Cal whispered. "It's a big wall. The only gates are this one and the one south of Lukus. The rest of it is solid stone. We'd have to go around to the ocean."

"Not necessarily," Anna said. "The Vasbrute got through somewhere. If we can pick up their trail, we can find out how."

"Maybe they just punched their way through the stone," Cal grumbled.

"Then they left a hole for us." Anna rolled her eyes.

They turned around and moved west through the trees until they found the spot where the river ran under the wall, a large stone arch over the top of it.

"Look." Anna stepped to the front. There was a large area on the riverbank that had been trampled, and a distinct trail leading from the north. "Of course," she said, looking at the grated opening in the stone where the river passed through. "They went through with the river."

"What about the iron bars?" Cal asked, leaning over the riverbank to get a better look.

"They might be loose," Anna suggested, "or they've removed some of them under the water."

Cal and Will looked at each other, frowning.

"Fine," Will gave in. "We'd all have to take a dip to get through, anyway."

The half-dwarf grinned in triumph. Anna sat with Cal at the side of the river while Will took off his armor. He stared at the slow-moving water before turning back to look at them.

"If I'm not back in five minutes, assume I'm dead."

"So dramatic," Cal sighed.

Anna laughed.

Will winked at her before he turned and waded into the river. He took a deep breath and then ducked under. His dark shape moved into the shadow under the arch and disappeared.

"Sometimes I feel like the third wheel on a handcart," Cal said, narrowing his eyes at Anna teasingly. "What happened between the two of you arguing at the breakfast table and you dying?"

Heat rose to her cheeks. "Nothing. I don't know."

One dark eyebrow lifted. "Uh-huh."

She leaned back onto her palms and looked away from him. Her mind turned to her time with Will in the forest outside of Kastarus. That's when she'd started to let her guard down. He had, too. He'd offered to teach her how to dance at the ball. They'd talked about their mothers on the ship. All the little moments in-between.

"Is it the constant sarcasm?" Cal asked. "Or maybe you're stunned by his long, shining hair?"

Anna swatted his breastplate, and her annoyed scowl turned into a wince as her shoulder twinged with pain.

He laughed, his white teeth shining in his dark face. Through his laughter, he said, "You should be careful with that arm."

"I'll start sitting on your other side."

Will returned, confirming their suspicions. Half the gate had been removed, enough space for a Vassian man to get through. He'd popped up on the other side and looked around.

"We'll lose the forest as we move further from the wall, and it opens up into a grassy valley. There's a big camp about a mile south. I could see it through the trees."

"How big?" Cal asked.

"The size of a small city."

Anna frowned.

Cal reached for his necklace. "We'll have to sneak in, but this should lead us right to them."

Face stern, Will looked at the pendant between Cal's fingers, then at Cal, and then at Anna. His eyes jumped to the bandages that peeked over her collar, and then met her eyes.

She couldn't tell what he was thinking. "I can be quiet," she told him. "My wounds won't hinder me there."

"I'm more worried about if we get separated. You got lost in the capital several times, and that was after you'd been there a month."

She knew he was right, but she couldn't let herself say it. "We won't get separated."

"We *can't* get separated," Cal said. "Neither of you knows where you're going."

"Then it's settled." Anna stood and wiped her palms together to clear the dirt.

Will sighed, looking at her. "You're sure you wouldn't rather stay here? Cal and I are more than capable—"

"No." She crossed her arms. "No way. I won't leave the two of you, *or* them."

The half-elf looked at Cal, hoping for support, but he just shrugged. "She'll be fine as long as we aren't caught."

"So simple," Will rubbed a hand over his face. "Of course."

50

THEY WAITED UNTIL LATE INTO THE NIGHT TO BEGIN THEIR RESCUE. They'd hidden their bags in bushes near the river, and Anna had left all her weapons except for her little hunting knife. Will had loaned her a dagger, and both hung at her belt.

The moon was bright and high as they dipped into the river, Will leading them through to the other side. The water was cold in the dark, and Anna's damp clothes clung to her as they moved from the water to the cover of the trees. Cal and Will dripped water from their armor as they began to move south. Copses of trees gave way to tall grass, and firelight dotted the Vassian camp in the distance.

The camp sprawled in the valley, bigger than Wallset. Tents filled the space in reds, oranges, and yellows. A tall, spiked fence surrounded it. Gray shapes moved along the paths between the tents, even in the middle of the night.

"A patrol," Will pointed out in a hushed voice. "Stay low."

Two figures walked around the outside of the wall, which rose another five feet over them. Will, Cal, and Anna stopped a hundred feet away, hiding in the tall grass.

"We've cut the shorter tree tonight," one said to the other. "Meat is roasting and drinks are flowing, and we're pacing the outer wall. Can't hear or smell anything over the party inside."

"They were roasting and flowing last night," came the reply. They put a hand to their head. "I had my fill, though I'm regretting it today."

There was a gruff laugh, and then, "You're no cub. You should know better than..."

The voices trailed off as they walked away, unaware of the eyes in the field.

"They're definitely in there," Cal said. The small beam of red light from the pendant pointed toward the center of the camp.

"It's now or never," Will said lowly, as he glanced back at Cal and Anna. "Last chance," he told Anna, holding her gaze.

She shook her head.

"All right." Will crept forward. "This is the stupidest thing I've ever done. Come on."

They reached the fence where a large tent butted up against it, leaving about three feet in between wood and canvas on the inside. The fence itself was built with logs stacked one over the other, alternating with the next section and creating a tall, thick ladder topped with spearheads.

Indistinguishable conversation and laughter floated out of the tent. They could smell incense and roasting meat. Smoke hung in the cool air.

"You go first," Will told Cal. "I'll follow Anna."

The half-dwarf nodded, and then he began his climb.

Anna wiped her sweaty palms on her damp pants. "You should go. If I fall—"

"You won't fall." Will's eyebrows rose at her, his mouth set. "You won't fall, and you won't get lost."

Anna took in a deep breath, as if she could draw in his certainty, and then she let it out in a huff. She nodded and turned, starting her climb. Carefully, she placed her feet on one log, then the next, until her fingers hovered over sharp steel. Cal paused with her, already on the other side to start the climb down.

"You good?" he asked.

She nodded stiffly. Then she sucked in a sharp breath as she bent her body, pain shooting through her chest and stomach as her wound bent onto itself. Jaw clenched, she grunted in pain as her feet climbed, and then she swung them one at a time over the top. Stars shot through her vision as she looked at the ground, two stories below. She took in short, shallow breaths through her nose. She moved to place her feet on the next log down, to straighten her body and stop the pain, but the world tilted.

"Woah," Cal cried out in a hiss of a whisper. His arm reached out to hold her against the fence. Her feet slid.

Will's long arm reached through the gap. It wrapped around her waist and pinned her to the fence, the wood slamming into her chest to hold her there.

She gasped in pain and her vision went white as her hands clawed at the log in front of her. When she could see again, her eyes found Will's face, strained from the effort of holding both of them up.

"You won't—fall—" he hissed through clenched teeth.

"I'm all right!" She pulled herself up by her arms, and her feet found purchase. Sweat trailed from her brow as she hugged the log in front of her and took gasping breaths.

Hesitantly, Will let go. He stared at her for a moment, waiting to see if she'd fall again, and then he hurried up the rest of the way himself. "Help her down, Cal."

"Go slowly," Cal told her, his hand on her back. He glanced at the tent behind them.

I have to move. They'll find us if I don't move. Gritting her teeth, Anna started her descent. When she reached the bottom, she sat down and tried to catch her breath. Raucous, gravelly laughter reverberated from the tent behind her, followed by clinking metal cups. She peeked under her shirt at the bandages. Blood seeped through the damp cloth.

Will hopped down and crouched next to her, his right hand massaging his left wrist. "Are you all right?"

"Yeah," she swallowed, and she turned her eyes to meet his. "I'm fine. Thanks."

The concern fled his face, replaced by anger. "I told you that you couldn't do this," he scolded in hushed tones. "Why couldn't you have stayed back?"

"I'm seeing this through." She stood, grimacing. "I'm here now, anyway. What do you want me to do? Climb back over that fence?"

"You'll have to when we leave."

"Shut up," Cal said, watching the red light from his pendant. "Someone's going to wonder who's out here bickering."

Will shot Anna a pointed look, and then he moved noiselessly to the corner of the tent and peeked around the side.

"Must be celebrating something in there," Cal told Anna with a nod toward the opening.

"We'll have to avoid the main paths and make our way between the tents. Look out for stakes and rope. The last thing we need is one of you pulling down a tent," Will said after returning, looking to Cal. "I'll lead. Keep Anna in front of you."

Cal saluted.

Will shot Cal a dry frown. "Watch for my signals." Then he took a deep breath and rounded the tent.

Anna stuck close behind, and then Cal followed. Will stopped them at the path and signaled for them to lean close to the canvas next to them. A couple of Vasbrute walked by, their features difficult to distinguish in the low, flickering firelight.

The three of them darted across the opening behind them and into another grouping of tents. Many of these were dark and quiet, the lanterns at their fronts extinguished.

"Does that thing tell you how close she is?" Will turned back to ask.

"No. Only direction."

"Great."

Will led them through to the next path, where they paused. A Vassian woman dressed in loose orange pants and a matching shirt pulled a Vassian man in leather pants and a tight orange shirt by the hand, laughing. They stumbled slightly, and then she drew him between the tents across the path. He pinned her to a thick tent post and then they started kissing.

Will wrinkled his nose and then turned. He signaled for them to go back the way they came.

"Who knew they'd be so lively tonight," Cal whispered.

"Let's hope this isn't about our friends," Will started around the other side of a tent.

Anna crouched as he checked the path was clear. Her hand rested across her middle as if it would help hold her together. There was darkness staining her fingers when they left the fabric. Blood was soaking through her old gray shirt. Quickly, she wiped her hands on her pants and hoped the others wouldn't notice in the dark.

They continued this way until they were near the center of the camp. All the tents ahead of them were colored bright goldenrod, washed out to pale yellow in the moonlight. The tents were arranged in a circle with a short fence around them, separating them from the rest of the camp. She could see armed Vasbrute stationed at the only opening in the fence. The barrier was only waist high—more of a marker of a restricted area than it was a physical deterrent. It was quieter here than the other groups of tents. The air smelled even stronger of incense. Anna could feel it drying her eyes and lungs.

"She's definitely in there." Cal shifted side to side, and the little red light pointed toward a smaller tent next to the biggest one at the back of the circle.

"Of course," Will sighed and turned back to them. "We'll have to make our way around and jump the fence. We'll be exposed if someone walks by, but I haven't seen or heard anyone over here besides those two guards. We need to be fast and quiet. Got it?"

They nodded.

"Stick close." Will turned, darted across, and hopped the fence as silently as an owl in flight. He helped Anna over. She clenched her jaw as her wound flared with pain, holding in the cry that wanted to escape. Cal was next. He made the jump easily.

Anna peered between the tents, toward the center of the circle. She realized what she was looking at by the smell before her eyes could make out the shape. It overcame the incense. Hundreds upon hundreds of flowers were piled in bouquets, lit by bright flames somewhere in the middle of them.

"I don't care!" Clara's voice carried through the tent and to them. "If they're going to hold us here, the least they could do is feed us an actual meal. I'm tired of camp food and tents!"

Anna glanced at Cal, who was smiling from ear to ear.

The walls of the tent were held down by stakes driven down at every foot. If they were going to slip underneath, they'd need to pull some out of the ground.

"There's no one in here that can change anything," Ben's voice said. "All you're doing is shouting at *us*."

"Well, I need to shout at someone!"

"Anna, watch the front. Cal, watch the fence. I'm going to get this wall free." Will knelt and started pulling at the tent stakes.

Anna moved forward until she was ten feet from the front of the tent. She didn't see anyone there, but it was easier to see the display in the middle of the space. Two large braziers lit an altar surrounded by flowers. A rainbow of petals flanked a path from the largest tent to the altar. Closest to the thick piece of solid stone were white blooms, until paxmortiums cascaded from the stone itself. Atop the altar lay a large Vassian body. His hands clasped the hilt of a greatsword on his chest. His leather pants were dyed a deep yellow. A band of brushed gold rested like a halo on his head.

Recognition brushed at the back of her mind. The little five-petalled flowers around him glowed in the firelight. Cold raced through her veins as his head turned toward her—

"Anna!" Will hissed.

His hand was on her shoulder, and he turned her around. "Come on. They're—" He cut himself off, staring at her eyes.

"What?" Anna looked at him, focusing on his face to pull herself out of her strange daze.

"Your eyes," he said, his hand sliding down to hold her upper arm gently. "They're glowing like fireflies."

"Glowing?" She looked over her shoulder at the body. It was still, its head pointed up at the sky. She returned her gaze to Will.

"It's gone now," he said, surprised again.

"Maybe the firelight..." Anna trailed off.

"Come on." Will was pulling her to the loose spot in the tent wall when his eyes snagged on the blood on her tunic. "Gods, why didn't you say something!?"

"I'm fine." Anna winced at the raw concern in his voice. "Let's go."

She could feel him boring a hole into the back of her head as they crouched down to the opening in the tent. Will held the material up as she slid underneath on her back.

"Anna!" Clara cheered. "Mother's Children, what happened to you?"

Standing, Anna looked around the dark room. Half the tent was occupied by an iron cage, and the rest of their team was gathered inside. They had no armor or weapons, and they were covered in blood and dirt. Clara stood at the bars of the cage, holding her brother's hand. Her left pant leg had been torn away at the knee, and her lower leg was wrapped in thick bandages. Ben stood just behind her, somehow the cleanest of the bunch even in his sweaty, dirty robes. There were metal bands around his wrists, strung together by a short chain.

"What happened to you?" Anna asked Clara, staring at her leg.

"That woman tried to hack off my foot," she answered indignantly. "But my healing is better than her hacking." She grinned smugly.

"Anna," Pyran hurried to the bars as Will came into the tent. "When I heard you scream, I thought Morterra was taking you."

"You could say that." Will moved to the door of the cage and inspected the lock. "Everyone needs to shut up so I can figure this out, or we'll all be in the cage together."

Pyran scrunched a brow at Will. Anna hugged him through the bars, and his arms wrapped around her.

"You're all okay?" Anna asked, looking through the bars. Ros and Merry were cross-legged on the ground next to each other. Captain Heiser sat with his back to the bars at the rear of the tent, taking them in with surprised, joyful eyes. His salt-and-pepper hair was singed.

"All good," Merry said.

"Why haven't you healed her?" Clara asked her brother.

"I can't."

Clara's brows jumped to her forehead.

"It's a long story," Cal sighed.

"Shush." Will was kneeling in front of the lock with his tools in his hands.

Anna heard metal clicking above them and looked up. A crow hopped to the front of the cage. It turned its head at an angle and looked down at Will. A short length of familiar string dangled from its left foot.

"Did you follow us here?" she wondered aloud.

It clacked its beak at her.

Will glanced at Anna, attention following hers to the top of the cage. He blinked at the crow, then shook his head and returned to working on the lock.

"What's taking so long?" Cal asked.

"You all won't shut up, for one," Will grumbled. "I've never picked a Vassian lock. It's complicated."

The crow fluffed up and let out a coo.

"I think it likes you," Anna whispered to Will.

"Let's hope it likes me enough to keep its beak shut," Will mumbled back. "There are too many tumblers. This thing was made by some kind of miniature machinist. Hold on." He scrunched up his nose as he concentrated, and then there was a loud, metallic *clunk.*

"Ah-ha," Will whispered triumphantly.

The crow jumped in surprise at the sound. It leaped from the top of the cage to land on Will's head, crying, "Careful! Careful!"

Will attempted to grab it, but the bird flapped its wings and cawed in protest. "A little help!" he hissed.

"Here, birdy!" Anna coaxed quietly as she lunged for it. The bird drew blood when it pecked at her hand, then continued its cacophony.

Anna and Cal tried to wrangle the crow as Will tried to pull the lock off the door while protecting his eyes from beak, claws, and wings.

"Shut up, you noisy black chicken, or we'll be found out!" Cal hissed.

The lock fell to the ground in a clatter, slamming against an iron bar.

"Shit!" Will ducked down after it.

"We have to go *now,*" Anna said, one arm reaching for the door as the other blocked flapping wings.

"You are going nowhere," a deep, rough voice sounded from the entrance of the tent.

51

ANNA'S SHOULDERS TENSED AND HER HAIR STOOD ON END. SHE TURNED TO see three Vasbrute at the end of the tent, their hulking forms filling the room.

"Gemma, come," a lighter voice called, and the crow flew towards it.

Then they charged. The man in the front lunged at Anna, pinning her to the iron bars with his thick forearm. She cried out in pain and clawed at his skin. Her vision went white as he put pressure on her bleeding wound. She heard the sound of scuffles, distant and far away, as her heartbeat pounded in her ears. Lightning flashed across her vision as her sight returned.

Cal was restrained by another Vassian man, one arm wrapped around his throat and the other pinning down his arms. Will was in a similar predicament. He struggled against the woman holding him, panting hard.

"Let her go!" Will shouted. "She's already bleeding!"

The Vasbrute man was baring his sharp teeth at Anna. "I should tear out your throats for trespassing."

Will threw his head back, catching the woman's nose. She gasped and released him, clutching at her face. He lurched toward Anna.

The Vasbrute that held her threw a punch at Will so fast, there was no time to dodge. With the sound of rock colliding with flesh, the fist made contact, and Will fell face down with a groan. The woman kicked him over, trapped his arms behind his back, and pinned him down with her knee.

"Careful!" the crow cried.

"Hush," the woman called.

"Get a good hold this time, Tash," the man in front of Anna spoke to the Vassian woman, and then leaned over his arm toward her. The golden ring around his head caught the dim light. "You have one chance to explain why I should not break your necks, and the necks of all your friends, for my trouble."

"Can't—breathe—" Anna gasped.

He glanced at her feet dangling off the ground, then let her slide down the bars until she could stand. His arm pulled back enough for her to get a lungful of air.

Anna gulped like a fish thrown back into water.

"Well?" he growled.

Tell him you can help. A smooth, familiar voice drifted into her consciousness from the back corner of Anna's mind. *You can assist the tribunal.*

"Talk!" he shouted in her face.

"I can help!" She screwed her eyes shut in fear. "The tribunal! I can help!"

"What do you know of the tribunal?" he shouted at her, pressing into her ribs again.

You can speak to his brother.

Anna coughed, then gasped, "I—can talk—to your—brother."

"My brother is dead!" he shouted, his gray face reddening. "You mock me before you die?" There was venom in his ruby eyes.

"No, no." Tears fell from Anna's eyes as she shook her head.

I sent you.

"Morterra sent me!"

He froze. His eyes widened, searching her face. They moved to the ring on her left hand, where it was clinging to his arm. "The Son of Death sent you?" he asked in a quiet, uncertain voice.

"Yes."

He stepped back, and she fell to the ground. She landed on her knees, and her right hand caught the ground before she fell on her face. Her left hand fisted in her bloody shirt as she gulped air through the pain.

She saw Will through the strands of auburn hair that had fallen from her braid. He was pinned to the dirt next to her. He looked at her with wide, frightened eyes. One side of his face was already darkening into a bruise, and the skin was split by his eyebrow.

She shut her eyes to stop his face spinning and push back the nausea.

How the fuck are you inside my head? she cried out inside her mind.

You're my champion. I'm never far from you.

I didn't give you permission.

You did when you accepted my deal. It's a good thing, too.

"Anna!" Pyran hissed through the bars in warning as the Vassian man returned.

Her muscles clenched in fear before she was unceremoniously pulled up by the arm and hauled out of the tent. She could hear her friends protesting behind them. Her feet stumbled as they went, but his grip on her was too tight for her to fall. A small crowd of Vasbrute were gathering at the end of the path of flowers leading to the altar. He threw her down in front of them.

There was a man and woman at the front of the group, dressed in finer clothes than the others. The man wore a gold band on his head that matched those on the body on the altar, and on the man that had dragged her out here, except that his held one large yellow gemstone. A bright goldenrod silk sash crossed from his shoulder into his belt. The woman's head was painted like the other women Anna had seen, but instead of a simple ring, her head was covered in a swirling gold design. She wore loose goldenrod pants with a thick sash tied across her chest as well. A sheer, golden silk shawl wrapped her in an ethereal light that glowed with the braziers. The intensity of the incense and flowers this close filled Anna's nose.

They stared down at her with wrinkles around their hard, red eyes.

"She says she can speak with Branik," the man that brought her spat.

The older man's eyes widened and the muscles in his jaw worked.

The woman's eyes narrowed.

Help me.

I thought you didn't want me in your head.

Help me! We can have the consent talk after you help me out of the situation you've put me in!

Tell her the Son of Death sent you to put her son's soul to rest.

Hands shaking, Anna looked up at the woman. "The Son of Death sent me to put your son's soul to rest."

The woman glanced at the altar, then turned her eyes back to Anna. "Stand." Her voice was softer than Anna expected.

Anna stood the best she could. Her shoulders hunched from the pain across the front of her body.

The woman looked her over. Her eyes caught the blood on her shirt, the wound beneath it, and the ring on her hand before landing on her weary green eyes. "Who are you?"

"Anna Hale." Her voice felt so small and shaken compared to theirs.

"Anna," the woman inclined her head in a fraction of a bow. "I am Khaleena, and this is Malaki, Crowns of Vassa. Bartok is our son, heir to the Crown."

Unsure what to do, Anna bowed her head. When she lifted it, Khaleena was holding out her hand, palm up and waiting.

Left hand, the god of death urged.

Anna placed her left hand atop Khaleena's. The woman's Vassian hands were bigger than hers, but still slender. The graceful thumb bent to touch her ring. When it did, Khaleena sucked in a startled breath and her eyes widened. "She speaks the truth."

"How?" Bartok growled behind Anna's right shoulder. "Branik is dead. He cannot speak."

"He can speak to *her*," Khaleena told her son as she placed her free hand over Anna's. "She has been touched by Death. She wears his ring and carries his blessing."

"She is a liar and a lich!"

Khaleena and Malaki turned to look at the man that shouted behind them. A Vassian man pushed his way to the front of the crowd, and Anna recognized him as the leader of the group they'd met north of the wall. She went rigid.

"Kolik split her in half. She should be dead, and now she fools you with her perversion of the weave," he continued.

"You question the Crown's sight, Stoiko?" Malaki challenged.

"You would trust a necromancer? A manipulator of the Children's will?" Stoiko returned the challenge, his burgundy eyes burning into Anna.

"This woman is no lich," Khaleena called to the crowd. "She is not a manipulator of the Children's will, but an executor of it. I can feel the Son of Death's hand on hers."

A murmur went through the crowd.

What does she mean, she can feel your hand on mine?

He didn't answer.

Khaleena turned back to Anna. "Follow me. Show them who sent you." She led Anna by the hand toward the altar.

"You defile Branik by bringing her to him," Stoiko shouted.

"You will be silent before your Crown," Malaki growled.

Khaleena smiled gracefully as she led Anna toward her son's body. The crowd hushed, and suddenly there was only the sound of her boots on the ground and the fire crackling in the braziers.

She thinks I'm going to talk to him.

You are.

Anna's breath was shallow as they stepped up to the unmoving form. Khaleena kissed her fingers and then touched the body's forehead. She inclined her head toward Anna, and then took a step back.

Anna looked at the dead prince. His face was bruised and cut, his knuckles scraped.

What do I do?

Touch him. And don't forget to breathe.

52

FINGERS SHAKING, ANNA REACHED OUT TO THE CORPSE. SHE PLACED HER left hand over the body's hands on the hilt of his sword. At the contact, her shaking stopped. Something was holding her hands steady. That same *something* filled the air around her, quieting the noise as if she were wrapped in padded velvet.

She breathed in. As she did, the braziers' light shifted from orange to a pale green, and the chest beneath her hand rose. Branik's eyes flickered open, and his head turned to look at her.

You get five questions.

Her heart stuttered in her chest. *What do I ask?*

No answer.

What do I ask!?

Trust yourself to find the right threads to pull.

She swallowed hard, and then she asked her first question.

"Who killed you?"

"There were four that night." Branik's mouth opened, and he answered in a wheeze. "Three to kill, and one to curse. Darkness hid them from me."

Her brows drew together. "What were they wearing?"

"Cloaks of shadow and night," came the rasping reply.

Three questions left. She took a couple of rattling breaths as she puzzled over how to find the right ones.

"How did you die?"

"They stalked me as wolves stalk a bear. When I was alone and distracted, they struck me down."

She chewed on the inside of her cheek. Her right hand fisted at her side and her nails dug into her palm. "What were their weapons?"

"The big one swung a pointed club, to busy my sight. The little one played with fire, to drop my sword. The shadow manipulated my flesh, to pin me down. The thin one struck with golden knuckles and knives, to steal my blood."

Anna gasped. *Golden knuckles. One big, one short, one thin. Who is this shadow? Ask.*

"The shadow," Anna said. "What can you tell me about the shadow?"

"A vile creature. From my spirit, she wrought her curse of anger. She mocks death, is driven by greed of life itself. Half-present and formless, she travels as mist and brings rulers to their knees. No blade will strike this fiend..." His voice trailed off as the last of the air in his dead lungs pushed its way out. "Thank you..."

Something cold within him released. The surrounding shadows grew brighter. His jaw fell slack and his eyes went flat and foggy. The firelight shifted back to its usual orange and the air around Anna thinned.

She pulled her hand back from his cold skin and stared at Branik's still, lifeless face. "I know who killed him."

Low chatter filled her ears in a rush. She turned, hands clasped at her chest, and found a hundred red eyes on her. Cal and Will stood at the edge of the tents, surrounded by a handful of Vassian guards, and she could see their fear.

Khaleena drew her attention, saying loud enough for the crowd to hear, "Branik has spoken. The tribunal begins with the return of the sun!" There were wet tracks from tears down her cheeks that reflected the firelight.

"What of the Death-Speaker?" a voice from the crowd called.

"She will be fed and she will rest before she is called for testimony." Khaleena held a hand out to her.

Anna blinked at the hand before taking it. She let the woman lead her away from the altar, leaning into her as a wave of exhaustion moved through her.

"Wait," she stopped abruptly, looking up with wide eyes, "The others—"

"They will be uncaged and cared for," Khaleena told her. "There is nothing to worry about."

Anna worried anyway.

ANNA WAS BROUGHT TO A YELLOW TENT WHERE TWO VASSIAN WOMEN WAITED with a warm bath. She flinched away from their hands, only able to see the gaping wounds on Lucy's body, but they explained what they were doing and waited for her to concede to it. Reluctantly, she did. She tried to cover herself even when she stepped into the water, but her nudity was forgotten as they started to clean her. They massaged her muscles around the bruises and scabs with fragranced oils. She felt small, like a child under their hands in the oversized tub. After she was clean, they treated her wounds and re-bandaged them. They left her with an outfit similar to what they were wearing and told her there was a bed waiting for her in the next room. After she was dressed, she stepped through.

There was the bed—a massive mattress covered in red and gold blankets—and sitting atop it was Pyran, his head in his hands. He looked up as she appeared. In the next moment, he was holding her in a hug, his head on her shoulder.

Anna breathed him in. He smelled like sweat and dirt and leather. She could feel the bruises on her back and chest, but she squeezed him as her eyes watered.

"Fuck, Anna. I thought they were going to kill you. I thought you were lying, telling them what they wanted to hear."

"We both know I'm not that quick." She grinned against his shoulder.

He pulled away to look her over at arm's length. Her bandages were visible around her stomach and chest and forearms. "Mother, is there any part of you that isn't bleeding?"

"My arms are all right. And the cuts on my face healed over." She touched the scabs under her right eye, thinking about falling out of the tree.

He took a noisy breath in and out through his nose.

"Where are the others?"

"In another guarded tent. I told the Vasbrute you wouldn't eat or sleep without your brother."

"My brother?"

He smiled and chuckled.

Anna laughed.

"Come on, I'm starving." Pyran sat on a cushion next to a short table spread with cooked meat.

She hesitated, and Pyran looked up at her.

"You're not scared of me?"

"Why should I be scared of you?" Pyran asked, confusion clear on his face.

She tugged at the edge of the bandage near her neck, her fingers shaky. "I just spoke to a dead guy. I would think Cal or Will would've said something."

"I know," Pyran said, "but you're still Anna."

Her eyes widened as she looked down at him.

"Do you remember that day, months ago, when I was training you and you fell and started crying?"

Anna's face flushed, and she looked down at the plush rug under her feet. There was a pattern of geometric lines, overlapping and braided together. "Yes."

"I knew you weren't crying because you were hurt or couldn't do the move. I know you were crying because you knew you *had to* do it. It was your only option. You couldn't fail. I know *why* now, but...of course that Anna Hale is the same Anna Hale that made a deal with death to keep going."

She looked at him. He was wearing a sincere, boyish grin.

"You're not stubborn about much, but you are stubborn about that," he continued. "And I'm not afraid of you."

"Even if I have scary death powers now?"

He shrugged. "Even with the scary death powers."

She sat next to him and picked up what looked like a chicken leg. They ate ravenously until her stomach hurt from eating too much.

"So," Pyran sighed and leaned back, "what happened? How did you get the scary death powers?"

Anna took a drink from the large mug of cool water in front of her. She wondered if anyone was listening behind the canvas, and then decided she didn't care. She told him everything. She explained her death, talked through her conversation with a god, and how she and Cal had convinced Will to come. He hugged her again when she told him about Lucy's grave.

She explained that magic couldn't heal her. In a hush, she told him about Will and the Black Hand. How they followed Cal's necklace south and then found their way past the wall to the camp. Pyran listened quietly through to the end, his brows furrowed in thoughtfulness and concern.

"Somehow," she finished, "we managed to sneak through the camp and to you without being seen. I think the people here were celebrating or something. The whole camp smelled like cooked meat and incense, and anyone awake was distracted." She yawned and arched her back in a stretch. Her bones popped, and she grimaced. "Ow."

"Come on," Pyran said gently. "They're going to get you up for that tribunal thing, and you need some sleep."

She groaned in agreement and stood. He helped her to the bed and eased her onto it. Then he blew out the candles in the candelabra over the table and laid down on the other side.

"I could sleep for a year," she said after another yawn.

"I bet you could," he said. "I'm glad you're all right."

"I'm glad you're all right." Her left arm reached out until it poked him in the ribs.

He took her hand and folded it around his arm. It was easy to fall asleep to the sound of his breathing.

53

THEY AWOKE THE NEXT MORNING A LITTLE AFTER SUNRISE. THE PRINCE, Bartok, came to collect them with a retinue of guards. He was quiet and anxious as he led them into the largest yellow tent. Inside, a crowd of Vasbrute old and young, big and small, spoke in hushed voices that, together, rose to a constant thrum. They sat on long benches divided in the middle by a path, and they faced away from the entrance. Ahead of them was a short stage. Malaki and Khaleena sat on two large, ornate wood chairs, facing the crowd. A single empty chair sat on the stage in front of them.

Eyes turned to Bartok, Anna, and Pyran as they entered, and the chatter dimmed. The prince walked them to the front, where the rest of Anna's team was sitting on the right side of the aisle.

"Oh, Anna!" Clara gasped and jumped up to embrace her, ignoring the scolding from her brother as he told her through clenched teeth to stay seated.

She hugged Clara back, the moment brief before the half-dwarf was pulled back to the bench. Will sat near the end. His face was still a little swollen, but much better than Anna had expected. *The twins must've healed him.* He stood when Anna sat, insisting that Pyran take the seat next to Clara. Pyran raised an eyebrow, but he took the seat. Will took the next spot, and finally Anna sat on the end, as directed by Bartok.

She avoided Will's gaze, but he was watching her carefully. "How are you?"

"Fine," she answered, wiping her nervous hands on her strange yellow pants. They were surprisingly soft and airy, but the material had weight. "How are you?"

"Cal fixed my face," he said. "You, uh, talk to dead people now?"

Anna tensed and chanced a glance over. He didn't look scared of her. He looked concerned for her. His dark eyes were trying to read hers.

She looked down at the ring on her finger and spun it around the digit. "I guess I do."

"You saved our hides."

Anna tilted her head to the side, unsure. *Morterra saved us. And we're still not free.*

The prince stepped onto the stage and addressed his parents in a booming voice that filled the tent and silenced the crowd. "All attendants are accounted for. Let the tribunal begin."

Khaleena nodded to her son, and he moved to stand at the front of a line of guards that encircled the crowd. No one was leaving until whatever was about to happen was over.

"The Crown calls on Stoiko Gok," Malaki's resonant voice declared.

Stoiko stood from where he had been seated across the aisle. His red eyes glared at Anna before he turned and approached the chair. He stopped next to it, his back turned to the crowd. The muscles of his broad back were tense.

"Who are you?" Khaleena asked, her gentle tone carrying across the room.

"I am Stoiko Gok, cousin of the Crown, fourth pride leader."

"Sit, Stoiko."

He sat in his chair straight-backed, with his fists on the arms.

"Tell us of the day of Branik's death," Khaleena ordered.

"I was taking over wall-watch that night. Branik was not on the trail. I knew something must've kept him, and I went looking with Tasha. We found him two miles westward."

Khaleena swallowed. "How did you find him?"

"Branik was dead." Stoiko shifted in the chair. "His face was beaten and there were thirteen knife wounds in his gut. His claws were bloodied and his—" He broke off, then started again in a growl. "His face was full of fear."

Khaleena's eyes shut, and her head turned away.

"Did you find anything else?" Malaki asked.

Stoiko turned his head at an angle and cracked his neck. He took a breath, then answered, "When I touched Branik's body, I was...overcome. Anger does not begin to describe it. I acted rashly, and I now plead forgiveness." His head bowed.

"Your case will be heard at another time," Malaki said sternly, "but your plea is heard. Thank you for your voice."

They called Tasha to the chair next. Will recognized her as the woman that had broken his wrist, now that he could see her in the light, and he mentioned it to Anna. The Vassian woman confirmed Stoiko's story and repeated what he'd said about the anger they felt when they found Branik. Ben mumbled something to Ros, who relayed it to the captain, but their voices were too hushed for Anna to make out what they said.

"Thank you for your voice," Khaleena told Tasha.

"The Crown calls on Anna Hale," Malaki's voice rang.

Anna swallowed hard and glanced at Will.

"Go on," he whispered, so quietly that only she could hear. "It's just talking."

She stood stiffly and then walked up to the chair, the weight of a hundred eyes on the back of her skull. She almost rounded the chair to sit, but remembered that the others had paused and stopped herself.

"Who are you?" Khaleena asked, her tone gentle and her burgundy eyes encouraging.

"Anna H-Hale."

Go on.

She flashed a frown at the voice in her head before she added, "Champion of the Son of Death."

She felt a smile at the back of her mind.

Khaleena grinned at the title as well. "Sit, Anna."

The chair was bigger than it looked. She was a little taller than the average human, but her back didn't reach the chair's back when the bend of her knees found the front of the seat. The arms were too long, too wide. She again felt like a child. *I must look like one.*

She sat rigidly and put her hands on the arms. Countless hands had worn the wood, and claws had raked grooves into them. As settled as she would be, she looked up at the Crown.

Khaleena looked at Anna, but spoke to the crowd. "I have read the girl's presence and have felt the touch of the Son of Death on her. I verify her power."

Hushed chatter spread behind her.

"What did Branik tell you?"

She tried to recall the dead man's words and provide them as closely as she could. "Four figures attacked him in the dark. Three men and a shadow." She swallowed, her mouth suddenly dry. "They attacked him with weapons and magic. The shadow held him down—pinned him with magic—and cursed him as the men killed him."

Khaleena took in a labored breath.

"Did he describe the men?" Malaki asked, leaning forward.

"One big, wielding a club, one little, using fire magic, and one thin, with a knife and brass knuckles." Anna's stomach knotted as a cold smile with a gold tooth flashed across her memory. "I know these men," she said in a low tone that rose from her chest. "They work for Governor Woulfe."

The chatter behind her grew louder.

"What?" Clara's hushed voice sounded before Cal shushed her.

Malaki's brow lifted, creasing his forehead. He raised a hand, and the crowd quieted.

"Did the shadow have a face?" Khaleena asked.

She thought back to Branik's words, shaking her head. "He called the shadow a she, but he did not call her a *person*."

Khaleena's brows drew together, and her lips curled slowly in disgust.

"I believe," Ben spoke, and Anna turned to see him stand from the bench, "that I could be of some assistance here."

"Too smart for his own good," Ros muttered under their breath.

Malaki and Khaleena turned their vibrant eyes on him. Malaki held a hand out to stop the guard that had moved toward the mage.

"And who are you?" Malaki asked.

Ben swallowed, glancing around at all the red eyes trained on him, many of them angry at the disruption to their proceedings. He looked up at the Crown and answered, "My name is Bennett Day. I am a trained mage from the University of Eysa."

One of Malaki's eyebrows rose. "We are familiar with the institution."

Ben cleared his throat nervously. "One focus of my study has been necromancy—"

There was a gasp in the crowd and aghast whispers. Anna glanced forward and found Malaki's face had fallen into disapproval, his brow low over his dark eyes.

"*Not* that I may wield it!" Ben clarified quickly. "So that I might recognize it and counter it."

Khaleena looked amused. "A noble cause."

"Thank you." Ben bowed his head. "Uh, may I?" He gestured toward the open stage next to Anna.

Malaki scowled in annoyance, but then inclined his head in a nod.

Ben bowed slightly again, and then hurried around the bench, muttering *excuse me* as he went. Captain Heiser looked flabbergasted, Ros was shaking their head, and Will looked like he wanted to laugh.

The mage stopped at Anna's right side. "As I said, I have trained myself to identify necromancy." He paused to be sure they followed, and then continued. "When my team and I, uh, met S-Stoiko and his team, I could sense a dark energy around them."

"They *were* trying to kill us," Merry mumbled.

"I believe that energy to be a curse. Judging by the testimony here, I would theorize a curse of wrath that was born from your son's death and set upon the first souls to touch his body."

Another murmur passed through the crowd.

"This theory is supported by the loss of aggression after I cast out the spirit."

Anna recalled the inhuman scream she'd heard before she died.

Khaleena sat forward. "Your point, mage of Eysa?"

"Right," Ben glanced at Anna, his cheeks pink. "The shadow. A necromancer could have cast that curse on your son." He turned to Anna. "Would you say that any of the men possessed necromantic powers?"

"No, I don't think so."

Ben nodded. He seemed to have expected that answer. He turned back to the Crown. "The shadow, then, not a person. A necromancer strong enough to craft such a wrath curse would also have the skill to create a dark simulacrum. A shape, a creature, a piece of themselves, half-real and half-ethereal, that they can cast spells through. Your shadow was a *shade*."

Khaleena looked at him thoughtfully. "Such magics have not been seen in centuries."

"Seen? No," Ben agreed. He glanced at Stoiko, then Anna, then looked up at Khaleena. "Somewhere in Telluth, there is a necromancer woman who wants war with your people."

KHALEENA AND MALAKI ENDED THE TRIBUNAL SHORTLY AFTER BEN'S REVELATION. They told the crowd that Branik's murder had been solved, and therefore, the tribunal was complete. Stoiko and his group were asked to stay, along with the crew from Telluth. Most of the guards followed the crowd out of the tent. The prince and handful of soldiers stayed.

Anna stood from the chair.

Stoiko sat with his arms resting on his thighs, staring at the group across the aisle with irritation showing in the twitch of his jaw muscles.

When the crowd finished filing out, Malaki spoke to Ben. "If what you say is true, we have all been deceived."

"Yes, highness." Captain Heiser stood. He bowed and introduced himself. "Captain Nathaniel Heiser, leader of this troupe. We have suspected treachery since receiving our mission."

Malaki released a thoughtful sigh and glanced at his partner. "We believe you."

"Stoiko and his pack are not usually so rash," Khaleena said. "I knew that something must have happened, but there was very little trace of a curse left behind on Branik's body, and his death had been so...dark."

"The effects of the curse may linger," Ben explained. "It could take some time for them to return to themselves."

"It is upsetting to hear of such possession," Malaki said, "but yet, I am glad that my nephew and the others affected do not bear the full fault of their actions."

"They killed someone," Anna found herself saying. "They killed Lucy."

"*They* killed Zrinko." Stoiko glared at Anna.

Khaleena sat forward with a frown, raising a hand toward Stoiko. "We would wish to resolve that debt."

The captain spoke up. "Restitution can be arranged with the woman's family, as well as your cooperation in what happens next."

"Yes," Malaki frowned. "I fear your Council will not be as graceful in their understanding."

Captain Heiser looked to Ben and Anna. "Is it possible to *show* them?"

Anna's eyes turned to Ben, and she could see he was rolling the question around in his brain.

He looked at Malaki. "It may be possible. I could sense the curse. Lord Inwood should also have the ability. If at least one of your men were able to accompany us..."

"The treaty—" the Crown started.

"Our Writ of Duty supersedes the treaty," Captain Heiser told him. "As long as they are with us on official Council business, the treaty holds."

"They have to honor the Writ of Duty," Pyran said in realization. "Those papers grant us and anyone under our protection free course to complete our mission, all the way through to the end."

"Precisely," the captain nodded. "The Council's guard has no authority to stop us. They are, in fact, duty-bound to aid us."

Malaki nodded. He looked at his nephew. "Stoiko, you will join them alongside Bartok's pack."

Stoiko frowned, but nodded.

Ben looked at Anna apprehensively. "They will not believe Anna's powers." He turned to Khaleena. "You can sense Morterra on her. How?"

She looked down at Anna. "I am familiar with the Son of Death. Malaki's house treats with the sun, but mine has been a home of the final peace. I am attuned to his touch, although it is strange to feel it on the living."

"Would you show me?" Ben asked reluctantly. "So that I might show the Council."

Khaleena blinked at him, and then frowned.

"She could talk to another dead guy," Merry suggested, brow furrowed.

"His powers are not to be spent on such shallow displays," Khaleena's frown deepened, and she turned to Ben. "I can tell you have much knowledge of the weave, mage, but the gods are not familiar to you. What I know, I have learned from a lifetime of communing with death. It would be impossible for you to learn in such a short time."

Ben's face fell, disappointed.

"The fact that magic can't heal her might be convincing enough," Cal said.

Clara turned to Anna with her brows furrowed. "Surely there is some way to—"

"There is." Will stepped toward Clara. "The natural way."

"But that *scar*—" Clara argued.

"We can't do anything about the scar," Will said, clenching his teeth as he squared his shoulders to the healer.

Eyes wide, Clara looked past him at Anna.

She shrugged in an attempt to look nonchalant. "There will be a scar, and I will live. It seems like a winning trade."

"Who cares about the scar?" Ros scoffed, their pale eyes looking around the group. "We were discussing how to present our evidence to the Council without looking like we've gone mad."

"The existence of the shade will be difficult to prove," Ben said.

"But the men will be easier. They can be found and apprehended, put on trial and forced to confess," the captain thought aloud, and then looked at Anna.

"Who are these men? How do you know them, and what is their connection to Lord Woulfe?"

The men who took my home from me. The reason I'm here at all. "I know them as debt collectors. The big one is a man named Luke, the little one is a dwarf named Cricket, and the thin one is an ass named Crocker. He's in charge." His brass knuckles flashed in her head, and she curled her hands into tight fists at her sides. "It seems they do all sorts of Woulfe's dirty work."

"If they all confess on trial to being in league with a shade," the captain said, "we wouldn't need to prove anything."

"We know nothing about this necromancer except that she is a woman," Ben said. "She could retaliate before the trial, or during it."

"Not if she doesn't know that she's been found out," Captain Heiser said. "Keep your sending spell brief, vague. Tell them we've discovered the reason behind the wandering Vassians, and we're coming back to report."

As they worked out the details, Anna's cognizance moved inward. *The Vassian, Woulfe, my mother's loan, Khaleena's link to you. It's all connected, isn't it?*

Everything is connected by a web of circumstance. The image of a shimmering spiderweb filled her mind's eye. *Some threads are stronger than others. As the ultimate fate of all things, I can see the threads, and—very occasionally—I can shift them.*

One of the spider's threads vibrated, resonating with a clear hum, and it moved.

The weave?

Anna felt his disagreement before she heard it. *The weave is a collection of energy that surrounds life. Life winds its own tapestry, separate from the weave, separate from us.*

The weight of the word *us*, and the gods it encompassed, echoed around inside of her, hollow. *I don't understand.*

There is too much you do not, and could not know.

Anger crept into her response. *Then you'd better start teaching me.*

His response was gentle, almost sad. *In time. If I were to let all my knowledge, my boons, fill you at once, you would be lost to its swollen tide, fractured and scattered, no longer yourself.*

Her hair stood on end, even as she felt his presence recede.

People were moving around her. Anna saw everyone leaving the tent. She was turning to join them when Khaleena stopped her.

"Would you stay with me a moment, Anna?"

She looked up at the beautiful six-and-a-half-foot-tall woman, still short for Vasbrute, and then glanced at her friends. Will and Pyran had paused to wait for her. The captain stopped behind them. She nodded at them and signaled for them to go, then turned back to Khaleena.

It was just her, the Vassian queen, and two of her guards.

"I would like to personally apologize for the actions of my nephew's pack. We may be strong, but it is not our way to commit violence for violence's sake. For the pain caused to you and your team, my people owe you a debt. For your death, and the power granted to you through it, I am forever in *your* debt. If there is anything you ever need, Anna Hale, you may call on me."

Surprised, all she could say was, "Thank you."

"I am one of the few prognosticators of our people, connected to threads that connect us all," she said. "When I touched you, I could see that your future will be awe-striking and tremendous. My abilities are not particular—that is, I cannot see specific danger in your future and warn you of it. However, I may be able to offer insight during a time of need." She held her hands up, palms out, between them. "Would you allow me to aid you in this way?"

Anna looked down at the hands uncertainly. Days ago, she hadn't believed in gods, and certainly not in fortune-tellers. *But now…*

She lifted her hands, and then hesitated as she remembered Lucy's torn flesh.

Khaleena looked at her with a great sadness in her deep red gaze. "If there is one thing I wish to accomplish now, it is the chance to win your trust. My people have hurt you and yours in an immeasurable way. I cannot give your friend—Lucy, you called them—back to you, but please know that I will be praying for their peace alongside the peace of our own we have lost."

Her son. Anna looked into Khaleena's eyes and found only earnestness. She nodded and placed her hands into Khaleena's.

"Thank you, Death-Speaker."

The Vassian woman shut her eyes, and her thumbs bent over Anna's hands, holding them gently in place. She inhaled deeply. "I see a darkness to the north." She frowned, her dark lips pressing against each other in discomfort. "It is cold, strange. You are at the center of it, blind." Her brows pulled together. "There are so many voices calling for help. Your ears are the only ones that hear them."

She swallowed. "Time passes. The darkness grows stronger, but so do your eyes and your ears. Vigilance will keep you keen, cutting." She blinked, and her eyes looked to Anna, a pale gray-green light fading from them until burgundy irises focused. She exhaled, and the strain left her. Her thumbs rubbed the back of Anna's hands. "You walk a strange path. There were champions before the war, revered and respected, but now..."

Anna grasped at the strand of information. "There were others like me?"

Khaleena smiled, her sharp teeth shining. "Perhaps not *like* you, but blessed in the same way. Their existence has been lost to time, now trapped only in books and spoken tales."

"I've never heard of them."

"I suppose you wouldn't have," Khaleena said thoughtfully. She released her hands. "But that is a story for another time. I understand your mage needs space and components to complete his sending."

Disappointment filled Anna's face, and Khaleena chuckled. "Don't worry, little champion. The Son of Death will surely show you in his time."

54

ANNA FOLLOWED KHALEENA TO ANOTHER TENT, WHERE BEN WAS SETting up his ritual. The mage was so focused on the task that he only gave a nod of his head in greeting.

He was stooped over a large wood table, drawing with a stick of white chalk. Anna stepped around the table to the other side to watch him. He traced a circular pattern of shapes and runes with a precise hand.

Khaleena spoke with a Vassian guard in the room, looked over the materials sitting next to the table, and then smiled at Anna before she left.

"Can I...help you?" Anna asked as Ben put the chalk down.

His forehead was pulled into serious lines as he checked his work. He wiped away a curl of a line and redrew it. She couldn't see a difference between the new mark and the old. Satisfied, he stepped back and looked at her. "You could hand me what I need."

She moved over to the small pile of spell components.

"The gem dust in that velvet bag, please."

She handed it to him.

He measured some of the dust into his hand and then carefully piled it at one end of the many-pointed star he'd drawn in chalk on the table. He did this at each, and then dragged the remaining dust from the points to the center of the drawing.

"The wire." He held out his hand.

She picked up the small spool of copper wire and handed it to him. He trimmed it into five pieces and shaped each into interlocking circles, which he placed at the center of the drawing.

"Letter."

Anna handed him the piece of folded parchment, so fine that it was bone white. The wax seal was bright yellow, with the impression of a six-pointed star. The words *The Council of Telluth* covered the front in Ben's elegant handwriting. The ink was the blackest color Anna had ever seen—blacker even than her Writ of Duty.

He placed the letter at the center, atop the copper wire. He glanced at Anna. There was an excited smile tugging at his lips and a sparkle in his eyes. He extended his hands over the table, palms down and fingers splayed.

He shut his eyes and spoke in an unfamiliar language, his voice low and heavy. His hands glowed white. Static filled the air.

There was a *pop*, and she smelled charcoal. The Vassian guard at the side of the entrance jumped.

The mage lowered his hands, and the letter was gone. The copper wire had patinated to green and the white chalk had turned black. The gem dust was gone.

"Woah," Anna breathed. She inspected the table with wide eyes.

Ben was beaming.

"You do spells like this all the time?" she asked.

He laughed. "No! I just used hundreds of gold worth of gem dust."

She cringed. "Did it go through?"

"I'm as sure about it as I can be," he told her. "Mind helping me clean up?"

"Not at all."

It felt good to be doing something mundane. The copper wire was warm to the touch, and brittle. They washed away the soot on the table with wet cloths. The table beneath looked untouched.

"That was your first time casting that spell?" she asked.

"I've done it once before, at the university. It was part of an exam."

"Do you think," she wondered aloud, "you could do it with a person? I know Will has that dagger, but that only works as far as you can throw it."

"Actually," he grinned, "there are several senior mages working on person displacement. From what I recall, they're close to finding a solution to travel limitless distances within six seconds, give or take."

She whistled, impressed. The guard took their dirty rags from them when they finished.

"So..." Ben picked at a crack in the grain on the table.

"So?"

"The gods are real," he said slowly, like he was tasting the words on his tongue.

"Very real," she sighed.

He looked at her with his bright gray eyes, like storm clouds full of lightning. "Are you okay? Really?"

She snorted. "No." Her smile faltered. "Are you scared of me?"

His grin crinkled the corner of his eyes. "I'm not scared of you. It's just another puzzle to solve."

"I could use all the help I can get."

"You've got me," he said, "and the others."

She nodded halfheartedly.

"Why are you worried?"

She glanced at the guard standing nearby and spun the ring on her finger. "I made a dead body talk. I'm terrified of *myself.*"

Ben frowned and his eyebrows tilted somberly. "You helped a grieving family find closure and completed our mission, saving all of us while you were at it." His hand settled on his hip. "I don't think anyone's scared of that."

"It doesn't freak you out?"

He shrugged. "It's magic. I don't know how you did it, but I'd like to."

"You said you could feel the curse. Do you…feel anything like that on me?"

He motioned for her to come closer. She rounded the table. He put both hands on either side of her face, his thumbs resting on her temples, and then he shut his eyes. His face set in focus.

She flushed at the unexpected closeness. Ben's face lit with a dim light from his hands, and then she felt a static rush from her head to her toes.

"Hm."

"Hm, what?" she asked.

He opened his eyes and lowered his hands. "Usually, I can feel the weave in a living thing if their power is strong enough, but this feels alien to me. Cal was vague when he tried to explain. When you made your deal with Morterra, after you…"

"Died," she finished for him.

He nodded, and his eyes flashed with sadness. "What happened?"

She took a deep breath, going over it in her head. "We were in limbo. He called it Intervallum, the gateway between life and death. He gave me a choice, death or life as his champion. Said he needed someone to help him affect the world directly, that something bad was working against the Well."

"Why you? No offense."

"I asked the same thing. He said it was because I was wearing his ring." She held up her hand. "And ley lines. Do you remember what we talked about on the ship?"

"Of course."

"He said it was like the opposite of a cong-conv—"

"Convergence?"

She nodded. "The weave opened enough that he could reach through, basically."

"Then it's true," he mumbled. "The weave is the wall between the world and them." He lifted a fist to his chin and thought. His eyes widened with some inner realization, and then narrowed at her thoughtfully.

"What?"

"I have a theory about your powers—why you can't be healed."

She waited expectantly.

Ben swallowed and his expression shifted to nervousness. "Cal and Clara pull their power from the weave. I have a theory that the person being healed is able to because everyone is connected to the weave.

"Anna, I don't think Morterra connected you to the weave to grant you power. I think you've been *disconnected*...and connected directly to Morterra instead. Your powers come from him. That's why they feel so foreign."

She blinked at him, processing.

"It's only a theory," he added.

Is that why you're in my head?

There was no answer.

She spun the ring on her hand again. She thought about mentioning the conversations she'd had in her mind, but she was wary of the Vassian guard and tired of the topic. "Okay."

"Okay?"

She shrugged. "I don't know. I'll think about it." Her stomach rumbled.

Ben huffed a laugh. "Come on. I think the others are eating."

He led her out of the tent, and the Vassian guard followed behind. They crossed the circle of yellow tents to a medium-sized one. The guard that followed them stopped and stayed outside next to the two guards stationed there. Inside, there was a long, low table in the center of the room, surrounded by rugs and cushions in warm colors, red, orange, gold, and pink. The team sat at the table eating, dressed in Vassian attire. As they entered, everyone turned to look.

"It's done?" Captain Heiser asked Ben.

The mage nodded. "They should have it in Kastarus."

"Well done," the captain praised.

Ben walked over to the table and took a seat at the end. Anna lingered near the entrance.

"You must be starving!" Clara jumped up and took her by the arm. "Come sit next to me and I'll build you a plate."

"Okay." Anna swallowed past the lump in her throat and then gave Clara a small, fragile smile.

Clara pulled her down at the middle of the table, next to Merry. Pyran and the captain sat across from them, with Ros to the captain's left. Cal sat on Clara's other side, and Will took the spot at the end.

Clara hummed to herself as she put food on a plate.

"How did you die?" Merry asked.

"*Mother*, Merry!" Clara froze in her task to look aghast. "You can't just ask that!"

Merry's face turned red. "I'm sorry! You don't have to answer! Cal wouldn't say, and I just thought—"

Shoulders stiff and hands balled into fists on her thighs, Anna smiled nervously at the tall woman. "It's okay. I'm sure you all want to know. I might as well answer."

Everyone stared expectantly.

"A sword." Her hand moved over the bandages from her right shoulder to her left hip. "Went right through my leathers, like they weren't there." When she looked up, Cal and Will were both finding the food in front of them very interesting.

"What is Morterra like?" Clara asked gently.

She considered how to answer in a way that made sense. Finally, she shrugged. "I don't know. Warmer than I would've thought. Infuriatingly...nice."

She thought she heard a chuckle in a corner of her mind.

"How did you know you could speak with the dead?" Ros asked.

Anna tucked a stray hair behind her ear. "He told me to."

"What else can you do?" Merry asked excitedly.

"I don't know." As she looked around the table, she realized they weren't scared of her. They were mostly in awe.

"That's enough for now." Captain Heiser lifted his goblet and said, "To your return!"

The table lifted their glasses, and Anna joined them. "Thank you."

As she ate, Clara chatted to her about their time in the cage. Ros talked about the curse, how it had seemed like a living thing when Ben pulled it from the Vasbrute and destroyed it. Ben talked about necromancy. They talked about Vassian culture, how they were carnivorous and nomadic. The Crown was a diarchy, traditionally held by a bonded couple that shared responsibility. The Vassians—it turned out—were kind to people that weren't their enemies. After they were freed of the cage, they'd all been kept clean and well-fed.

After lunch, Captain Heiser was called away to help plan their trek north and determine what supplies they needed. He took Pyran with him. The swordsman had ruffled Anna's hair on his way out, and she'd taken it out of her braid.

Anna looked down the table at Will. He was frowning and twisting a dagger around in his hands.

Clara caught her looking and leaned in to whisper, "He's been quiet these couple of days. I mean, I get it, but he's full-on sulking."

"It *is* weird," Merry agreed. "Not even a joke."

Maybe he is *scared of me. Or is he mad that I made him stay?*

The conversation shifted to the first thing they'd do when they returned home, and Anna's mind wandered to her mother.

THAT NIGHT, ANNA WAS GIVEN ANOTHER BATH AND REBANDAGED. THIS time, she told herself not to flinch at the Vassian hands. What wounds had opened during their infiltration of the camp were now closed again. When she walked back to the tent the group was in, she found Will walking out.

He looked up at her, surprised. "Anna."

"Will," she mimicked his greeting. "Were you going for a walk?"

"Just needed some fresh air." His right hand lifted to the back of his neck and he strained a smile.

Anna's nose wrinkled at his expression. "What's wrong?"

"What do you mean?"

"I don't think I've ever seen you fake a smile."

His smile turned wry. "I'm that obvious?"

Her eyebrows raised as she waited for an answer to her question.

"I've been thinking about...everything."

"I thought you'd be happy. We're going back alive. After the meeting with the Council, things can go back to normal."

He glanced back at the tent, and then looked at Anna. "Would you walk with me?"

"Oh. Sure."

Will led her around the circle of yellow tents, his voice quiet and unsure.

"I didn't want to go back."

Anna hummed thoughtfully. "Right. You know, I think we'd all be okay with faking your death."

He shot her an amused smile.

"I mean, Ben or Clara might talk, but by then, you'd be gone." She thought of Will disappearing, and felt heat climb to her neck and into her cheeks. She turned away to look at one of the lanterns around the circle. "We'd miss you."

"We?"

When she looked back at Will, he was smirking cheekily. The heat in her face burned. "Sure. Merry would be lost without her grumpy sidekick."

"Grumpy?" He feigned offense. *"Sidekick?"*

"Grumpy, sarcastic, pessi—"

"I get it, I get it," Will interrupted, rolling his eyes. When he was done, he turned a thoughtful gaze on her. "Anyway, that was before. Now..."

She waited for him to continue.

"Well, for one, I still have to teach you how to dance."

Her heart skipped a beat. She was sure he could see her blushing now, even in the dark. "I never accepted your offer."

"Someone should teach you before we get back. They'll be lining up to dance with death's champion."

Anna grunted. "Yeah, right. *Death-Speaker* doesn't exactly ooze friendliness."

"You underestimate the court's desire to be close to power. You could use somebody on the outside to keep your head on straight."

"You want to come back just to be my dance instructor and counselor?" she asked skeptically.

Will sighed and stopped walking. "Before all of this, I was ready to give up on everything." His deep brown eyes turned to Anna. "Maybe you showed me I don't have to."

Her eyebrows rose. "Maybe?"

He started walking again. "I'm giving it a trial run."

A smile crept across her face.

55

THE NEXT MORNING WAS SPENT GATHERING SUPPLIES FROM THE VASSIANS for their journey. For Anna, this meant sitting and watching while everyone else filled packs. Whenever she tried to get up and help, someone would scold her and force her to sit back down.

It was infuriating.

It gave her a good vantage point to watch, though. The crow, Gemma, had joined them with the Vassian woman, Tasha, and the bird's interest in Will was comical. It perched on his pack as he turned to grab something to put inside, and he had to shoo it away multiple times. At one point, the bird tried to land on Will's shoulder, which led to more shooing and a scolding from Tasha to the bird about personal space.

"Really," the Vassian woman told the crow. "I don't know what's gotten into you."

After an awkward lunch with their Vassian travel companions and a courtly goodbye from the Crown, they paraded out of camp and back to the wall.

They avoided the gate again, so they wouldn't tip anyone off as to who they were traveling with and where they were. Once they'd crossed the wall, Prince Bartok asked for a guide from Captain Heiser's crew.

Anna stepped forward immediately, and told her worried friends, "I walked all the way here bleeding. I can do it backwards in better condition. It's just walking."

Will joined her. This time, he stuck close, no further than ten feet from her at any given time. Gemma joined them at the front, gliding from tree branch to tree branch or circling overhead. The rest of the group was never far behind, either.

They followed the river north until they had to split from it to turn toward their previous camp. It was long dark by the time they reached the spot, but they'd been making great time and Anna wanted to take advantage. Her friends were tired, but the Vassians were doing just fine.

She sat by the firepit and started on lighting the fire while the others set up their remaining tents. The Vassians quickly set up one large tent on an edge of the camp, and the others set up theirs across the clearing.

It didn't take her long to start the fire. Once that was done, she found Pyran. "She's over here."

He followed her to Lucy's grave. The sword and shield hadn't moved, but the paxmortium plant still reached out of the dirt and was beginning to loop around the sword.

"She'd like that," Pyran gestured at the sword and shield. He swallowed past something in his throat and added, "And the flowers. Did you plant those?"

Anna frowned. "Yeah."

"It's a good spot."

Anna pulled in a shaky breath.

He nodded at Anna, and then glanced at the Vassians beginning to settle in by the fire. "The one that killed her isn't here. He should have to see this."

"I think she killed him." Anna shook her head, her eyebrows pressing together. "He was cursed. Possessed. There should be repercussions, but he wasn't in control of himself. I'm sure that what he did would haunt him." She paused, then said, "They all lost their prince, too. The way that Branik talked about being pinned down with magic—I think it's similar to the curse. It's something in their brains, pushing them to violence rather than preventing them from moving."

Pyran's lips rose in a snarl. "Then we find those men. Make them pay."

Anna nodded. She put a hand on his tense shoulder, then turned. She left him, gave him a moment alone, and returned to the fire. She avoided the Vassian eyes on her as she grabbed one of the roasting sticks she'd prepared, and then sat down about four feet from Prince Bartok.

"You know the woods well," the prince complimented.

She glanced at him. His red eyes watched her with interest. She thought of the anger she'd seen in them when he'd pinned her against the bars of the cage, and she turned to the fire again. "Thanks."

Heavy quiet hung in the air. The snapping of the flames and the sound of crickets filled the space. She sat tensely, warming up some of the meat they'd brought. Her eyes darted back to him before returning to the stick she held over the fire.

The other Vassians joined her in warming up dinner, occasionally casting glances at her. Stoiko did not appear, apparently choosing sleep over dinner.

Anna swallowed nervously, then sighed stiffly. She pulled the meat from the fire and held it out to the prince. He thanked her and took it. The other Vasbrute watched the exchange carefully.

She leaned toward him and asked quietly, "Why are they staring at me?"

He grinned as he answered. "They do not think you should be cooking."

Anna blinked. "Because I'm not Vassian?"

"No," Bartok's grin grew. "Because you are Death-Speaker, Champion of the Son of Death. They consider it beneath you."

She laughed softly. "Beneath me?"

He nodded.

"That's ridiculous," she said. "I cooked before. I'll keep cooking now."

"I doubted you, at first," he said. "But I was not seeing, then. Now I believe you are the right choice."

That makes one of us.

"Is the food ready?" Pyran walked up with Cal, both of them eyeing the Vassians around the campfire.

"Help yourselves," she said, nodding toward the roasting sticks.

They sat on Anna's other side with their dinner over the coals.

Will walked up next, looked around the circle, and then planted himself in the gap between Anna and the prince. Gemma called from the trees and then swooped down to hop nearby, head tilting at them all. Slowly, everyone else joined the circle. Awkward silence filled the air again as they ate. Will looked at the crow nearby with a dubious frown, and then he tossed a small piece of meat to Gemma, who hopped over and plucked it from the ground before fluffing happily.

Anna thought about the stories her dad used to tell by the fire, and had an idea.

She cleared her throat and then leaned forward to look around Will at the prince. "When I talked to your mother, she told me there were champions a long time ago. Do you know any of the stories?"

He considered her question and then replied, "There are many stories of champions and of gods. We tell them to children to teach them. I do not know which are history and which are fiction. There are few that study such things."

Anna nodded, a little disappointed.

"Where would one study them?" Ben asked. "I've never seen anything about that in the libraries in Eysa."

"Your kind has erased the old truths," Bartok said with a frown. "There are some tomes and records with our knowledge-keepers, but they are far south of the wall, deep within Vassa for preservation. Outside of that, you might try with the elves or dwarves to the north, but they do not share easily."

"Would you tell us a story?" Merry asked. "One of the children's stories?"

Bartok smiled and turned to his companions. "Malik?"

A Vassian man looked up. He wasn't as thick with muscles as Bartok or Stoiko, but still cut an intimidating figure. "I remember one story that would be relevant, prince." He looked at Anna and then his red eyes drifted over their heads, unfocused at the darkness as he recalled the tale.

"There once was a man full of fear.
It was his life he held dear,
but life passed him by.
One day he did die,
and the Son of Death's voice he did hear.

'Your story, as written, is complete.
I come here to offer you sleep,
yet you do not agree,
you offer a plea,
but the payment I ask for is steep.'

The man did not heed Death's advice.
He offered to pay any price.
So Death took his due,

and kept his word true.
The man returned with his life.

But all things for him were now changed.
His very fate rearranged.
Of time he grew tired,
while his family expired.
His mind became quite deranged.

The man took his second chance
to continue life's haphazard dance.
His body was whole,
but his soul took the toll.
And so he cried out for Death's lance.

Death heard his shout and returned,
saying, 'Now, I see, you have learned.'
The man did agree,
with humility,
'For death, it is now that I yearn.'

So we trust the master of ends.
It is dangerous when fate bends.
When we are finished,
our light diminished,
the world's order, he defends."

The children's rhyme sounded almost sinister, rolling off his stony tongue. They sat quietly as he spoke. Merry laughed nervously and glanced at Anna.

"Wow, that's really..." the strong-woman started, and then trailed off, unable to find the words to finish her statement.

"Eerie?" Will offered. "Foreboding?"

Anna shifted uncomfortably in her spot on the grass.

"No, no," Bartok shook his head. "True, it is a warning not to wish for more after death, but it is also a lesson in trust. The gods know things we do not. They are connected with forces we cannot see. It is a lesson in trusting their judgement, particularly the judgement of the god of order. You did not argue for a second life." He looked at Anna. "The god of death gave it to you. It is different."

THE NEXT MORNING, THE GROUP CONTINUED THEIR JOURNEY NORTH.

Pyran spent the day asking the Vassians questions about strategy. He wanted to know everything about their approach to battle and how they use their many strengths. Anna listened from ahead as she led them through the trees.

When they stopped for lunch, she sat with Pyran and the Vassians, talking about war and customs and things she had little experience with.

It was common for Vassian military leaders to be challenged to combat, she learned. If they won, they proved their position, but if they lost, positions were reevaluated.

"Physical strength isn't the only mark of a good leader, though," Pyran said. "Sometimes it's not even all that important."

"It is also not the only way to win a test of combat," Prince Bartok said. "All skills are considered and celebrated. Stoiko has won several challenges, and each test required different approaches. Right, Stoiko?"

Stoiko looked up from where he leaned against the trunk of a tree. "Yes, prince."

"Celebrated?" Anna asked. "What do you mean?"

"After a challenge, there is a feast held in the winner's honor," the prince explained. "It is the same reason we bare our skin. The marks there are trophies of our strength and what we have overcome."

Clara, who had been listening with her brother, wandered over. "Do these feasts involve music and dancing?"

"Yes," the prince nodded with an amused smile, "but it is not the kind familiar to you."

"Well," Pyran said, "maybe Anna would be better at a Vassian feast than a Council ball."

One of Bartok's bald brows rose. "You dislike the parties of the court?"

Anna shook her head and jabbed Pyran with her elbow. "Yeah, I'm not a dancer. Considering that's the main event, I get pretty bored at balls."

"Takes a whole task force to get her dressed up, too," Pyran leaned forward, mock gossiping.

Her elbow jabbed him in the side again, and he laughed.

Bartok grunted in what may have been a laugh. "We are not all made to look pretty, but I'm sure you have no trouble."

Clara giggled at Anna's flushed cheeks. "Days ago, you only had three baggy outfits," she told the redhead between her laughter. "Now you're getting compliments from foreign princes!"

Pyran laughed with her.

Embarrassed, Anna walked over to Will. She found him sitting with his back against a tree trunk, feeding Gemma berries from her perch on his knee.

"Does Tasha know you're feeding her crow?" Anna asked, wearing an amused smile.

"I do," Tasha called from nearby. "She is *enthralled* with him. It is bewildering."

Anna hummed thoughtfully, then teased, "Maybe it's because they match."

Will glanced up at her, a berry between two fingers on its path to the bird's beak. "You're just jealous you can't pull the look off."

Gemma looked at Anna, her head tilted curiously, then clacked her beak.

"Wow," Anna laughed. "Your sense of humor is rubbing off on her."

THEY CROSSED THE RIVER WEST OF EFFLEY AND MADE CAMP IN THE WOODS there. Clara seemed to feel more comfortable after their lunch conversation, and spent some time asking the Vassian woman, Milenka, about the fabrics they used in their clothing. Merry joined, and they compared the size of their arms and thighs.

After dinner, they sat around the fire, telling drinking stories. Anna didn't have any, but she listened and laughed. Pyran told a story of a birthday party gone awry. He and his friends had ended up naked in the lake, their clothes missing. Milenka talked about a feast when she had danced with both princes, only to wake up the next morning and remembered none of it, and then Bartok filled in the details. Clara talked about a ball where she'd accidentally let slip that their distant cousin was getting divorced, and Cal explained all the damage control he'd had to do. Ros' story started with their tolerance training. Apparently, the fledgling Krakens would get drunk to build their alcohol immunity, but this took time, and there were always mishaps.

After the captain spoke of his first ball, and how he had knocked over the cellist, Clara said, "They'll have to throw another ball in our honor, and I'm sure we'll all be expected to be active participants. That means *dancing*." She turned to Anna and grinned.

"We all know how good I am with footwork." Anna pulled at her bandages. Her crew laughed, but some of the Vassians stiffened. She cleared her throat nervously.

Clara smiled and rolled her eyes, taking back the attention. "Dancing isn't complicated. You're being dramatic. Here, come with me." She stood and held out her hand.

With a sigh, Anna let the half-dwarf pull her up. "Can't I just decline to dance?"

"No, they'll think something's wrong with you."

She was pulled to their tent, where Clara dug through her bag. She pulled a small box out of the bottom and brought it outside. She turned a little crank on one side, and then Anna heard the soft tinkle of music. The music box played a slow, spinning melody.

Anna glanced at the people sitting at the fire, many of them turned to watch her.

"You scared little dove," Clara huffed and pulled her behind the tents. "I swear, I don't know where your white belly hides, but it comes out at the strangest times."

Anna frowned at her.

"Okay." Her hand waved Anna's irritated expression away, and she set the music box on the ground. "I'll show you. I'll be the lead." She held Anna's waist with one hand and her right hand with the other. "Put your left hand on my shoulder. Good."

Clara slowly moved through the steps of a simple waltz. Her feet were sure, but her left leg moved a little stiffly.

Anna tried to follow. She tripped over her own feet and then stepped on Clara's. Her partner remained a stone-faced instructor through all of it. Gradually, she picked up the pattern. Her movement was clunky, but she had figured out where she needed to put her feet as she stared down at her boots.

"Could I cut in?"

Anna looked up at Will, and they paused.

Clara raised a skeptical eyebrow at him, but she shrugged and released Anna's hand. "Sure."

As she walked away to find another partner, Will took her spot. He took Anna's hovering left hand in his right and laid it on his shoulder. His left hand delicately held her fingers. His arms arched, elbows slightly lifted. "Ready?"

"Yes."

He led her into the first step, and Anna's attention turned back to her feet.

"Are you going to stare at your boots the whole time?"

"I don't want to trip."

"If you're partnered with the right lead, you won't have to worry about your feet." He squeezed her hand to grab her attention.

Heat rose from her neck as she looked up into his face. He was half a head taller than her, which hadn't felt like much before, but with only a foot of open air between them, it was much more obvious. He was watching her, his dark eyes lit golden with interest.

His hold on her was firm. As he stared, his feet moved further, their dance wider, but Anna didn't trip. It was as if he carried her through the motions, knew where her foot wanted to go, and guided it to where it *should* go. She felt her muscles loosen as the dance shifted from a repetition of steps into an ongoing, fluid motion. A smile grew across her lips.

"See?" he smirked.

His expression snagged at the breath in her lungs, but she managed to say, "I thought it was impossible for me to move like this."

"Miracles happen."

She gave a little laugh.

The music box tinkled next to them in the low light of the distant fire. Merry laughed as the captain told another story. Crickets and an owl sounded in the darkness of the trees.

"You know," Will said, "I think you look more alive now than you did before you died."

"More sarcasm?"

"No." His eyes traveled over her face before returning to her eyes. "There's a light that wasn't there before."

She hummed thoughtfully. "Maybe it's you that's changed."

One dark eyebrow rose. "How so?"

"For one, the Will Grey I met in Kastarus would not be dancing with me in the woods."

The music box stopped, its song spent. They stopped dancing. Anna lifted her hand from his shoulder, but he held onto her other hand and her waist. His arms relaxed, pulling her a little closer.

"And two?" he asked, his eyes searching hers. His head tilted slightly, and his eyes glanced down to her lips.

Her heartbeat quickened. Her left hand still hovered above him. The urge to cup his neck and trace his jawline with her thumb came to her suddenly. Instead, she swallowed and rested her hand on the side of his arm. "Two," she said slowly, and looked over at her left hand. "The old Will wouldn't have cared that I have to go back to Hillcrest when this is over. I think the new Will does."

When her eyes met his again, he took in a little breath through his nose, like the smallest gasp. And then he was leaning in.

His lips met hers softly, hesitantly. When she kissed back, he became more sure, his kiss more confident. Her fingers fisted in the fabric of his sleeve. His hand released her other hand and moved to the back of her neck, where his gloved fingers cradled the back of her head. Something tugged inside her chest, warm and growing, as his hand at her waist pulled her against him. Her right hand wrapped around his side to press against the back of his shoulder, holding them together.

A low whistle sounded, and then a Vassian shouted, "We're under attack!"

Anna and Will pulled abruptly apart, but the half-elf's hold on her tightened. They looked at each other with wide eyes for half a moment as time skittered and jumped around them.

"Hide," Will said through a ragged breath, before turning toward the campfire. With a throw of his magical dagger, he slipped through her fingers.

56

ANNA HEAVED TWO BREATHS WHILE STARING AT THE EMPTY SPACE WILL had left behind. The sound of growls and banging metal slammed into her, throwing her into motion.

She crouched and scurried toward the back of the tent she shared with Clara and Merry. She lifted the canvas and dove underneath. Her eyes scanned the darkness as her fingers fumbled for her pack.

I need light.

The ring on her hand warmed and began to glow, illuminating the space around her in a pale cast. She grabbed her shortbow and threw her quiver over her shoulder. She knelt in front of the tent's entrance and peeked through.

Everyone was scattered, caught in frenzied combat with people in dark clothing, wielding glinting blades. The camp invaders wore leather armor and carried multiple weapons. All of her friends were without armor, and mostly without weapons.

Shit.

She spun, hooking her bow to her quiver. She grabbed Merry's shield and

Clara's mace.

You there? she called into her mind.

Yes.

If I die again—

You will not.

Perfect.

She ran from the tent, toward where Clara was fighting with a swordsman. The knife in her hand was doing little to block and parry. Her opponent's reach was much greater than hers.

Anna ran up behind the man. Her shoulder and chest erupted in pain as she lifted Skullcrusher with all the strength she had in her right arm—shouting with the effort—and then brought the weapon down onto the man's back. There was a muted *crunch,* and he stumbled, howling in pain.

"Take it!" she shouted at Clara, holding out the mace with a shaking arm.

"Mother, Anna!" The half-dwarf grasped her weapon and spun toward the stumbling man. "You're going to hurt yourself!" She ducked as the man swung his sword at both of them.

Anna took the shield with both hands and thrust it at the flying weapon, teeth clenched against the pain. A loud *clang* rang through the trees and reverberated up her arms as she was knocked backwards. She heard a louder *crunch.* When she regained her footing, she looked around the shield to see the man in a heap on the ground, one side of his head caved in and blood trailing from his mouth and nose.

"Merry," she said, gaze fastened to the man's crushed skull. "Her shield."

Clara took hold of her left shoulder and spun her toward the battlefield. "Merry's in there by Ros. You're not going in there."

There were several separate battles between her and the strong-woman. A Vassian man growled at two opponents before lunging at one, picking them up, and throwing them at the other. The captain fought off an attacker with quick, graceful strikes of his rapier before spinning to slice at another attacker. Pyran and a Vassian woman stood back-to-back as they dodged attacks. The woman struck out with her claws, but Pyran was weaponless, until he broke the arm of his attacker and claimed their sword. Ros, too, swung a stolen sword near where Merry wielded a flaming torch. She tried to dodge an attack, but her opponent was faster, their sword slicing into Merry's arm.

"She needs her shield," Anna asserted.

Clara turned, and her mace collided with the gut of an attacker, sending them flailing backward. "I'll take it to her!"

"No," Anna glanced at Clara's left leg. After the attack, the half-dwarf shifted her weight to her right leg. "I can do it."

Clara glanced at her leg as well, and then let out a huff. "Fine. But I swear to the Well, if you die again, I will learn necromancy, bring you back, and then kill you *again*!" She stepped toward the attacker she'd knocked away as he got back to his feet.

"You're not the first to offer it!" Anna called back before she turned and started cutting a route to Merry.

Everyone she scurried past was already engaged in combat, their attention focused. She moved through them in a stuttering dance, avoiding blades and eyelines. Her feet faltered when she saw a tall, familiar man in the crowd, throwing around a spiked club.

She stumbled into a figure in black, who turned and dragged their hooked dagger across her upper arm. She screamed and shoved with the shield as hard as she could. The attacker shouted back and pushed her, until their voice was cut off abruptly. A thin sword pierced through their chest, hot blood splattering onto the shield and Anna's face.

"Careful, Anna." Captain Heiser pulled his sword from their back and turned to face the next attacker. The body fell in a heap. "Or Morterra will have to bring you back again!"

Panting, she nodded at the back of his head, and then restarted her rush towards Merry. By the time she reached her, Merry's torch was a flameless splinter.

"Shield!" Anna shouted at her, and she held it out.

Merry's blue eyes glanced in Anna's direction, and a grin spread across her face when she saw her shield. She turned her attention back to the enemy in front of her and kicked forward. Her foot landed on their chest and sent them backwards ten feet, arms pinwheeling.

She took the shield from Anna and then stepped up to her opponent as they were getting up. Her shield crashed into their head with a *clang* that echoed like a dull cymbal. The strong-woman looked back at Anna, but then her smile fell. As she shouted a warning, Anna felt a spark at her collarbone. She turned and dove forward, landing in a sloppy roll. Her bow caught her as she landed on her back, digging into the earth and into her spine. When she looked behind herself, a figure in black stood where she had been, two swords slicing through what would've been her heart.

Just as suddenly, Ros whirled at the figure, their sword glancing off both of the enemy's blades as they blocked. "Why do I find you in the center of the battlefield with only your bow?"

Anna scrambled to her feet, breath coming hard. Before she could formulate an answer, Merry moved forward to assist, saying, "She brought my shield!"

"Right," Anna agreed.

She scanned the battlefield and unhooked her bow, then nocked an arrow. The clearing was churning with chaotic motion, but there were bodies clothed in black scattered across the ground. The Vassians had dispersed across the camp, and the numbers looked closer to even now. There was a five-foot wall of ice in a semicircle at Ben's back. The mage was casting explosions and wind gusts at the nearby attackers while Cal stood with him, shooting his crossbow into the frenzy. Ben's face was set into a grimace, and she could see blood trailing down his robes from his shoulder.

Will was across the camp, fighting a short man whose red hair shone even in the low light.

Dwarf. Anna's mouth went dry. Her eyes raked across the bodies until they found the familiar, tall man she'd spotted earlier. Luke swung his spiked club at Clara, who dodged, barely. There were other dark figures around them. Her friend was cornered.

"Cover me," Anna told Merry as she lifted her bow and took aim. One breath in. A half-breath out. Release.

The arrow whined through the air, biting across Luke's forearm. His swing went wide as he instinctively pulled his arm toward his chest.

"Someone needs to get to Clara!" Anna shouted.

"I'll go," Ros said.

The person they'd been fighting lay on the ground, two dark ribbons of red across their gut. Ros held their fallen enemy's swords as they started toward Clara.

"We want him alive!" Anna called out to them.

Ros glanced back with a pale eyebrow quirked. "He is one of them?"

"Yes!"

Anna caught Pyran's eye, and the swordsman looked at Ros, then at Clara. "On my way," he shouted, forcing his way through the crowd.

Merry caught a sword with her shield, and she shoved back. Anna startled, then took off running toward Will.

"Where are you going?" Merry asked.

"There's another one!"

Will and Cricket were locked in battle. The dwarven mage deflected each of Will's cuts or stabs—twice by some invisible force—and his hands were flaming as he swiped at Will. They were both out of breath when Anna reached them.

"Hey!" Anna shouted. "Cricket! Where's Crocker?"

She was successful in drawing the dwarf's attention. His head swiveled to face her, sweat glistening on his brow—but so did Will's. His brown eyes were full of alarm.

Cricket caught the half-elf's reaction, and the corner of his mouth lifted in a smirk. "Hello, again," he said, then raised his hands toward Will.

Will's daggers glowed red hot, and he hissed a curse as he dropped them.

Cricket moved much faster than Anna remembered. He leaped at Will, his hands aflame and grasping.

"No!" Anna dropped her bow and pulled her knife from her belt as she charged forward.

They rolled, flames dancing between them. The dwarf had a hold of Will's leathers and they caught fire.

"Fuck!" Will rolled them again so that he was on top and tried to shove his thumbs into Cricket's eye sockets.

The mage cried out and released one of his hands to shove it into Will's face. They rolled again.

Anna didn't know where to stab the knife, so she ran up and kicked Cricket in the side as hard as she could. He grunted and let go, rolling off Will. In the next moment, Will was on top of him with the jump dagger at his throat.

"Wait!" Anna shouted. "We want him alive!"

Will's dagger stopped, pressed lightly against the dwarf's skin. Panting, with eyes still locked on Cricket, he asked, "You're sure his friends can't speak for him?"

"I guess it's his choice." Anna's voice hardened. "He can either die or he can stand trial. He'll confess to the Council. Won't you, Cricket?"

The dwarf glared at Will, then at Anna, his mouth curled into a snarl. She thought he might not answer, but he finally said, "I haven't had a confessional in years. About time."

A ragged scream ripped into Anna's ears, and her skin prickled. She turned to find Clara standing across the camp, staring at Pyran, who lay unmoving at her feet. Clara recovered in time to block a sword with her mace. A battle cry broke from her lips as she swung Skullcrusher so hard that it knocked her opponent over and she kept spinning.

Anna was already running, halfway there before she realized she was moving. She narrowly avoided the swipe of a sword as she slid across the bloody grass and crawled the last few feet to her friend.

He was face down with a large stab wound in his back. With a grunt, she rolled him over so that she could see his face. Blue eyes stared out at nothing as a dark red stain on his shirt grew. Her hands pressed against the gushing wound, but blood forced its way between her fingers.

"Clara!" she shouted, "Cal!"

"Shit! Shit!" Suddenly, Cal was kneeling on Pyran's other side. He put his shaking hands over Anna's. His fingers glowed.

A moment passed. Then another. "No, no, no." Cal pressed harder as his voice broke.

A shock went through Anna. She looked at Pyran's glassy eyes and put a bloody hand on his forehead. "You don't die today. Not you, too. Not today, Pyran Taggert."

He does not die, you hear me? she shouted into her mind, and then more softly, almost a whimper, *How do I fix him?*

To give life, you must take life. But be careful, Anna. There's no going back.

Tell me how!

Look around you.

Anna looked around. The grass was bloody, and bodies littered the area around her. Pyran had taken out several attackers before—

Most of them were still, but the stuttered rising and falling of a chest caught her eye. It was the man Clara had knocked over. He probably had shattered ribs, internal bleeding, maybe a punctured lung.

Him?

Yes.

She stood and grabbed the man under his armpits to pull him. He was heavy, and she was so sore. "Help me," she told Cal.

"What?" he looked up at her in frightened confusion.

"Please," her voice cracked.

Cal blanched, but stood and grabbed the man's legs. They laid him next to Pyran.

"Now what?" Anna asked aloud, her panic making her forget that the conversation was in her head. She panted as she knelt between the bodies. The stranger's eyes were rolling back.

"What?" Cal asked, "What are you doing?"

Are you sure?

Yes!

Morterra seemed to sigh, and sadness flooded her thoughts. *One hand on the living, the other on the dying.*

She placed a hand on each of their chests.

Pull the life from one to the other. This...will hurt.

Anna's brow drew together. She glanced between them. She didn't know how to *pull life,* but she imagined a river travelling across her arms from the stranger and into her friend, a flow of energy. As she drew in a breath, her lungs froze.

It was more like lightning than a river. White-hot pain filled her palm, pooled in her hand, and tore into her bones.

Do not remove your hands until the rite is complete, or you could burn away.

She fought the instinct to pull her hand back, like when she'd accidentally touched a hot pan. The energy filled her arm, shattered into her chest, stopped her heart, and kept going. But she didn't need her heart to beat, didn't need to breathe, because the pain that filled her was the power of life itself. Like thunder clapping, her awareness spread, encompassing everything around her.

Every person around her burst into blinding light, and when she shut her eyes against it, they were still there, burning through her eyelids. Beyond the suns that surrounded her were dimmer lights. A few people on the ground, the man under her right hand, even the grass and trees and animals.

Her body rigid with pain and sentience, the energy continued to fill her. She felt tight, stretched beyond her limits to contain another life force. In the small corner of her mind that was still her, she worried about losing consciousness or violently exploding.

And then she heard the screaming. A man's voice broke through the pain, through the light, and stabbed into her mind. She was vaguely aware that she, herself, was screaming, but it was like she was watching through a distant window. Shooting pain coursed through her chest, and her lungs couldn't fill with air. She wasn't breathing, needed to breathe, *couldn't* breathe. Her vision at the window fogged.

Stay here, Anna Hale, a forceful, deep voice commanded her, grounded her. *Do not give in to another man's end.*

She crashed through the window and flew from her mind—no, his mind—and she was back in the pain and awareness and tightness again. Her scream died out as her lungs emptied, and then the man's scream stopped. She was filled with him, but not *him*—his life force. Briefly, for no longer than the blink of an eye, she saw glossy threads swaying between the lights around her, only visible as they moved, thin as spiderweb.

And then the energy within her pushed against what held her together with renewed force. She clutched at the vision of the river in her head, focusing on the flow of the water. Even as she felt it might disintegrate her bones, the white-hot pain moved, forcing into her other arm, her hand, and finally into Pyran.

As it left her, a growing ache formed in her chest. A drum sounded. She realized her heart was beating again. A whining gasp left her mouth as her lungs pulled in air.

When the energy left her, she felt burnt from the inside, hollowed out and empty. The world was dark, and she had been stretched too far, unable to spring back. She blinked at the nothingness in her vision.

Am I blind? She knew she should be scared, but she was too tired.

Well done. Like soft fur brushing against her skin, Morterra's voice reached into to her mind, pleased.

TOUCH RETURNED FIRST. SOMEONE WARM WAS CRADLING HER IN THEIR arms, and someone was holding her hand. Something wet and sticky rubbed against her arm.

Then she regained smell. There was iron and dirt in the air, and something smoky. Next came hearing. Someone was sobbing, others were arguing. Finally, her eyes cleared.

Pyran's head rested against her shoulder, his body racked with his cries, and his blood soaked through his shirt and into her sleeve. Her tired head rolled to the side. Will was holding her hand. Her fingertips were purple.

She squeezed his hand, and his head lifted. His dark eyes stared at her fingers, and then found her face. He held her hand tighter.

"You need to stop dying on me, Anna," the half-elf told her with watery eyes.

"I didn't die that time." Her voice was quiet, hoarse. She held Pyran's arm with her other hand when he lifted his head. "Just passed out, I think." She took a breath. Her lungs ached.

"What did you do?" Pyran asked through his tears. "I thought you died for me. What did you do?"

"Kind of the opposite." She glanced at the dead body next to them, and she winced.

"Ah," Clara squealed, appearing over her head. "She's alive!"

She blinked up at Clara, and then her brain caught up. "Cricket. Luke. Did anyone find Crocker?" She tried to sit up, but Pyran held her too tightly.

"We've got the two," Will said. "The Vassians are hunting down the third."

"Okay." She relaxed again. "Mother, I have a migraine worse than whoever's skull Clara's mace found tonight."

"You were on fire." Clara glanced at the dead man, and then turned back to Anna. "There were green flames! And your eyes!"

Senses now fully returned, she felt a pulsing pain in her hands and up her arms. Her muscles and joints were stiff. She could hear the man's scream in her head again, a memory. A ghost.

She took a shaky breath and looked at Pyran. Voice thick, she said, "I'm glad you're all right."

"I'm glad you're all right," he replied.

"Thank the Mother." Cal knelt next to his sister. "Anna, what the fuck was that?"

"I think I took that man's life energy and...gave it to Pyran."

Cal blinked down at her.

"So you can just save our lives now?" Clara wondered.

Cal swatted her shoulder.

"Maybe?" Anna sighed. "But let's avoid dying. I never want to do that again."

"Right, of course," Clara agreed.

"Ah." The captain stood over the twins, eyebrows raised. "Our miracle has returned. How do you feel?"

"Like I've been struck by lightning."

"You look it," he grinned. "Why don't we move you into a tent? They've fared all right. Cal, you and Clara see if there's anything you can do here."

Pyran shifted, and Anna watched him wince. "Maybe some healing here," he told the twins.

"On it," Cal nodded, and then looked Anna over. "Can you stand?"

"I've got her." Will answered before she could. He tucked his arms under her knees and shoulders and picked her up. Pyran let him, leaning on Cal and Clara to stand. Anna wrapped her arms around Will's neck.

Even in her worn-out state, she felt heat rise to her neck and she turned her head away. "You smell like a campfire."

"Your friend's a real hothead," he joked, then said in a lower voice, "I told you to hide."

"You should know by now that's a command I don't follow."

When she glanced up, a small grin flickered at the corner of his mouth.

The twins healed Pyran. Apparently, her spell had brought him back from the edge, but it hadn't *healed* him.

Will sat with them when the twins left to tend to the wounds of the rest of the team. Pyran scolded Anna halfheartedly for doing something so dangerous, and then he thanked her.

She had a difficult time focusing on what was happening. She felt as if someone had filled her with boiling oil or coals and she was left a sensitive, brittle husk. Her mind replayed the experience over and over, flashes of pain and visions of light. She had felt almighty during that brief moment of…of what, she wasn't sure. It was like she had risen to a higher plane of existence, seeing and feeling things she hadn't known were there. She had played reaper, decided who lived and who died.

But at what cost?

Exhausted, she drifted to sleep with Pyran by her side.

57

A SCREAM HAUNTED ANNA'S DREAMS. SHE WOKE IN A COLD SWEAT, PYRAN snoring softly next to her, and sunlight peeking through the gap at the entrance of the tent. She stretched, and then groaned at the soreness in her limbs. Her bloodied sleeve was dry and crusty, and the air smelled like old blood. She crawled out of the tent.

A handful of people were sitting at the campfire, Vassians and Tellans. She could smell breakfast. She turned and looked for the rest of them.

The grass was painted with blood. Someone had gone into town for a cart, and they'd piled the bodies onto it and wheeled it into the trees a little ways off. She could still smell them. She found two Vassians standing guard over the attackers that had lived—a handful of strangers, an irritated Cricket, an exhausted Luke, and—

Anna froze.

Crocker smiled across the camp at her, gold tooth glinting in the morning sun. There were dark circles under his eyes and his hands had been tied behind him, but he looked otherwise untouched.

Jaw clenched and eyes set into a glare, she walked toward him. Halfway there, Will joined her.

"Don't try to stop me," she told him.

"I wasn't going to. Should I?"

Fifteen feet away, Crocker called out to her. "Well, you look like shit. How's Ma?"

Before the Vassian man at his side could step in, Anna stomped up to him, and her fist stuck him in the nose.

He cried out and blood spilled over his mouth. "You bitch!" He tried to wipe the blood on his shoulder. Cricket laughed.

The Vassian next to him kicked his foot. "You *do not* talk to the champion that way."

Anna raised her fist again, but before it could make contact with Crocker's eye, Will grabbed her and pulled her back.

"Woah, woah, woah! He needs to breathe to stand trial, and if you break your hand, the twins can't heal it, remember?"

"That was for my mom, you absolute piece of shit," Anna spat, shoving against Will's arm.

Crocker laughed. "I sure got under your skin, you redheaded skank. Was it your hate for me that kept you alive this long?"

Anna sucked air into her nose and pushed harder against Will, who picked her up off the ground to get her to stop. The Vassian guards glanced at each other, and then one of them turned and kicked Crocker to the ground. Boot on his now-silent face, he said, "I told you not to speak to the champion like that. Now you don't speak at all." Satisfied with the frightened look on the thin man's face, he lifted his boot and stepped back.

"Go get some breakfast." Will set her down and turned her toward the campfire.

She started walking, but turned back when she heard a pained grunt. Will jogged to catch up to her, and Crocker lay curled on the ground, his knees bent over his stomach.

"Here." Will took the hand she was cradling against her chest. He looked at it, then poked it gently. "Make a fist."

She did. Her knuckles were sore, and she knew they'd bruise.

"Not broken," he told her, and released her hand. "Feel better?"

"No."

"Yeah," he sighed, "it usually doesn't. Let's eat, champion."

THEY MOVED SLOWER THAT DAY. THOSE THAT WERE HEALTHY TOOK TURNS guarding the people they had apprehended, and Will and Pyran took turns keeping Anna away from them. The Vasbrute pulled the cart. When Anna asked why they didn't just burn or bury the bodies, Captain Heiser told her that the Council would want to identify who they could.

When they made camp, the captain washed and shaved, and he encouraged the rest to clean up as well. He wanted to make a good impression addressing the Council when they returned the next day.

At dinner that night, Pyran asked Anna what she had meant when she'd told Crocker her punch had been for her mother. When she'd explained shortly that the man had beaten her mother, Pyran offered to break his nose again and knock his teeth in, but she told him not to.

"He's going to spend the rest of his life in chains," she'd said. "He'll hate every moment, and it'll be what he deserves."

He hugged her by the fire.

As she slept that night, the dying man's screams echoed as a woman called for help—the same woman she had seen in her dreams since dying.

THE NEXT DAY, PYRAN LOANED ANNA A SHIRT AND ROS LOANED HER A PAIR of pants. The shirt was too big and the pants a little short, but it was better than being covered in dried blood. She was officially out of clothes.

She walked with Will in the middle of the group that day. They made a game of seeing who Gemma would take a treat from, her or Will. The half-elf won most of the time, but the crow came to her outstretched hand more than a few times.

Spotting Kastarus in the distance was like seeing a friend of a friend out on the street. She knew that it was friendly and safe, but she didn't know it well enough to be enthusiastic about seeing it again. The crowd at the city gates was near-silent as they made their way through, staring at the Vassians they travelled with and the cart of dead bodies.

Captain Heiser and Prince Bartok met the guards flanking the doors, and the captain presented his Writ of Duty. The guards, terrified and wary, sent for the general, who recognized the captain and called for an escort to bring them through to the Council. They left the cart with the soldiers at the gate, handing off their prisoners to the general's men. The strange resulting parade drew fascination from the people passing by and those that stepped out of their shops and restaurants.

The return plucked a bittersweet cord inside of Anna. The last time she'd made this walk, she had been a different person—someone small and curious, but inconsequential. Now, it felt like she had shed that skin and was stepping out as something bigger, unable to turn back after crossing that threshold. Walking into the city now felt like a kind of announcement.

Even though most of the eyes were staring at the Vassians, she felt them on her, as if by seeing her, they could tell who she'd become. She reached into the corners of her mind for that now-familiar presence, but he was quiet.

The guards at the castle were expecting them. The gate was open when they arrived, and they traded escorts. They were joined by several rushing advisors as they traversed the long hall toward the Council chamber. This time, there was no waiting to be announced. The door opened for them, and they stepped inside.

The furniture was positioned the same as it had been, as were most of the governors. Lords Inwood and Finke were not present, and neither was Lady Cate. Instead, three advisors sat at each of their tables. Behind them, a crowd of counsellors rustled papers and spoke in hushed tones. The buzz went quiet as they entered.

Anna's eyes met Lord Woulfe's and he seemed surprised to see her. His shock was quickly replaced by a stony anger as he held her stare. So far, she had been irritated by his willful ignorance of her, but his sharpened gaze aimed at her felt worse, as if he was silently telling her that she had at last earned his attention and the ire that came with it. She went stiff as her arms bristled with goose bumps.

Lady Gratadia stood. Her eyes widened briefly at the Vassians walking into the room behind them, before a practiced calm took over her features. "Welcome to the Tellan Council, Prince Bartok, Captain Heiser, and your companies. Please forgive the rushed state of our meeting. Perhaps if we had received word of your arrival earlier, we could have been more accommodating. If you would please explain the suddenness of our assemblage, and why, prince, you and your envoys have ventured not only past the wall, but directly into the heart of our country."

Prince Bartok stepped forward and smiled. The expression would have looked graceful on someone else, but his sharp teeth gave it an intimidating air. "Myself and my people come to your Council today in collaboration with the agents you sent to investigate a group of Vassian soldiers, for members of this circle have deceived us both."

Hissed questions ran around the room before Lady Gratadia raised a hand to silence them, her face pulled into stern lines. "That is a strong accusation. Do you possess evidence of this treachery?"

"We do, lady," Captain Heiser stepped forward with a smooth bow. "Before we proceed, I would ask that we barricade any opportune exits from this traitor to our nation."

Her eyebrows rose.

"If the Council finds our information to be incorrect, all may leave freely at the conclusion of this meeting, and I will offer myself for interrogation," the captain offered.

The governor looked at him thoughtfully, her jaw working as she took in his words. She waved a hand and said, "Very well. Guards at the doors, please. Ms. Brooks, a barricade against any magical means of exit, if you don't mind."

"Y-yes, Lady." Irene stood suddenly. Her hands drew circular patterns in front of her as she spoke quietly.

"This is ridiculous," Woulfe complained. "You bring strangers into the very gut of this country's institutions, and then lock them in with its leaders."

"Lord Inwood," a man at the Eysa governor's table spoke up in a shaking timbre, "would like to voice concern about the safety of such measures. To be locked in with..." he cleared his throat as he glanced at the Vassians in front of him, "*foreigners* of such unknown motives and great physical strength is treacherous in itself."

"You are forgetting," Lady Dato cut in, "the great power we hold in this room, governors, and the security protocols in place." She looked at Prince Bartok and said, "You'll find any plans for treachery thoroughly quashed, prince. Be cautious with how you proceed."

The prince's smile sharpened with irritation, shifting what could have been an attempt at friendliness into a silent snarl, and he replied, "Duly noted, but it is not for me to proceed. We are only present to support your Captain Heiser in his explanation of his case."

"Complete," Irene said, and the room suddenly felt smaller, even though nothing had moved. There was a deadened quality to the air, like they were packed into a cotton-lined box.

"Please," Lady Gratadia motioned toward Captain Heiser, "unravel this mystery you have tangled for us."

He cleared his throat and nodded. Then he clasped his hands behind his back and paced as he told the story.

He began with the missing supplies in Dore and moved on to the suicide at the orchard and the violence that had preceded it, and then his team's collision with Stoiko's pack. He asked Ben to come forward and describe how he had identified the wrath curse and then destroyed it. One of Lord Inwood's mages came forward and inspected Stoiko, confirming traces of the blood-cursed spirit within him before almost running away from the hulking figure in fear. The captain then had the prince describe his brother's death and Stoiko's part in finding the prince's body.

"Stoiko's pack brought us to the Vassian Crown so that they might decide how to proceed, but not all of us. Three were left behind. Anna, please come forward."

With her fingernails digging into her palms, Anna stepped up to stand next to the captain. She met Irene's eyes. The mage was watching the exchange curiously, and looked surprised to see Anna brought forward.

"Thank you." The captain put his hand on her left shoulder and turned back to the Council. "Anna, Callum, and Will followed us, found us, and attempted to bring us home. They were caught, and Anna was given a chance to find the truth. How were Stoiko and his pack cursed? Why were they cursed? Who killed the prince?

"What I am about to tell you may seem impossible, but we can verify all of it. Anna Hale *died* during our altercation with the Vassians," he told them, his voice calm and clear. His eyes travelled to each representative.

"She is standing in front of us, alive," Lord Moineau said, gesturing at her.

"It seems we waste our time on the theatric delusions of...an old veteran and the foreigners he has roped into his game." Lord Inwood's speaker winced as he repeated his governor's words, then cleared his throat. "What evidence could you possibly provide?"

Anna swallowed, drilled her eyes into the table in front of her, and then pulled at her collar and the bandages underneath, revealing the top of her scar. "I was cut through from shoulder to hip. Our healer could not heal me. I met Morterra, and he brought me back."

Several people gasped, including Irene. When Anna looked up, her gaze met Lady Gratadia's, whose eyes were narrowed at her as if they could break her down into smaller bits, something easier to understand. Anna watched the governor's fingers drumming on the table.

"A mage, please," Ben called out. "I myself am able to tell that her powers do not come from the weave."

"I would volunteer." A woman sitting at Lord Finke's table stood and turned to Lady Gratadia. She was dressed in dark violet, and her long, dark hair fell to her elbows, shining and straight. Her face was thin, with high cheekbones and arching eyebrows.

One of Gratadia's eyebrows lifted as she turned to the woman. "You may, Ms. Basilia."

The woman nodded respectfully and walked around the tables to stand in front of Anna, gray eyes searching her face. There was an air of extreme calm around the woman, and the room held its collective breath as she lifted her pale, slender fingers toward Anna. The ring on Anna's left middle finger buzzed as the woman's cold thumbs pressed gently against her temples.

She shivered as static washed through her, Ms. Basilia's gray eyes boring into hers. They widened and the mage released her, turning toward Lady Gratadia. "It is as they say. I do not feel the echo of the weave within her, yet I sense a fountain of power."

"And yet," Lord Moineau said, "what does this young woman's power have to do with the Vasbrute?"

The mage walked back around the tables as Anna spoke up again. "I was able to speak with Prince Branik, and he told me who killed him."

After another burbling of shock and disbelief, Prince Bartok said, "I can vouch for her honesty. I was there. I heard my brother's voice."

"Preposterous!" Lord Woulfe bellowed. "They are in league against us. Surely, they stand to gain from this committee's mistrust in itself."

"And yet, they have not named the accused." Lady Gratadia's eyes narrowed at him, and the room quieted. "Please continue, Ms. Hale."

Anna's fingers pressed harder into her palms, and she looked at Lord Woulfe. The man was sweating and shifting in his seat. *We've got him. He's cornered.*

Like a hungry wolf to a lost lamb, justice finds us all.

With a confidence fueled by the god of order in her head and her own anger toward her governor, she said, "Prince Branik described his killers to me. There was a shade woman, who trapped him with blood magic and cursed his body, and three men I recognized as under *Lord Woulfe's* employ." She tried to keep from snarling the name. "These same men violently came after my family as his debt collectors. But you don't have to believe me."

She turned to Lady Gratadia. "They attacked us on our journey here, alongside a small army—their one last chance to stop the truth. They weren't expecting our Vassian friends, though." She glanced at Prince Bartok. "Rather than killing us to pin it on the Vassians, as they intended, most of them were killed when we defended ourselves. We captured the men that survived."

She turned back to Woulfe, whose face was red and shaking. "Leonard Crocker, Cricket, and Luke, along with a handful of the rest that *you* sent."

"Absurd!" Woulfe shouted as all eyes turned to him. He looked as if his eyes might pop out of his head. "Complete lies! They attempt to frame me. I move to take these traitors to court for slander and treason, I motion for a vote of—"

"Governor Woulfe, you speak out of turn!" Lady Gratadia said, with a pound of her first against the table.

"You cannot believe these—" he tried again.

"Ms. Brooks, some assistance?" She turned and found her mage advisor behind her.

Blinking, Irene responded, "Certainly." She raised her right hand, fisted her fingers, and then dragged her fist across the air in front of her, facing Lord Woulfe.

The governor's mouth opened and closed, but no sound escaped. As he floundered silently, Lady Gratadia turned to a guard near the captain. "Can you verify that they have brought these prisoners?"

"Yes, lady," the guard nodded stiffly. "We have them in custody."

The governor of Kastarus and chief of the Council sighed, frowning down at the table in front of her. When her head lifted, she had set her expression into stern lines again. "With the information provided, I move to sanction an official investigation of Governor Woulfe and all of his dealings. In the meantime, he shall be detained in custody of this committee until a trial is held and his role in these matters established."

A wave of something like relief washed over Anna, giving her goose bumps.

Woulfe stood, knocking his chair back. It made no noise as it hit the ground. He made several angry gestures at the captain and Anna as he argued, even though no one could hear him.

"All those in favor of the motion, please indicate." Lady Gratadia lifted her hand.

Lady Dato lifted her hand, followed by Lord Moineau and the man sitting in for Lady Cate. Finke's proxy raised their hand, followed by Inwood's.

"The motion succeeds unanimously, with the exception of its subject. Guards."

Two large knights stepped to either side of Woulfe, their armor going silent when they came within ten feet of him. The governor huffed and puffed as they each took hold of an arm.

"Will there be any other motions before we conclude this inauspicious meeting?" Lady Gratadia glanced at her fellow governors.

"I move to negotiate, at a later date, the reparations from the Vassian emissary and Governor Woulfe's coffers to the family and workers of the orchard where the first attack took place," Lord Moineau said.

"We would be happy to oblige." Prince Bartok bowed his head.

"All in favor of the motion, please indicate," Lady Gratadia said, and lifted her hand.

The governors all raised their hands.

"The motion succeeds. If there is nothing else..." Gratadia paused, but the others were quiet. "Very well. That concludes our business." To her advisors, she said, "Please prepare rooms for our Vassian guests."

She turned back around to say, "Prince, captain...Ms. Hale and company, please be prepared for a messenger to inform you of the date of trial so that you may be present for testimony. Until then, you must only discuss these matters between yourselves or our advisors."

She moved to step away from the table, then stepped back in again. "We appreciate what you have done for Telluth, and what you have been through. When the trial is over, we will discuss adequate compensation. Thank you. You are dismissed."

58

LADY GRATADIA HAD MEANT IT WHEN SHE'D SAID THEY WEREN'T TO DIScuss anything with anyone else. Anna was assigned a guard and told she shouldn't leave the Barracks unless it was vital. They also read through the letter she sent to her mother to tell her she was alive and well, but not coming home yet.

They were all being watched closely. Besides Anna's own guard, there were two positioned in their hallway, one at each end. They followed when they went to meals and waited by the doorway of the cafeteria.

Anna was again faced with having no clothes. After she wrote to her mother, she wrote to Irene Brooks and explained the situation. The next day, the mage showed up at the Barracks with several trunks carried by city guards who had been told she was on official Council business. One trunk contained an extravagant packed lunch for everyone stuck in the Barracks, and the others were full of clothes for Anna. While the others had sandwiches and tea in the cafeteria, Irene turned Anna's room into a dressing room, and they snacked as they went through the trunks together.

"I told you I didn't need much, didn't I?" Anna asked as she stared at the clothing overflowing around her room.

"Oh, of course you did, but now is not the time to be humble! Here, anything you like is yours to keep."

Anna laughed. "I don't think we'd fit everything I like into one closet."

"Atta girl!" Irene laughed. "Dream big! Now, you try something on and tell me all about being a god's champion."

"There's not much to tell. I don't understand what I'm capable of. I've only used the power twice, and both times he was in my head, telling me what to do as I was doing it."

"In your head?" Irene's eyes widened, and she laughed nervously. "The god of death?"

Anna sighed. "Sometimes."

"You can talk to dead people. What else can you do?"

"I think I stopped someone from dying, but I had to take a life to do it." She shivered.

"Interesting. So even the gods have rules—balance and all that."

"I guess." Anna stepped out in a dusty blue two-piece. The skirt was full, and she liked the way it swished as she moved. The top was a thickly strapped tank top that had a short V neckline, which covered most of her scar. She would hold onto it, but she needed more practical clothing. "Did you bring anything better for moving in?"

"Ah." The mage stood and pulled out a folded stack of clothes. "This is the style I wear when I'm exercising."

They were tighter than what Anna was used to, though that could be said about most outfits compared to her father's modified things. The pants were stretchy and fit tightly at her waist and ankles, similar to Ros' pants, but with less fabric. The shirts were sleeveless, with straps that crisscrossed between her shoulder blades, rose up over her shoulders, and pulled back together across her cleavage. It was a supportive style. Her scar peeked out from either side of the strap.

"That looks great on you." Irene joined her at the mirror. She hummed thoughtfully and then said, "I've hidden scars before. If you like, I could hide yours."

She thought about it. Now that she was standing in front of a large folding mirror Irene had brought and really seeing it, the scar was jarring. The wide, silvery slash across her front clashed against the warm tones of her skin and the light freckles across her shoulders. But the thought of someone else changing her appearance so greatly, controlling the way she looked, didn't sit right with her, either. She thought back to what Prince Bartok had said about their scars in the woods. *Besides, I'm different now. Maybe I should look it.*

"No. I mean, thank you, but I think it should stay. It's a reminder."

"A reminder that you died?"

"No. That I came back."

She looked at herself in the mirror, her left hand gently running over the edge of the scar. It was strange, new. So was she.

THEY SPENT THE FIRST WEEK RESTING. THE TWINS TAUGHT ANNA HOW TO take care of her scar, which mostly involved massaging it with perfumed lotion. Eventually, the others grew bored and resumed training. Pyran insisted she work on conditioning if she was up for it, and everyone else agreed, saying they wouldn't want something to happen to her. When Anna suggested that the reason Morterra had chosen her was because she was a lost cause, they would have none of it.

Soon, she was spending the long days strength training with Pyran and Merry, taking breaks to learn more about natural healing remedies from the twins, or to have brief, frustrating lessons about magic with Ben, and then ending by balance training with Ros and Will. Some days, a familiar crow found the courtyard and watched them.

The half-elf acted cool, collected, normal. Anna thought of their kiss whenever he adjusted her posture or accidentally brushed against her. She wanted to talk about it, but they never had a moment alone, and she didn't know what to say, anyway. She was sure that everyone had caught her blushes.

Some nights after dinner, Ben would sit with her, magically reading her vitals or sensing her aura and taking notes. A few days after they returned, he had walked into her room while she was sitting with Pyran, his arms loaded with all the books he'd brought with him from Eysa. When she told the mage that she heard the god of death in her head, he had fainted.

"You can talk to him all the time?" Pyran had asked while fanning Ben. They'd picked him up and laid him on her bed.

"Not all the time. I haven't heard him since we met with the Council, but he said something about *never being far away,* whatever that means."

"Could you ask him questions for me?" Ben asked, blinking his eyes open.

"I can try, but like I said, I haven't heard him since."

"How does he funnel power to you? Is it some kind of conjuration magic?" Ben began a long list of questions.

Each time Anna asked into her mind, she received no answer. They eventually gave up, but by the end of breakfast the next day, everyone knew that she occasionally had her patron in her head.

IT HAD BEEN ALMOST TWO WEEKS, AND ANNA HAD RECEIVED NOTHING from her mother. She worried that the post had lost her letter, that they were holding her letters and not telling her—or worse, that something had happened to her mom. She wrote a second letter, similar to the first, and she sent it out.

THERE HAD BEEN NOTHING TO SAVE, BUT ANNA STILL MISSED HER OLD CLOTHES.

Her nightmares grew worse. Now, she had started *becoming* the woman calling for help, walking the dark alleys of Kastarus in a frantic search for something. Then she was surrounded by death, and the scream—there was always that awful scream. She could feel her hand on his body as she stole the life he had left, his punctured lungs struggling for air.

One night, she woke to someone shaking her. Her eyes opened and found the guard in the hallway holding her shoulders, telling her she couldn't leave in the middle of the night.

"What happened?" she asked him, glancing down the dark hallway. The glow of the mage lights was low. She could still hear that scream in the back of her head.

"You kept saying you needed to leave," he told her.

She turned her gaze on him and focused on his face. He had a square jaw and a dark moustache. Judging by the wrinkles across his forehead and around his eyes, and by his graying hair, he was around her mother's age.

"It's like you weren't hearing me," he added.

The door across the hall opened, and Will stuck his head out. He looked at the guard, then the guard's hands on Anna, and quirked an eyebrow. "What's going on here?"

The man pulled his hands back and lifted them in the air, palms out. "She was sleepwalking! I stopped her before she tried to walk into the city."

Will looked at Anna.

She shrugged. "It's the truth."

His dark eyebrows pushed together, and he stepped into his doorway. "That's new."

"It's these dreams I've been— Never mind. Let's just go back to sleep." She rubbed her tired eyes and turned toward her room.

"Hold on." Will glanced at the guard, and then gently pushed Anna into her room and closed the door behind them. "What dreams?"

She felt that if she told him, if she admitted to them, it would make them more real. Instead, she said, "They're just nightmares. I didn't mean to wake anybody up."

Will sighed, and she knew he could tell there was more to it. His eyes narrowed as he noticed her top, and she felt heat rise to her cheeks.

"What?" She crossed her arms over the shirt Pyran hadn't asked for her to return yet.

"Here." He started to pull off the baggy cotton tunic he was wearing over his loose pants.

"What?" Anna blushed harder. "What are you doing?"

He held the shirt out to her, chest and abdomen bare in the dim moonlight coming through the little window. "I know it's not your dad's, but it might be more comfortable. For sleeping."

"Oh." Anna blinked at the shirt, and then took it. "Thanks."

He held onto it as she tried to pull it away. "If you want to talk about your nightmares, I'm just across the hall," he said, and then let go.

She nodded. Something clutched at her heart and her gaze fell to his lips. Her mind jumped back to their kiss in the woods. She quickly averted her eyes to the shirt in her hands. *Mother, I need to calm down.*

She noticed the small smirk across his lips as he left the room.

THE TRIAL STARTED AT THE END OF THE SECOND WEEK. THE COURTROOM and offices were in a building on the castle grounds near the city guards' offices.

Anna spent three days in the courtroom. The room was laid out similarly to the tribunal in Vassa. Half the room was seating for an audience, and the other half was where the trial took place. This room was full of old woodwork, from the paneling on the walls to the furniture itself. Two ornate desks stood facing a raised platform where a judge presided, dressed in black robes. The paneling in front of them was carved with trailing ribbon and paxmortium flowers, a nod to the god of order. A chair next to the judge faced a row of tables in front of the crowd.

That's where Anna sat to give testimony on the second day, after swearing to Morterra to speak the truth. There had been a chuckle in her head, and she had almost laughed along. She talked through her story again, from the beginning. The counsellor representing Telluth and the Council asked her detailed questions about her death and following resurrection. Will and Cal were called forward to verify her death. Both were uncomfortable talking about the incident. Cal's voice broke as he recounted his multiple failed attempts at healing her. Will avoided meeting her eyes as he recounted his side of the story. Woulfe's counsellor attempted their own line of questioning, stumbling through questions about the minute details, attempting to catch them in a lie, but failing.

Finally, Anna was asked to demonstrate her power. Two mages, one a senior administrator from Luminport and the other a tenured professor from Eysa, read her energy. Similar to when Ben and the mage woman from Altumburg had done it, they each placed a hand near her temples. A buzzing passed through her.

She had felt Morterra with her since she stepped into the room. Still, she asked, *Are you there?*

Always.

The mage from Luminport gasped and she looked up at him. He was staring at her, and she could see two glowing green lights in the reflection of his startled gaze.

My eyes are glowing.

I thought I'd put on a show.

There was a row of seating at the back of the room reserved for press. There were a few papers in Kastarus, and each had brought a journalist and sketch artist. All of Telluth would meet her on paper and learn of Governor Woulfe's fate by the end of the month. She wondered how they'd capture her glowing eyes in ink. Once the courtroom was convinced of her abilities, Prince Bartock testified, validating what his dead brother had said. The sketch artists had worked furiously that day to get his likeness just right.

On the third day Crocker, Cricket, and Luke were made to testify. Cricket and Luke described how they were coerced into work as debt collectors, and Anna felt an echo in their stories—a financial mistake too big to correct on their own. For Luke, it had been his father. The man had become so addicted to solim that he'd taken out a loan just to get his hands on more. Cricket's home had burned down. Though he did not explicitly say it, Anna wondered if it had been his own powers that had started the fire. His family had done the only thing they could—give the child away to work until their debt was paid.

Still, Anna wasn't completely endeared to them. They'd killed people—at least one Vassian prince and who knew who else, and Cricket and Crocker had seemed to enjoy the violence.

Next was Crocker's turn. When he sat next to the judge, he found Anna in the crowd and winked. Oil dripped from his words as he explained how he had been under duress as well when acting for Governor Woulfe.

"If I didn't do as I was told and kept my mouth shut, they would kill me." He shook as he spoke, his generally cocky attitude replaced by an outward display of fear and shame. It made her stomach turn.

They had all confessed to the killing, and the partnership with the shade, but all argued that they were forced to act, that it was kill or be killed themselves. Before the governor took the stand, the Council brought out their lead investigator to talk through all the evidence they'd found in his home and offices, and there had been plenty. Correspondence between him and Crocker, vague notes from some third party—presumably the necromancer—and large investments in Hillcrest's steel foundries and factories. By the time Woulfe was called forward, there was no use refuting the evidence. He fumbled through his testimony, unable to gain any ground.

"That's not mine!" he argued of the correspondence between him and the unknown third party. "I've never seen it before in my life. Someone planted it!" His face was red with anger.

It didn't matter. It was Woulfe himself who had ordered Crocker, Luke, and Cricket to kill the Vassian prince, no matter what was argued about the correspondence. The result was a guilty plea. It appeased Anna to see Lord Woulfe brought low, sputtering on the stand and then begging for mercy as he admitted to the crime, but it wasn't as satisfying as she had hoped. Sentencing would take place at a later date.

As they were leaving, Captain Heiser and his troupe were called to the castle for a private meeting with Lady Gratadia. They met her in her office, a grand wood-paneled room above the Council chamber with its own tall windows looking out over the Solanis Ocean. She was sitting at her desk as they entered, the bell sleeves of her black silk shirt dancing as she stacked papers and slid them into a drawer.

"Welcome," she greeted as the messenger left them. "Please come in. I'd offer you all a seat, but I don't have enough chairs here, I'm afraid." She stood herself.

There were three navy velvet chairs in front of her desk. Clara sat in one, Ben sat in another, and everyone else gathered around them.

Gratadia grinned. "Now that the trial is over, I'm able to share some good news. The first bit is that we're pulling back our watch over you. You're free to go where you will, without escort."

"Thank the mother," Clara sighed.

"The second is a…job proposal. You have all proven to be people the Council can trust. Your integrity and your abilities make you great candidates as a permanent strike force for the Council. We're extending an offer of employment indefinitely. We would provide residences here in Kastarus for you and your families. Any previous work contracts would be paid out, along with the payment promised for this mission, though you will receive that even if you decline."

Her eyes met Anna's, "This includes debts," she said, and then turned to Will.

The half-elf was leaning back against the wall, his arms crossed. His lips were pressed together as he took in her words.

"This is wonderful!" Clara cheered. "Right, Cal?"

"I guess it would be nice," he said, glancing around at the others.

"Lord Moineau has agreed to this?" Ros asked.

Lady Gratadia nodded. "I believe his thoughts were that if there is going to be such a squadron, he'd prefer you on it."

Ros nodded.

"I'm in!" Merry smiled.

"You don't have to answer now," the lady smiled at the strong-woman. "Take two weeks. Be with your families, and then let me know. Also." She shifted and grabbed something from another drawer. She held out nine crisp white envelopes, each of their names written in dark ink across their fronts. "We're holding a ball in your honor two days from now. Your families have been invited. I'd personally like the chance to thank you all. I've never liked Governor Woulfe, but I'd always seen him as too dim to be dangerous."

The captain took the envelopes and distributed them. "It is our highest honor to serve our country. I hope that you would include the investigation of the shade and the necromancer in our new duties."

"Yes, I see that as the next logical course of action," she agreed.

59

After their meeting with Lady Gratadia, the group made plans to meet for dinner in town the next night to talk about the offer. The captain split off to return to his apartment, and the rest walked back to the Barracks.

Clara and Merry chatted as they made their way. Just as they reached the building, Clara turned to Anna to say, "You've got to stay! They'll clear your debt!"

"That's not for you to decide!" Cal scolded. "I'm sure she's thinking very hard about it."

Anna smiled halfheartedly. "I'm not sure what I want to do yet. My mom... she's never been far from home." She glanced at Will, who had stopped to lean against the stone wall and stare down at the cobblestones.

Clara followed her gaze and hummed thoughtfully. She leaned in to whisper, "You should talk to him." Then she turned to her brother and pulled him inside, saying, "Come on. Let's see what we have to wear for the ball. Maybe we could all color-coordinate?"

"That would be fun." Merry followed.

"I don't think so," Ben said, trailing behind.

Ros snickered into their hand as they came after.

Pyran paused. He turned to Anna. "I'm going home after the ball to talk with my family, but I think I'd like to take the offer."

Anna put her hand on his shoulder. "You deserve it, Pyran."

"Thanks." He glanced at Will and said quietly, "I get it, he's attractive, but—"

She swatted at his arm as heat rushed up her neck. "Go on! I'll find you later."

Pyran smirked, and then disappeared into the building.

Anna huffed and turned to face Will, who was watching her. "What was that about?"

"Pyran was trying to be funny," she said, and then walked over to him. "What are you thinking?"

His eyebrows furrowed. "That I'm tired of being under someone's thumb."

She sighed. "You don't want to take the offer?"

He tugged at the glove on his right hand. "I'd be stupid not to."

"So you're taking it?"

"Are you?" His golden eyes lifted to meet hers.

"I...don't know."

He nodded, and then asked, "Is he in there?" His chin jerked toward her.

She shrugged. "I haven't heard him since yesterday."

A smirk tugged at the corner of his mouth. "Can I take you somewhere?"

Anna quirked an eyebrow. "Where?"

"Come on." He pushed off the wall and started walking. "You got somewhere to be?"

"Uh." She glanced back at the Barracks, and then hurried to catch up.

He smiled when she reached his side. "You're a very curious person."

"I thought you figured that out when I told you I like to spend my time exploring dusty basements in the woods."

He grunted a laugh. "That's true."

"Where are we going?"

"To my home."

He led her north, through the second wall, and into the noise and hustle of the outer district. It differed from the neighborhood around Left Leg. Instead of bustling shops, restaurants, and theaters, the apartments here were tightly packed, and corner grocers tucked into gaps between buildings. People stared as they passed by, a couple nodding at Will in greeting.

He took off his gloves and tucked them away, saying, "Stay close."

A man on a street corner in pale Creed robes shouted at passersby about the love of the Mother, and her hatred of disbelief and sin. He asked them as they walked by, "Have you taken time today to seek Her out? Talk with her Children?"

"Not today," Anna told him. "Not yet, anyway. Morterra can be surprisingly chatty when he wants to be."

The man stared, mouth agape, as Will pulled her along.

Will led her around a bend and down an alley, where he pushed past a solim dealer and their buyer, and then brought her out onto a sunny, quiet street. A horn sounded, and Anna turned to see smokestacks rising over the houses in the distance.

She heard children's laughter. Will took her hand and pulled her toward a wide, two-story building with a little yard encircled by a short, rusting, wrought-iron fence. Children were running, playing tag, in simple cotton shirts and pants. The little gate let out a *screech* as Will opened it, and they all stopped to look.

"Willy!" a boy cheered, and then they were all running up to him. He let go of Anna's hand to catch a little girl that jumped at him.

"Willy?" Anna laughed. She saw his ears go red where they peeked out of his hair.

"Who's that?" the little girl in his arms asked, staring with wide hazel eyes at her.

"This is my friend Anna," Will told her. "Anna, this is Jane, Billy, Jasper, Carol, and Robert."

"Is Annie your girlfriend?" the same boy that had greeted Will asked. Anna thought this was Jasper. He was taller than the rest, with brown skin, dark, curly hair, and gray eyes.

Color crept onto Will's cheeks. "Anna is a friend. Now, come on and show me where Mr. Slatton is."

Jasper eyed Anna, then started toward the large front door. "He's helping with dinner now."

Carol took Anna's hand with a smile and pulled her along with little, pink fingers. "I'll show you! The kitchen is this way, miss." She had a missing tooth that whistled, and her brown hair had been pulled into two braids.

They stepped inside to a dark interior. As her eyes adjusted, Anna saw a long chalkboard at the end of the room and a handful of long tables spread in two lines. Older children sat at the tables, talking amongst themselves.

"Willy's here for a visit!" Jasper announced as they entered.

All eyes looked toward them, and a boy who looked about twelve turned to Anna and asked, "Who's that?"

"She's his girlfriend, Annie," Jasper declared, as if it were obvious.

The kids erupted into questions, many of them hurrying over.

Will stepped in front of her, saying, "Don't be rude. *Anna* is not my girlfriend, she's my guest, and I'd like you to all be polite."

"Sorry, miss," a couple of children chanted.

"Now," Will sighed, "Mr. Slatton?"

"Come on." Jasper waved them forward.

Anna was trailed by a group of children who were very curious about her outfit. She was wearing the dusty blue two-piece, and they poked at the hem of her skirt as they moved toward a doorway to the right. The kitchen was past a wide set of stairs. A robust woman in a simple gray dress and apron stood at a butcher-block table, chopping vegetables. An old man stood beside her, picking up the vegetables she chopped to put into an oversized pot.

"Willy's here with—"

Will cut Jasper off, "A friend."

The man and woman looked up, and a smile broke across the old man's face when he saw Will. "Willard."

Will sighed and glanced at Anna. "Mr. Slatton, this is Anna Hale."

"Oh, welcome!" His bushy white eyebrows shot up to his receding hairline. "Welcome to Northside Home! It's not often we get visitors. I'm George Slatton, and this is Nelly Caerby, our cook. Will you be staying for dinner?"

"Please, *please*," the little girl in Will's arms begged.

"Just for dinner," Will agreed.

While Nelly finished cooking, Mr. Slatton joined them in the main hall. Will put Jane down and discreetly handed him a small coin purse as they shook hands.

Mr. Slatton said, "What would we do without you?"

"Same as you've always done," Will replied. "Your best, and nothing less. Could I talk with you for a moment?"

"Of course," Mr. Slatton smiled. "We can go to my office. Will your friend be—"

"I'm sure the kids can keep her company, right?" Will asked the small crowd.

"Oh, yes!" Carol cheered.

"Will she tell us a story?" Jane asked.

"You'll have to ask her very nicely," Will told them, glancing at Anna with a smirk, and then he followed Mr. Slatton up the stairs.

Anna hadn't been around children since her school days, but when Jane took her hand and asked, "Please, would you tell a story, miss?" she couldn't say no.

She sat on a bench and asked them, "What kind of story would you like to hear?"

"Adventure!"

"Pirates!"

Anna smiled at the boys that shouted and started a story about a ship captain named Ivette Crawford, who ran into some pirates on the open ocean.

WHEN WILL AND MR. SLATTON CAME BACK DOWN THE STAIRS, THEY HELPED set out dinner. Nelly had made a stew with fresh, flaky rolls. It was good, but the stew was a little thin. Anna complimented her on the rolls, and her round cheeks flushed.

And then it was time to go. The children begged Will to spend the night, and she watched him regretfully decline and say his goodbyes, explaining that he needed to take Anna home.

"Thanks for coming to see us," Carol told her. "I liked your story."

She thanked Carol, thanked Mr. Slatton and Mrs. Caerby, and then said goodbye. Some of the kids followed them to the gate, waving.

Anna waved back, Will's hand in hers as he pulled her along.

"So that's where you go missing to," she said as she turned to face him, a smile on her face. The sun was setting over the rooftops, turning the sky pink.

"Mystery solved," he agreed.

"Do they keep you awake asking for stories, *Willy?*"

He stopped and turned toward her. "You breathe one word of any of this to anyone and you'll lose your tongue."

"These lips are sealed," she laughed. "What did you talk about with—"

"Ah, there's our crow." A woman stepped out of an alley in dark clothes, and Will stiffened. "And he's found a finch. Charming." She was pale, with thin lips and a sharp nose. She eyed Anna with an eyebrow raised. Her light brown hair was pulled into a short ponytail.

"Lacey," Will sighed and turned to look at her, releasing Anna's hand. "Long time, no see."

"Who's the chick?" she asked. "I saw you two *canoodling*." She wiggled the fingers of a black left hand.

"She's a friend. What do you want?" He shifted his weight to one side and crossed his arms in front of Anna.

"Touchy," Lacey said with a smirk. "Just checking in. We heard you made it back, heard about the trial. I already know who she is." She looked around Will at Anna. "The papers got your nose wrong." She turned back to Will. "Champion of chattin' up dead people. A little creepy, even for you."

Anna saw Will's jaw clench. "If you already know everything, why are you here?"

She put her black hand on her hip, bored. "Boss says hello. They're curious about this shade, say its bad for business. Thought they'd warn you in advance that they might drop by."

"I'm done with the Hand. They sold me out to the Council, remember?"

"Figured you'd say that. They said to remind you that as long as you've got that hand, you're theirs."

Will scoffed.

Lacey lifted her hands, palms out, and widened her brown eyes innocently. "I'm just the messenger!" Her expression shifted to a smirk as she turned back to the alley, waving the black hand over her shoulder. "Toodles!"

Will stared after her, unmoving.

"Are you okay?" Anna asked.

"Not here." Will took her hand again and started moving, his eyes scanning the streets and then the rooftops. After a few minutes, he ducked into an alley and stopped at an iron ladder. He swallowed and turned to face her.

"I hadn't seen them in weeks before we left. When we got back, I thought maybe they didn't know. But the trial..."

Anna frowned. "I'm sorry, Will."

"It's not your fault." He smiled ironically and shook his head. "They were waiting outside the orphanage for me. Mother, I should've known better. They must already know about the governor's offer. They'll want me to take it, give them another man on the inside."

"What if you tell them no? What happens?"

Will grimaced. "They hunt me down and cut off my hand, and maybe stick a knife in me while they're at it."

Her brows knit together as she looked up at him. She wanted to comfort him, but she didn't know how.

His ironic smile returned as he looked at her. "I'm sorry. I shouldn't have brought you."

Her eyes widened. "Don't say that! I loved meeting your—your family."

"Don't do that." He huffed a laugh.

"Do what?"

"Look at me with those green eyes and make me want to kiss you."

Her breath caught. She blinked at him, heat rising into her ears.

He laughed airily. "Not helping."

The heat grew, spreading across her chest. "I'm not— I'm just—"

Will sighed and wiped his black hand down his face. He took a step back, nodding toward the ladder. "Climb up. There was something else I wanted to show you."

Anna swallowed, still flushed. "All right." She started up the ladder, and he followed.

"Be careful at the top. It's a little loose."

The ladder shook as she climbed onto the roof. Most of it was sloped metal, but there was a foot-wide catwalk at the edge and a short railing. She stared at her feet as Will climbed up behind her, and then he held her shoulders as he guided her forward.

"Are you going to look up?" he asked.

She lifted her head and gasped. She was facing west, over the outer wall of the city. Past the farm fields was the forest they had spent time in together. A blanket of sunset covered all of it. "It's beautiful."

"I used to sit up here when I ran away." His hands fell from her shoulders. He took a deep breath and said, "I can't ask you to stay. I wanted to show you there are good things about this city. The whole thing went off course, though."

She turned and found him watching her, a frown on his face.

"Do you still want to kiss me?" she asked him.

His eyes widened, glowing with the sunset. "Anna, I—"

"Because I'd like to kiss you."

He inhaled softly, and then they were holding each other, his lips on hers. His arms wrapped around her waist, pulling her against him, as hers wrapped over his shoulders, her fingers in his long hair. He leaned over her, and then his hair fell around her. She sucked at his bottom lip and he groaned low in his chest, his fingers finding the skin under the hem of her shirt. When they pulled apart, they were both panting lightly.

"Mother's Children," Will breathed. She could feel his heart beating fast in his chest, pressed as it was against hers. A smile spread over his mouth. "You learned to kiss like that in Wallset?"

Anna scoffed, but she couldn't stop her own smile. "See if I kiss you again," she laughed.

His dark eyebrows rose, and a familiar smirk tugged at his lips. "Again?"

"Not after *that* terrible joke."

He groaned in fake pain and pulled back. "You wound me," he said, putting his left hand against his chest. "No wonder the most wet-blanket god chose you. You can't take a joke."

She rolled her eyes. "Maybe if you told better jokes."

"You can help me work on that, if you stay," he said, searching her face.

She sighed. "I... It depends on my mother. I can't leave her alone."

"But you *want* to stay?" he asked.

She bit her lip to hold back a nervous grin, and she nodded hesitantly.

He smiled. He pulled a strand of hair out of her face with his left hand, and then rested his palm against her cheek. "Can I kiss you again?"

She nodded, smiling as their lips met. His hand slid under her shirt, pressing her closer again. She held the back of his head with both hands, and her right thumb traced the edge of his ear. A sigh escaped her as one of his fingers drew small circles onto her back.

He pulled away, smiling at her and catching his breath.

"What?" She chuckled at his expression.

"We never finished our dance lesson."

"No, I guess we didn't."

He took one of her hands and pulled her toward the ladder. "One more stop."

He took her to a dance hall in the outer district. She'd never seen anything like it. It was similar to a tavern but the tables were pushed to the edges of the room and the space was full of dancers. Will knew the bartender, an older man that glanced at her and made a joke she couldn't hear before pouring them both a beer. They were dark and tasted almost creamy. Will called it a stout.

The band was livelier than the band at the ball. Every song was faster, punchier than anything she'd heard before, and the couples who danced spun and moved at a dizzying speed. She was reluctant to join them, but she couldn't say no to Will's outstretched hand and the honest smile across his face. He carried her across the dance floor, the skirt of her dress pulling as it caught up to her, just for them to change direction again.

She laughed like she hadn't laughed in a very long time.

All of the stars were in the sky when they returned to the Barracks. He held her in the dark hallway outside their rooms and kissed her on the forehead. "Goodnight, Anna."

"Goodnight, Will."

He let go and disappeared into his room. She took her aching feet to bed.

60

THE NEXT DAY, PYRAN KNOCKED ON HER DOOR, SHOUTING THROUGH IT TO say that she should get up if she wanted breakfast.

She sat up and rolled her sore ankles, and then stretched her legs. "Coming!" She threw off Will's shirt and put on one of the exercise outfits from Irene, then pulled on her old boots. Her hair fell in waves from the braid it had fallen out of. After smoothing the messy bits, she opened the door.

Everyone was in the hallway waiting for her, including a smirking Will. He leaned against his closed door, arms crossed smugly. "Good morning," he greeted, brown eyes looking at her knowingly.

She blushed.

"I *knew* something happened last night!" Clara exclaimed, looking between Will and Anna.

Pyran rolled his eyes. "Can we eat now?" He shoved Anna gently down the hallway.

She spent the day brushing elbows with Will, and when it was time for balance training, Ros rolled their eyes so many times at Will's hands-on adjustments and Anna's subsequent blushes that she thought they would walk off and leave the two of them alone.

As they headed back to their rooms to clean up for dinner, Clara asked her, "Are you going to stay? I mean, it's poor timing if you're not, but I can understand a kiss goodbye."

"Clara!" Anna scolded. "I'm going to try, but I need to talk with my mom."

"This city could use a good baker," she smiled.

"How would you know?" Anna laughed.

The half-dwarf shrugged. "*Any* city needs a good baker."

Anna laughed again.

That night, they all went out to the Left Leg. Clara and Callum looked as skeptical as Anna and Pyran had been their first time, wrinkling their noses at the smell around them, but they didn't say anything. The captain seemed excited. He smiled at a table full of people as they passed by, greeting the locals with a nod.

Pyran stuck close to Anna. She'd gotten a few looks on the walk there, and it was the same inside the busy restaurant. Will was quiet. He had argued that the Left Leg wasn't for everyone, but Merry had insisted.

"I didn't think this was your kind of thing, Captain," the half-elf said as he took a seat next to Anna at the end of the table.

Pyran sat on her other side, and then Merry next to him. The captain sat across from Will with Ros, then the twins, and finally Ben at the other end of the table.

"I like to think I can tell a good dive when I see one. I've traveled for long enough. It's a skill you pick up when you're always looking for somewhere new to eat or sleep."

"Tell us another story!" Merry urged. Anna was reminded of the children at the orphanage.

"Maybe after a glass," he told her.

"Welcome back to the Leg!" a waiter greeted Will. "Ah, but you're new," he smiled at the captain. "Who'd you bring in, Will?"

"This is *Captain* Heiser," Will gestured with a flourish. "Leader of our happy troupe."

"A *captain*," the waiter smiled. "And you look it, don't you? What'll it be, captain?"

"We'll all have the usual with a mug," Will answered.

"Making it easy for me," he turned to nod at Will, and his eyes caught on Anna. "Do I know you?" he asked. "You look familiar."

"I've been here before," she said, "twice."

"No, that's not it." He hummed thoughtfully, then turned to the waitress walking by with her hands full of mugs. "Hey, Lo, does she look familiar to you?"

The woman glanced at Anna, then stopped and stared. "She's from the paper, isn't it? You're much more colorful in person."

"That's right!" The waiter pointed at her. "You're that girl that can talk to dead people, right? They didn't quite get your chin right, either."

Anna's eyebrows rose and she glanced at Will, who shrugged. "What happens if I say yes?" she asked the man.

"I'll give you a round on the house," he said with a smile. "It's been a while since someone did something worth printing 'round here! I'll give you another round if you can tell me about the Vasbrute."

"Careful!" The waitress adjusted her hold on the mugs. "She's got Morterra whispering in her ear now."

The waiter waved a hand after his coworker dismissively. "Anyone that puts a greedy governor in chains is all right in my book. I'll put this in for you."

"I haven't seen the paper yet," Merry said.

"I wonder how close your picture is," Clara said to Anna. "It must be good if you're getting recognized."

"Yeah," Anna agreed, frowning at the table behind the twins. The men there were talking in low voices and glancing in her direction. They stopped a waiter, frowning as they spoke. The waiter glanced at her, shrugged, then gestured around at the full room. Her brows pushed together as the table stood with disapproving glares and left.

"Wow," Merry said, "They don't like *you* even more than they don't like Ben."

"Hey," the mage protested, then looked at Anna. "Don't worry about them."

"Right," Clara agreed. "Let's just enjoy dinner." Her smile faltered as a table nearby broke out into laughter because one man had fallen over while trying to empty his mug. Anna held in a laugh.

"Wait until you try the food before you cast judgement," Ros said.

"I promise it's worth it," Anna added.

"I agree," Pyran said, drumming his fingers on the table impatiently.

"You eat anything on a plate." Cal rolled his eyes.

"Ouch," Anna laughed, turning to catch Pyran's eye.

"Hilarious," he said, dripping sarcasm.

Their food came quickly, along with mugs full of ale. The waiter introduced himself as Jack and leaned against the table, asking questions about the trial that Anna and the captain answered as they ate. The twins were quiet, enjoying the food. After dinner, the waiter brought another round of drinks and told them they were on the house for answering his questions. They raised glasses to their safe return, and then again to their offer from the Council.

"But you have to tell us where you went last night!" Clara said to Anna and Will. "It must have been late when you got back."

Anna glanced at Will, who seemed to be waiting for her to answer.

"He took me dancing," she said, smiling.

"Really?" Clara asked with a contented sigh.

"Really?" Cal asked, skeptical.

"Shut up, Cal," Will rolled his eyes.

"What color are you wearing tomorrow?" Clara asked Anna.

She shrugged. "I don't know. I'm going to find something in Irene's closet."

"Don't you want to match Will?" the healer asked.

Anna felt heat in her cheeks.

"Black is a safe bet," Ros teased with a smirk.

"Ah," the captain smirked as he looked at Will. "You two are...?"

Anna looked back at Will, who shrugged nonchalantly and said, "We can match if she'd like to." He looked at her with pink in his cheeks himself, and a smirk masking the blush.

Anna turned back to Clara and said, "Sure, I think black would be fitting."

Pyran mocked a gag.

"Because you died?" Merry asked.

"It's still summer," Clara whined. "Don't you want to wear some color? We could find Will a matching pocket square or something."

Anna laughed and shook her head.

Clara sighed in defeat.

"Look what I found!" The waiter returned with a newspaper in his hand. He slapped it on the table, his hand over the drawing of Anna. "I heard you hadn't seen it yet!"

He picked up his hand and...it *was* her, but it was a little off. Her chin wasn't the right shape, and there was indeed something off about her nose.

"Oh!" Clara stared at the picture. "Are you going to frame it?"

Anna huffed a laugh. "No, I don't think so."

MERRY BROKE OUT INTO SONG ON THE WALK BACK TO THE BARRACKS. AS the twins joined her, Pyran put his arm around Anna's shoulders and pulled her to the back of the pack.

"I'm glad you're going to stay," he told her, "even if it's partly because of him."

"Don't you have a boyfriend?" Anna asked teasingly.

Pyran blushed and sputtered, "Th-that's not relevant right now."

She laughed and shook her head at him. "It's not guaranteed, me staying."

Pyran shrugged, and the motion pulled her closer. "Your mom will want to do what makes you happy."

"I want her to be happy, too."

"From what you've said of her, I think she'll be happy wherever you are," he told her.

Anna thought about that as they walked quietly behind the others. Will glanced back, caught her eye, and then turned back around.

"When you come back, after you see your family," Anna said, "you should bring Adrian for a visit. I'd like to meet him."

61

THE NEXT DAY BEGAN MUCH LIKE THE MORNING OF HER FIRST BALL. SHE ate breakfast with those that chose not to sleep in—Ros and Ben—and then walked to Irene's townhouse. The door opened after she knocked, but this time, there was a person opening it. It took her a moment to register who it was, and then she was convinced she was seeing some kind of illusion until arms were wrapped around her.

"Lynnie!" her mother shouted, hugging her tighter than ever before.

"Mo-Momma?" Anna's voice broke as she stood still, unable to comprehend what was happening. Her arms lifted hesitantly, and then she squeezed her mother back with all the strength she had.

"Oh!" Bren Hale laughed, then sniffled. "You're so much stronger!"

"Mom," Anna spoke into her mother's shoulder. "What are you doing here?"

"I asked her to come."

Anna looked up and found Irene in the entryway, hair in rollers and a smile on her face. "What do you mean?" she sniffled through the tears she was fighting back.

"I knew about the ball before you did," the mage explained, "and I knew there was no way your mother would make it without a little help. I hired a carriage for her and sent them with a letter from me, explaining the situation."

"I just arrived yesterday." Her mother pulled back to look at her. "I'm so proud of you, Lynnie." Tears filled her eyes again.

"I'm sorry," Irene said with a little wince. "I'm sure you wanted to be the first to tell her things, but I thought it was more important to get her here. I only said what I needed to."

"All Mother's Children." Anna rested her head on her mom's shoulder. "Don't apologize. I can't believe you're here."

"Me, either," Bren Hale laughed through her tears.

"Come in, come in." Irene pulled them inside. "You don't have to cry on the porch." The door shut behind them and she ran off to get something bubbly.

"What do you know?" Anna asked her mother.

"Just that you've returned from a very dangerous mission, and the Council is throwing a party for your whole team. I'm looking forward to meeting them."

"A fancy carriage pulled up and asked you to get in, and you said yes?"

"Her letter was very convincing," Bren argued with a grin. "And it lined up with what you had told me in your letters." A sigh left her lips, and then she giggled. "I felt a bit like a long-lost princess in a faetale."

They laughed together, and then Irene returned with three glasses full of pink, sparkling liquid. "I'm sure you want to hold each other for a very long time, but first, take these so that we can salute your reunion properly."

Mother and daughter each freed a hand to take a glass, but kept an arm each wrapped around the other.

"To you," the mage smiled, "and the love you share."

"And to you!" Bren put in, before they could drink. "You have no idea the peace of mind it's brought to know that our Lynnie wasn't alone here. Thank you for being so good to her."

"She makes it easy to be good to her," Irene winked at Anna.

And then they drank. Bren started asking Anna all her questions, and to answer them, Anna started from the beginning. She told her about the people she'd met in Hillcrest, particularly Pyran, and how they had both been leaving home for the first time. Then she described the whole group to her mother, saving Will for last.

"He's, uh, half-elf," she started, then cringed. "Well, he's more than that. He's always lived here in the city. We spent a lot of time together because the captain made us both scouts, and...and I taught him how to navigate the woods. He picked it up quickly—"

Bren stifled a chuckle, and Anna looked at her with a small frown.

"What?"

"Nothing." Her mother shook her head as the seamstress measured her, still trying not to laugh.

"No, tell me," Anna insisted.

Bren shared a knowing glance with Irene, and then sighed. "It's just that it's clear you like the young man."

Heat rose to Anna's ears, and she glanced at Irene, who shrugged and held up her hands. She turned back to her mom and said, "I was going to get to that later."

"Sure, honey." Bren shot her a grin, a laugh still in her eyes.

"*Anyway*, when we left, we took a ship down the coast to Osborough."

Bren's smile fell. "Oh, no. Were you all right?"

"I was fine," she said, puzzled, "once I got used to it. Why?"

"Your father," Bren said. "Before you were born, he took me on a dinner cruise on Long Lake for our anniversary one year. He couldn't keep anything down, and you're so like him, I just assumed."

"Oh."

Anna moved on to talk about the colorful houses in Dore and then paused. Her mother glanced at her expectantly.

"Mom, I, um, don't want you to get upset, because everything's fine now. I think."

"Is that supposed to be reassuring?" Bren laughed nervously.

"It's just that," Anna glanced at Irene and then down at her hands. "I, uh, got really hurt. I *died,* actually."

Bren gasped.

"But-it's-okay-because-Morterra-brought-me-back!" she added as quickly as her breath would let her.

The baker blinked at her daughter, trying to comprehend what she'd said. "What are you talking about, Lynnie?"

Anna looked up at her mother and winced. Her eyes watered, and her voice shook as she said, "I heard Dad, Mom. I died…and I heard him. He said it would be okay." Her voice broke, and she wiped aggressively at the tear racing down her cheek.

"Lynnie." Bren swatted the seamstress's hands away and rushed to wrap her arms around her daughter again. "Oh, Lynnie. I'm so sorry." She ran her hand over Anna's hair.

Anna sobbed once, then reeled herself in with a long sniffle. An ironic laugh bubbled up, and she said, "I'm sorry."

"No, honey." Her mom was crying, too. "If I hadn't cared so much about trying to do better, about that stupid fucking oven, it never would've happened."

Another laugh bubbled up at her mother's swearing, and she squeezed her mom back. "That's not all of it. I have a nasty scar, and I'm, uh, a champion of Morterra now, whatever that means."

"You're what?" Bren pulled back, teary eyes wide.

"Morterra said I had a choice. If I came back, I'd be his champion, or I wouldn't come back."

Her mother stared at her.

She sighed, and her tense shoulders fell. "That's how we made it back. I was able to talk to a dead Vassian prince—"

"Vassian?"

"—and figure out who killed him. Turns out it was the same fuckers—"

"Lynnie!" Bren scolded.

"—that came after us. You just said *fucking*, mom. I think I'm allowed to say *fuckers.*"

Bren was frowning at her, but let it go with a sigh. "Fair point."

"And now Governor Woulfe is in prison," Irene added, "the ringleader of the show and all-around greedy bastard. That's thanks to your daughter." She handed them each a handkerchief. "It's in the paper."

"You're in the paper?" Bren asked.

Anna nodded.

"I'll show you later," Irene said.

They gave her mother back to the seamstress, who brought out a deep green gown for her to put on. Her reflection in the mirror left her entirely tickled.

"Any thoughts on what you'd like to wear this time?" Irene asked Anna.

"What do you have in black?"

IRENE AND BREN WALKED TOWARD THE CASTLE ARM IN ARM, GOSSIPING like schoolgirls. The mage waved at the guards as they passed through the gate. They greeted her with a smile before their eyes found Anna, and then they openly stared. She frowned at them and continued on, fighting the urge to leave.

When she'd chosen her dress, Irene had asked if she was sure. It had been easier to be brave in the mage's closet, but here, in the castle courtyard, she felt exposed.

The material was shining black silk. It gathered at her waist before falling in smooth lines over her hips to the ground. She stared down at the sparkling black slippers that peeked out under the hem as she walked, avoiding the eyes around her that she felt burning into her bare right shoulder.

The dress was one-shouldered—her left. From there, it fell to her cleavage before wrapping around her side and dropping again to her lower back. The boning in the dress's front, beneath the gathered fabric, kept everything in place, and she felt secure—but her shining scar was laid bare from between her breasts to the top of her shoulder.

She'd insisted on wearing her teardrop necklace again, even though Irene had offered countless other options, and she had borrowed the same earrings as last time.

While her mother marveled at the landscaping, Anna shifted her eyes to her mother's back. She tapped her little white invitation between her fingers as they climbed the stairs. Two attendants dressed in black pulled open the doors to the ballroom, glancing at Anna's scar and then away.

Irene handed two envelopes to the man standing in the doorway.

"Irene Brooks, Mage-Counsellor to Lady Gratadia, and Bren Hale," the man announced into the room.

Irene glanced over her shoulder at Anna with a reassuring smile as they walked into the room.

"Invitation, please." The man held a hand toward Anna, his gaze trained on her face.

She gave him the envelope. He read it silently, nodded, and then called out, "Anna Hale, hero of Telluth and Champion of Morterra."

She froze at the titles, and all eyes turned to watch her. Her face burned before she took a deep breath and joined Irene and her mother in the room.

"Welcome." Lady Gratadia found them first, looping her arm with Anna's and steering her toward the tables covered in food. Through her smiling teeth, she said, "You looked a little like a frightened animal, but I doubt many people were looking past this gorgeous dress."

"I wasn't expecting the titles," Anna told her, glancing back at her companions as they followed behind. She turned to look at Gratadia, who stood a head shorter than her. The yellow-gold gown she wore reminded her of the style the Vassian women wore, though she was showing less skin.

"I thought I might swoop in and give the crowd time to get used to you," she went on. "At least, they shouldn't all swarm at once. A benefit of my position, I suppose."

"Lady," Veronica Sico stepped up to the governor's other side. "Captain Heiser and the rest of his team are hovering around a table nearer the balcony."

"Excellent. Thank you, Veronica."

The advisor bowed her head and turned to walk away.

"These events are like one very long, complicated dance," the governor told Anna as she waved and smiled at someone. "But if you do the dance right, you have the chance of leaving better for it."

"Irene told me something like that."

"She's smart," Lady Gratadia smiled at Anna. "Stick close to her and you'll learn a lot. Here we are."

Anna looked ahead to find most of her friends staring at her and the governor. When her eyes found Will's, his cheeks darkened and his throat bobbed.

"I thought I would deliver your last member to you," Gratadia said, then laughed a little. "It seems you're all as stunned by her as the rest of them." She patted Anna's arm. "Guard her well. My power only extends so far."

"Thank you, lady." Captain Heiser smiled graciously. "I'm looking forward to speaking later on." He bowed, and the baby blue satin trim on his deep navy jacket shone with the movement. This military jacket had silver buttons that reflected light like tiny mirrors as he straightened.

"Cut in if you find me cornered by Lord Inwood for too long," she said quietly, conspiratorially. She turned and acknowledged Irene and Bren, and then she left.

"I wasn't sure they could outdo your last ensemble," Clara glanced between Anna and Irene, "but I know *this* tops it." The half-dwarf woman was wearing a pale green gown with a plunging neckline. There was a layer of something sparkly over the base fabric. It made her look like dew glittering on new leaves.

"Thanks, Clara." Anna smiled and let out the breath stuck in her lungs. She turned to gesture with an open hand. "This is my mom, Bren Hale."

"Wonderful to meet you all." Bren smiled so widely that her nose wrinkled.

"Oh." Clara looked behind her at a tall, dark-skinned man and a short, dark-skinned woman. He looked to be fully human, and she seemed fully dwarven. "These are our parents, Tomas and Carina Phaon."

"A pleasure." The man grinned and bowed as the woman inclined her head.

"What do you do?" Carina asked.

"I'm a baker. And you?"

Carina smiled at her husband. "Tomas is mayor of Delphia."

Bren let out an impressed, "Oh."

"I'm Pyran Taggert." The swordsman stepped forward in a gray suit and introduced himself. "This is my family. My dad, Spencer, my mom, Grace, and my little brother, Rory." They looked just like the portrait he kept, if a little older.

"We're accountants," his father said, with a nervous glance at the Phaons.

"Ah," Bren smiled and laughed.

"I'm Ben, and this is my wife, Larrissa." Ben smiled, his arm around a pretty woman with brown hair and blue eyes. They matched in violet, Ben in mage's robes and her in a light gown.

"It's nice to meet you," Anna said. "Ben's said all kinds of nice things."

"You, too," Larrissa nodded.

"My father's here somewhere," Ben said, glancing around the room. "He's a professor at the university in Eysa."

"I'm Merry." Merry thumbed at herself as she smiled at Bren. "Merritt McGill." She was wearing a pink dress with floral appliques across the corset and thin straps that crossed over her muscular shoulders.

"Nice to meet you," Bren returned the smile.

"Ros Dixon," Ros introduced themself. They were wearing a shirt so pale blue it was almost white, and their tailored pants were an iridescent blue. "I'm from Lakoona."

"I'm Cal." Callum stepped up next to his sister. "I'm the one that's been holding your daughter together after she gets herself hurt." His tan suit contrasted well with his deep skin, and his vest matched his sister's dress.

"Well, I could've used you when she was growing up. Always tripping and falling out of trees, this one," Bren laughed.

"I could see that." Cal grinned at Anna, who rolled her eyes.

"And this is Will," Anna gestured toward the half-elf standing quietly in the middle of everyone. He was wearing the same suit as last time, and she was glad, because that was what she had planned for. Her black satin dress matched the satin trimming his suit perfectly. There was a silver chain hanging from a buttonhole of his jacket and disappearing into the pocket at his breast.

He smiled at her mother. "Will Grey. It's nice to meet you."

"Hm." Bren grinned and glanced conspiringly at her daughter. "You, too."

As Anna blushed, the captain spoke up. "Captain Nathaniel Heiser. Would you like a drink, Mrs. Hale, Ms. Brooks?"

Irene nodded.

"Yes, thank you."

Anna caught the light blush on her mother's cheeks and felt her own darkening again.

The captain left to fetch drinks, and Clara turned to Will. "You're awfully quiet. Suddenly respectful with our parents in the room?"

"Hm?" He turned to her with his eyebrows raised, as if he had missed her question. "Oh, sorry. I couldn't hear you over the glitter covering your dress." He grinned at her. Cal snickered.

Clara scoffed. "It's not glitter, it's— Ugh, whatever."

The half-elf's smile narrowed his eyes as he chuckled at her frustration. His gaze met Anna's briefly before he lifted his glass to his lips.

"Here you are." The captain returned and handed the glasses he held to Irene and Bren.

"I'm going to get something to eat before the dancing starts," Clara announced, and then turned to Anna's mother. "Would you like to come?"

"Oh, yes!" Bren smiled. "I'm curious what they've made."

As Clara took her mother's arm, she said, "Anna has told me nothing can rival your food, but we'll see how these compare."

"I'll come, too," Merry agreed.

"Hungry?" Cal turned and asked his parents, the Taggerts, and Ben and his wife.

They all followed toward the food.

Captain Heiser's head lifted as the announcer called a name, but Anna missed it. When she turned around toward the entrance, she saw a woman with a dark bob walking into the room. The captain excused himself and made his way toward her.

"Did he say *Crawford?*" Will asked.

Ros' pale eyebrows rose as they watched their captain. "You're correct. That is Captain Crawford."

"Do you think they'll be glued together like they were on the ship?" Anna asked as she walked over to stand between Ros and Will.

"There's a strong possibility," Ros smirked. They drank the last of the wine in their glass, and then said, "Look at that. I'll have to get another." Then they walked away, leaving Will and Anna.

"And then there were two," Will said, watching Anna and turning the glass in his gloved hand.

She hummed in agreement, pointing at the silver chain he wore. "What's that?"

He pulled out a simple silver pocket watch and showed her the time. "I've been given strict orders to not leave before eleven, but when I see that time on this watch, we are out of here." He glanced at Anna, then quickly added, "Unless you'd like to stay."

"I'm sure I'll be ready to leave," she said with a little laugh, glancing at a small group of people nearby who were staring at her.

"We've got four hours. Can I get you a drink?"

"Yes, please. I'll walk with you."

Will offered her his elbow, and she took it as they walked toward a table spread with full glasses.

"Did Mr. Slatton get an invite?" she asked as she took the glass he held out to her.

"No." Will was surprised by the question. "But even if he had, I doubt he would've come. A ball isn't really his thing."

"I'm sure he's proud of you. He might've come just to show support."

He hummed thoughtfully. "Maybe." He lifted his glass, smirking. "To that dress."

She felt herself flush again as she rolled her eyes, then she lifted her own glass. "To well-tailored suits."

He inclined his head in a small bow, and then touched his glass to hers. They each took a drink.

"If I could have everyone's attention, please."

Lady Gratadia's voice filled the room, and they turned to find her standing in front of the small orchestra with a mage next to her, amplifying her voice.

"Before the music and dancing starts, I'd like to say a few words. I'll start with the reason we're here, our guests of honor. I'm sure I speak for all of Telluth when I say how thankful I am for what they've been through, and for rooting out an enemy to the nation. Their mission was harrowing, and its only by the grace of the gods they've returned to us, and I do mean that quite literally." She paused as laughter filled the room.

"I say this with all due respect to the gods," she went on, and raised an open hand toward the sky, "but it wasn't *just* the gods that made their mission a success. They built a team that came together so well, if someone was lacking or had a weakness, another would fill the gap. A team that picked each other up when they fell and supported each other through *each and every* trial. A group of people from all over this country, all walks of life, banded together to accomplish something that would have been impossible alone."

The crowd applauded.

Will leaned toward Anna and whispered in her ear, "She's laying it on a little thick."

"I think we could all use their example as a model for our own goals. One of the great things about this nation is our diversity. Each of us has different strengths and skills we bring to the table. Let's utilize the wonderful force that is community to accomplish something greater. Imagine the possibilities within Telluth and beyond.

“I’m sure most of you have seen Prince Bartok and the Vassian envoys in attendance. I encourage you to make them feel welcome tonight. Their help during this sensitive mission was invaluable.”

Anna found the prince in the crowd. He was sporting an amused grin as his pack watched Lady Gratadia.

“Finally, I hope you all enjoy yourselves. Let’s carry this energy with us as we create a stronger Telluth.” She picked up the glass Veronica held out to her and raised it into the air. “Cheers!”

Anna raised her glass, then turned to Will as she drank. The orchestra started playing, and the surrounding applause faded. He set his glass on the table and offered her his hand.

“Can I steal the first dance?”

62

ANNA GRINNED AT WILL AND HIS OUTSTRETCHED HAND. “ALREADY?” SHE set her drink down on the table next to them and put her hand in his.

“Wouldn’t you rather be dancing with me than standing here? I know I’d rather be dancing with you.” He pulled her onto the dance floor.

His arms held her like they had when he was teaching her to dance in camp—raised, rigid, formal. They turned with the other dancers, spinning toward the middle of the group. She glimpsed Captain Heiser’s jacket and then Captain Crawford’s hair, and she nodded her head in their direction to point them out to Will. He glanced over his shoulder, and then turned back to her with a quiet laugh.

She floated over the stone tiles as he pulled her over the dance floor. She couldn’t keep the smile from her lips. Nothing had ever felt as easy as dancing with Will. He smiled too, small smiles as he watched her laugh. The song ended too quickly, and he led her toward where her mother was standing, watching.

“I’m impressed,” Bren told Will. “I’ve never seen Anna move like that.”

“Anyone can dance with the right lead,” he told her, and then winked at Anna.

Her mother shook her head, a smile across her face. "I bet I'd give you a run for your money," she joked.

Will's eyebrows rose, then settled again as a glint caught in his eye. "I'll take that bet."

Bren laughed. "I couldn't."

He held a hand out to her as the next song started.

Bren looked at Anna skeptically. Her daughter shrugged and gestured for her mother to take the outstretched hand. Bren giggled nervously as she did. Anna laughed to herself as she watched them go, then turned to get another drink.

AS ANNA WATCHED THEM DANCE—HER MOTHER SMILING BRIGHTLY AS Will led her around the dancefloor—she realized she'd made a mistake. She didn't know what they were talking about, but she was sure it was about her. An approaching governor interrupted her failed attempts at lip reading.

"Ms. Hale," Lord Inwood greeted as he stood beside her in deep blue robes with swirling, embossed patterns that shone under the mage lights. "How are you?"

"Governor Inwood." She returned the greeting, turning to face him with a reluctant smile. "I'm well. How are you?"

He nodded politely and glanced at the glass in his left hand. His mouth pressed into a hard line behind his beard. "I would like to speak with you about your abilities. Your power hasn't been seen in hundreds of years and there is so much to *learn* from it." He stroked his beard thoughtfully, staring out at the dancers.

Her eyebrows rose at the old half-elf. "You know about the champions, from centuries ago?"

"I know little beyond their existence before the Great War. Our oldest books speak of a champion for each Child, with unique abilities, but these histories are vague and speak of them only in passing. That is *why* it is imperative we learn what we can from you."

"I don't think you'll get your answers from me," she told him, scanning the crowd for Ben. "Ben has been trying to understand what he can, and he's more familiar with the, uh, lingo." She winced at the only word that came to mind. "I have no personal experience with magic, outside of what Morterra has shown me how to do."

His white eyebrows rose and he locked his gaze to her face. The surprise passed, replaced with lowered brows and narrowed green eyes. "You say Morterra has *shown* you these things? How?"

She stalled by taking a drink. When she was finished, she laughed nervously, unsure what to say. "Well, he told me what to do, step-by-step. Uh—"

"Are you saying, Ms. Hale, that you continue to converse directly with Morterra?"

She waved her free hand between them. "No, no! Well, yes, but it's not really up to me. He kind of pops in whenever he wants."

"*Pops* in?" Lord Inwood stared at her.

Anna took a deep breath, sensing that if she said anything else, she would just be digging a deeper hole.

"I do hope you comprehend the gravity of your situation. Your acquired power marks the end of an age of the person as separate from the gods, and the beginning of a time when the gods again meddle in even the smallest of our affairs. If we are to understand why, and what this means, we must understand *you*." He paused to look her over again, and then went on, "As it is likely you are unable to decipher such things on your own—"

Rude. She scanned the crowd for help. Her eyes made contact with Prince

Bartok's from where he stood at the end of the buffet. He was wearing a cream button-down shirt and brown pants. His gold circlet rested on his head.

"—I would ask that you come to Eysa. Our researchers at the university are much better equipped to study your condition, and we hold some of the oldest tomes in the country. I am sure the High Priestess could be persuaded to share the Creed's private library, as well. It is vital that we learn the motive behind this development. There may yet be time to combat it."

Anna's eyes whipped back to the governor. "*Combat* it?"

He sighed, his mouth dropping into a frown and shoulders sagging slightly. "Yes. As I understand it, you were not a woman of faith before your...transformation. Surely you understand the importance of maintaining our separation from deities that would be more than happy to tamper. Wars have been fought and won over—"

"Champion." Prince Bartok smiled from Lord Inwood's other side, and the governor stopped talking, his eyes widening at the giant standing there. "Governor, do you mind if I speak with her? Alone."

Lord Inwood glanced at Anna. "Not at all." He bowed slightly to the prince, and Bartok inclined his head in dismissal. He glanced back as he walked away, one eyebrow raised obstinately at Anna.

"He is old," Bartok commented, watching him go, "and not entirely wiser for it."

She wrinkled her nose. "He said a lot of strange things."

The Vassian grunted in acknowledgement, turning to look at her. "I think you threaten him, and he is frustrated further that you do not know your own power."

"You heard him, then?"

He tapped a finger on his double-pointed ear. "I could hear any conversation in this room if I chose to."

"Right." She grinned. "You'd make a great spy."

He shook his head. "I do not like to hide."

"Some hide in plain sight, or so I've heard."

He shot her an amused grin, and then he looked her over and said, "I see you have chosen to display your strength."

She nodded.

"It looks good on you," he told her.

"I could use a snack," she said, changing the subject.

He offered his elbow. "I recommend the skewered meats."

"Lead the way."

AS ANNA PICKED AT FINGER FOODS WITH PRINCE BARTOK, LADY DATO APPROACHED with a young man at her side, wearing a military jacket similar to Captain Heiser's but in a deep green.

"Ms. Hale, prince." The governor bowed, her blonde bun dipping.

Bartok acknowledged her with a bow of his head.

"I would like to introduce myself formally," she told the Vassian. "I am Aurelia Dato, Governor of Luminport. It is good to meet you."

"Thank you. I'm glad to meet you outside of Council chambers. It is like finding a lion in its den."

The governor smiled at the expression. "I apologize if I came off as aggressive. I take my job very seriously."

"As you should," he agreed.

The governor turned to Anna. "I hope you're thinking quite hard about our offer."

"Absolutely."

Lady Dato gestured to the man beside her. "I wanted to introduce General

Jonas Adair. He's one of the youngest generals in Tellan history, and he's earned his role."

The general bowed to her. When he stood back up, there was a smile on his face set with perfectly straight, white teeth. His hazel eyes looked at her from under golden blonde hair that had fallen across his tan forehead when he bent forward. "It's a pleasure to meet you."

"Same to you." Anna returned the smile.

"If you choose to stay, you may find yourselves together frequently, so I thought I should make the acquaintance," the governor explained. "The general will be assisting in our search for the necromancer."

"I'm looking forward to working together," he told Anna. "I've heard great things about your team."

She gave a little laugh. "They're Captain Heiser's team more than they're *mine*, but you're right. They're great."

Lady Dato turned back to the prince. "I hope you've enjoyed your time here."

"I have," he replied, "but I'm looking forward to returning home."

"I can understand that," she nodded and adjusted her glasses. "Kastarus has its charms, but I prefer Luminport. It's brighter there, and not so tightly packed."

"Is it true that you see both sunrise and sunset over the water?" Bartok asked. "I've heard stories of the peninsula where your people race the sun."

"It's true," General Adair said. "We have a race on the shortest day of the year when our fastest ships travel around the peninsula, following the sun in honor of Sollis."

"A worthy tribute to the Son of Day."

ANNA WAS WALKING OUT OF THE HALL THAT HELD THE RESTROOMS WHEN a woman in cream-colored robes of the Creed and a white headdress trimmed in gold stopped her.

"Ms. Hale," she greeted with a smile that emphasized the wrinkles around her eyes. "It is an honor to meet you. I am High Priestess Clement, leader of the Creed in Telluth." She bowed her head.

"Oh, uh, I'm Anna Hale, but you already know that."

The woman laughed lightly, the wrinkles deepening across her olive-toned face. "Most of Telluth knows who you are now, thanks to Morterra's blessing. I was hoping to talk with you. Have you been to the cathedral? It would mean so much if you would join us for Monday mass."

Anna looked over her shoulder, but she was too far from the party to catch anyone's eye.

"I know we aren't your home congregation, but if you plan on staying in town to work with the Council, we could easily have you transferred."

Anna smiled and shook her head. "Unfortunately, I can't attend Monday." *I'll be doing anything else.*

"Oh," the priestess's face fell. "There's always the next week—"

"Ms. Hale." General Adair appeared from the hallway, glancing between the two women. "I'm sorry to interrupt, but I was hoping to ask you to dance."

Anna blinked at him.

He smiled as he looked pointedly at the High Priestess, and then back at her.

"Oh, a dance!" Anna said with realization. "Thank you." She turned to the priestess and said, "Maybe another time," and then she took the arm the general offered.

When they were out of earshot, she sighed in relief and told him, "Mother, that was good timing."

He chuckled and said, "I respect the church, but I wouldn't want to be stuck in a conversation with a priestess at a party, let alone the High Priestess."

She smiled at him. "She was asking me to attend mass every week."

His eyebrows rose. "The only people who do that are the clergy and the old folks who have nothing better to do."

She laughed.

"You looked like you could use a rescue."

"I'm glad you were there." When they rounded the buffet tables toward the dance floor, she said, "Oh, you were serious."

He laughed at her reaction. "Did my rescue earn me a song?"

"Sure," she told him. "Why not?"

She could already tell he was a tall, strong man with wide shoulders, but when she put her left hand atop his shoulder, she could feel the muscles beneath his jacket. His warm hand was large against the side of her waist.

"I'll warn you," she told him as she tried to maintain her smile through the heat rising to her face, "I'm not very good at this."

"Really? You were all grace during the first song."

Her flush grew stronger. "I had a very good partner."

"Let's see if I can measure up."

He left his arms more relaxed, which brought them a little closer than when she danced with Will. She could feel the warmth through his jacket as he turned her across the floor, as smooth as a breeze.

When her smile returned, he asked, "How am I doing?"

"Good, general. It's no easy feat to keep me from tripping over myself."

"I'll expect my medal in the post."

She laughed.

He watched her, and when she was finished, he said, "I didn't expect the Champion of the god of death to be so..."

"Lively?" she suggested.

"Yes," he agreed.

"I guess that's what happens when you're given a second chance."

"I guess so."

As the song continued, his hand at her waist slid further around, and by the end, she could feel his fingertips against her lower back. He held her as they slowed to a stop, and then he continued holding her.

"I don't think you're a bad dancer at all," he said. "You just need a little help finding your footing."

She felt herself flush again and shook her head. "You haven't seen me with a sword."

He tilted his head thoughtfully, his hazel eyes staring into her, then said, "Maybe you haven't found the right partner."

Anna almost jumped as someone cleared their throat next to her.

"May I cut in?" Will asked, one eyebrow arched.

General Adair released her hand and her waist to step back, smiling at Will. Before he walked away, he looked at Anna and said, "Thanks for the dance."

She smiled back.

Will was frowning when he took her hand.

She narrowed her eyes at him as her smile turned amused. "Are you actually upset that I was dancing with him?"

"No," he said, his cheeks darkening. She quirked an eyebrow at him, and he sighed.

"You are," she laughed lightly as the next song started. "He saved me from an awful conversation."

They started dancing, and Will said, "I'm fine."

"It's not like he danced with my mother," she joked. "What were the two of you talking about, anyway?"

A familiar smirk crossed his lips and there was a glint in his eyes again. "All sorts of things."

"You're not going to tell me?"

"Nope."

Her eyes narrowed at him.

"You're not very intimidating."

She rolled her eyes, and then scanned the crowd. Her mother was talking with Irene and Captain Heiser. She didn't see Captain Crawford. Clara, Cal, and Merry were chatting with a younger group of people, Anna recognized one as a merchant she'd met at the last ball. Pyran was standing with his family and Ros, and Ben was dancing with his wife. The Vassians stood together out on the balcony.

"Do you think they'll go back south tomorrow?" she asked Will, nodding her head toward the small circle of giants.

He glanced at them. "I don't think they have a reason to stay." When Anna frowned, he asked, "Are you going to miss them?"

She turned her gaze back to his. "I will, actually."

He grinned at the answer.

The song ended and Will checked his pocket watch. "Quarter after ten," he sighed.

"Let's get some fresh air," she suggested.

Will took her hand, and they walked out onto the balcony. With the Vassians outside, it was clear of other guests.

Tasha approached as they crossed to the railing, Gemma at her shoulder. The crow clacked at Anna and Will in greeting, rustling her wings.

"Hello," Tasha greeted stiffly.

"Hello," Anna replied.

The Vassian woman took a deep breath and turned to Will. "Gemma has been distraught without you."

Anna fought back a surprised giggle.

"I, uh...I'm sorry," Will said, glancing nervously at Anna.

"I believe she has bonded with you," Tasha said, frowning slightly. "She is still young, two years old. It is possible that she finds you to be some kind of...kin."

Anna put her hand over her mouth and turned her laugh into a cough.

"I also find this ridiculous," Tasha told her with a withered look. She turned back to Will. "It may be best if Gemma were to stay here, with you."

Will blinked at her, then looked at the crow. Gemma's head was tilted curiously. She let out a little, crackling call and the feathers around her neck fluffed.

"I see," he said uncertainly.

"She's been with me for just over year," Tasha explained. "Never has she had this reaction with anyone else."

Will swallowed. "I—" he stopped and started again. "I suppose I could—"

Tasha sighed in relief. "Thank you. I will be sad to say goodbye, but she is excited for her next adventure."

"Come, come," Gemma croaked excitedly. "Go!"

Will laughed. "All right. Should I...?" He started to lift a hand, then hesitated.

Tasha shook her head. "I will find you tomorrow. Tonight, I will say goodbye."

Will nodded.

Tasha ran a finger along the crow's wing as she turned to walk back toward her pack. "You must not give him a hard time. You shouldn't yell when you should be quiet, or ignore him. Do not be so stubborn, little one."

Anna laughed as she led Will over to look out at the water, away from other people. Waves crashed a hundred feet below them, the sound rhythmic, yet random.

"I didn't think I would like the ocean," she said, leaning a little over the stone wall to look down at the moonlight on the water.

"Well, it's nothing like the woods." His arms braced on either side of her, and he looked over her bare shoulder. She felt his hair brush her arm.

"Ha-ha."

She felt him exhale against her shoulder, and her ears grew hot. "Somehow," he said into her ear, "after weeks in the city, you still smell like pine."

Heat spread across her face and down her neck. She turned her head slightly toward his.

He pulled back, standing straight again. When she turned around, his dark eyes were on her face and he was grinning.

She took a deep breath to calm herself and raised a challenging eyebrow.

Both of his eyebrows rose in response. "You can't blame me for wanting to make a pretty girl blush."

She swatted lightly at his chest.

"What?" he asked. "I'm just trying to make you feel the way I have all night."

"Even when you were dancing with my mom?" she laughed.

He blinked at her. "Well, no. I—"

She laughed harder.

"Wow," he chuckled, and one of his hands lifted from the wall to rub the back of his neck. "You really ruined my moment."

"I'm sorry," she said as her laughter eased. "I was nervous."

"So it *was* working," he smiled.

She smiled back, leaning against the wall behind her.

He let out a gentle sigh, his eyes searching her face. They caught on her lips before meeting her gaze again. The hand on his neck moved to hold her hip. When he leaned forward, she did, too.

As she kissed him, her hands reached for the lapels of his jacket. Her fingers took hold of the satin trim and pulled him close. His body pressed hers against the wall, and she let out a little gasp. His tongue licked across her lip and then pressed into her mouth while his gloved hand wrapped around to her bare back. Heat pooled low in her stomach as she pulled him closer, as close as she could get.

Will pulled his head back. Between heavy breaths, he said, "Gods, I wish I wasn't wearing gloves."

Completely flushed, she let go of his jacket. "Sorry," she said, smoothing out the little wrinkles she'd made.

He shook his head at her, smiling as he caught his breath. "You're just borrowing this dress?"

She nodded.

"Good," he nodded back.

One of her eyebrows rose in a silent question.

He shook his head, his own smile turning into a smirk as his eyes lit up. "I don't think I could stand it if you wore it again."

WHEN THEY RETURNED TO THE PARTY, THEY FOUND ANNA'S MOTHER, WHO was talking with the rest of the team. Pyran mouthed the word *sorry* as Bren greeted them.

"Anna!" Bren smiled tightly. "Your friends were just telling me that the Council has offered you all employment here in the city."

Anna looked at the others, who mostly seemed apologetic. "Yeah, I didn't really have a good chance to mention that earlier when we were talking about how I died."

"Why don't we give them a moment to talk?" Ros suggested.

Will joined them as they walked away, his hand sliding from Anna's arm.

"You could've told me, Lynnie."

"What I did tell you was overwhelming enough. I was going to talk to you about it tomorrow."

Bren nodded in understanding, her eyes on the glass in her hand. Then she looked up at her daughter. "It sounds like the rest of your friends have decided to stay."

"Oh. Did Ben already make up his mind?"

"Yes. I think his father's a little overbearing. He was excited to move."

"Yeah." Anna smiled a little, her eyes turned down to stare at a tile on the ground.

"Why haven't you told them that you're staying, too?"

Anna looked up at her mother. "I haven't decided yet. I don't want to leave you alone."

"I'll come with you," Bren shrugged.

"But—" She collected her thoughts and restarted, "But the house, the bakery...?"

"I can start a bakery here, and I can live with you again."

"What about Wallset? What about...Dad's grave?"

Bren sighed, her brows pushing together as she looked at Anna. "It's only a grave. We'll make sure it's taken care of, but that's not where your father is. He's with us."

Anna swallowed back the water gathering in her eyes, her throat tightening.

Bren put her hand on Anna's arm. "We'll go back, see it again when we get our things for the move. And it will always be there if you want to visit."

Anna nodded, blinking through her blurring vision.

"He'd be so proud of you, Lynnie." Her mother's voice cracked, and she looked up to see tears in her brown eyes. "He'd want you to be here. There's so much *more* for you here."

Anna nodded and wiped at the tear that escaped and rolled down her cheek. Then she hugged her mom.

Bren laughed lightly. "We've hugged more today than we have all year."

"I'm sorry. I should've hugged you more. I should've talked to you."

Bren shushed her gently. "We were both trying to cope." She released her daughter with a sad smile, pushing a strand of Anna's hair out of her face. "I don't think it goes away. I think you just get better at it."

63

THAT NIGHT, ANNA HUGGED HER FRIENDS, EVEN CAPTAIN HEISER, AND told them she would take the Council's offer. She told Pyran she'd like to go home again first, and that she'd like to travel with him if that was all right. He told her he wouldn't have it any other way.

She said goodnight to Will in the courtyard outside the castle, then went with her mother to spend the night at Irene's.

A few days later, they began the journey home. Pyran's family had left the day after the ball, but he had waited for the Hales. They walked back the way they had come, camping along the way. Bren taught Pyran how to make a pie over the open fire, and he was hooked. They stayed at the inn at the crossroads, and then with the Taggerts in Hillcrest. Pyran introduced Anna to Adrian. As the highest-ranking officer in Hillcrest, the commander was now filling in for Lord Woulfe. The governor had no children, nor had he claimed an heir, so the Council had agreed to run an election.

The next day, the Hales made their way to Wallset. They stopped at the Wilcott's inn to tell them they were moving, and Jo and Alvin made Anna tell them how she'd ended up in the paper. She watered down her story a little, but they got the main points. She knew it would be all over town by the next morning.

It only took them a couple of days to pack up what they wanted to take with them.

On the morning of the third day, they visited her father's grave. Her mother said a few words, ran her hand over her daughter's hair, and then gave her a moment alone.

Anna sat next to the large, round river rock that sat in place of a headstone, crossing her legs. The paxmortium was in full bloom—a hundred small, white flowers hanging toward the ground, as if they were on display for the bones in the dirt. She ran her fingers over a small bloom. It seemed to rise at her hand, and then it was looking at her.

She pulled her hand back, wrinkling her nose. "It's weird. Since I heard you, I don't feel you as much here." She cleared her tight throat. "So much has changed. I've met so many people, lost someone else close to me." Her lungs pulled in a deep breath, then let it out. "I don't think you would've believed it if someone had told you back then that I'd be moving to Kastarus to work for the Council. I know you wouldn't have believed I'd be a champion to some god." She smiled wryly. "I thought I'd always be in Wallset, with you."

Her hand lifted to flatten on top of the smooth, cool stone. "I think a part of me will be, the part that never wanted to leave the woods." She swallowed past the lump in her throat. "I've seen the capital, the ocean, the wall. I scared off an angry hedgebear! I've even seen Vassa, a little of it. There's one thing that never changed. There's always birds. They might be different birds, but they're always there. I'll keep counting them for you."

She pressed up against the stone to stand, wiping at the trails of tears falling down her cheeks.

"I love you, Dad."

Then she walked away.

64

BREN HALE PULLED A LARGE SHEET OF QUICHE OUT OF ONE OF HER DOUble ovens. She carried it out of the kitchen and into the long dining room, where she set the steaming tray onto a large hot pad. Other fresh bakes surrounded it. She sat down at the head of the table.

"That smells amazing," Pyran said, looking like he might start drooling. He turned to Anna and asked, "How are you not just eating constantly?"

"You think I'm not?" she asked.

"She can't, with all the training you two put her through," Adrian said, glancing between his boyfriend and Will. "She could use a break."

"Thank you!" Anna looked at Pyran and said, "Your boyfriend's very smart."

Adrian beamed.

"Champions don't get breaks," Will told her. "Not until they can beat me."

Anna rolled her eyes.

A *ding* sounded in the kitchen, and Bren stood up again. "That'll be the rolls!" She hurried back out of the room.

There was a knock at the front door. Gemma squawked from her perch on the back of Will's chair.

Anna sighed. "I told Ben not to bring his giant notebook over today." She stood and walked to the front of the house, mumbling, "All that man does is magic-this or weave-that."

When she opened the door, however, it was not Bennett Day standing on her porch. Jen Parker stood there in city guard leathers, catching her breath.

"Oh, good, you answered. The Council is requesting your presence urgently."

"What for?"

"I'm afraid I can't say, but they're waiting for you. Champion business." She glanced inside, over Anna's shoulder.

"I'm going with you," Will said, his chest pressing against her back.

"They've only asked for Ms. Hale."

"She's not going alone."

Anna glanced at Will, then back to the messenger.

Jen let out a huff. "All right, but we need to hurry."

"Just a moment." Anna held a hand out to the woman, then hurried back to the dining room. "The Council is asking for me. I've got to go."

"I'll go with you," Pyran said, starting to stand.

"No, stay with Adrian!" Anna insisted. "And my mom. Someone's got to eat all this food." She grabbed a cinnamon roll, then promptly dropped it as it burnt her fingers. "Ow!" She jumped back from the table and knocked into the wall. She turned and straightened the framed picture of her from the paper.

"Here." Her mother handed her a cloth napkin. "Wrap it in this."

"Thanks." Anna grabbed the roll with the napkin, then another, and wrapped them up. "Love you."

"Love you, too, Lynnie!"

Clack, clack. "Come. Go!"

She scratched the crow's neck as she passed by. "Not this time, Gemma."

She ran back to the front of the house, handing the rolls to Will so she could shove her boots onto her feet. "Okay, let's go!"

It wasn't a long walk from their townhome to the castle. As they went, Anna ate one roll and gave the other to Will. When they stopped in front of the chamber doors, Will made her wait so he could wipe the frosting from the corner of her mouth with his thumb.

"Thanks," she told him as he licked it off his finger.

The doors opened, and they stepped inside.

Lady Gratadia was standing at her usual position in the center of the room. The only other governor present was Lord Inwood, who was also standing at the table in his usual spot, but he was wearing a scowl. In the open space in front of them stood six people, three in fine robes and three in leathers that looked like a scale mail made of hundreds of little leaves. They were all fairly tall, and all except for one had long, straight hair. They looked barely older than Will. Poking out from their shining strands were ears sharper than Will's. At the front of the group was a man with silvery blonde hair, as light as Ros's, wearing pale robes. His striking green eyes turned to Anna and Will. Next to him was a man with dark hair, wearing leaf-like leathers gilt with gold. His golden-brown eyes were wide as they took in the pair in the doorway. Anna's eyes froze on his face. He looked like an older, sharper version of Will.

"Ms. Hale," Lady Gratadia greeted. "I see you brought Mr. Grey with you."

Anna reluctantly pulled her eyes from the stranger's face to turn to the governor. "Yes. We were...having brunch."

"I see." The governor's cool exterior faltered briefly before it was recast. "These are emissaries from the elves to the north. This is Mr. Sallinor—"

"Sallinor is fine," the man with the pale hair said with a smile.

"—from Mythellon, the temple of Morterra, to be precise."

Anna's eyebrows rose as she turned back to Sallinor.

"I am keeper of his temple," he told her. "I've come with two acolytes under the safety of the Wild Hunt to meet you. This is Ailmar—"

"Fuck," Will let out in a breath at Anna's shoulder.

"—leader of the Hunt. I hope his presence conveys to you the earnestness with which I ask. I would like to extend an invitation to you to return with us to Mythellon. There is much for you to learn from us and the previous champions."

"Previous—" Anna glanced at Lady Gratadia, then back to Sallinar. "You have information about them?"

"Of course." Sallinar's smile grew amused, and she felt like she'd asked a stupid question. "We've kept all records for thousands of years."

"I'm human," Anna said. "I thought only elves were welcome in the north."

"There are exceptions," Sallinar told her. "Your position as champion is one of them."

Anna looked at Lady Gratadia, hoping for any kind of help.

"I cannot keep you from leaving," the Chief of the Council said. "Your role as champion is not confined to Telluth's borders, but I would argue that there is much for you to do here."

Anna looked at Will, who was attempting to stare a hole into the blue carpet, his jaw clenched. She drew in a heavy breath and turned back to the temple keeper. "This is sudden. I…"

"I understand. We will stay for a week. Please take that time to consider what we offer."

Anna nodded.

"We've prepared rooms for you here," Lady Gratadia told the elves. "Please make us aware if there is anything lacking. I'll have someone show you the way."

"Thank you, governor." Sallinor swept his arm out as he bowed.

Anna and Will moved to the side to let them pass. As they did, Ailmar's eyes flickered to Will, and then away. When the doors shut behind them, some of the tension in the air released.

"We find ourselves in strange times," Lady Gratadia sighed, staring at the closed doors.

"Be wary." Lord Inwood's eyes were on Anna. "The elves are known to wield words as weapons, and their almost ageless existence warps their perception of time. Your lifetime is but a passing season for them."

"What they offer could be invaluable to you," Lady Gratadia said, "but Governor Inwood is correct. Be cautious in making agreements with them, even conversationally."

Anna's fingernails pressed into her palms as she nodded, unable to come up with a response worth saying aloud.

"We have nothing further for you. If you wish to speak with them, you can ask for them here. My door is open to you as well." Lady Gratadia sighed, and then her lips lifted into a small smile. "You may return to your brunch."

Anna could feel Lord Inwood's eyes attempting to drill into her mind as she thanked them before they left.

"Are you okay?" she asked Will, halfway down the long hallway outside the chamber.

The half-elf took a rough breath in through his nose, and his eyes flickered to Anna, his jaw muscles working. "I think that was my father."

About the Author

E. C. TAYLOR IS THE AUTHOR OF THE NEW NOVEL SPEAK WITH THE DEAD. A professionally trained engineer, her love of all things fantasy has fueled her reading and writing since childhood and given her books a depth of setting and character. She's spent her days living near the woods, waiting for the day the trees call her to join them. Until then, she spends her time playing Dungeons & Dragons with her friends and camping in Michigan with her husband, lounging in a chair with a book in her hands.

You can find her on social media as @etay_1010, where she posts silly memes and teases her writing.

To get the latest information on E. C. Taylor, visit her website at www.ec-taylor.com or scan the QR code below:

www.ingramcontent.com/pod-product-compliance
Lightning Source LLC
Chambersburg PA
CBHW021938110726
47901CB00003B/885